COVERING FIRE

JONATHAN MOELLER

DESCRIPTION

An unexplained suicide. An accidental death. Neither are what they seem.

Private investigator Cormac Rogan just wants to keep his head down and work his way out of debt. But when a wealthy widow offers to hire Mac to investigate her husband's suicide, the money is too good to say no.

The widow is the only one who believes her husband didn't kill himself.

But Mac thinks she might be right.

And the undetected killer is willing to kill many more people to remain undetected, starting with Mac...

Covering Fire

Copyright 2021 by Jonathan Moeller.

Published by Azure Flame Media.

Some cover images copyright themacx | istockphoto.com & Coverkit.com

Ebook edition published August 2021.

All Rights Reserved.

This novel is a work of fiction. Names, characters, places and incidents are either the product of the author's imagination, or, if real, used fictitiously. No part of this book may be reproduced or transmitted in any form or by any electronic or mechanical means, including photocopying, recording, or by any information storage and retrieval system, without the express written permission of the author or publisher, except where permitted by law.

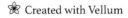 Created with Vellum

1

A FAVOR

Mac Rogan did not want to return Dave Wester's message. That wasn't fair, though. Dave had been a good friend of Mac's father and had stood by John Rogan when much of the police department had turned on him. For that matter, Dave was Mac's friend as well. Ever since John Rogan had been murdered, Mac had done various jobs for Dave's private investigation firm. Dave was an excellent investigator, but he hated computers. As the twenty-first century progressed, more and more actual investigative work involved computer fraud, much to Dave's dismay, and Mac had done a lot of work for him over the last few years.

So that was probably the reason for the call. Dave had another job for Mac. God knew that he needed the money. The last call with the insurance company had said they would finally pay out his claim after the apartment fire, but he probably wasn't going to get the money until next year.

No, the reason Mac didn't want to return the call, he could admit to himself, was that he was in a foul mood and didn't want to talk to anyone.

He was in a foul mood most of the time these days.

But Dave was a friend, and Mac really did need the money, so in the afternoon of Monday, October 22nd, 2007, Cormac Rogan picked up his cell phone, flipped it open, and scrolled until he found Dave Wester's number.

He sat in the bedroom of his new apartment. Not that he ever actually slept in here. Mac had laid a plastic chair mat along one wall and set up three white plastic folding tables to form a wrap-around desk. His computer equipment occupied the tables – some of it new, some of it scavenged. The newest and most expensive item was a nineteen-inch flatscreen monitor, which currently displayed the programming code for a smartphone application that was ninety percent finished.

Well. Maybe eighty percent. Seventy-five at worst.

His clamshell phone's screen was scratched, but it still worked, and Mac didn't want to replace it. The phone had been one of his few possessions to survive the fire. Not that it had any sentimental value for him – he just didn't want to shell out the money for a new one.

He hit the call button and lifted the phone to his ear.

Dave picked up on the third ring. "Mac, that you?" Dave had a deep voice with a drawl, overlaid by the clipped tone acquired by a man who had spent a full twenty-five years in the police force. Whenever Mac talked to him, he half-expected Dave to start reading a crime report and giving a description of a suspect.

"Got your message," said Mac. "What's up?"

"Interested in a job?" said Dave.

"I'm always interested in a job," said Mac. "What do you have? Another forensic computer audit?" The last job he had taken from Dave had involved an accountant suspected of embezzling. Mac had found the accountant's hidden books on his employer's servers. The embezzler had been a good accountant – he had meticulously recorded every penny he had stolen, a fact he no doubt now regretted.

"Not quite," said Dave. "It's a bit unusual."

"Unusual?" said Mac. "Unusual is bad."

"Sometimes," said Dave. "I've got a potential client, and I don't have the time to handle the kind of investigation she wants." Between insurance fraud, Medicare fraud, and various divorce cases, Dave and the assorted employees of Wester Security kept busy. "But you've still got your PI license, right?"

"Right."

"Come meet me for a drink," said Dave. "Eight at Becker's. I'll introduce you to the client, and you can see if it's the kind of thing you want to do."

"I don't know," said Mac. "I'm pretty busy right now…"

"With RVW Software?" said Dave. Mac glanced at the code on his monitor. "You can't be making any revenue yet. I bet you could use the work."

Mac glanced around the bedroom. Dave was right about that.

"And you are a good investigator, Mac," said Dave. "You'd have made a great detective, but you saw too much of how the sausage gets made with your dad."

John Rogan's voice played through Mac's memory.

"Time to do some digging, Mac."

John Rogan had, hadn't he? He had done some digging, and it had gotten him killed. Mac had done some digging this past summer, and it had nearly gotten him burned alive.

Then again, if he hadn't gone digging, he might have gotten killed anyway, and thousands of people would have died if that bomb had gone off at Greenwater Community Church. As angry and disillusioned as the experience had left Mac, as much as it had cost him, he knew that it would have been worse if he had not gone digging.

Much, much worse.

And Mac was honest enough with himself to know that he did like investigating and was good at it.

"All right," said Mac at last. "Eight PM at Becker's. You're paying for the drinks, though."

Dave laughed. "Fair enough. See you there, kid."

Mac ended the call, closed his phone, and stood up, the plastic mat beneath his makeshift desk smooth and cold beneath his bare feet. He crossed to the window and pushed open the blinds, looking into the parking lot three stories below.

It was a cold gray day, drizzling a little, the ground covered with wet leaves dropped from the trees. On TV, autumn days were always bright and crisp, but today it looked damp and dreary, like the weather wanted to shift from rain to snow and couldn't quite find the energy to commit. Through the window, Mac saw the rest of his apartment complex, several three-story buildings that looked like oversized shipping containers with windows, and beyond them, the lights of Timmerman Airfield blinking in the late afternoon gloom.

He stared out the window, wondering if agreeing to the meeting had been a good idea.

RVW Software, at the moment, was nothing more than some incorporation filings and a mostly finished smartphone app, and Mac should be focusing on that.

Not on a mysterious case from Dave Wester.

But Mac needed the money, and he liked the work. If he was idle for too long, he started thinking too much, thinking about what had happened over the summer. Then he started to get angry about it all over again.

No, better to work.

Speaking of that, it was barely five PM. Mac could put in a good two hours on the app before he had to get ready to meet Dave and his client.

He skipped dinner – Mac found that his head was clearer, and he was less likely to make mistakes when he was a little hungry. He spent the next two hours working on the code for the app, pausing every so often to get up and do some pushups to keep his joints from aching and to get his blood moving. Once seven PM drew near, Mac reviewed the changes he had made, realized he had made more progress than anticipated, and uploaded the new code to RVW Software's servers, along with a quick email to Nikolai with updates.

After a shower, Mac got dressed. Nearly all his clothes had burned with his old apartment, and his new wardrobe had been assembled slowly through visits to thrift stores when time permitted. He pulled on jeans, a T-shirt, a black hooded sweatshirt, and running shoes. The jeans had fit when he had bought them back in July, but now they were too loose, and Mac had to tighten his belt an extra notch. Over the sweatshirt went the only coat in his size he had been able to find, a black pea coat with epaulets that looked like something that either a naval officer or an artist with pretensions would wear.

He checked his reflection in the bathroom and grimaced. His black hair had needed a trim three weeks ago, and it had gotten thick and shaggy. His blue eyes were bloodshot, and his face looked a little bony because of the weight loss. Mac didn't look like a private investigator, or a computer programmer, or a network technician. Honestly, he looked a little like a drug addict.

Though he did smell better than most of the drug addicts he had known. That was going for him, at least.

Mac locked his apartment behind him and headed to his car, a battered blue Chevy Corsica that had seen 129,000 miles and better days. He really hoped he could squeeze another year or two out of it, though that was looking optimistic. But the car started on the first try, and Mac left the parking lot.

He had moved into the same apartment complex as his brother Tom. It faced a small airport, and between the noise from the nearby state highways and the occasional planes and helicopters, it wasn't quiet, and the neighbors tended to be loud and troublesome. It was what he could afford, and at least he didn't need roommates. Mac didn't want any roommates to share the rent, partly because he preferred to be alone and partly because his last apartment building had gotten burned down when someone tried to kill him.

No one had died, thankfully. Well, no one innocent, anyway. But thinking about that was one of the things that made Mac angry, so it was better to live alone.

The drizzle intensified to pounding rain, the asphalt of the highway gleaming in his headlights. Becker's was a sports bar in downtown Wauwatosa, with a large patio overlooking the Menomonee River. Given that Wisconsin's weather made the patio unusable for half the year, Mac wasn't sure why the owners had put it in. He found a parking spot three blocks away and headed to the bar, turning up his coat's collar against the rain and keeping beneath the shop awnings when he could.

Mac walked into Becker's at about six minutes before eight. A large man in a tight-fitting T-shirt sat close to the door, his arms covered in tattoos. His hard eyes rested on Mac for a moment, and then he gave a sharp nod. Mac nodded back and stepped past him. The room was dim, with a long bar running along the left-hand wall. A hard-eyed woman with an easy smile worked the bar, a black tank top revealing toned arms and shoulders. A few people ate late dinners at the tables, but most of the patrons were at the bar, watching Indianapolis play Jacksonville in football.

Dave Wester was at the end of the bar, and he waved Mac over.

"Mac," said Dave. "Thanks for coming out."

"Dave," said Mac, and they shook hands. Dave was dark-skinned and dark-eyed, with graying black hair, a thick gut, and equally thick arms and shoulders. He looked like he could have taken the bouncer at the front door. Dave had spent twenty-five years in the Milwaukee police force, ending his career as a lieutenant of detectives. He had found retirement boring and had started his own private security company that had rapidly become successful. Dave almost always wore a suit and tie, and he was fond of saying that people found a large black man frightening, but a large black man in a suit was an authority figure.

Mac suspected the real reason was that Dave had dressed in a suit every day for twenty years and didn't own any other clothes.

"How's the RV software business going?" said Dave.

"It's RVW Software, and you know it," said Mac. Dave grinned. "We named the company after our last initials – Rogan, Volodin, and Williamson. And right now, it's an unfinished app." He shrugged. "We'll see if Paul and Nikolai are right about iPhones."

"I don't know." Dave produced his own phone. "I've gotten pretty used to my Blackberry. Dunno if I'd like a touchscreen phone. Definitely not dropping five hundred bucks on one."

"I don't think you called me down here to talk about phones," said Mac.

"Nope." Dave looked towards the door. "Here's the client."

Mac turned his head just as the woman stepped inside, carrying both a purse and a black leather briefcase. She looked like a Midwestern blonde – about five foot five, fifteen to twenty too many pounds that she nonetheless carried well, and a round, pretty face. The woman wore a black pantsuit that said either lawyer, senior accountant, or realtor. The bouncer nodded her in and then watched her ass as she walked to the bar.

She looked back and forth from Dave to Mac, nervousness clear on her face.

"Dave," the woman said. "Is this..."

"Yup," said Dave. "This is Cormac Rogan. Mac, this is Julie Norton, a senior partner and chief legal counsel at Morgan Properties."

A realtor and a lawyer, then. Mac's guess had been right.

"Good to meet you," said Mac, shaking her hand. There was a wedding ring on her left hand. Her grip felt soft and a little damp despite her effort to squeeze – she really was nervous.

"I saw you on the news this summer," said Julie. "You were the guy at Greenwater Community Church, right?"

Mac didn't want to talk about that.

"That was me," he said.

"Oh," said Julie. She seemed impressed. "You work for Dave? His company has done some work for Morgan Properties, but I haven't seen you before."

"I do freelance work for Dave from time to time," said Mac.

"Why don't we get a table?" said Dave. "I'll get us some drinks, and then we can talk about your problem and see if we can do something about it."

Mac asked for a beer, Julie for a Manhattan, and Dave put in their order. The bartender produced the drinks, and Dave said something that made her throw back her head and laugh. Mac led the way to a round table on the far side of the room, out of earshot of the bar, and he and Dave waited until Julie had seated herself, arranging her purse on her lap and her briefcase beneath her chair. She turned the glass with the Manhattan in it, her wedding ring occasionally clinking against the glass.

"You're…" Julie shook her head. "You're younger than I thought."

"I turn twenty-nine next month," said Mac. "I don't think it should concern you, since I'm at least a year older than you."

Julie blinked and then smiled with genuine amusement for the first time. "You're right, that was rude. If you must know, I'm about to turn thirty-five for the second time." She looked at Dave. "I'm not usually so nervous. I don't know where to start…"

"Why don't you tell Mac about it?" said Dave. His voice had switched to that of a cop gently prompting a witness. "Start at the beginning."

"The beginning. Okay." Julie took a deep breath. "Okay." She looked at Mac. "Are you familiar with Northwoods High School in Brookfield?"

"No," said Mac.

But it triggered something in his memory, something he had seen on TV, though he couldn't place it.

"You might have heard about it on the news," said Julie.

"Recently?" said Mac. He didn't watch the news. His dislike of reporters had begun after Tom had been wounded in Iraq. Journalists had shown up and wanted to know how he felt about his brother's wounds or if he blamed George Bush or Donald Rumsfeld, and there had been a hungry, vulture-like gleam in their eyes as they asked the questions. After his mother had murdered his father and tried (ineptly) to frame Mac for it, the same ghoulish process had repeated.

That was nothing compared to the media circus after Senator Kelsey's death and Mac's testimony to Congress over the matter. His dislike of journalists had turned into full-on loathing, and he had refused to speak to the media, knowing that anything he said would be twisted out of context.

To make things worse, every story and news article in which he had featured, every single one, had something wrong in it, with errors ranging from comical to egregious.

But he had heard about Northwoods High School before, and the memory finally clicked.

"The school shooting," said Mac at last.

Julie nodded. "April 14th, 2005." Her smile was brittle. "I thought finalizing a tax audit would be my biggest problem that day. It wasn't. Someone opened fire on Northwoods High School from across the street as class let out for the day. Five students were killed and seven more wounded."

"And the perpetrator was never caught," said Mac with a sinking feeling. He had some recollection of the police or maybe the FBI arresting and then releasing the wrong suspect, but he didn't know any details. Mac really hoped Julie Norton didn't want to hire him to catch the shooter. If the police and the FBI hadn't managed it, he wouldn't have any better luck.

"No, he wasn't," said Julie. "For a while, the police were certain that they had the students responsible, but it was proven that they couldn't have done it, and one of the kids committed suicide. It was a huge scandal and fouled up the investigation, but..."

"Did you have a child at Northwoods?" said Mac.

"No," said Julie. "My kids are still in grade school. But my husband Doug was a teacher at Northwoods. Um, a history teacher and the head football coach. It was a terrible day, Mr. Rogan. We had been married for eleven years, and I had never, ever seen him cry before. But he cried that day."

"I'm sorry," said Mac. Julie tensed up as she talked about her husband, and Mac suspected they were coming to the point.

"Doug was found shot to death in his classroom on January 24th, 2006," said Julie.

"I'm sorry for your loss," said Mac. The words always felt useless, but there was nothing else to be said.

"The police thought he killed himself," said Julie, "and the medical examiner ruled his death a suicide. But I know he didn't kill himself. I know he was murdered." Her hands kneaded the purse in her lap. "If Dave recommends you, I would like to hire you to look over the case and find proof that my husband was murdered. He didn't kill himself, Mr. Rogan."

Mac said nothing, carefully keeping the alarm from his face. He had hoped Dave would have something simple for him, but he should have known better. Dave wouldn't have called him down here for anything less than a mess.

"Mrs. Norton, I'm very sorry for your loss," said Mac. "I need…"

Julie's smile was hard and bitter. "You don't believe me."

Mac didn't. He had neither reflexive respect nor autonomic disdain for the police. Granted, a lot of his experiences with the police had been bad, but that had been because his father had been a crusader who liked to take on corruption and had gotten murdered for his efforts. But the police, by and large, were not stupid. For that matter, it was very, very difficult to kill someone and make it look like a suicide.

"It's too early for me to make that kind of judgment," said Mac instead, which seemed to mollify Julie. "I just need a word alone with Mr. Wester before we decide whether or not I'm the right choice for this sort of work."

"Oh," said Julie. "Yes, of course. Please, take all the time you need."

Mac jerked his head towards the patio door, and he rose to his feet. Dave grunted and stood, and they crossed the bar to the patio and stepped outside, staying beneath the awning. The rain had intensified to a steady soaking, and the deck and the metal patio furniture gleamed.

"Okay," said Mac. "I don't want to do this."

"Why not?" said Dave in a reasonable tone. Likely he had used the same tone of voice when dealing with recalcitrant detectives.

"Because this is a bad idea," said Mac. "There's a ninety-nine percent chance her husband killed himself, and she's in denial about it."

"And how do you know that?" said Dave.

"Because the medical examiner ruled it a suicide," said Mac. "And because Julie Norton seems like she badgered the police until she got the complete case file and autopsy report. She would have given them to you, and you looked at them, and you think Doug Norton killed himself."

"Yes," said Dave. "I do."

Mac sighed. "Goddamn it, Dave. You'd be taking her money for no good reason."

Dave shook his head. "I know Julie reasonably well. My company has done a lot of work for Morgan Properties – background checks, due diligence, that kind of thing. She won't give up, Mac. If my company doesn't take her case, she'll find someone who will. There are PIs who will take her money and string her along to max out their billable hours. I'm not going to do that, and neither will you. That's why I called you. You'll give her a fair and honest look at the case in exchange for her money. A lot of people wouldn't do that."

"I don't know," said Mac. "This won't end well."

Dave shrugged. "It already didn't end well when they found Doug Norton with a bullet in his head. Look at it this way. You might help Julie get some closure, you'll keep someone from ripping her off, and you'll make some money in the process."

"What do you think?" said Mac. "You read all the files. Do you think her husband killed himself?"

"Yes," said Dave. "But there are some anomalies in the report, some things that don't make sense."

"Like what?" said Mac.

"I'll let you read it and make up your own mind," said Dave.

Mac chewed on that for a moment, staring into the rain.

"Did your detectives like it when you told them that?" said Mac.

Dave's grin flashed in the light leaking from the windows. "They hated it. But I was the lieutenant, which meant they had to suck it up and like it. But you've got a choice, Mac."

Mac sighed. "I'm going to regret this."

"No, you won't," said Dave. "You'll make a couple of thousand dollars out of it, and you'll help put Julie Norton's mind at ease."

"So I'll be scamming a poor widow out of a few thousand dollars," said Mac. "Swell."

Dave grunted. "She's a widow, but she's not poor. She's a vice president at Morgan Properties. Julie Norton has more money than you and I ever will unless your software for RVs takes off." He shrugged. "Guess real estate always does go up after all."

Mac stared at the rain falling into the river, the lights of the city bleary in the weather. He didn't want to do this. On the other hand, he needed the money. RVW Software didn't have any debt, but neither did it have any revenue. Mac had some income from consulting jobs and the occasional case from Dave, and while he had made some progress paying down his debts, he still needed the money. Taking money from a mourning widow in denial about her husband's suicide felt dirty, but Dave was right. If Julie didn't go with Wester Security, she would go with someone with fewer scruples who would drag the case out to pad their billable hours.

"Fine," said Mac. "But I have some conditions for her."

"Thought you might," said Dave. "I've got some paperwork for you to sign before we're done."

"You were so sure I would do it?"

Dave grinned. "Thought you might."

They went back into Becker's. Julie Norton remained where they had left her. She was sipping at her drink. Some of her nervousness returned as Mac and Dave sat across from her.

"Mrs. Norton," said Mac. "I will take your case."

She nodded and eased a little. "Good."

"Two conditions, though," said Mac. "One, I will tell you the truth about whatever I find out." Julie nodded at that. "Even if you don't want to hear it. If when I'm done, I think that your husband did kill himself, I will tell you that."

"I don't expect anything less," said Julie. "But Doug didn't kill himself."

Again, Mac had the feeling that this was a mistake, but he had committed himself.

"The second condition," said Mac. "We set a time limit. This isn't going to be cheap, and I don't want to take advantage of you. This is exactly the sort of situation where it would be easy to pad the billable hours."

Her smile was flinty. "I'm a lawyer, Mr. Rogan, and I work for the best commercial realtor and development firm in the state of Wisconsin. You might wind up working for free if you're not careful."

"Right," said Mac. "I'll do my best, but it's possible there is nothing to be found. I'm afraid sometimes things simply don't make sense."

"I know," said Julie, her voice quiet. "But I am absolutely certain my husband didn't kill himself." She hesitated. "Say...the end of the year? December 31st, 2007? If you haven't found anything by then, then you likely won't."

Mac glanced at Dave, who nodded.

"Fair enough," said Mac. "If those terms are agreeable, I can start tomorrow."

"Good," said Julie, lifting her briefcase. She opened it and produced a thick tan envelope. "A copy of the police report on my husband's death and the medical examiner's report." Mac wondered if she had looked at the photographs, and for her sake, he hoped not. Gunshot wounds were never pretty. "You'll need those."

"Yes," said Mac, taking the envelope. "Also, I'll need to interview you to get things started. Probably tomorrow, if you have time free."

"Of course." Julie produced a Blackberry and began thumbing through it. "Would ten AM at my office at Morgan Properties work?"

"Yes," said Mac. "I will see you then."

"Before you go," said Dave with an apologetic smile, "we do have some papers to sign, and there is the matter of the retainer..."

2

SUICIDE NOTE

Dave produced his standard contract, and Julie signed it. She paid the retainer, and just like that, Mac was once again a contract employee of Wester Security. After some more small talk, Mac promised again to visit Julie's office at Morgan Properties tomorrow for the first interview, collected the files, and headed for his car.

The rain hammered down, and Mac tucked the envelope beneath his coat, keeping again to the awnings. He got to his car, tossed the envelope on the seat, and headed out, driving a few miles below the speed limit because of the wet roads. Halfway to his apartment, he stopped at a gas station and bought a bottle of Coke and a bag of cinnamon gummy bears. The cashier, a dark-haired woman a few years younger than Mac, smiled and made small talk until she handed over his change.

As Mac drove the rest of the way to his apartment, he belatedly realized the cashier had been flirting with him. She had been pretty, but his mind had been full of the problem Dave had handed him and RVW Software's challenges, and Mac hadn't noticed. He started to wonder what the cashier would look like in something other than a blue polo shirt and black work pants, but soon found himself thinking about the case and software development again.

Mac's life had enough complications that he didn't want to add to them by finding a girlfriend.

"Get a girlfriend, Mac," his brother's rough voice said in his head. "Gotta do something other than work all the time."

Mac rolled his eyes and kept driving.

One of the many vexatious features of his apartment complex was a lack of assigned parking. It was almost ten by the time Mac arrived, so he had to park a good distance from his building. He crossed the parking lot, the envelope with the file under his arm, the bag from the gas station dangling from his hand. Three Hispanic men stood in front of the door to his building, smoking cigarettes and talking in Spanish. They glanced at Mac and ignored him, and he returned the favor as he opened the door. The sound of a steady bass beat from an apartment on the ground floor came to his ears, and he caught a whiff of marijuana smoke.

He climbed to the top floor and let himself into his apartment. Mac changed to a T-shirt and sweatpants and went to the kitchen. He retrieved a bottle of vodka from a cabinet and mixed it with some ice and Coke in the glass, opened the bag of gummy bears, and took a long drink. It burned down his throat, and he ate one of the bears and took another drink.

File and glass in hand, Mac went to the living room. He had two couches obtained from various thrift stores, draped in blankets to cover their unattractive upholstery. They faced his TV, which sat on a rickety wooden table with a DVD player. Mac put on an old movie for background noise and seated himself at the end of the couch.

With that, he took another drink, picked up his laptop from the end table, and booted it up.

A flicker of uneasy memory went through his mind. His laptop had survived the fire that had destroyed his old apartment because it had been in his car. Mac had been under suspicion of murder, and he had been investigating to clear his name.

Digging. Just like his father had done.

What was he going to dig up this time?

Mac had been involved in investigations since the death of Senator Jack Kelsey the past summer. But they had been odd jobs for Dave – insurance fraud and embezzlement and divorce proceedings, the bread and butter of a private investigator's business.

Not anything where people had been killed.

The problem with digging was that you might not like what you find.

Mac pushed aside his misgivings. The bald fact was that Doug Norton had probably killed himself, and this was a way for his widow to come to terms with the fact.

God knew there were worse ways to grieve.

He took another drink and ate a gummy bear to cut the bitter taste. From the end table, he drew out a new reporter's notebook and a pen. At the top of the first page, Mac wrote DOUG NORTON INVESTIGATION in capital letters.

Then he opened the envelope that Julie Norton had given him and started going through the files.

His eyes flicked over the relevant facts. Douglas Alan Norton had been born on January 3rd, 1964, making him forty-two at the time of his death. He had attended the University of Wisconsin-Madison on a football scholarship, playing for all four years, and after graduation had embarked on a brief and unspectacular career in the NFL. Norton had played for Kansas City as a defensive lineman until a combination of a knee injury and generally poor performance had ended his time as a professional athlete. Reading between the lines, Mac suspected that Norton had just barely qualified to play for the NFL and hadn't been able to keep up.

Norton had made the best of it, though. His degree had been in education, and he had soon gotten a job with the Brookfield school system. Norton had been a history teacher and head football coach at Northwoods High School for eleven years before his death. He and Julie had been married for ten years and had two daughters.

He had no felonies, no misdemeanors, no drug habits. Doug

Norton's criminal record consisted of speeding tickets every few years and one citation for disorderly conduct during college that seemed to have been a bar brawl. Mac's impression was that Norton had been one of the unassuming but necessary people who kept the wheels of society turning.

Things changed with the school shooting.

Large portions of the envelope's contents were excerpts from a much larger file dealing with the Northwoods High School shooting. On April 14th, 2005, soon after classes concluded for the day, someone opened fire on the school's front doors from a house across the street. Many students had been leaving for the day, making them easy targets for the sniper. Five students were killed, seven wounded, and thirty more were injured in the panicked stampede.

The shooter had never been caught.

The file included the statement Norton had made to the police, along with the interviewer's notes. Norton had conducted himself with bravery during the shooting, getting students to the classrooms and keeping them away from the windows until police arrived. The interviewer noted that Norton had been found physically blocking the door to the classroom. The usual ugly mess had followed the shooting – the grief, the media circling like vultures, political activists using the dead as an argument to advance their particular viewpoint, the civil lawsuits, all of it exacerbated by the fact that killer had never been found.

On January 24th, 2006, Doug Norton shot himself in the head.

Mac read the relevant pages, making notes as he did. Norton had been found dead at his desk in his classroom at around 5 PM by a colleague. He had shot himself in the right side of the head, and the suicide weapon was found on the floor near his hand. Specifically, a Smith & Wesson Model 910 semiautomatic pistol. The angle of the bullet was consistent with Norton having fired it himself, and the powder burns on his right temple meant the muzzle of the weapon had been against his skin. Norton's fingerprints were all over both the weapon and its magazine.

Doug Norton had almost certainly killed himself.

Except it hadn't been his gun.

The pistol had been registered to a man named Winston Marsh who had been killed in an accident six months prior. Marsh had left no heirs, and the pistol hadn't been found among his possessions when his apartment had been cleared out. There had been no connection between Norton and Marsh that anyone could find, and no one had any idea how Norton had ended up with Marsh's gun six months after his death.

That was strange. But not unexplainable. It wasn't that difficult to buy a weapon illegally. Maybe someone had broken into Marsh's apartment after his death, the pistol was the only thing worth stealing, and Norton had bought it from the thief with cash. It was strange that Norton would have Marsh's gun, but there were any number of plausible explanations.

The suicide note was even stranger. Such as it was.

Suicides, Mac knew, did not always leave notes. Sometimes those inclined to suicide planned it out carefully, leaving a detailed note apologizing for their failings. But it was disturbing how often suicides took place on the spur of the moment, when someone was in a dark mood and the opportunity was right in front of them.

Norton had written the words KRISTIN SALWELL on his day planner on the page for January 24th, 2006. He had used the planner extensively, and KRISTIN SALWELL was written in the last appointment of the day. He had circled and underlined the name as if making a point.

Which opened up another can of worms.

Kristin Salwell had become a person of interest in Norton's death, but she couldn't have been involved because on January 24th, 2006, she had been serving a one-year prison sentence for blackmail and extortion. Salwell had graduated from Northwoods High School the prior May in the delayed ceremony after the shooting, and she had done it with a 4.0 GPA. She had achieved this not through academic prowess but by sleeping with two of her teachers, recording the encounters, and blackmailing them. She had also extorted both teachers for thousands of dollars and made the mistake of doing so when she was eighteen and no longer a minor. When the mess settled, the two teachers went to prison for statutory rape, and Salwell went to prison for a year for blackmail. All of that had come out in the summer of 2005 as any hope of catching the school shooter dwindled.

The past two years, Mac reflected, had not been good ones for Northwoods High School.

He finished his drink, got up, and poured himself another. Why would Doug Norton have written Kristin Salwell's name in his final moments before his death? The conclusion was obvious enough. He had been involved with Salwell in some way, maybe had slept with her, and then guilt had overwhelmed him, and he had shot himself in the head.

Of course, that was a lot of assumptions.

Mac took a long drink from his glass and paced to the window, pushing open the blinds with a finger. The parking lot below was dark, the only illumination coming from the security lights near the building doors. A few cars went past on the street. He idly wondered if anyone driving those cars was thinking about suicide, dismissed the thought as both morbid and unproductive, and returned to his couch. The buzz from the alcohol was starting to drag at his thoughts, and he wanted to finish glancing over the contents of the envelope before he went to sleep.

The detective assigned to investigate Doug Norton's death had spoken with Kristin Salwell in prison, asking if she had any involvement with Norton. Salwell had flatly denied that she had ever slept with Norton and claimed she had never attempted to extort him. In the transcript of the interview, she said that while she had been in Norton's history class, he had too much of a "stick up his ass" to even consider sleeping with a student.

Mac came to the final pages of the files. Due to the position of the bullet wound and the fingerprints on the gun, Douglas Norton's death had been ruled a suicide. No one knew how Norton had gotten Winston Marsh's gun, and there had been no reason for Norton to write down Salwell's name before he died, but the preponderance of evidence suggested that Norton had killed himself.

He stared at the pages, and a wave of anger, shocking in its intensity, went through him. It had little to do with what he had just read. Ever since the events of the summer, ever since Senator Jack Kelsey and Katrina Hobb had died in front him, Mac had felt a constant low-level irritability interspersed with bursts of overwhelming anger. Tom thought it was a form of post-traumatic stress, but Mac suspected that Tom was overthinking it.

It had all been such a waste. Kelsey had gotten away with his crimes for years and ruined a lot of lives along the way, and Katrina had died for nothing. Doug Norton's death had been a pointless waste as well. He had killed himself for nothing, and his grieving widow had latched onto the stolen gun and the day planner to explain the tragedy, clinging to the hope that her husband had not killed himself rather than continue life with her.

Suddenly Mac was so angry that he wanted to smash his laptop. Which would have been stupid. He needed the laptop and couldn't afford a new one. Instead, he closed the laptop, put the files away in the envelope, and got up and paced, finishing the rest of his drink. Mac had a definite buzz, and it was almost eleven by now. He needed to get some sleep before his interview with Julie Norton tomorrow.

Bit by bit, he calmed down, the anger fading into weariness.

He had a plan for the investigation. If he found out how Norton had gotten Marsh's gun, that might be enough to explain the suicide. If Norton had been thinking about killing himself, perhaps he had bought a stolen gun to avoid raising any red flags with his family.

Mac cleared the laptop and the files off his couch, ate a dozen more gummy bears, and washed them down with two glasses of water. Hydration and blood sugar were the best ways to avoid a hangover, and he needed his wits about him tomorrow for the interview.

He turned off the lights, lay down on the couch, and pulled a blanket to his neck. Mac had never gotten around to buying a bed for his new apartment. He slept on his back most of the time, and the couch was comfortable enough. No sense in buying a bed, he mused, when he was too busy to try and get anyone else into it.

Mac drifted off to sleep. Sometimes, frequently, he had bad dreams about the events of the summer, but not tonight.

Vodka and gummy bears were good for that much.

3

DISTRACTIONS

The woman who had killed Douglas Norton drove alone through a bad part of Milwaukee.

Arianna Crest ought to have been thinking about her plan, she knew. She had broken the law not once but many, many times, and she had always gotten away with it because she thought things through well in advance. She liked to think her father would have been proud of her. Arianna had never been caught, and though she had done things that would have put her in prison for the rest of her life – assuming the sniveling parents of all those dead teenagers at Northwoods High School did not kill her first – no one even suspected her.

People were so stupid, and it was easy to do what you wanted if you just thought things out.

Arianna ought to have been thinking about the plan, but instead, she found herself thinking about the psychopath test.

She had read it in a magazine years ago, a trashy article in the sort of trashy magazine that appealed to the insecurities of the modern American woman. A bottomless market if there ever was one, and Arianna had read it in the dentist's waiting room to pass the time and amuse herself by sneering at the obsessions of her inferiors.

But one article had caught her attention. It claimed there was a simple test to determine if you were a psychopath or not. A woman is at her mother's funeral and meets a man she finds attractive but doesn't get his phone number. A few days later, the woman killed her own sister. What was her motive?

If you answered that she hoped the handsome man would come to the sister's funeral, apparently you were a psychopath.

Arianna had thought it a stupid test. There were many, many more effective and subtle ways for the woman to have found the man, especially in the era of the Internet. It was possible to get away with murder (Arianna had), but it wasn't something to do lightly and without careful planning. The "psychological test" struck Arianna as wasteful, not insightful.

And yet.

Arianna had been an only child, but if she had had a sister, and killing the sister would have been a step towards something Arianna wanted...

Maybe the article had been on to something.

Arianna didn't think she was a sociopath. She had loved her father, after all, even in his decline when he had been more interested in alcohol, potato chips, and television than anything else.

But a psychopath?

Maybe.

Or perhaps "psychopath" was the word stupid and weak people used to describe their superiors.

She smiled at the thought and maneuvered the van into a parking spot.

Like many American cities, Milwaukee had a prosperous downtown surrounded by a variety of low-income neighborhoods. This particular area was on the edge of Marquette University's sphere of influence, a mixture of student housing, shabby bars, and apartments for the workers who staffed the restaurants and the businesses that catered to the university community. If Arianna had wanted, she could have bought a variety of illegal drugs without much effort.

She was here for a different reason.

The van had stopped in front of a shabby three-story apartment building. A rail-thin man in a gray utility coverall similar to Arianna's own emerged from the building, a canvas tool bag slung over one shoulder. Arianna unlocked the doors, and the man dropped into the passenger seat with a grunt. He smelled of cigarette smoke and unwashed clothing. No liquor odor, though, which was more important.

"You have everything you need?" said Arianna.

"Yeah," said Rod Cutler. "You bring the money?"

Arianna stared at him with distaste. Rod was balding, with a lined face and an unfortunate mustache that resembled a cheap paintbrush. He looked like the sort of man who frequented prostitutes, which was fair enough because his addiction to them had destroyed his life. Once Rod had been a married man with a prosperous home-improvement business. Then he had embezzled a little too much money to pay for his appetites, and the discovery of that fact had cost Rod Cutler his marriage, his business, and five years of his life in state prison.

But he still had a variety of useful skills.

Rod looked away first, pretending to glance at the sidewalk.

He was too frightened of Arianna to make much trouble. Rod was a liability, and she would have to get rid of him one day, but for now, he was still useful, and he was too scared to betray her.

It helped that she had killed someone in front of Rod about five seconds after they had met.

"Yes, of course," said Arianna, and he looked back at her. "A thousand dollars up front." She passed him an envelope with a gloved hand. "And four thousand more if we pull this off." Rod took the money at once, tucking it into a pocket. "Have I ever not paid you?"

"No," conceded Rod, grudgingly. Arianna always kept her word. That way, if she found it necessary to employ treachery, it was all the more unexpected. For now, he was still useful, and he was smart enough to realize that betraying her would end very badly for him. But the day she decided Rod was no longer of use, he would never see the bullet coming.

"Good," said Arianna. She smiled, using the expression she practiced in the mirror before important meetings. Rod knew her well enough that the smile completely failed to relax him. "Then let's get to work."

She put the van into drive and pulled into traffic, Rod settling the tool bag on the floor between his work boots.

Arianna headed for Waukesha, a small city to the west that made up part of the extended Milwaukee metropolitan area. It would have been twenty minutes by freeway at this time of night, but she kept to the surface streets. Fewer cameras and fewer chances of running into a speed trap. Rod shifted uneasily in his seat, and Arianna finally told him to turn on the radio to amuse himself. He complied and switched through the stations until he found one discussing football, which he listened to with interest.

"Those idiots," said Rod as Arianna turned onto a county highway, the van's headlights illuminating empty fields on either side. "Don't they know their defense won't work?"

"Guess not," said Arianna, who had memorized just enough about football to maintain a conversation when necessary. God, but the subject was tedious. She only cared about things when they offered her a chance to accumulate money and power, and since she had no desire to go into sports gambling, football offered neither.

Rod shook his head with dismay and went into a long, rambling speech about various defensive plays and the failures of the coaches who lacked the wisdom to see things Rod's way. Arianna listened with half an ear, most of her attention focused on the road and watching for any police cars. It wasn't likely that she would run into any police, but bad luck could ruin even the most careful plan.

She drove to a new subdivision on the outskirts of Waukesha proper, a cul-de-sac lined with large houses. Arianna had been involved in some of the deals that had gotten the subdivision approved, and she knew that the houses were ridiculously overvalued, especially since they had been built as cheaply and as shoddily as possible.

Her target, Nathan Rangel, lived in one of those houses.

Arianna circled around the subdivision, turning north, and got back on the county highway. It was almost midnight by now, and a sea of darkness surrounded the subdivision's lights. The only other light came from Arianna's van.

"There's the transformer," said Rod. He had been paying attention after all.

Arianna pulled over to the shoulder of the road. In the distance, she saw the lights of the subdivision's shoddy mini-mansions. Illuminated in the lights of the van was a slab of concrete surrounded by a chain-link fence. Within were two large cabinets of gray metal covered with DANGER and HIGH VOLTAGE signs.

She shut off the engine and headlights. Darkness swallowed the landscape around her.

Rod lifted his tool bag. Arianna picked up a heavy flashlight and an empty duffel bag, and Rod took a second flashlight. They got out of the van and picked their way over the damp ground. The rain had finally stopped a few hours ago, but everything was still sodden. Just as well that Arianna had thought to put a pair of plastic booties into her pockets, the sort crime scene technicians wore to avoid contaminating evidence.

She, too, wanted to avoid contaminating evidence, just in a different way.

Arianna waited as Rod produced a pair of bolt cutters and cut first the padlock on the fence gate and then the lock on one of the big metal transformers. The boxes gave off an ominous humming sound that made Arianna's skin crawl. She didn't know exactly how electrical power worked, but she stood a safe distance away in case Rod accidentally fried himself. If he did, she would have to remember to search his body to make sure the corpse had nothing that could link him to her company.

"All right," said Rod. He nodded to himself and looked at her, the flashlight casting harsh shadows over his bony face. "I can cut the power to the entire subdivision. Shouldn't be a problem." He jerked his head towards the houses. "Of course, all those rich assholes, the minute the power goes out, they'll pick up their phones and make a stink. I'd say we've got an hour before the power company sends someone out to check."

"Stopwatches," said Arianna. She produced a small digital stopwatch, and Rod dug one out of his bag. "Fifteen minutes. When it hits zero, cut the power."

Rod nodded and started the timer. He knew better than to ask what she would be doing.

Arianna started through the empty field towards the subdivision, taking slow, careful steps so that she would not lose her footing on the wet grass. She wasn't terribly worried about anyone seeing her. It was an overcast night, and the empty meadow north of the subdivision was mostly flat, with large pieces of fieldstone jutting from the ground here and there.

She picked her way step by step towards Nathan Rangel's house. Arianna knew Rangel passingly well – businessman, entrepreneur, Waukesha city councilor, and insufferable blowhard. Rangel owned several different businesses throughout the Milwaukee metropolitan area, mostly fast food and restaurant franchises, and she had dealt with his company a few times.

Rangel liked to talk, which meant that Arianna knew that he and his family were on a trip to Florida this week.

She also knew that he was a gun nut. He boasted about his hunting trips, and he collected weapons.

Arianna had a better use for the weapons than shooting deer.

Her heart rate picked up, the familiar tingle going down her nerves. This was a risk, and Arianna was honest enough with herself to realize that she loved risks. She never felt more alive than when doing something dangerous.

Perhaps that meant she really was a psychopath. Arianna had read somewhere that excessive risk-taking was a common symptom of psychopathy, and she had taken some extreme risks in her time. Killing all those teenagers at Northwoods High School, or the day she had murdered her mother, or shooting that moron Douglas Norton in the head and making it look like he had killed himself.

Arianna hadn't done that because she enjoyed killing. She didn't have strong feelings one way or another, like it was a chore she simply had to do on occasion, like filing quarterly taxes or remembering to floss before bed. But those killings had made her millions of dollars in the end. If shooting them hadn't brought her profit, Arianna wouldn't have done it.

But she had, and in the moment...God, it had been a thrill.

Some of that thrill came back now. This wasn't as dangerous as some of the things she had done. But she was robbing a gun nut's house, and any number of things could go wrong.

Arianna stopped about a dozen yards from Nathan Rangel's home. It was two stories, with five bedrooms, a three-car garage, and an expansive deck on the back of the house. Security lights bathed the yard and the house's sides with bright white illumination. She checked her stopwatch, its digital numerals glowing dimly in the darkness. Seven minutes left until Rod cut the power, assuming he didn't screw it up. Arianna took those seven minutes to prepare, sliding the plastic booties over her shoes, pulling a hairnet on, and donning a ski mask to conceal her features. It was doubtful the police would do DNA testing for a simple burglary, and she didn't think anyone would see her, but it was best to think things through.

She waited, watching the house. Some of the lights on the first floor of Rangel's house were on, but none of the upstairs lights and the illumination didn't have the distinctive flicker of television. Arianna was reasonably sure that the house was empty, that Rangel's entire family was on vacation.

The stopwatch ticked down to zero, and Arianna waited.

About fifteen seconds later, the power went out, the subdivision plunging into darkness.

The best security system in the world didn't do much without electricity.

Arianna strode forward, passing onto the deck. She saw the plastic dome of the home security camera over the back door and smiled. The camera would do little good without power. She reached into a pocket of her coverall and drew out a lock rake gun, one that was technically illegal for anyone but a law enforcement officer to possess. Arianna lined it up with the lock on the back door, and it opened on the sixth try.

She slipped into a large kitchen, the counter and the appliances shadowed in gloom, and listened. Rangel and his family were in Florida, but it was always possible they had left behind a house sitter, or maybe one of the teenage sons had stayed behind to "study" while fooling around with his girlfriend. But the house was silent, with the stillness of an empty building.

Nothing. She was alone.

Arianna crept forward until she was out of sight of any windows and flicked on her flashlight, sweeping it over the floor until she found the cellar door. She opened it and clomped down the stairs, the plastic on her shoes leaving little puddles on the floor and steps. That was unfortunate, but it was much better than leaving behind footprints, and by the time the Rangels returned, the water would have evaporated anyway.

The basement was in excellent condition – painted cinder block walls and polished concrete floor. It had been a while since Arianna had sold any houses herself, but she could just imagine herself emphasizing the basement during a showing. Ample storage space, concrete floor, included washer and dryer, a drain in the floor to prevent any flooding, modern furnace and water heater, and...

She smiled behind her mask as she swept the flashlight beam over the walls.

And room in the corner for a hunter's workshop.

Rangel had a dozen stuffed deer heads mounted on the walls, no doubt banished to the basement by his wife, who though vapid and insufferable, did have better taste than her husband. A table held gun cleaning tools and several black plastic storage totes. An easy chair faced a small flatscreen television on a wooden stand. A black metal gun cabinet with a glass door caught Arianna's attention.

Inside were the weapons she sought.

Nathan Rangel, she reflected as she broke the glass door with the butt of her flashlight and opened the lock from inside, really ought to have invested in a proper gun safe. No doubt he liked to admire his weapons through the glass. Arianna unrolled her duffel bag and took several weapons – two AR-15s, a modified Ruger rifle with a scope and a larger magazine, and a Mossberg pump-action shotgun. For what she had in mind on Halloween, Arianna only needed one of the AR-15s, but it was best to confuse the trail a bit.

Besides, you never knew when another gun might come in handy.

Arianna opened the storage lockers, found boxes of ammunition and shotgun shells, and stuffed several of them into her duffel bag. With the weapons and ammunition secured, she stared up the stairs. The bag was heavy enough that she needed both hands to carry it, and she felt the strain in her arms and shoulders.

She hauled the bag out the back door, making sure to close it behind her, and then started across the patio and across the field to the county highway and the van. A quick glance around the subdivision showed a car driving past, a few people coming out of their overpriced houses with flashlights to see if the entire neighborhood's power had gone out. But in the darkness of the overcast night, no one saw her carrying the duffel bag of weapons across the field.

A few minutes later, she reached the power station. Rod flinched as she strode out of the darkness, but Arianna walked past him and tossed the duffel bag into the back of the van. Her arms and shoulders burned from the exertion, but not that badly, and the sensation would pass soon enough.

"Get the power back on and let's go," she said. She started to climb into the driver's seat and decided that it would be more efficient to make sure Rod didn't leave any evidence behind. Arianna masked her intent by shining her flashlight beam where Rod was working. He looked at her, blinked in surprise, and then grunted his thanks.

Arianna swept her flashlight back and forth over the gray metal cabinets at Rod's direction. Finally, he nodded to himself, pulled a large black metal switch with an insulated handle, and stepped back as the transformers began to give off an angry buzz. For an alarmed second, Arianna thought they were about to explode, but the buzzing grew less strident, and lights began to flick back on throughout the subdivision.

"Power's back on," announced Rod.

"Good," said Arianna. "Get your tools. We're leaving."

She watched as Rod gathered his tools and scuttled to the van. Arianna took one last look at the power station, satisfied that they had left behind nothing incriminating.

A moment later, they were gone, driving back to Milwaukee.

"So," said Rod, clearing his throat. "About my four thousand dollars…"

Without taking her eyes from the road, she reached into her coverall, produced another envelope, and passed it to him. Rod let out a satisfied sound, took the money, turned on the overhead light, and started counting it.

"Use your flashlight for that," said Arianna. "I don't want anyone to see our faces when we go past."

Rod flinched but nodded and turned off the overhead light. "You going to tell me what's in that bag?"

"Drugs and gold coins," said Arianna. "About a million dollars of cocaine."

"Fine, don't tell me," said Rod, but he knew better than to press the point. He was smart enough to realize that the less he knew, the less likely it was that Arianna would decide to kill him.

Rod finished counting his money and tucked the envelope away, satisfied. They returned to Milwaukee, the streets mostly deserted, and Arianna stopped in front of Rod's decrepit apartment building.

"You have any other work for me?" said Rod.

"I might," said Arianna. She had planned out Halloween well in advance, and the guns she had taken from Rangel's house were the final step. But one never knew what might come up. "Leave your phone on. I'll text if I have something for you." They communicated through two cheap prepaid cell phones Arianna had bought at a Wal-Mart in Minnesota. Arianna only used that phone for communicating with Rod, and if necessary, she could destroy it swiftly.

Best to never leave any evidence behind.

"All right." Rod looked at the envelope, at his apartment building, and licked his lips. "I won't be available tomorrow. Gonna have to spend this all."

Arianna kept herself from rolling her eyes. Rod was enslaved to his lust for prostitutes, just as her father had been enslaved by his gluttony in his final years. The weakness disgusted her, but she kept it out of her voice. "Fine."

Rod nodded, collected his tools, and exited the van. Arianna waited until he had disappeared into the apartment building and then put the van back into drive and set off across Milwaukee.

A short drive brought her to the boundary between Brookfield and New Berlin, to where the Crest Development office building stood, a long, wide rectangle of gleaming concrete and glass. Arianna owned the entire building, though her company only occupied the top floor, and she leased the bottom three floors to other businesses.

Waste not, want not.

Arianna's own construction people used the yard behind the building to store their vehicles and equipment, and Arianna parked the van in its usual spot. She stopped inside long enough to let herself into the security office and turn the cameras back on. Thieves tried to steal tools and equipment from the trailers in the yard on a regular basis, but Arianna had wanted no record of her use of the van.

With that finished, she took the duffel bag of guns to her SUV and drove home.

Arianna lived in a Brookfield, in a five-bedroom, two-bath, three-car garage home she had built herself through Crest Development and was currently valued at just over eight hundred and fifty thousand dollars. It had gone up considerably in last year – the boom in real estate prices had benefited both her company and her personally.

She thought of the little three-bedroom bungalow she had grown up in, the house her mother had sneered at, and Arianna smirked to herself as she did every time she thought of her mother. A pity that the late Jacqueline Crest hadn't lived to see her daughter's success. Arianna would have loved to rub her nose in it.

If she had lived. Jacqueline Crest had been Arianna's very first kill, and you had to start somewhere, didn't you?

She lugged the duffel bag of guns and ammunition into her basement workshop. Before her father had become too fat to walk, he had been a prison guard (a "corrections officer," he insisted), and one of the things that Arianna had learned from him was to never, ever keep anything you used to commit a crime, and especially don't keep it in your own house. Many of the inmates in Andrew Crest's care would have gotten off scot-free if they had only disposed of the gun, the knife, the drugs, or the stolen goods before the police had caught up to them.

With a few tactical exceptions, Arianna followed that advice religiously.

Arianna had no intention of ever having children, so one of the bedrooms had been converted to her home office, the second to a personal yoga studio. The rest of her gym equipment was in the large, spacious basement, a treadmill and an elliptical and free weights. She kept her workshop down here, along with her guns and their maintenance equipment. Arianna enjoyed guns just as much as Nathan Rangel, though she was quieter about it.

Come to think of it, she probably enjoyed guns more than Rangel. She had killed a lot of people, and Arianna bet Rangel had never even shot anyone.

Later she would examine the weapons. Right now, it was almost two in the morning, and Arianna had a day full of meetings ahead of her. She went upstairs to the master bedroom, showered off, and sprawled in her king-sized bed. Sometimes she entertained company in her bed, occasionally to amuse herself and burn off her urges, more frequently to help persuade someone in a deal, but she preferred to have the bed all to herself.

Arianna awoke at six, worked out in her basement, and dressed in a black pencil skirt, a form-fitting black jacket, and a crisp white blouse. Tasteful jewelry went on her ears and around her neck –

enough to suggest wealth, not enough to be garish. She had three angled mirrors by her vanity, and she turned, examining herself from every angle, and was pleased with the way the clothes fit snugly against her. At Arianna's age, her mother had been fifty pounds overweight, and in his final year of life, her father had been so fat he could barely get from his bed to his couch. Arianna found obesity repellent on a visceral level, both aesthetically and as a sign of weakness, and she found weakness and lack of self-control disgusting.

The United States, she thought, had too many useless people. Too many people were a waste of the oxygen they breathed. Perhaps governments that had purged their societies of the unfit or rounded them up into camps had been onto something. Still, it was so easy to separate the unfit from the money they didn't deserve to have, so maybe she was overthinking it.

Arianna collected her purse, which as always contained a small revolver, and drove to her office building. She arrived promptly at seven-fifty, her heels clicking against the polished floor of the lobby. The security guard greeted her, and Arianna favored him with a smile as he held the stairwell door for her. She always took the stairs, ostensibly for exercise, in reality because she disliked the loss of control in an elevator.

Her personal assistant Helen waited with a cup of coffee, and Arianna took it and stepped into her office. She had the corner office on the top floor, sunlight streaming through the windows. Arianna paused halfway to her desk, examining the mockups that stood on a pair of easels near her door.

The Westview Mall development. Currently pursued by both Morgan Properties and Crest Development.

Arianna's company would get it.

The project would make her millions of dollars. If it went really well, it might make her into Wisconsin's first female billionaire.

And all she needed to do was to kill a few high school students.

After all, she had done it before.

4

WEIGHTS

Mac awoke at five forty-five AM when the alarm clock on his end table started buzzing.

He had a mild headache, a dry mouth, and a full bladder, but no hangover. It was a trick that he had learned in college from a man whose alcohol consumption had been legendary yet never seemed to suffer a hangover. The student, a premed, had explained to Mac that hangovers were caused by a combination of dehydration and a change in blood glucose levels, both of which could be mitigated by remaining hydrated and consuming sugar. Mac didn't know if that was actually true or not, but the former premed student was now a respected family practice doctor, and Mac didn't have a hangover.

After taking care of his full bladder, Mac got a cup of coffee and sat at his computer. He checked his email, noting that Nikolai agreed with the changes that Mac had made to the app code and suggested a long list of his own. Mac worked through the changes until six-thirty, and then it was time to get ready.

He stood and turned, and as he did, stubbed his toe against the legs of one of the folding tables that served as his desk.

The anger that exploded through him caught Mac off-guard, and for a second, he was so furious that he wanted to flip his tables over and start smashing things with his bare hands. He just barely stopped himself – he really needed his computers and couldn't afford to replace them. Instead, he paced in circles through the living room, shivering with fury, hoping he didn't hear someone playing loud music or shouting somewhere else in the building. That might set him off, and he didn't need to lose his temper with strangers right now.

Bit by bit, the rage abated. Ever since the troubles in June and the death of Senator Kelsey and Katrina Hobb, Mac had been subject to bursts of explosive temper. Tom thought it was a form of PTSD. Mac didn't want to hear about that…

Shit. Tom. He was going to be late.

Mac sighed, forced down the anger, and changed in haste. He dressed in a loose tank top, shorts, running shoes, and grabbed his gym bag and a tattered old coat from the closet. Pausing only long enough to fill up a plastic water bottle in the kitchen, Mac locked the apartment, descended to the parking lot, and headed out.

A short drive of a few blocks took Mac to a strip mall. It was unremarkable – a Subway on the corner, a Chinese restaurant next to it, an accountant's office after that, and then a space currently used as a Democratic Party field office. But a full third of the strip mall was taken up by Iron Oswald's Gym, and the harsh light from its windows shone into the gloom of the overcast fall morning.

Mac got his gym bag and opened the front door.

Some gyms had cheerful lighting, carpeted floors, upbeat music, and vending machines with colorful sports drinks. Iron Oswald's Gym had none of those. The floor was sealed concrete, stark and gray, the fluorescent lights stark and unflattering. A row of treadmills ran along one wall, and the rest of the floor space was taken up with rows and rows of free weights and weight racks.

A desk stood near the door, equipped with a computer and a monitor showing security camera feeds. A sullen-looking Turkish man sat behind the desk, playing solitaire on his computer. Mac thought he was one of Osman's numerous brothers or cousins.

Osman had come to America twenty years ago and owned numerous businesses around the Milwaukee area, all of which provided employment for his extended family. For some reason, Osman named his gym Iron Oswald's to appeal to the American market, though the gym's complete lack of amenities meant that it appealed mostly to men with a serious interest in weightlifting, much like Mac's older brother Tom.

Osman's brother and/or cousin nodded to Mac, and he walked past the desk to join Tom Rogan at one of the squat racks.

Tom was a big man in a tank top and loose shorts. He had a Semper Fi tattoo on his left bicep, an enormous bushy beard, and dirty yellow hair pulled back into a ponytail. The beard and the hair almost, but not quite, managed to conceal the heavy scarring on the left side of his face.

"Mac," said Tom. His voice sounded a lot better these days. His speech therapist clearly knew her job. "You're almost late."

"Almost is not the same as late," said Mac. "You gonna lift weights, or are you going to complain about the clock?"

Tom grinned at him, and they went to work.

They started with three rounds of pushups and unweighted squats and then switched to the weights. Mac had never really gotten into weightlifting, and his interest in organized sports had been lukewarm at best. In high school, he had played on the freshman and sophomore basketball team, less out of love for the sport and more out of a desire to meet girls. But he had been bored with the game, and during his final two years of high school helping his father with his growing private investigation business had been more interesting.

He hadn't met many girls doing either sports or investigating, come to think of it.

But after the events of the past summer, Tom had suggested weightlifting as a way to deal with his frustrations. Mac had been dubious, but he had taken Tom up on the suggestion, and he had been surprised that it worked. He felt better after a weightlifting session, less angry, his mind clearer. There had been other benefits as well. Mac had gained seven pounds since the summer, but it had been muscle, and all his clothes fit looser.

They started with a round of deadweights. Mac had started in June able to deadlift a hundred and fifty-five pounds, and he had increased that to two hundred and twenty-five pounds. Tom expected he would max out around two hundred and fifty or maybe two hundred and seventy-five.

"So you never progress after that?" Mac had asked.

"Nah," grunted Tom. "Eventually, you get injured or pull a muscle. Then you recover, and you start all over again. Part of the fun."

Mac finished his deadlifts and then spotted Tom through his. After they took a short break, drinking from their water bottles. Mac always brought his own water since he thought the water from the drinking fountain tasted funny, and it wasn't the sort of thing Osman was likely to fix anytime soon.

"I've got a new job," said Mac.

Tom grunted for him to continue.

"From Dave Wester," said Mac.

Tom's eyebrows rose. "Thought you didn't like digging." He coughed. "You were going to focus on software development with the lawyer and that Russian guy."

"Dave persuaded me," said Mac. "Woman named Julie Norton. Know her?" Tom shook his head. "She works for Morgan Properties."

"Do know them," said Tom. He took another drink of water. "Big commercial developers. Behind that Broadlawn Acres development I was working on all summer after I got my electrician's license." He grunted. "Morgan Properties spends their time competing with Crest Properties. Good for contractors like me."

"Last January, Julie's husband killed himself at his desk," said Mac. "Julie thinks it was a murder, not a suicide, so she hired Dave to look into it, and Dave hired me."

Tom stared at him. "You think he did kill himself."

"Yeah."

Tom snorted. "Let me guess." He coughed and cleared his throat.

"Dave said she was going to spend a lot of money to look into the case anyway, so she might as well pay it to you since you're honest and wouldn't cheat her."

"Pretty much. You know Dave."

"That's Dave." Tom set down his water bottle and gestured towards the equipment. "Let's do the bench presses. Then I'll tell you what I think."

They switched to the bench press. Tom loaded up his bar, and Mac spotted him while he worked through his presses. By then, business was beginning to pick up at Iron Oswald's Gym. The clients were entirely male and ranged from angry-looking men about Tom's age to middle-aged and elderly guys with thick paunches and muscular arms. Tom finished his sets, and Mac removed some of the weights from the bar and took Tom's place. He couldn't lift as much as Tom, but he could lift fifty pounds more in a bench press than he could have in June.

"Okay," said Tom after they had returned the bar and the plates to the racks. "Here's what I think."

"Yeah?" said Mac.

"You say you're done digging," said Tom. He coughed and took a drink of water. "But. You keep taking these jobs from Dave."

"I don't like digging," said Mac. "I'm broke and paying off debts. Dave pays on time, and he's a good man to work for. Once I'm out of debt, I'm done. No more playing private investigator."

Tom looked unconvinced. "Eh. If you didn't like it, you wouldn't keep doing it." He coughed and took another swig of water. "You could do other things to make money."

"Dad liked digging," said Mac, "and look what it got him."

Tom shrugged. "That's like saying because Mom was a psycho bitch, you're never getting married."

"And yet neither one of us are married," said Mac.

"You haven't had a date since college," said Tom.

"I have too," said Mac. He just hadn't had a relationship that had lasted more than a few dates since college. "And you're one to talk."

Tom only smirked.

"Wait," said Mac. "You have a girlfriend? Since when?"

Tom put down his water. "Time for squats."

"Christ," muttered Mac, but he followed Tom to the squat rack. He spotted Tom through his set, and then Mac adjusted the weights and did his own reps. His muscles were definitely feeling it by the time he was done, an ache in his shoulders and legs, his shirt sticking to his chest and back with sweat.

After he finished, they took another quick break with their water bottles.

"So you have a girlfriend?" said Mac.

"No," said Tom. "But you should be more open to the possibility."

"Sure," said Mac. "Worked out real great for Dad."

He wondered if that had been a stupid thing to say. Their mother had murdered their father and tried to pin it on Mac. She had done a bad job of it, however, and currently was spending the rest of her life in state prison. But Tom only shrugged.

"Don't marry a crazy actress like Dad did," said Tom. He coughed and drank some more water. "You going to stick with this investigation?"

"I said I would," said Mac.

"You think the husband killed himself?"

"Probably," said Mac. "I want to focus on how he acquired the gun. Doesn't make any sense. The pistol he used belonged to a janitor who died in an accident several months before. If I can figure out how he got the pistol, I can probably convince the widow it was a suicide."

"Careful," said Tom.

Mac shrugged. "This isn't like the Kelsey thing from the summer. No crazy environmentalists. No corrupt political machines. I won't have to testify to Congress."

"No. I mean the widow," said Tom. "One of two things will happen." He rubbed his throat and took another drink. "One, her husband killed himself, and she's in denial, and she'll lose her shit if you prove it. That's more likely." He pointed at Mac. "But if someone did kill him and you start to figure it out..." He coughed and took another drink of water. "They won't like it."

"Yeah," said Mac.

"Give a call if you need help," said Tom.

"I will," said Mac.

"I'm tired of talking," said Tom. "Let's finish up."

They wiped down the weights and returned them to the racks, and then headed to the treadmills. Tom's preferred workout program ended with a two-mile run, and Mac ground it out in the treadmill, sweating heavily the entire time. He preferred weightlifting to running, but he nonetheless finished before Tom.

At last, the run ended, and they wiped down the treadmills.

"Want to grab some breakfast?" said Tom.

"Nah," said Mac. "I'm doing the first interview with the widow at ten. Need to look presentable by then." He grimaced. "It'll be fun."

"Gonna ask if she and her husband were cheating on each other?" said Tom.

"Yup," said Mac. "Maybe it will help that the cops already asked her that when her husband shot himself." He corrected himself at once. "Or allegedly shot himself. She's paying enough money for this, I should keep an open mind."

Tom snorted. "Decent of you. Beer on Thursday?"

"Yeah, unless something comes up," said Mac. "What are you up to?"

"Remodeling some rich lady's bathroom," said Tom. After leaving the Marines, Tom had become a carpenter and did work for a number of different construction companies in Wisconsin. He had acquired numerous other practical skills along the way and never seemed to lack for work. "Suppose we've got that in common. We're working for rich women who have more money than sense."

"They're the foundation of the American economy," said Mac.

Tom laughed at that, hard, which turned into a coughing fit that he suppressed with another drink of water.

"How's the throat?" said Mac, a little worried.

"Better," said Tom. "New speech therapist helps. Government's even paying for it." He clapped Mac on the shoulder. "See you on Thursday. Give me a call if your case gets tricky."

"Let's hope not," said Mac.

They left the gym, nodding to Osman's relative at the desk, who glowered back but offered a curt nod. It was brighter outside than it had been when Mac arrived, but it was still going to be another gloomy fall day. Tom got into his new truck, a gleaming 2005 Ford F-150. It was substantially nicer than Mac's battered Chevy Corsica.

Maybe he was in the wrong line of work.

Mac drove back to his apartment, showered, and sat in front of his computer for an hour, working through some code changes in the app. Then it was time to get ready for his interview with Julie Norton. Mac loaded up the tools he would need in a laptop bag – his notebook, pens, and a digital voice recorder. He took his laptop along since he would likely type up his notes immediately in the car after the interview. Good record keeping was the foundation of investigative work, especially if he wanted his results to stand up in court. Not that he expected this to end up in court, but it was always wise to cultivate sound work habits.

Mac dressed in his interview suit, which also happened to be his only suit. From what he had heard about Morgan Properties, Mac suspected it would not go over well if he walked into the building wearing jeans and a T-shirt.

The suit was looser in the waist than it had been this summer but tighter in the shoulders and arms. Mac grimaced, rolled his shoulders a few times, and checked his reflection in the bathroom mirror. He looked sufficiently presentable to walk into a rich commercial development firm. Though he still really needed a haircut. Well, he would have time for that later.

Mac collected his laptop bag and left the apartment, locking the door behind him. He started humming to himself as he descended to the parking lot, and he blinked in surprise.

Why was he humming?

He felt interested, like an intriguing puzzle had just dropped into his lap.

"Time to do some digging, Mac," his father's voice murmured in his memory.

"Hell," muttered Mac, blowing out a breath. Maybe there was something wrong with him. Or something wrong with his family that had been passed on to him.

There had definitely been something wrong with his mother.

At least it had stopped raining. Mac walked to his car, brushed wet leaves off the windshield, dropped his laptop bag onto the passenger seat, and headed out.

Investigating the death of Douglas Norton was probably a bad idea, but Mac was committed, and he set off for Julie Norton's office at Morgan Properties.

5

THE INTERVIEW

The Morgan Properties building was in a much nicer neighborhood than Mac's apartment or Iron Oswald's Gym. Mac drove into a business park that he suspected Morgan Properties owned to judge from the MORGAN BUSINESS PARK sign along the main entrance. The sign rose out of a large retaining pool, a pair of submerged fountains sending plumes of spray into the air on either side. Currently, several dozen ducks floated serenely in the pool in front of the sign. Mac wondered if Morgan Properties had paid extra for them or if the waterfowl had simply shown up on their own.

He drove past several sleek office buildings of glass and steel and white concrete, all of them looking tasteful and expensive. Foreign cars filled the parking lots – BMWs and Audis and a few Italian cars, alongside older domestic vehicles that no doubt belonged to the janitors. Mac came to Morgan Development's own parking lot and slid his car next to another Corsica that was even more battered than his.

Morgan Development's building was two stories tall, the windows made from greenish-tinted glass that made the entire thing look somehow crystalline. With all that glass, Mac wondered how much it cost to heat and cool the place. He got out of his car, collected his laptop bag, and headed for the front door.

The lobby was decorated in shades of industrial white and gray, complete with a snowy white marble floor. A receptionist's desk was on the other side of the room, and Mac headed towards it. A nervous-looking young woman in a dark jacket occupied the desk, watching three other people warily. Two of them were middle-aged men in suits. The third was a short, thin woman of about fifty wearing a blue pantsuit and subdued jewelry. She had a cap of styled blond hair. Mac never really liked short hair on women, but she had the bone structure to pull it off. Her hands were on her hips, and she seemed to be fighting back her temper as she glared at the two men.

"I don't care what they said," said the short woman. "We are getting that contract. I am not going to let Crest undercut us yet again. God knows what kind of lies she's going to say during the meeting."

"She can be very persuasive," said one of the men.

The short woman threw up her hands in disgust. "She'll say anything. Why am I the only one who can see her for what she is? I think..."

Right about then, she noticed Mac, and all four of the people looked at him.

He gave them a polite nod and stepped to the receptionist's desk. "Good morning. I'm here to see Julie Norton."

The receptionist nodded, shot a quick, nervous look at the blond woman, and then lifted her phone and spoke into it. "She'll be down for you in a moment."

"Thank you," said March.

The short blond woman looked at him, a faint line of suspicion forming between her brows. "And just who are you?"

There was no reason to lie. "Cormac Rogan."

"The private investigator," said the blond woman with annoyance. "Do you know who I am?"

People who asked that question, Mac reflected, were invariably about to cause problems.

"I'm afraid we haven't had the pleasure of an introduction," he said.

A thin smile flickered over her lips. "Angela Morgan."

Mac had seen her name referenced in the case file he had read through last night, and he had heard of Angela Morgan before that. Morgan Business Park and Morgan Properties had been named for her. She was the majority owner of Morgan Properties, one of the richest women in Wisconsin, and friends with half the state legislature, regardless of their party affiliations.

Angela Morgan, Mac suspected, was a good friend and a vengeful enemy.

"Ms. Morgan," said Mac. He held out his hand. "A pleasure."

Morgan shook it. She had a thin, hard hand and squeezed with more force than Mac would have expected from a woman of her size.

"So," she said, releasing his hand. "I suppose you're here to prey upon Julie's grief?"

"It wouldn't be appropriate for me to discuss client details, Ms. Morgan," said Mac.

"Ah." Morgan glanced to the side, and Mac saw Julie Norton hurrying into the lobby. "Well, Mr. Rogan, I look after my people. Just so you know, if you defraud Julie, I will take it badly." She offered a chilly smile. "I'm told it's unpleasant to get on my bad side."

Great.

"I wouldn't have taken the job if I wasn't going to do it honestly," said Mac.

"Angie," said Julie, come to a stop. Mac couldn't imagine anyone addressing this imperious woman as 'Angie,' but Morgan showed no offense. She handed a leather portfolio to Morgan. "Here is the proposal for the Drummond property."

"Thank you," said Morgan, opening the portfolio and glancing over the papers. "You know Crest will just lie about it anyway."

"We can't do anything about that," said Julie. "We just have to lean on the facts, our track record, our relationship with the banks."

"True," said Morgan. She closed the portfolio and tucked it under her arm. "Well, it's time to meet the lawyers. Wish me luck." She looked at Mac. "Remember what I said, Mr. Rogan."

Mac said nothing as Morgan walked away, followed by the two middle-aged men. Julie sighed and shook her head.

"This way, please," she said. They took the stairs to the second floor, and Julie led him down a carpeted hallway to her office. She had a corner office, Mac noted, which no doubt was a sign of status, though her windows only offered a good view of the parking lot and the office building next door. The office was tidy, with an enormous desk and a sleek white Apple computer, though large stacks of files occupied much of the desk's surface. Framed pictures held shots of Julie and her daughters, and Mac recognized the picture of Douglas Norton from the file he had read last night.

Julie sat and gestured at one of the guest chairs, and Mac slid it a little closer to the desk and seated himself.

"I'm sorry about Angie," said Julie. "She's very protective and thinks I'm wasting my money with this." Mac was inclined to agree, but he knew better than to say so. "Did she threaten you with legal action?"

"Not quite," said Mac. "But I wouldn't care to get on her bad side."

"She's in a bad mood anyway because of the Drummond property and the mall development," said Julie.

"Mall development?" said Mac. "What's that about?" He wanted to ease Julie into answering questions. Best to start with something relatively innocuous.

"Our company mainly does commercial real estate development and management," said Julie. "Recently, an elderly farmer named Robert Drummond died. He owned a prime parcel of farmland in western Wauwatosa, and he had refused to sell to anyone for years, even after he was too old and sick to work the farm. Well, he was a widower with no children, and eventually, the court determined that the land went to some cousins in Oregon who don't want to deal with it."

"I assume the land is in a good location for commercial development?" said Mac.

"Oh, God, yes," said Julie. She picked up a sheet of paper and held it out to him. Mac took the paper. It was a mockup of a large shopping mall of gleaming glass surrounded by asphalt parking lots. The legend along the top read PROPOSED WESTVIEW MALL – ARTIST'S CONCEPTION.

"Looks nice," said Mac.

"It might be, but right now, it's a mess," said Julie. "The cousins don't want to deal with the land and are eager to sell. We're competing with Crest Development to buy the land outright." She blew out a breath. "Don't repeat this…"

"I won't unless compelled by a subpoena," said Mac, which was his usual answer to that statement.

"But Arianna Crest is a nasty piece of work," said Julie. "She's a serial liar and charming enough that she can get people to believe her. Crest and Angie have butted heads before, and Crest's come out ahead a few times. That's where Angie was going, to a meeting with the lawyers. Basically, she has to try and outbid Crest for the land."

"Sound complicated," said Mac.

"It is," said Julie. She sighed and seemed to steel herself. "But you didn't come here to talk about land development."

"No," said Mac. "And I am charging you by the hour."

A wry smile went over her face. "I suppose we had better begin, then."

"Yes," said Mac. "Before we do, I want you to understand that I will have to ask you some awkward and unpleasant questions. I need to get a full picture of what happened to your husband."

She didn't look away from his gaze. "After they found Doug's body, I sat through days of police interviews, Mr. Rogan. I learned how an investigation works. You have to go through everything over and over again until you find the connections."

That oversimplified things but was accurate enough.

"I would also like to take notes and record this interview for future reference," said Mac.

"You have my permission," said Julie.

Mac nodded, drew out the case file for reference, opened his notebook, started the digital recorder, stated the date and time – October 23rd, 2007, 10:15 AM – and the interview began.

He started by walking Julie through the events of Tuesday, January 24th, 2006, the day that Douglas Norton had killed himself. Or had been found dead, Mac reminded himself. Julie was paying a lot of money for him to keep a clear mind. Mac had already read the police report, but he heard the same facts from Julie. It wasn't uncommon for Doug to work late, and she had only grown concerned by 7 PM. She tried calling his classroom phone, but no one picked up. Worried, she had called Northwoods High School's central number and had been routed to the police officers who had responded to the discovery of Doug's body, who informed her that her husband was dead. Julie answered all the questions in a calm voice, though her face grew paler, and from time to time, a muscle jerked near her eye. It was clear the topic was a painful one.

Mac understood. After his mother had murdered his father, he had sat through numerous interviews like this one.

"All right," said Mac. "Who found Doug's body?"

"Raul Torres," said Julie. "Another faculty member. He was also Doug's assistant coach for the football team. Raul said he wanted to stop by to chat with Doug about ordering new equipment for next year's season. They were planning to put together a presentation to the school board about it, but…" She sighed and shrugged.

"You don't think Raul had anything to do with it?" said Mac.

"No," said Julie at once. "He and Doug had been friends for years, and his death shook Raul up badly. Especially after the shootings and the business with the blackmail. Northwoods High School has had a rough couple of years."

"Yes," said Mac. "Speaking of that, the very last note in Doug's planner was just a name…"

Julie nodded before he could finish. "Kristin Salwell. She's as unscrupulous as Arianna Crest but not nearly as smart."

"Do you know why Kristin Salwell's name was the last thing Doug wrote in his planner?" said Mac.

"I don't," said Julie. Her smile was tight. "I suspect we're coming to the awkward questions phase of the interview, aren't we?"

"There were some details about Salwell in the file you gave me," said Mac. "She graduated with a 4.0 GPA by extorting good grades from two teachers who committed statutory rape with her."

She nodded. "That's right."

"Do you know if your husband had a...relationship of any kind with Salwell?" said Mac.

"She was in one of his classes," said Julie. "Doug said she was bright and worked hard, but he thought she might be a sociopath. Which turned out to be true. But that's not the kind of relationship you mean. No, I'm entirely certain Doug didn't sleep with her. That would have been out of character for him. A wife knows her husband. I realize that won't convince you, so think about this. When Salwell was arrested, she had every reason to tell the police everything. She tried to paint herself as the victim, but the recording destroyed her credibility."

"Recording?" said Mac.

"She went too far," said Julie. "She had already gotten good grades from the teachers she slept with, and she moved on to extorting money from them. One of the teachers cracked and told his wife everything. The next time Salwell called and demanded money, they recorded her, and she made the mistake of threatening violence against their children." Julie shrugged. "The whole mess came out then. Doug said that 2005 had been a shit sundae for Northwoods High, and the Salwell case was the cherry on top."

Mac could hardly disagree with that assessment.

"Then you don't believe Doug had any kind of inappropriate relationship with Kristin Salwell?" said Mac.

"I'm certain he did not," said Julie. "Doug was a man of integrity, and he wasn't stupid. In this day and age, he knew a male teacher has to be careful around female students. He would never meet with them alone, or if he did have to meet with one alone, he would use one of the study rooms of the commons, the ones with glass doors. In fact, he joked to me once that if it wasn't illegal, he would videotape every meeting he ever had with a student. The US has become so litigious, and one false accusation can sink a teacher's career."

"There's also the fact that Salwell was in prison on the day of your husband's death," said Mac. "Do you think she might have convinced someone to attack Doug?"

"I can't imagine why," said Julie. "She was in one of his classes, but that was it. Could I see her killing someone? Yes. But she had no reason to kill Doug, and I can't imagine how she could have managed it."

"You don't seem to like Salwell very much," said Mac.

Julie raised an eyebrow. "She tried to portray herself as a victim in the trial. You know, the innocent high school girl seduced by two teachers in exchange for higher grades. But that's exactly backward. She knew precisely what she was doing. Yes, those teachers were idiots and should have known better, and they are also to blame. But Salwell initiated the encounters. Do you know what she did once she got out of prison? She's working at that club by the airport, the Graymont, as a dancer and probably a high-priced call girl. Kristin Salwell is going to either become rich or dead in a hotel room by the time she's twenty-five."

Mac supposed that explained Kristin Salwell. Except, of course, why Douglas Norton had written Salwell's name down before he died. But he suspected that Julie had no idea why Doug had done that.

"There's also the matter of the handgun," said Mac.

Julie let out a breath. "That puzzles me. It puzzled the police, too. They could never figure out how Doug had gotten it, and I had no idea that he even had a pistol."

"Did he own any legal guns?" said Mac.

"No," said Julie. "Doug was very anti-gun. He didn't used to be. When we first got married, he owned a couple of shotguns and a pistol. Everyone in his family owns guns, and some of the people he met in the NFL," a sardonic smile flickered over her face, "had lots of guns and liked to pose with them and the cheerleaders at the same time. But after the Columbine shooting and some of the copycats, his opinion changed. He got rid of all his guns and started to get involved in some anti-gun groups." She sighed. "He could be really long-winded about it. Never thought I would miss him lecturing on one of his high horses."

"Do you currently own a gun?" said Mac.

"Yes, a Smith & Wesson nine-millimeter pistol," said Julie. "I got it ten years ago and kept it even after Doug changed his mind about guns. I think every woman should own a handgun, to be frank. It's a dangerous world out there, especially for women. Doug never really understood that. He was a big, strong man, so he always felt safe, but he didn't have a malicious bone in his body and didn't understand people who did. I don't think he understood what it felt like to be a woman walking alone at night and a bunch of strange men start following you."

"Or a car pulls up to the curb next to you," said Mac, who had heard similar stories.

"Yes, exactly," said Julie.

"You have no idea how he might have gotten Winston Marsh's pistol," said Mac.

"Like I said, it baffled me," said Julie. "Doug knew how to get a gun legally. I have no idea how he might have gotten Winston Marsh's pistol." She leaned forward. "I think whoever killed him and made it look like a suicide obtained the handgun and left it there."

"Only Doug's prints were found on the pistol," said Mac. He paged through the thick file and found the report on the handgun.

"But only on the grip and the trigger," said Julie. "Everything else was clean. There were no fingerprints on the barrel or the magazine. He would have needed to load the weapon."

"It might have been loaded when he obtained it," said Mac. Still, she had a point. He had handled guns frequently himself, and they picked up fingerprints quite easily.

"I think that whoever killed Doug wiped down the gun first and then pressed it into his hand after he was…was dead," said Julie, stuttering a little over the last word. It was the first real break in her composure he had seen during the interview.

"The angle of the wound was consistent if he had pulled the trigger himself," said Mac. "So was the position of the bullet casing."

"Which could have been moved," said Julie. "And Doug was sitting at his desk. It would have been very easy for someone to walk up and place the gun to his temple at the correct angle." She hesitated. "Especially if it was someone he knew and didn't suspect."

Mac said nothing. On balance, he still thought that Douglas Norton had killed himself. And yet...the fingerprints on the gun were odd. The fact that Doug had been found with a pistol that had apparently been stolen from a man who had died six months earlier was also strange. But all those things most likely had simple, logical explanations. If Doug had been suicidal, he would not have been thinking clearly, and he could have bought a stolen gun and wiped it down.

Yet it confirmed Mac's earlier hunch that the best course forward would be to find how Doug had gotten that gun. If Mac explained how Winston Marsh's pistol had ended up in Douglas Norton's possession, perhaps that could establish the suicide to Julie's mind. And in the unlikely event that Doug had been murdered, maybe it would show the path to his killer.

"It said in the file that Winston Marsh died in an accident six months before your husband," said Mac. "How did he die? It wasn't included in the file."

"He fell down a flight of stairs while he was drunk," said Julie. "If I remember correctly, he lived in an apartment over a convenience store. The stairs to his apartment were in the alleyway. Marsh was trying to unlock his door at two in the morning and slipped and fell, and that was that. The owner of the convenience store found him at about six. I was able to get a copy of Marsh's file as well. Would you like to see it? I can tell you anything you want to know."

"Please," said Mac. "I would like to have that copy as a guide to my memory." Julie nodded and made a note on a legal pad. "Did Marsh have a drinking problem?"

"A severe one," said Julie. "He stayed mostly sober while he was working, but once he retired at the end of 2004, he started drinking again. Marsh had a semi-estranged daughter, and she told the police he spent most of 2005 in one long bender."

"Was he a cop?" said Mac. He had seen that kind of reaction before in men who retired from stressful jobs.

"No, a janitor," said Julie. "Wait, that's not quite right. A maintenance technician. I think he was qualified with HVAC or something like that, and he did property inspections. He worked at Crest Development before he retired."

March blinked. "Crest Development? Morgan Properties' main competitor? The company that Ms. Morgan was complaining about in the lobby?"

"That's right," said Julie. "You don't think that's connected?"

"Do you?" said Mac. "You've had longer to think about it."

"That's true," said Julie. She was silent for a moment and then shook her head. "I think it's a coincidence. Maybe not even all that unlikely of a coincidence. If you include all our contractors, both our company and Crest's have employed thousands of people over the years. There must be something like ten thousand people connected with both our companies. I mean, Arianna Crest has absolutely no scruples, but I can't see her killing anyone. She's too cold for that… and she's the sort of woman who would get a man to do it for her."

"Okay," said Mac. "I want to ask a few more questions, but I'm afraid they will be awkward."

"I'm ready," said Julie.

"There was no sign of a struggle," said Mac. "If Doug was murdered, then he was shot by someone he knew. Can you think of anyone who might have had a grudge against him?"

Julie shook her head. "I've asked myself that again and again. I can't think of anyone who would do that. Sure, Doug had disagreements with some of the other faculty at Northwoods, and sometimes I've wondered if someone angry at Morgan Development took it out on him. But that doesn't make any sense. Angie's the face of the company, not me, and anyone wanting to go after Morgan Development would come for her."

"Could Doug have had a lover?" said Mac. "Someone who didn't want their affair to come out?"

"No," said Julie. "I'm absolutely certain that my husband never cheated on me." She looked right into his eyes. "I believe that with all my heart and soul."

"Okay," said Mac again. A lot of people, he had learned, believed things that weren't true, often in the face of all evidence to the contrary. "Another awkward question. One possible motive for murder could be the elimination of a romantic rival. Did you have a relationship with a man who might have viewed Doug as competition?"

Julie let out a humorless laugh. "Did I have an affair, do you mean? The police asked me that several times."

"Did you?" said Mac. "You hired me to find out what happened to your husband, not judge your personal life."

"I never had an affair, and after I married Doug, to this day, I have never had a romantic or a physical relationship with another man," said Julie, still looking into his eyes.

Mac nodded. "What about someone who thinks otherwise?"

Julie's brow furrowed. "I'm sorry?"

"Say, a family friend, or a relative of Doug's," said Mac. "A man who might have viewed Doug as a rival for your attention."

Julie sat back in her chair, surprised. "I never thought of that. Neither did anyone else. That's the first time anyone ever asked a question like that." She thought for a few seconds and shook her head. "No. There hasn't been anything like that. People have been friendly since Doug died, but not...like that. I haven't dated at all," she shrugged, "and no one has asked. Not that I've really wanted to. I mean, I do have a few male friends and acquaintances who would probably sleep with me if I let them. Most women do. But they've never pushed or been inappropriate."

"Well, please think it over," said Mac. "One other thing I need to ask, and then we'll be done."

"Go ahead."

"Do you think Doug's death had anything to do with the mass shooting in April 2005?" said Mac.

"I wondered when you were going to ask that," said Julie with a cynical smile. "If the trauma of the experience led Doug to take his own life, how I could miss the signs and all of that."

"That's not what I asked," said Mac. "That's one possible interpretation of the facts, yes. But I asked if you think that Doug's death was connected with the mass shooting."

Julie sighed and picked up a pen, fiddling with it. The pen looked heavy and expensive. She set it back down and straightened up in her chair.

"I don't know," said Julie. "Truly, I don't. The shooting…did you see any of the news coverage?"

"Some," said Mac. He had not paid close attention to the story. He had been preoccupied with his own concerns, struggling with the debts left by his father's death and his mother's imprisonment. He had never been to Northwoods High School, nor had he known anyone connected with it. The shooting had soon faded from his mind, though not from public consciousness.

"It was awful," said Julie. "I think it was some of the worst days of Doug's life. Seeing a parent lose their child…it's horrible. I want to see my girls grow up, but I also want to die before they do. I couldn't bear it the other way around. It was a terrible situation, and the fact that they never caught the shooter made it worse." She sighed. "One of our employees lost her son. Clarissa Chartwell. She was one of the best agents we had, but losing her son just ripped the heart out of her. Clarissa quit a year later, and she and her husband moved to Indiana to be closer to her parents. It was like she aged ten years in a day, and she was never the same after that."

"It wasn't the usual kind of school shooting, was it?" said Mac. "Normally, the shooters go room to room. This was a sniper firing from a house across the street."

"That's right," said Julie. "Whoever did it used .223 rifle rounds. Five killed, seven wounded, and thirty more students injured in the panic." She shook her head. "The FBI got involved in the case, and they concluded that two of the less, mmm, popular students were the most likely suspects. Ryan Walsh and Parker McIntyre. Fit the standard psychological profile of a school shooter or something like that. Their names leaked to the media, and the two kids and their families started getting death threats. Walsh was attacked by the parents of a murdered student. He couldn't deal with the attention and killed himself. Then it was proven that Walsh and Parker couldn't have been behind the shooting because they were truant at the time and playing some sort of online computer game. Parker's mother sued the FBI and the national media for a lot of money, and I think they settled out of court for a big sum."

"I hadn't heard any of that," said Mac.

"So you see why the investigators think Doug killed himself," said Julie. "He and the school had two awful years, and they think he just snapped. They told me that a significant portion of suicides don't leave a note and don't give any warning beforehand. But I know that he didn't kill himself. I know that he was murdered, and it was made to look like a suicide."

The certainty of it all but radiated from her face. Mac wasn't sure how to respond. Once again, he wondered at the wisdom of agreeing to take this case. The evidence mostly looked like Douglas Norton had killed himself and Julie was in denial about it. Mac wondered if anything would ever change her mind, if she would eventually fire him and Dave Wester and go from private investigator to investigator until she bankrupted herself in pursuit of a delusion.

And yet, there were things that didn't make sense. How had Doug gotten Winston Marsh's gun? For that matter, the fact that Marsh had worked for Crest Development was an odd coincidence. It might have just been that, only a coincidence, but maybe it wasn't. Mac's father had been fond of saying that any coincidences in an investigation were automatically suspicious, and Mac had seen that proven right again and again.

"So you can't think of any reason that someone might have attacked Doug over the mass shooting?" said Mac.

Julie blinked and then let out a quiet laugh. "I keep failing to answer your questions, don't I?"

"All part of the job."

"But, no, I can't think of any reason someone might have wanted to shoot Doug because of it," said Julie. "He...well, the media portrayed him as kind of a hero after, because he helped get the students under cover. He refused to give any interviews, and he was absolutely furious at the way the media went after Parker and Ryan." She shook her head. "I can't think of a reason why anyone would go after Doug, but I know he was murdered."

"All right," said Mac, and he said the date and time again and shut off the digital recorder. "I think that's all I need for now."

"What are you going to do next?" said Julie.

"I want to see if I can figure out how Winston Marsh's pistol ended up in Doug's classroom," said Mac. "That makes absolutely no sense. If we find out how that happened..."

Maybe Julie would accept that Doug had killed himself.

"Maybe we can determine what happened," said Mac instead. "I will keep you updated."

"Thank you," said Julie. "I don't expect daily reports. Weekly will be fine. I know this process can take a while." She craned her head to look at the window in her office door. "I think my assistant's back if you want a cup of coffee before you go."

Mac frowned. "Where did your assistant go?"

"I sent her to get groceries to restock the break room," said Julie. "She doesn't approve of this. She will in a kind, albeit passive-aggressive way, give me a stern lecture about grief and moving on."

"Ah," said Mac. "Good luck."

"I would prefer if you took all the luck with you," said Julie.

Mac said his farewells and walked back to his car. He sat in the passenger seat for a moment with his laptop, typing up his notes from the interview. Dave would expect good record-keeping, and Mac knew firsthand how critical good records could be to an investigation. And in the unlikely event any of this resulted in criminal prosecution for someone, Mac would need to document his findings properly.

His conversation with Julie had given him several avenues to pursue. Figuring out how Doug had gotten Marsh's gun would remain his priority. But regardless of what Julie thought, Mac wanted to talk to Kristin Salwell. Julie might have believed that her husband had never cheated on her, but Mac knew better than to assume. For that matter, Doug had been a middle-aged former NFL player, fit and strong for his age. It wasn't unreasonable to suspect that Salwell might have seduced him.

Mac also wanted to find out more about the Northwoods High School shootings. Maybe something stemming from that incident had triggered Doug's suicide. He should also learn more about the two students who had been falsely suspected of committing the shooting. One of them had committed suicide, and maybe Doug had blamed himself.

Maybe the surviving student blamed Doug and had somehow contrived to shoot him.

Mac finished typing up his report and saved a copy to a thumb drive which he dropped into the interior pocket of his coat. He closed down the computer, secured it in the trunk, and took a moment to look at the Morgan Properties building, his mind wandering over what Julie had told him.

Northwoods High School. Somehow, Douglas Norton's death was connected to Northwoods High School and probably the mass shooting.

But how?

The shooter had never been caught.

Maybe Doug had figured out who the shooter was and had been killed for it.

Mac snorted. Real life was never that tidy.

He checked his watch. The interview with Julie had taken only a little longer than he had thought, which meant he had time to make his next appointment.

For the next hour or so, he would need to focus on his other job.

6

LOOKING OUT FOR NUMBER ONE

Arianna's lip curled in disgust as her destination came into sight.

It was a chain motel just off an exit on westbound I-94, surrounded by the usual array of fast-food restaurants and gas stations. Her father had loved fast food, and in the final years before his death, he had been so fat that he could barely get from the couch to the bathroom and back. Granted, breaking both his legs at work had contributed to his spiraling obesity, but he had smothered his pain with cheeseburgers and alcohol.

Her father had been perhaps the only person Arianna had ever actually loved, but many of his lessons to her had been examples of what not to do.

She would sooner go hungry than eat at any restaurant with a drive-through window.

The chain motel, she supposed, was a nice enough example of its kind, with a well-kept lawn, a pothole-free parking lot, and the flags of the United States and the state of Wisconsin flying from metal poles before the main doors. It also boasted an attached Business & Convention Center, as if it was the sort of place where important work was done, rather than a hotel where traveling sales reps and adjunct professors on their way to conferences could check their meaningless emails.

She found the place tasteless, though if she had been left with no choice, it would have been preferable to sleeping in her car. And Arianna did own two of them in the Milwaukee area, both of which generated a nice profit, so she couldn't complain too much.

Still, the fact that the Drummond family's lawyers wanted to have the meetings here only reinforced Arianna's low opinion of them. Apparently, Robert Drummond's cousins and heirs lived in Portland, Oregon, and were ultra-liberal vegans who referred to the earth as their "Mother Gaia," abstained from caffeine and alcohol, and regularly ranted about the patriarchy and colonialism. Arianna herself ate a diet designed for maximum health and fitness and only drank for social obligation, but she found the Drummond cousins whiny, weak, and contemptible.

She was going to enjoy screwing them out of the land, building the Westview Mall, and making millions of dollars off it that the cousins would never see.

Arianna parked her car, a blue Audi S6, far enough out in the parking lot that she wouldn't need to worry about dings in the paint job. One last glance in the mirror to check her makeup, and she collected her briefcase and headed for the motel. She walked into the lobby, favored the clerk at the desk with a bright smile, and proceeded down a carpeted hallway into the convention area of the motel.

Arianna found the conference room they had booked. It was a symphony of inoffensive business décor – beige walls, gray carpet, a long table that looked like real wood, and a side table with coffee and pastries.

Some of the participants were already there – the Milwaukee county supervisor, keen to prove that he was interested in economic development and providing jobs for his constituents, a lawyer from the city of Milwaukee and another from Wauwatosa, and the head of the zoning board. Arianna knew them all and had worked with them in the past. The counsel for the Drummond cousins was there, with no trace of the cousins themselves, since they were too lazy and stupid to leave their precious coastal city even with millions of dollars at stake. Unfortunately, while the lawyer was a man of limited imagination, he was nonetheless scrupulously honest, so Arianna couldn't bribe or bully him.

But that was all right. Arianna had another way to guarantee that she would develop the Westview Mall.

In another few days, Angela Morgan would be too crippled by grief to function.

Arianna had arrived before Morgan. That was both good and bad. It made her look needier, hungrier, and less experienced. On the other hand, it gave Arianna a chance to chat with the various lawyers, which she did with aplomb. It helped that they were all men. She had a much easier time charming men than she did women, who tended to subconsciously see her as a rival. Arianna kept the bright smile pasted on her face like a mask while she traded anecdotes about golf and how the Packers had performed and the Bucks would likely fare.

Not that it really mattered. The guns she had stolen from Nathan Rangel would decide the contract, not anything that happened here.

Angela Morgan and two of her employees walked into the conference room precisely four minutes before the meeting was scheduled to begin. Arianna's smile sharpened as she looked at her chief competitor. Morgan was fifteen years older, but Arianna respected how she had kept herself in shape. The blue pantsuit she wore fit her very well. She had short hair, though, and the only way Arianna would ever cut her hair that short was through medical necessity.

The lawyers and officials greeted Morgan, and then Arianna shook her hand. They both squeezed hard. Morgan's smile was cold and clear and bright, like an icicle in January, and none of it touched her eyes. Much as Arianna detested Morgan, she could at least acknowledge Angela Morgan as a formidable adversary. Morgan Properties had gotten numerous contracts that should have gone to Crest Development.

Well, payback was coming.

"Arianna, dear, so good to see you again," said Morgan.

"And you, Angela," said Arianna. "You're looking well." She was tempted to ask how Morgan's son Charlie was doing, but that would be too obvious. In a few days, Arianna would need to feign shock and distress, just as she had done after the first Northwoods High School shooting in 2005.

With the pleasantries out of the way, they seated themselves at the conference table with coffee and pastries (both Arianna and Morgan avoided the doughnuts), and the meeting began.

"All right," said the unimaginative lawyer for the Drummond cousins. "Ms. Crest, Ms. Morgan, thank you for coming. As you know, the Drummond family wants to make the best possible use of Robert's land. The family feels this would be the best way to honor Robert's legacy." Arianna kept herself from laughing. The Drummond cousins hadn't spoken to the dead farmer in decades and wanted to cash in on his land without doing any work themselves. "Robert Drummond was a lifelong resident of Wisconsin and the Milwaukee area, and the family feels that an ecologically responsible commercial development that generates jobs for the state..." The lawyer droned on for some time about the cousins' wishes. Arianna listened with half an ear, instead thinking about the guns she had taken from Nathan Rangel's basement. "We've decided to proceed in alphabetical order. Ms. Crest, if you would like to go first."

"Thank you, I would be delighted," said Arianna.

She rose and spent the next twenty minutes laying out her plan for the proposed Westview Mall, describing costs and potential tax benefits to the city, county, and state. The members of the zoning board had pointed questions for her, but Arianna answered them all. She had done this before and knew what kind of questions they would ask. Mostly they wanted to know how much sewer and water hookup would cost.

Arianna finished her presentation, and Morgan stood up to make her pitch. Again, Arianna had to concede that Morgan made a formidable competitor. She had charisma, and she knew her material.

The thought of killing her was a temping one.

But, no. It would accomplish nothing, and Arianna would be a key suspect.

She had learned a few things from her previous kills.

The very first person that she had killed had been her mother.

Which, Arianna conceded, sounded shocking, but Jacqueline Crest had deserved it. She had been vicious, lazy, and gluttonous, with no redeeming qualities whatsoever, and Arianna's own tastes had been formed in direct opposition to anything her mother liked. When Arianna had been twelve, the marriage of Andrew and Jacqueline Crest had finally broken down, and Jacqueline had threatened to take everything in the divorce (not that there had been much to take) and planned to claim abuse and battery, even that Andrew had abused Arianna.

That had been the final straw for Arianna.

Her father had never raised a hand to her. He had taken her hunting, teaching her to shoot and numerous other useful skills, treating her as the son he had never had. Which Arianna appreciated because while she liked being a girl (especially after she discovered boys and how easy they were to manipulate), she detested most other women.

Jacqueline's threats had been intolerable.

Something had to be done.

It had proven simple enough. Jacqueline liked to drink a lot, and she had only avoided DWIs through sheer luck. Arianna had taken her father's deer rifle into the woods and waited. Jacqueline's favorite bar was a three-mile drive outside of town along a narrow, curvy stretch of county highway. At two in the afternoon, Jacqueline's car had come down the slope too fast, heading towards one of those sharp curves. From Arianna's position in the trees, it looked as if the car had been coming right at her.

Her bullet had gone into Jacqueline's front right tire, which exploded from the impact. The car had been going downhill at the time, twenty miles over the speed limit, and Jacqueline had been drunk. Her car slewed sideways, flipped over, smashed through the guardrail, and tumbled into a wooded gully.

It crashed upside down into a hundred-year-old maple tree, crushing the roof of the car like one of her father's empty beer cans.

Jacqueline Crest, in a final act of stupidity, hadn't been wearing her seatbelt, and the county medical examiner concluded that she had been killed immediately the first time her car flipped. Everything else had just been overkill. No one ever found the rifle bullet, and Arianna made sure to locate the casing and take it with her. The sheriff's department investigated, and the conclusion came quickly enough. Jacqueline had been drunk, and her car had been in poor repair. The tire burst as she came up to the curve, and she had lost control of the vehicle and gone over the guard rail and into the gully. She had been dead of a fractured skull before the car tumbled off the road.

That had been that.

Arianna watched Morgan speak, remembering the crunch Jacqueline's car had made as it had slammed into the tree and imagining the same happening to Angela Morgan.

No, too risky.

Arianna had learned that with her father.

The years after Jacqueline Crest had gotten smashed to a pulp inside her wrecked car had been good ones. Both Arianna and her father had been relieved to be rid of her, and Andrew Crest grew more cheerful. Arianna had worried that her father would seek a new romantic partner, and he often commented that he could find a better woman now that Jacqueline was dead, but nothing ever came of it. The bald fact was that between his increasing obesity, tendency towards laziness, dead-end job, and general truculence, Andrew Crest was not a catch.

But father and daughter had enjoyable days hunting and fishing together and frequently visited the shooting range. Andrew's experiences working as a security officer in prison had convinced him that the collapse of the United States was imminent, so he had a lot of guns to defend them from the starving hordes that would come out of Milwaukee, Madison, and the Twin Cities once food distribution collapsed. Arianna was an excellent shot, as Jacqueline's fate had demonstrated, but she enjoyed the practice, and she liked guns a lot.

As pleasant as those years had been, Arianna had already been thinking about the future. She had no desire to spend the rest of her life working at a menial job in a small town in northern Wisconsin, or worse, to marry one the local single men. She wanted money and a lot of it. For that matter, Arianna suspected that she and her father would not get along so well once she was an adult. He had already been making snide comments about how much time she spent exercising, joking that maybe she was anorexic just because she didn't stuff her face with a double cheeseburger and two orders of fries the way he did when they went to dinner at the town bar.

Of course, since she carried most of their equipment when they went hunting and could haul a deer carcass out of the woods on her own, he didn't complain all that much.

The problem came to a head soon after her eighteenth birthday in early 1990. Andrew had been trying to subdue a troublesome inmate at work. Unfortunately, he had done so on the stairs, and in the altercation, he had fallen down the steps and broken both his legs and his knees. Since it had happened on the clock, the state of Wisconsin had been obliged to pay for his medical bills, and Andrew went on disability. Once the surgery and physical therapy were done, he could walk, but barely. He developed an addiction to painkillers, and the constant drinking and overeating did not improve his health.

Arianna found the situation intolerable. She had to drive Andrew everywhere, and while he could get to the bathroom unassisted, he frequently drank himself senseless and threw up in his sleep, which she was obliged to clean up. The smell of vomit soon permeated their house. Worst of all, the next year Arianna had planned to attend UW-Madison and start a degree in business. She wanted wealth, and the opportunities to acquire it in their small town were limited.

But Andrew assumed that she was going to stay at home to take care of him. There was absolutely no way Arianna was going to do that, and she supposed her father's life had become intolerable.

Wouldn't resolving the situation be an act of mercy?

It had been easy enough to arrange. She had made him a heavy dinner, enchiladas and tortilla chips with lots of cheese and hot salsa, accompanied by copious amounts of his favorite liquor. Andrew ate and drank too much, staggered off to bed dead drunk, and as Arianna had expected, he had thrown up in his sleep. It had been simple to take a wet towel, roll it around in the vomit, and spread it over his face.

She had waited until Andrew had stopped breathing and then kept the towel over his another fifteen minutes just to be sure. Arianna supposed this was the best thing she could do for her father, to give him a merciful, quick death. He hadn't felt anything at all, and certainly it was a better death than her mother had received.

Satisfied, she disposed of the towel, took a shower, and slept soundly.

The next morning, she woke up at seven AM and called 911, working herself up into screaming hysterics. The paramedics arrived, took one look at her father, and pronounced him dead on the scene. Arianna cried some more. One thing she had learned was that when a pretty blond girl cried, and not delicate tears but ugly, body-wrenching sobs, people were sympathetic. It worked on the paramedics. It also worked excellently on the sheriff's department investigator who came out to question her. The county medical examiner ruled that Andrew Crest had died of asphyxiation due to choking on his own vomit in his sleep, and everyone assured a guilt-ridden Arianna that she had done the best that she could.

Everyone except for the investigator for the life insurance company.

Somehow, she had known.

The woman's name had been Michaela Simpson, and she had looked like a middle-aged girls' gym teacher – squat, burly, hard-eyed, with a short cap of iron-gray hair. For some reason, she disliked Arianna on sight, and she had questioned the death vigorously, making Arianna go over the details again and again. Simpson hadn't brought up the matter, but Arianna could tell that the investigator thought that she had killed her father and made it look like an accident. Fortunately, there were no cracks in Arianna's story, nothing that the annoying woman could use to pry apart her account, and in the end, Arianna had gotten the life insurance payment for her father's death. Once she sold the house, she had more than enough money both to graduate debt-free from UW-Madison and to start Crest Development.

Angela Morgan kept describing her vision for the mall development, and Arianna maintained a polite, interested smile on her face, even as she envisioned sending a bullet through Morgan's skull.

She wouldn't, though.

Simpson had taught her a valuable lesson. Arianna had been too close to her father's death. Given that between the life insurance policy and the sale of the house, Arianna had walked away with something like three-quarters of a million dollars, she was the obvious suspect to have murdered him. Arianna could concede that she had benefited from both good luck and good planning. If she had left any indication, any indication at all, that Andrew Crest had been murdered, she would have been in a lot of trouble.

What she needed was distance. To arrange matters so that she wasn't the obvious suspect, so there were numerous layers between her and the victim.

Arianna had refined that technique at college. At UW-Madison, one of her professors had been a fat plug of a woman like Michaela Simpson, and she had taken a dislike to Arianna. Of course, Arianna had been cheating outrageously, but the professor hadn't been able to prove it. Nevertheless, Arianna needed that class to graduate. Something had to be done.

The solution had presented itself neatly. The professor's life partner was a skinny woman who worked as an activist lawyer and liked to bicycle along the Lake Mendota trails near campus every morning. Arianna had watched her route for a few days, concealed herself in some convenient bushes with a shovel, and thrust the implement into the bicycle as the lawyer went past.

The results had been pleasing. The lawyer had vaulted over the handlebars of her expensive bicycle, landed on her face, and then the bicycle had landed atop her. She broke one leg and one arm, and the resultant investigation was everything Arianna could have hoped for. Both the professor and the lawyer were certain the attack had been a deliberate hate crime, and a minor media circus had resulted. The professor and her life partner were on the news every night for a week, state legislators and senators made fulsome speeches, angry newspaper editorials were penned, and there was even a small rally in front of the state capitol.

At no point in the furor did anyone even begin to suspect the actual motive and perpetrator. With the professor's full attention on the matter, Arianna sailed through the class without difficulty.

It reinforced the lesson Michaela Simpson had taught her. Had Arianna attacked the professor directly, she would have been a suspect. But by attacking the professor's partner, she had created too many layers between her and the target. Arianna had gotten what she wanted, and no suspicion had come in her direction.

That was why she had shot Joshua Chartwell on April 14th, 2005. His mother Clarissa had been an employee of Morgan Properties, and she had been the prime mover on a condominium deal that Arianna wanted for herself. So Arianna had prepared a little snipers' nest in the house across the street from Northwoods High School, waited until crowds of students gathered before the front doors, and shot Joshua through the head. She had then emptied her weapon, hitting as many students as she could to create a massacre.

The pattern of the professor had repeated itself but on a far larger scale. The media and the investigators assumed it was another of the school shootings that had plagued the United States over the last decade, and the investigation never came anywhere near Arianna. In fact, the FBI profile of two of the suspected students had leaked, and the press harassment had grown so intense that one of the students had killed himself, and the second had sued and settled for a lot of money. Arianna had been delighted with the outcome.

Especially when Morgan Properties' deal had fallen through, and Crest Development had seized the condo project instead. There had been some mutterings that it was in poor taste, but business was business.

The failed investigation of the massacre had given Arianna another opportunity. Julie Norton had been working on a deal for a property that Arianna wanted, so she had shot Doug Norton in the head and made it look like a suicide. Unfortunately, that hadn't worked. Angela Morgan had simply stepped into her friend's stead, and Julie herself had been back at work within a month. The deal had been delayed, and the owners of the land in question had been willing to wait rather than exploit a grieving widow in exchange for cheaper development costs.

Idiots.

Still, the investigation had concluded that Douglas Norton had killed himself, and no one even suspected that Arianna had been involved. No harm done. Even Arianna couldn't expect all her plans to work.

Angela Morgan finished her presentation, and the lawyers and officials applauded. Arianna was obliged to clap as well – Morgan had politely clapped at the end of her presentation, after all. Morgan looked over the room and smiled.

Arianna smiled back and thought of Morgan's son.

Charlie Morgan. A senior at Northwoods High School.

Morgan's only child.

Let Morgan smile all she wanted.

Her expression would be very different once Arianna shot Charlie through the head.

Halloween was coming soon.

7

RVW SOFTWARE

Mac drove across Brookfield, his mind turning over everything that Julie Norton had told him.

He decided to try and speak with Kristin Salwell as soon as possible. She seemed to have no connection whatsoever to Doug Norton's death and had in fact been in prison when that bullet went into Doug's brain, whether put there by his own hand or someone else. Yet nonetheless, the final words that Doug had written had been Kristin Salwell's name. There was something there, some link, but what?

The entire thing seemed like a suicide to Mac. If forced to decide right now, he would have said that he was eighty percent certain that Douglas Norton's death had been a suicide.

But when he had agreed to take the case, he had been ninety-five percent certain.

Mac put it out of his mind as he drove west on Bluemound Road until he came to a Starbucks near the mall. A quick glance at the dashboard clock told him that he had arrived with three minutes to spare. He had to park in the far corner of the overflowing lot, squeezing his Corsica between two white Toyota Highlanders, and grabbed his laptop and hurried into the Starbucks. It was crowded enough and the line was long enough that Mac figured the employees would not hassle him if he didn't buy anything, so he threaded his way through the crowd to a table in the corner.

The other two founding members and shareholders of RVW Software awaited him there. One was a thin, wiry man with pale blue eyes, pallid skin, and brown hair, and he wore worn jeans and a black hooded sweatshirt. His neatly trimmed mustache and beard made him look like a Bolshevik commissar, which was only half-accurate because while Nikolai Volodin was in fact Russian, he was rabidly anti-communist.

The other man was fat, outweighing Mac by a hundred pounds. He wore an expensive business suit, his red tie crisp and knotted to perfection. His hair had been slicked back, and he had grown a beard in a mostly futile effort to disguise his double chin. Between the suit and the beard, the overall impression was of some large, predatory animal looking for its next meal. His name was Paul Williamson, and he was a lawyer at the firm of Rottwald and Smith. He had immense ambitions that ranged from political office to enormous wealth, and it had recently occurred to him that smartphone software might be a potential pathway to riches or at least a handsome profit.

Which was why Mac was here.

He pulled out a chair and sat down, placing his laptop bag on the table. "Gentlemen."

"Cormac," rumbled Nikolai. He had a deep voice, with a Russian accent he deliberately let thicken when flirting with a woman who found foreign men exotic.

"Mac," said Paul. He took a sip of his coffee and set it next to a plate that held an enormous blueberry muffin. "You going to get anything?"

"Maybe on the way out," said Mac. In truth, money remained tight, and he did not want to spend any here, not when for the price of one coffee he could make six or seven pots of the stuff at his apartment.

"Suit and tie," said Nikolai. He drank a black coffee. Nikolai always drank black coffee and claimed he added vodka to it, though

Mac had never actually seen him drink anything stronger than a wine cooler. "A lady friend, you are taking her for a date?" He spoke English well, though sometimes his sentence structure came out oddly.

"No," said Mac. "I took another job from Dave Wester."

He expected his business partners to react with annoyance, but instead, they both nodded with approval.

"That's good," said Paul. "That's good. Adds to the...mmm, how do I want to say it? Social proof." He waved a hand in the air as if gesturing to a billboard or maybe a PowerPoint presentation. "Cormac Rogan, working private investigator, helped develop this software. The man who foiled the Greenwater Community Church terrorist bombing..."

"Don't mention that," said Mac. He really didn't like talking about it, and he definitely did not want to use it in marketing copy.

"Right," said Paul without missing a beat. He had helped get Mac out of some serious legal trouble right before that situation had nearly gone to hell, so he knew how it could have been much worse. "But, seriously. You being an actual licensed private investigator will only help with our bona fides."

"Cops generally don't care for private investigators," said Mac in a dry voice.

"Now you are thinking too much," said Nikolai, leveling a finger. "You Americans, you think cops are magic. Too many police movies with the shooting and the car chases and the hot lady detectives in leather jackets. The real life, it is more prosaic. Police agencies are government bureaus. Like the Department of Motor Vehicle or the DNR, but with more guns and rules. And government bureaus all want the same thing. They want the cheapest equipment possible from contractors without much hassle." He waved a hand over the table. "Which is why we are here."

Paul reached into the interior pocket of his jacket and drew out his iPhone. The device had only been released to the public in June, and Mac still hadn't seen that many actual iPhones. He always thought it looked like a fat little deck of cards with a glass screen.

"I still think there's no way that iPhones are going to become mainstream," said Mac. "They're too damned expensive. Five hundred dollars for a phone that will break if you drop it once?"

"That's why you buy a good case," said Paul.

"Technology, it always becomes smaller and cheaper," said Nikolai. "You know this, Cormac. Fifteen years ago, laptops were rare and the size of unabridged English dictionaries." He gestured at the tables around them, where half the patrons were typing away on Dell laptops or MacBooks. "Now everyone has them."

"I think we're at the start of a big revolution here," said Paul. "First the desktop PC, then laptops, and now smartphones. And we are perfectly positioned to take advantage of the change." He unlocked his iPhone and tapped the screen a few times. "And I think the new interface on the app works much better."

"Is much more intuitive," said Nikolai.

"Good," said Mac.

"I've already talked to three different sheriff's departments about the web version," said Paul. "They're very interested in the mobile reports feature, and I'm sure at least two of them will give it a trial."

"It is like I said," said Nikolai. "Reliable contractors."

Mac remembered the conversation that had led to RVW Software. It had been towards the end of the summer, not long after Mac had flown back from Washington DC after testifying before the Senate about Jack Kelsey's death. He had gone out for a drink with Paul, who had recently become the proud owner of a shiny new iPhone. He had been showing off his new toy when they had run into Nikolai Volodin. Like Mac, Nikolai did frequent freelance IT jobs, though he had better skills with software development, and Mac was stronger with server administration. Nikolai commented that he knew some people in California who worked for Apple, and sometime in the next year, Apple was planning to open the iPhone up to allow the installation of third-party apps.

"You know," Paul had mused. "I bet there might be some money in that."

From that conversation, RVW Software (named for Rogan,

Volodin, and Williamson, in alphabetical order) had been born. Their mission statement was to develop apps for law enforcement and private security to use on mobile devices, and each of the three partners brought different skill sets to the company. Mac had some knowledge of software development and a thorough grasp of the needs of both a law enforcement agency and private security. Nikolai had excellent software development skills, in particular the programming languages that the iPhone would employ. Paul's legal expertise would prove useful, and he had contacts with law enforcement agencies throughout the Midwest.

Their first app would allow officers to take reports on their mobile devices, which the app would export into the most popular case management software program. Both cops and private security guards spent endless hours writing reports, and Mac knew they would welcome any tool that would make the task easier and quicker.

So far, the company hadn't made any money. But they hadn't taken on any debt, either, since Mac and Nikolai were using computers and software they already owned to develop the code.

"Right," said Paul. "How close are we to a beta test?"

Mac and Nikolai both agreed that the initial web-based version of their software was ready for testing. Paul knew several private security companies that were willing to beta test the software in exchange for potential future discounts, and the discussion turned to practical details – timing, training, and so forth. There would be web hosting expenses for the beta version of the web client, and they agreed to split the cost three ways. Fortunately, the expense would be minimal, though it would scale rapidly if they had actual customers. By then, Mac hoped they would have some actual revenue to go with the customers.

"Good meeting," said Nikolai once they had finished. "Should have been a phone call."

"Then we wouldn't have gotten coffee," said Paul, lifting his own cup, "and I wouldn't have had an excuse to get out of the office."

"I would not object to a scone," said Nikolai. "Gentlemen, I shall see you later." Mac and Paul said goodbye. Nikolai packed up his laptop and got in line, which was getting shorter as the lunch rush ebbed.

"So what's your new case about?" said Paul. Mac wouldn't talk about his investigative work to most people. He had told Tom because he trusted Tom. Paul provided legal advice to Mac, which meant he was technically Mac's attorney, and therefore everything Mac said to him was protected under attorney-client privilege. That often meant little in the real world, but Paul knew how to keep a secret.

"Ever met a lawyer named Julie Norton?" said Mac.

"Mmm, sounds familiar, but I can't place it."

"She works for a company called Morgan Properties," said Mac.

Paul's eyebrows lifted. "Now I have heard of them. She's their in-house counsel, right? Rottwald & Smith did some work for them. Property law related to land development, that kind of thing, and we helped with a few of their lawsuits against Crest Development."

"They've sued Crest Development?" said Mac. Julie hadn't mentioned that.

"Morgan Properties and Crest Development have sued each other a bunch of times," said Paul. "They're the two biggest commercial property developers in Milwaukee. Companies at their level sue each other all the time and usually wind up settling. It's another form of negotiation. Of course, some of it comes from the fact that Angela Morgan and Arianna Crest absolutely hate each other."

"I picked up on that," said Mac.

"Did you meet them?" said Paul. He paused to take another bite of his enormous muffin.

"Morgan, not Crest," said Mac.

"Well, you'll remember it if you meet Crest," said Paul. "She is seriously hot. Like, blond fitness fanatic hot. Of course, she's probably crazy."

"Crazy?" said Mac. "Is that a legal term?"

Paul snorted. "It should be. She puts out this energy, man...like, I bet she would be amazing in bed, but if you said the wrong thing to her, you'd come home to find that she'd cut off your dog's head and left it in your refrigerator. That kind of crazy." He grinned. "Though you lucked out if you're doing investigative work for Morgan Properties. They're forever snooping around Crest Development and vice-versa. Whole lot of billable hours there. Just don't let Crest catch you doing it. She has a vindictive streak a mile wide."

"Julie Norton hired me personally," said Mac. "Her husband probably killed himself, and she thinks it was a murder."

"Huh." Paul took a bite of muffin, chewed, and swallowed. "That sounds messy."

"It's probably going to be," said Mac.

"Let me guess," said Paul. "You didn't want anything to do with it, but Dave Wester said that she had money and was going to hire a PI no matter what, so she might as well hire an honest one."

"Yeah," said Mac. "I ought to get a T-shirt that says CHUMP in big letters."

"Nah," said Paul. "You like investigating too much, Mac." He held up a thick hand as Mac started to protest. "No, no. I know you swore it off after this summer, but here you are, still doing jobs for Dave. It's how you make sense of the world. Me, it's documenting everything and then making sure the documents are organized properly. Good thing I'm a lawyer, huh? For you, it's investigating."

Mac only scowled and said nothing. That had more truth in it than he liked and was more than he wanted to think about right now.

"Anyway," said Paul. "Is Mrs. Norton in denial, or did her husband get murdered?"

"Last night, when I talked to her," said Mac, "I was ninety-nine percent sure that he killed himself. After reading the files and talking to Julie Norton…I think I'm only eighty percent sure."

"Eighty percent?" said Paul. "That's quite a jump. What changed your mind?"

Mac laid out the case for Paul – Winston Marsh's stolen gun, Kristin Salwell's name in Doug's day planner, Julie Norton's utter certainty that Doug had neither cheated on her nor killed himself.

"Huh," said Paul, thinking that over. "Man. If I can use another legal term, I believe Northwoods High School has some shitty luck. A mass shooting, teachers sleeping with students, and a probable suicide? If I have kids, I am definitely sending them to private school."

"If I can figure out how Doug got Winston Marsh's gun, that should go a long way toward clearing it up," said Mac. "For that matter, I want to know why Doug wrote Kristin Salwell's name in his planner right before he died, but Doug's the only one who knows why."

"And maybe Salwell," said Paul. "You're sure she was in prison at the time? She wasn't paroled or anything?"

Mac thought back over the file. "She served her full sentence, and the police talked to her. They confirmed Salwell was in prison when Doug was killed, and she claimed to have no idea why he wrote down her name."

"You know what happened to her?" said Paul.

"Julie said she had a job at a strip club called the Graymont," said Mac.

Paul raised his eyebrows. "The Graymont Gentlemen's Club near the airport?"

"Don't tell me you go there," said Mac. He half-expected Paul to tell him that Salwell was his favorite lap dancer.

"Of course not," said Paul. "But even better. I know the owner. Guy named Ernesto Diaz."

"How'd that happen?" said Mac.

"Legal case," said Paul. "He got sued by the county, and we represented him and won." He sketched out the basics of the case. "Guy's an enormous asshole, but he makes a lot of money. He's the American dream. Came here from Mexico when he was seventeen, and twenty-five years later, he's a millionaire from overcharging for drinks and food while tourists ogle women dancing on his stage. Diaz has almost been in serious legal trouble a couple of times, related to drug deals at his club, but so far, nothing has stuck. He's never been directly involved in anything illegal, but if anything happens at his club, someone pays him a cut under the table."

"Sounds like a model citizen," said Mac.

Paul shrugged. "Even somewhat less than model citizens deserve legal representation."

"Could you give him a call?" said Mac. "Ask if he could arrange for me to talk with Salwell?"

"Diaz really doesn't like to talk to cops unless he has no other choice," said Paul.

"I'm not a cop."

"Good point," said Paul. "I'll ask him to tell Salwell it's related to a life insurance case. Which is technically true because most life insurance policies don't pay out on suicide, and so Mrs. Norton didn't see a dime when her husband killed himself."

"Thanks," said Mac. "I appreciate it."

Paul made a show of unlocking his iPhone, noting how much easier it was to use the touchscreen to find contacts as opposed to the physical buttons of a flip phone. Since Paul was doing him a favor, Mac kept his thoughts on that to himself. Paul found the right contact, hit the call button, and lifted the phone to his ear.

"Mr. Diaz?" he said. "Hi, Paul Williamson. How are you doing?" Mac heard a gravelly, Hispanic-accented voice on the other side. A few minutes of polite chitchat followed, and then Paul got down to business. A friend of his was working on a life insurance case and wanted to talk to one of Diaz's employees, specifically Kristin Salwell. Several minutes of reassurance followed as Paul explained there was no threat to any of Diaz's businesses and that none of his employees were suspected of criminal involvement.

"In this matter, anyway," said Paul, and Mac heard Diaz's harsh laugh over the phone's speaker. Paul and Diaz talked for a few more minutes, and then the call ended.

"Diaz agreed," said Paul. "And you're in luck. Salwell works the dinner shift at the club tonight, and she's coming in at two to get ready. Diaz says you can talk to her then, though he doesn't guarantee that she will talk to you." He paused. "I got the impression that Kristin Salwell is something of a difficult personality."

"She seduced two teachers, blackmailed them into giving her passing grades, and was only caught when she was dumb enough to extort money after she had turned eighteen," said Mac. "Yeah, I'd say she qualifies as a difficult personality."

Paul snorted. "You be careful around her, Mac. You always did like ambitious women with sob stories. Like Kate."

Mac let out an irritated breath at the mention of his one and only long-term girlfriend. "Kate was smarter than that."

"Kate was too smart," said Paul. "It's a bad quality in a woman. You want a woman to be above average in intelligence because no one wants to go through life with someone dumb. But too much intelligence in a woman causes all kinds of problems. Intelligent women mostly use their intellect to find new ways to make themselves miserable."

"Half the lawyers are Rottwald & Smith are women," said Mac. "How have you not gotten fired yet?"

"Because, if you will forgive the crudity, I am smart enough not to shit where I eat," said Paul. "But, what, it's been three years since Kate?"

"Four," said Mac.

"As your friend, I would tell you to go out and get laid, but that might distract you from working on RVW Software, so it's really not in my financial interest," said Paul. Mac snorted at that. "But I'm going to follow my advice and chat up that barista."

Mac followed Paul's gaze and looked at the front counter. The lunch rush had died down, and no one was in line. Paul was looking at a red-haired woman standing near the milk steamer. Caucasian, red hair, green eyes, probably five foot four or five, likely one hundred and twenty pounds. Mac was amused to note that even when looking at an attractive woman, his mind defaulted to the sort of description in a police report.

"Nice, right?" said Paul. "Watch. I'm going to go get dinner with her."

"Sure you are," said Mac. "She probably gets hit on all day by guys in suits who think they're the masters of the universe."

"A key difference," said Paul. "I actually am the master of the universe." Mac laughed. "Well, one of them, anyway."

"Thanks for calling Diaz," said Mac.

"No problem," said Paul. "Speaking of which, you'd better get going if you want to make it on time." Mac collected his laptop bag. Paul did the same, and then they shook hands. "Good luck. Let me know how it turns out." He grinned. "And if Julie Norton decides to sue you for emotional distress once you prove her husband killed himself, give me a call."

"At least Dave will have to pay your fee this time," said Mac.

He headed towards the door, and Paul strode towards the counter and the barista. Mac hesitated, decided he didn't want to see Paul crash and burn, and walked into the parking lot.

His conversation with Kristin Salwell was likely to be much less pleasant.

8

WEBCAMS ARE THE FUTURE

Mac got onto the freeway and headed through downtown Milwaukee and then south towards the airport. Traffic was heavy, but it usually was on the downtown freeways and would only increase as the afternoon continued. Directly west of the airport were several commercial stretches – hotels and midscale restaurants and stores that catered to business travelers, like FedEx offices and print shops and a place that sold cheap cell phones.

Graymont Gentlemen's Club was discreetly tucked away behind the hotels, out of sight of the main roads. It did not look all impressive – a cinder-block building with a metal roof, the walls painted a shade of deep green. A small sign by the parking lot identified the club, and it looked more like an industrial building than anything else.

Mac had heard of the place turning up in the news a few times over the last few years, though he had never paid close attention. Both the city and the county of Milwaukee were not happy to have an adult entertainment venue so close to the airport, and he had read a newspaper article saying that the city intended to force Graymont to move. Given that the club was still there, Mac supposed the city hadn't succeeded.

A half-dozen cars were parked in the corner of the lot. The employees, most likely. Five of the cars were Fords and Toyotas, but the sixth one was a BMW. Mac suspected that car belonged to Ernesto Diaz.

He got out of his car, slung his laptop bag over his shoulder, and after a moment's consideration, locked it in the trunk. It would have been useful to record his conversation with Kristin Salwell, but he suspected that both Salwell and Diaz would react badly if he brought any recording devices. Mac would just have to write out notes quickly in the car after they finished.

The front door was a solid slab of steel set in a recessed niche. There was a sliding plate at eye level, which was unnecessary since Mac saw the plastic dome of a camera overhead. A metal stool rested next to the door's niche, no doubt where the bouncer sat and checked IDs. The door was locked, and an intercom had been built into the left side of the niche with a sign that read DELIVERY BUZZ FOR ACCESS.

Mac hit the button and waited.

About thirty seconds later, a rough voice came over the speaker. "We don't open till four."

"I have an appointment with Mr. Diaz," said Mac. "My name's Cormac Rogan."

There was a pause.

"Hang on."

Mac waited another minute, and then the locks clicked, and the door swung open. A Mexican man in black jeans and a black T-shirt stood on the other side, his heavy forearms covered with tattoos. His black eyes were flat and unfriendly and a little annoyed. Mac suspected he worked as one of the bouncers.

"Ernesto will see you," grunted the bouncer. "This way."

Mac followed him into the Graymont's main room. A long bar ran along one side, and two of the other walls were lined with booths. The fourth wall held a raised stage with four polished metal poles, a long line of multicolored spotlights mounted on the ceiling pointing at the stage. Tables and chairs filled most of the floor space. The only other people were a middle-aged Mexican woman running a vacuum over the floor and two college-aged white men wiping down the tables and booths. The air smelled of cleaner and disinfectant, which couldn't quite mask the odors of beer and old cigarette smoke.

It wasn't quite as seedy as Mac expected.

"You a lawyer?" grunted the bouncer as they crossed the room.

"No," said Mac.

"Cop?" said the bouncer, pushing open the kitchen door.

"No," said Mac.

That seemed to satisfy him. They crossed a kitchen with gleaming steel counters and appliances, again cleaner than Mac would have expected. With all the trouble the county had given him, maybe Diaz didn't want to offer the health department a lever to use against him. The bouncer crossed to a carpeted hallway off the kitchen, came to one of the doors, and knocked.

"Boss?" said the bouncer.

"Come in," came a voice like gravel.

Mac stepped into a nicer office than he expected. New carpet and the walls had been painting gleaming white. A row of file cabinets sat against one wall, and an expensive L-shaped desk of polished dark wood dominated the center of the room. Papers covered the arm of the desk facing the door, arranged in neat stacks, and a desktop computer with two monitors occupied the other arm. One of the monitors showed a grid of sixteen black and white camera feeds.

Ernesto Diaz sat behind the desk. He looked a lot like the bouncer, with the addition of two decades and about twenty pounds of fat. Nevertheless, he was still strong, and Mac would not have wanted to get into a physical confrontation with him. Diaz wore a crisp white shirt with no tie, the top two buttons open, a black sports coat, and a gleaming American flag pin on the lapel.

The bouncer began speaking in Spanish, and Diaz answered in the same language. Mac couldn't speak Spanish very well. He did, however, understand quite a bit of it. The bouncer expressed the opinion that Mac was probably a snoop from the city, looking to make trouble. Diaz responded that he would take care of it and told the bouncer to go help unload the beer truck that had just arrived.

The bouncer nodded and turned to go.

"Don't forget to lift with your knees," said Mac. The bouncer blinked at him. "Those cases of beer are murder on your back."

Diaz's mouth twitched once in something that was almost a smile.

"They're barrels, dumbass," said the bouncer in English, and he left, closing the door behind him.

"Please forgive our rudeness, Mr. Rogan," said Diaz. He spoke English clearly, though with a pronounced accent. One thick, callused hand gestured to a chair in front of the desk, and Mac sat. "Usually, we can have private conversations in Spanish."

"Bet the health inspectors love that," said Mac.

Diaz grinned. He had very white teeth. Apparently, the Graymont Gentlemen's Club made enough money to afford a good dental plan. "They're so afraid of getting called racist they stand there with these stupid smiles on their faces while we make fun of them in Spanish. Doesn't work so well on cops, though. Now." He folded his hands on the desk. "What do you wish to discuss? I normally wouldn't have this kind of meeting, but Paul said it would be helpful."

"I was hoping you could introduce me to Kristin Salwell," said Mac.

"You can see her dance here on Thursdays, Fridays, and Saturdays," said Diaz. "Or you can go to her website and book a private viewing session."

Website?

"Not as a client," said Mac. "Just an interview."

"Paul implied you were a life insurance investigator," said Diaz. His black eyes were getting harder, colder. The man had a good intimidating stare.

"How much do you know about her past?" said Mac.

Again, he almost smiled. "She was a very bad girl. Of course, good girls don't wind up working here."

"I've been hired by a woman whose husband committed suicide," said Mac. "The police think it was a suicide, but she believes it was a murder."

"A tragic story," said Diaz. "What has it to do with me and my business?"

"Nothing," said Mac. "But the last thing the dead man wrote in his day planner was Kristin Salwell's name."

Diaz's brow furrowed. "And you think she had something to do with this suicide?"

"I doubt it because she was in prison on the day he killed himself. But I want to know why he wrote her name down." Mac spread his hands. "Mr. Diaz, I don't want to make trouble for you or your business. And I don't see how this could. But if you can introduce me to Kristin, it might help a grieving widow come to terms with her loss."

Diaz stared at Mac without blinking. He could almost see the cold calculation going on behind his eyes. Finally Diaz shrugged and got to his feet.

"Why not?" said Diaz. "You have incited my curiosity, Mr. Rogan. Let us see what Kristin has to say. Of course, she might not wish to talk to you. She is a good worker and brings in the customers, but her temper is quite…mercurial, let us say."

"Thank you," said Mac, rising from the chair.

Diaz led the way into the hall and walked three doors down. He rapped on the door with his knuckles. "Kristin?"

"What?" came a woman's annoyed voice, muffled through the door.

"Are you recording?" said Diaz.

Recording?

"No, come in," said the woman.

Diaz opened the door, and Mac followed him inside.

He expected to see something that looked like a theatrical dressing room, a place where the dancers would prepare before they went on stage. Something with a row of wooden counters, a lot of mirrors, and bright makeup lights.

Instead, he found himself in a room that looked like a small television studio. One half held what looked like the set of a bedroom from a sitcom, with a row of spotlights mounted on the ceiling. Two high-quality cameras pointed at the bedroom set. The other half of the room held stacked plastic storage totes labeled COSTUMES or PROPS. A plastic folding table contained a Mac Pro tower connected to a pair of monitors and several external FireWire drives.

Kristin Salwell stood next to the table, hands on her hips, a thunderous scowl on her pretty face.

She was young. If Mac remembered right, she had been a senior in 2005, which would mean she was twenty or twenty-one now. She could be old enough to dance at a place like the Graymont while still too young to purchase alcohol. Salwell was an attractive, fit woman, her brown hair tied back in a ponytail. Mac could tell that she was fit because she was wearing black yoga pants and a skin-tight blue tank top that exposed both cleavage and several inches of flat stomach. A tattoo of roses and thorns wound up her right arm, and he saw part of another tattoo that looked like a dragon on her stomach, the ink stark against her pale skin.

He could see how she had seduced those two teachers. Salwell had a smoldering magnetism, a sort of charisma that compelled the attention of any heterosexual man. Certainly, Mac would have found her attractive if he hadn't known about her past.

Despite her beauty, there was a hard edge to face, a detached coldness to her eyes. Her face and neck also looked a little too thin. Mac wondered if she had a few plastic baggies of cocaine hidden in her car. He remembered Julie Norton's opinion that Kristin Salwell would either become a wealthy woman or die in a hotel room by the time she was twenty-five, and thought that Julie's prediction had probably been right.

"Who the hell is this?" snapped Salwell. "Someone wanting a private performance?" Her expression changed to a seductive leer. The rapid change from annoyed anger to come-hither was unsettling and had exactly the opposite effect on Mac than what Salwell would have wanted. "What do you like, big boy?"

"Just to ask some questions," said Mac.

"Questions?" said Salwell. Her voice lost its purr and returned to waspish irritation. "About what?"

"My name's Cormac Rogan," said Mac. "I'm a private investigator, and I was hoping I could ask you a few questions."

"You're not a cop," said Salwell. "I don't have to talk to you about anything."

She glanced at Diaz, but he simply leaned against the door, hands in his trouser pockets.

"No, you don't," said Mac. "But I would appreciate it if you could."

"Let me guess," said Salwell with a sneer. "Some fat housewife found her husband watching one of my videos, and she hired you to find out if we're having an affair or not."

"No," said Mac. "Do you remember a man named Douglas Norton?"

That took her aback. Surprise overrode her annoyance for a moment, and she blinked several times.

"Mr. Norton?" said Salwell. "He killed himself a year ago. Poor bastard."

"The police concluded that Douglas Norton killed himself," said Mac. "His wife believes that he was murdered and hired me to check over the case to see if they missed anything."

"The police already talked to me about that while I was in prison," said Salwell. Her smirk returned. "I couldn't have killed him because I spent all day working in the laundry room."

"Did you convince someone to kill him for you?" said Mac.

Salwell stared at him and then threw back her head and laughed.

"God! You're...what's the word? Cocky? Impudent? I don't know." She stepped forward, leaned against the table holding the computer equipment, and folded her arms across her chest.

"I've been called worse," said Mac. He decided to attempt some humor. "I imagine you have as well."

She smiled at that. "You have no idea. All right. Ask your questions. Let's see if I can shock you."

"How would you describe your relationship with Mr. Norton?" said Mac.

Salwell shrugged. "I took his class. That was about it." Her smirk returned. "I bet you know all about me, don't you?"

"I'm aware you had some legal difficulties," said Mac.

"Legal difficulties," repeated Salwell with some mockery. "You could say that. I told the judge I was so, so sorry for all the awful things I had done, that I had learned my lesson, and the asshole still put me in prison for a year."

"As I recall, you accused the teachers of raping you," said Mac.

"I was underage," said Salwell. "It was rape no matter what." That smirk returned. "Even if I could have made them do anything I wanted. Which I did. Want to know a secret, Cormac?"

"Sure," said Mac.

"Men are so stupid," said Salwell. "I figured that out about two weeks after I started growing breasts. I can make them do whatever I want."

Mac caught Diaz rolling his eyes. Salwell didn't notice.

"Like giving you a passing grade?" said Mac.

Salwell shrugged. "If I'm nice to them...why shouldn't they be nice to me?"

"Maybe you wanted them to be a little too nice to you," said Mac.

Salwell frowned but then shrugged again. "I got greedy. And stupid. I shouldn't have asked for money over the phone. Could have guessed that it would get recorded. Everything is recorded nowadays. But I figured out a better way to make money with recordings."

"So you're running a porn site?" said Mac. Pornography had never appealed to him. He knew that a disturbing percentage of the women who appeared in online pornography were victims of human trafficking, forced into it against their will. The women who participated freely were often people like Kristin Salwell, blackmailer and extortionist.

"Customized digital adult entertainment experiences," said Diaz from the wall. "It's a great business. By the end of this year, we'll have made almost as much money from the website as from the club, and I think in 2008, it will surpass the club's revenues."

"If you don't mind the question, how do you make money?" said Mac. "Porn is everywhere on the Internet, and most of it's free."

"Personalization," said Diaz.

"People pay for that?" said Mac.

"What do you think?" said Salwell.

She took a step forward, and her whole demeanor changed. Her eyes seemed to become hooded, her lips parted, and she did not so much walk towards him as sway. Her hands began sliding up and down her body with slow languor.

"Hey, Cormac Rogan," Salwell purred. Her voice had become softer, huskier. "I've been so lonely." Her eyes bored into his. "You want to help me be a bad girl, huh?" She gripped the base of her tank top and began to slowly slide it up towards her chest, exposing her tattooed stomach. "You want to see just how bad of a girl I can be for you, Cormac?"

She stopped when her shirt was maybe half an inch below what would have been public indecency, and her smirk returned. "Of course, you want to see anything, you'll have to pay for it. Tell you what. I'll give you a twenty percent discount on a personalized video. Maybe…mmm, ten percent discount on a live performance."

"That's coming out of your half," said Diaz.

Salwell gave him an exasperated look.

"Nice sales pitch," said Mac. "Did it work on Douglas Norton?"

Salwell gaped at him as if stunned he wasn't yanking out his wallet to see the rest of her show. For a second, she looked almost hurt, and then she huffed out a laugh, tugging her tank top back down.

"It didn't," she said. "Yeah, I tried flirting with him. I flirted with all the male teachers when I could, made them do things for me. And Mr. Norton…big burly football guy like him, I thought he would be fun in bed, and I could have him do favors for me. But it just bounced right off him. He never even tried to look down my shirt or check out my ass when he thought I wouldn't notice."

"You're saying he had integrity," said Mac.

Her eyes flared. "And you're saying that I don't?"

"Like I said, I'm not here to make trouble for your business," said Mac, though he thought it wouldn't be the worst thing in the world if Graymont and its website got shut down. "But I think we can all agree that teachers shouldn't sleep with their students. They should have known better."

Her smirk returned, and Mac wondered if her anger had been real or not. "But I can be very persuasive."

"Why do you think Mr. Norton wrote down your name before he died?" said Mac.

"I have no goddamn idea," said Salwell. "I wasn't even able to get anything out of it. When the cops talked to me about it, I thought I could use it to get out of prison sooner. But nothing. Waste of my time."

"I see," said Mac. "What do you think happened to Mr. Norton?"

Salwell shrugged. "He killed himself, didn't he? Seems pretty obvious."

"You said you know everything there is to know about men," said Mac. Her smirk returned. "With that in mind, why do you think Mr. Norton killed himself?"

Salwell opened her mouth, closed it. He could tell that the question had taken her off-guard.

"Hell if I know," said Salwell at last. "Sometimes people kill themselves, and it's obvious why they did it. Like, a fat loser with no friends shoots himself, makes sense, right? But Mr. Norton wasn't like that." She thought about it. "I think it was the school shooting. I know he really liked some of the kids who got killed. Joshua Chartwell got killed that day, and he was the best defensive player on the team. He really looked up to Mr. Norton. So Mr. Norton seems like he's okay, then one day he's sitting alone in his office and gets sad thinking about Josh, and then..." She put a finger to her temple and mimed shooting a gun.

"The school shooter was never caught," said Mac.

"What, you think I did it?" She laughed. "I've never fired a gun in my life. When the shooting started, I was in the bathroom, and I hid there until the cops brought us out."

"Who do you think was the shooter?" said Mac.

"Parker McIntyre and Ryan Walsh, obviously," said Salwell.

Mac thought back to what he had read in the file Julie had given him. "I thought it was proven they couldn't have done it."

"Oh, come on," said Salwell. "Parker's mom is some big-shot rich lawyer or something like that, and she made a fuss until the cops had to back off. Probably helped that Ryan killed himself, the big fat pussy."

"Sounds like you didn't like them," said Mac.

"I didn't," said Salwell. "I see guys like them all the time in the club, and they buy my videos on the website. Fat and sweaty, and if they found themselves alone with a woman, they'd probably start crying." The contempt dripped off her words like acid. "They always say they're nice guys deep down and why don't girls like their real selves, blah blah blah. Well, their personalities suck, too."

"Doesn't stop you from taking their money," said Mac.

Salwell barked out a harsh laugh. "What's that you always say, boss? Doesn't matter whether they're white, black, or brown, what matters is that the money is green?"

"Damn right," grunted Diaz.

"So there you go," said Salwell. "That's all I know about it. Still seems strange that Mr. Norton shot himself, though."

"Why's that?" said Mac. "Because he didn't seem suicidal?"

"No, because he hated guns," said Salwell. "Like, really hated them. Sometimes he'd go on and on in class about how the Second Amendment was obsolete, and the NRA was as bad as al-Qaeda. He wouldn't shut up about it. So if he was going to kill himself, I figured he would jump off a bridge or cut his wrists or something."

"I see," said Mac. "You don't know a man named Winston Marsh, do you?"

"No, never heard of him," said Salwell. She looked at Diaz, who shook his head. "Should I?"

"He was a retired janitor who died in an accident about six months before Mr. Norton was killed," said Mac. "Doug Norton shot himself with a pistol registered to Marsh."

"That's weird," said Salwell. She shrugged. "He probably bought the gun from somebody in a parking lot. That kind of thing happens all the time."

"Not here, though," said Diaz, a bit sharper than his usual tone.

"Right, right, not here," said Salwell. "Every always observes the law here."

"Thanks for your time, Ms. Salwell," said Mac, reaching into his jacket pocket.

"Ms. Salwell," she repeated mockingly.

"If you think of anything else, please give me a call," said Mac, handing her a business card with Dave Wester's number and website on it.

"Sure," said Salwell, dropping the card on the table. Mac suspected it would go in the trash in about two minutes. "Though... hey, maybe I just thought of something."

"Yeah?" said Mac.

Salwell grinned. Her teeth were very white, likely bleached for the camera, and something about her expression put Mac in mind of a piranha. "Maybe the reason Mr. Norton wasn't flirting with me was that he was having an affair."

"Why do you think he was having an affair?" said Mac.

"A couple of days before the shooting, I saw him talking with a blond woman," said Salwell. "I was coming out of the locker room. He was talking to a blond woman in an expensive coat."

"Maybe it was his wife," said Mac. "She's blond."

"Nah, I saw pictures of his wife," said Salwell. "She was taller and chunkier. This woman was shorter than me."

"Was she another teacher?" said Mac. "Someone who works for the school?"

"Don't know," said Salwell. "But I knew all the teachers. She wasn't one of them, and I never saw her there before or since." She grinned. "But the blond woman was pissed, I could tell. Maybe she just found out that Mr. Norton was married."

"Maybe," said Mac, though he doubted it. If Doug had been having an affair, and if he had been meeting the woman at the high school, someone likely would have seen something. The police and the FBI had conducted thorough interviews with everyone at the school after the shooting, and that likely would have pulled the affair into the light. Extensive investigations like that often dug up unrelated matters people wanted kept quiet. "Or maybe she was a parent who was pissed he'd given a kid a bad grade."

Salwell opened her mouth, closed it, and then shrugged. "Maybe. Her coat was expensive, so she was probably a parent. A lot of rich kids go to Northwoods High School."

"Thanks for your time," said Mac

Salwell had already turned away to adjust one of the cameras, dismissing Mac from her attention.

"I'll see you out, Mr. Rogan," said Diaz, opening the door. Which was likely a polite way to make sure Mac didn't do any snooping on the way out. They stepped into the hall, and Diaz closed the studio door behind them. "If I may offer you some advice?"

"Sure," said Mac.

"The woman who hired you is obviously in mourning and in denial," said Diaz. "Best let her realize the truth on her own. A man who snatches a delusion from a woman is like one who tries to steal a meal from a starving tiger."

"Good advice," said Mac. "Did that come from a fortune cookie?"

Diaz snorted as they walked back into the main room. The woman had finished vacuuming the floor, though the college students were still wiping down the tables.

"My turn for some advice," said Mac. "You should be careful around Salwell. She slept with two teachers when she was seventeen and extorted them for grades and money. She'll put in a knife in your back without even blinking."

"Mr. Rogan," said Diaz. "I appreciate your concern. But I have been in this business since before you were born. Salwell thinks she is tough. Some of the women I have employed could have pulled out her spine and used it as a toothpick."

"Don't think anyone would pay to watch that on the Internet," said Mac.

"You would be surprised," said Diaz. He held out his hand. "Good luck on your investigation."

"Thank you, Mr. Diaz," said Mac. He shook Diaz's hand and very carefully resisted the impulse to wipe it on the side of his pants. That would have been rude.

He stepped back into the parking lot, hearing the heavy locks thump back into place behind him.

After talking to Salwell and Diaz, Mac felt like he needed a shower, like he'd just spent the last half-hour wading through algae-choked water.

He wondered if Salwell had ever "performed" for Diaz and decided that he really, really didn't want to know.

Mac shook his head and started across the parking lot to his car. To his surprise and annoyance, he felt the start of one of the episodes of rage that had dogged him all summer, his hands starting to shake a little. He grimaced, got his laptop out of the trunk of the car, and made notes on his conversation with Salwell. That helped him calm down and focus. Mac supposed Diaz was watching to see if he left, but he didn't care, and he didn't want to drive until he had calmed down somewhat.

After fifteen minutes, he had made a satisfactory record of the conversation.

Mac hadn't liked either Salwell or Diaz, but that was irrelevant. He didn't think it likely that either one of them had anything to do with Douglas Norton's death. For one thing, Diaz wouldn't have even met Salwell until she had gotten out of prison. For another, Salwell had seemed mostly indifferent to Norton. She had neither been upset nor gleeful that he had died, and her chief opinion of Doug Norton seemed to be annoyance that he had refused to respond to her flirtations, which was itself a grudging admission that he had been someone of integrity.

Yet why had Salwell's name been the last thing Norton had written before he died?

For that matter, Mac wasn't sure what to make of Salwell's story of Doug Norton talking with an angry blond woman in private. Perhaps

Salwell had only been screwing with Mac, adding one last contradictory story to confuse him. Then again, he didn't think that Salwell had lied to him, save for her obvious self-justifications. But she was a very good actress, which meant she would be an equally proficient liar.

Nevertheless, he thought that Salwell believed that Doug Norton had killed himself in an episode of despair over the Northwoods shooting.

Mac was inclined to believe that himself.

Yet there was still the question of Salwell's name in Norton's day planner and how he had gotten ahold of Winston Marsh's gun.

Maybe Diaz was right, and Doug has simply bought the weapon from a thief in a parking lot for cash, a transaction that would be nearly impossible to trace.

Mac came to a decision and left the parking lot for Graymont Gentlemen's Club. He needed to make a phone call, and he didn't want to do it here. Mac drove a few blocks and came to a Taco Bell. The parking lot was only about a third full, and he slid into an empty spot and shut off the engine.

It was time to find out more about the Northwoods shooting.

Mac pulled out his cellphone, found the number for Agent Matthew Cole of the FBI, and hit the call button.

9

THE NORTHWOODS TRAGEDY

Mac wasn't sure if he would get Cole or not, but the FBI agent picked up on the third ring.

"Mr. Rogan," said Cole in his quiet voice. "It's been a while."

"Yeah, since Washington," said Mac. They had both been at the Capitol on the same day, testifying to Congress about the assassination of Senator Jack Kelsey.

"Testifying before a Senate committee is usually either a career highlight or a career-ending event for an FBI officer," said Cole.

"Well, you picked up the phone, so I'm assuming that it wasn't a career-ending event," said Mac.

Cole snorted. "That's true." The amusement faded. "I'm just glad it wasn't a life-ending event for us and a lot of other people. Most of the day-to-day work of an FBI agent is reports, research, and meetings."

"Not a giant fertilizer bomb under a packed megachurch," said Mac.

For a second, he remembered Jack Kelsey sliding dead to the ground, that shocked look still on his face, Katrina Hobb's weary smile as she died, the bodyguards shouting, the noise echoing off the concrete pillars...

"Well, I doubt you called to reminisce," said Cole. "What can I do for you?"

Mac had met Cole while the FBI had been investigating Senator Kelsey's corruption. Later, after the dust had settled and they had both testified about Kelsey's assassination and numerous crimes, Mac and Cole had a conversation outside the Capitol. Mac's actions, Cole said, had saved a lot of innocent lives, which was the important thing. They had also made the FBI look good in front of a lot of important people, which while less important, was still a significant consideration. Without coming out and saying it, Cole had let Mac know that if he needed unofficial help (within the bounds of all federal and state laws, of course), he could have it.

"I wanted to talk to you about the Northwoods High School shooting," said Mac.

There was a pause.

The FBI had looked less good with that case.

"What is your interest in it?" said Cole, his tone a little cooler.

"Do you know a guy named Douglas Norton?" said Mac.

"Not off the top of my head," said Cole. "But connected to Northwoods...oh, yes. He was one of the teachers, got his students to shelter during the shooting." He paused. "If I remember right, he killed himself."

"Yeah," said Mac. "His widow Julie thinks Doug was murdered and hired me to look into it."

"Ah," said Cole. "I'm afraid that's a common reaction among the relatives of suicides."

"I'm eighty percent sure that Norton killed himself," said Mac. Though after talking to Salwell, it had gone up to eighty-five. The fact was that Salwell's explanation made sense – Doug had been overcome by a fit of grief and shot himself.

But that didn't explain why Doug had written down Salwell's name before he died.

Or how he had gotten Winston Marsh's gun.

"When did Norton die?" said Cole. "It was relatively recent, wasn't it?"

"January 24th of 2006," said Mac.

"About eight months after the Northwoods killings," said Cole. "Why do you want to know about the shooting?"

"Because it's the only reason I can find for him to have killed himself," said Mac. "He and his family didn't have money problems, he wasn't on drugs, he didn't have a history of mental illness, and as far as I know, he wasn't having an affair. There was a female student who was sleeping with teachers and extorting them for higher grades..."

"Kristin Salwell, yes," said Cole.

"I talked to Salwell since her name was the last thing Norton wrote in his day planner before he died," said Mac. "She claims that she never slept with Norton and seemed personally offended that he refused to flirt with her. The most probable explanation is that his death had something to do with the shootings."

"I'll tell you what I can," said Cole. "I didn't work the case, though, so I can only tell you what I heard since. I was on assignment with a domestic terrorism task force in Washington at the time, which is how I wound up working on the Pure Earth and Kelsey investigations. Just as well, since the Northwoods case turned out to be an enormous unsolved mess. Which maybe isn't surprising since it was so strange."

"What was so strange about it?" said Mac.

"It didn't fit the usual patterns," said Cole. "Ever since Columbine, school shooters tend to fall into a common pattern. They're usually male, loners, unpopular, sexually frustrated, come from divorced parents, and are frequently on some kind of antidepressant medication. There have been exceptions, of course, but the pattern holds more often than not. They're also usually spree killers. They walk the school and shoot as many people as they can until they're killed, or they wind up killing themselves. It's extremely unusual to have an unsolved school shooting like this one, since the perpetrator almost always winds up dead or in custody at the end."

"The shooter was across the street, right?" said Mac.

"Right," said Cole. "The main building at Northwoods High School is this old-four story building from the Depression. The school district has been buying up the houses across the street in preparation for a new athletic facility. The shooter broke into one of the houses and fired from the third-story window. It was a perfect position. The window faced the primary doors to the school, and a large number of students were leaving the building. The front stairs were full of students and parents. It was only about fifty yards from the window to the front doors, and it would have been an easy shot."

"A shooting gallery," said Mac.

"Precisely."

"There was no trace of who had done it?" said Mac.

"No," said Cole. "None whatsoever. We're pretty sure that the shooter entered the house through the back door. Examination of the lock revealed scratches consistent with the use of a lock rake or a similar tool. The Milwaukee crime scene crew went over every inch of the house, and they couldn't find any fingerprints or any DNA traces. An alley ran behind the house, and we think the shooter had a vehicle parked there for a quick escape. I think between the Milwaukee cops and our agents, we interviewed something like seven hundred witnesses, and no one saw anything. A couple of people thought they saw a panel van driving through the alley, but they didn't get a license plate. And it was three in the afternoon, and traffic was heavy."

"That sounds unusually organized for a school shooter," said Mac.

"It was," said Cole. "For a while, we thought it might be a domestic terror incident or perhaps a racial hate incident, not a school shooting. Homegrown domestic terrorists usually try to get away and don't want to get caught. But no one ever claimed responsibility. For that matter, most of the victims were white. Northwoods High School at the time was something like ninety percent white, and only one black student was wounded out of the five dead and seven wounded. We decided a race-based or an extremist political motivation for the attack was unlikely."

"I understand things got complicated," said Mac.

"I'm only telling you this because I know how much you dislike reporters," said Cole. Mac had expressed his feelings on journalists to Cole at some length. He had flatly refused to speak to any reporters after Kelsey's death, which hadn't stopped them from following him around and making a nuisance of themselves until the news cycle had moved on to its next outrage. "After a week of investigation, the Milwaukee police had nothing. No leads, no witnesses, no suspects, not even any physical evidence other than the scratches from the lock rake. The investigators called us in for a consultation. Our team built a potential profile of the suspect and started considering which students weren't at school that day. The most likely candidates were two seniors named Parker McIntyre and Ryan Walsh."

"Why did they fit the profile?" said Mac.

"They were both loners and apparently were each other's only friends," said Cole. "They were unpopular with the other students, and both had divorced parents. Walsh was on antidepressants, McIntyre was not. We started taking a closer look at them, and then some idiot leaked their identities to the press."

"I take it that turned out badly?" said Mac.

"It was a shitstorm," said Cole. "You have to understand, at this point it had been two weeks since the shooting, and there had been no progress in the investigation. There were hundreds of grieving family members and thousands of upset people, and all of them wanted someone to blame. Leaking those names was like dropping a lit match into a bathtub of gasoline." His voice grew harsh. "To this day, we don't know if it was someone in the MPD or the Bureau. But we immediately had demands for the suspects' arrest. Walsh and McIntyre started getting death threats. One of the fathers who had lost a child confronted McIntyre and wound up breaking his nose. And then Walsh killed himself. I was still in Washington for this, but I heard about it, and it was a disaster. The worst part was that it was all for nothing."

"It was proven they couldn't have done it?" said Mac.

"Walsh and McIntyre skipped class that day to play an online computer game," said Cole. "Evidently their 'guild,' which is some kind of gaming club, had scheduled a session, and they decided to skip afternoon classes to play the game. We subpoenaed the game company, and the server logs proved that Walsh and McIntyre were both online and playing at the time of the shooting. McIntyre's mother had a lot of money and local connections, and she sued the MPD and the press. They wound up settling out of court for a very large sum."

"How did McIntyre's mother get her money?" said Mac.

"She used to be a commercial real estate developer," said Cole. "Worked for...let me see...Morgan Properties, that was it."

Mac felt an odd jolt. "Morgan Properties?"

"Surprised you haven't heard of them," said Cole. "They're one of the two biggest commercial development firms in Wisconsin."

"That and Crest Development," said Mac. "Julie Norton is a senior vice president and in-house legal counsel for Morgan Properties. Joshua Chartwell, one of the victims, was the son of Clarissa Chartwell, one of the best agents for Morgan Properties. Parker McIntyre's mom..."

"Maggie McIntyre," supplied Cole.

"You just said she used to work for Morgan Properties," said Mac. "And the gun that was found by Douglas Norton's corpse was stolen from a man named Winston Marsh who had died six months earlier. Marsh used to work as a maintenance technician for Crest Development before he retired. A lot of odd coincidences."

"True," said Cole. "However, both Morgan Properties and Crest Development are two of the biggest employers in the Milwaukee area, especially for white-collar workers and professionals. They must have employed thousands of people in various capacities over the last ten years. It's possibly no more significant than if they all turned out to have voted for George Bush or John Kerry in the last election. Data points that aren't indicative of any relevance."

"You're right," said Mac. Still, the coincidence nagged at him. It was probably just a coincidence, but it was an odd one. "I wish I could figure out how Doug got ahold of Marsh's gun."

"He probably bought it from whoever stole it," said Cole.

"Doug was apparently strongly anti-gun," said Mac. "But that was a recent change in his attitude. He would have known how to buy a gun legally."

"If he and his wife shared a joint account, said Cole, "he might not have wanted her to know about the purchase. Especially if he was developing a suicidal ideation and had concealed it from her. Given that his death caught her by surprise, I think he successfully hid it from her."

"Yeah," said Mac.

"The unfortunate fact is that Douglas Norton was probably traumatized after the shooting," said Cole. "PTSD and survivor's guilt are not uncommon in people who survive events like mass shootings or terrorist attacks, and there's often a cluster of suicides that follow in the months after. The most likely explanation is that Norton had traumatic stress, didn't deal with it well, and then finally ended up in a bad place and killed himself."

"I think you're right," said Mac. "Everyone I've talked to said Norton was dedicated to his students, and apparently Joshua Chartwell was one of his favorites."

"There you go," said Cole. "The trick will be convincing Mrs. Norton of that."

"If I can trace how Doug got a hold of Marsh's gun, that will probably do the trick," said Mac. "Though I wish I could figure out why Kristin Salwell's name was the last thing he wrote down before he died."

"There could be any number of explanations," said Cole. "Maybe he thought one of his other colleagues had been blackmailed by her. Maybe he'd slept with Salwell."

"Salwell says she didn't," said Mac. "I suppose she could have lied."

"I doubt it's a question that has an answer," said Cole. "Trying to track the handgun is your best bet. Though that will be difficult.

There are neighborhoods in Milwaukee and Chicago where you can get a stolen pistol for a hundred dollars without much effort."

"You're right," said Mac. "Still, I set a deadline with Julie Norton, so I'm obliged to look until I run out of time."

"How's the software company going?" said Cole.

"Well enough," said Mac. "We're out of alpha testing and into beta, and Paul's got some clients lined up."

"The iPhone," said Cole with a snort. "It's going to be an expensive fad. Just watch. People aren't going to give up physical buttons for a screen that cracks if you look at it wrong."

"Maybe," said Mac. "But even if the iPhone fizzles out, we can port the software to other platforms. The web-based client might be the way forward. Every law enforcement car in the country is going to have a laptop mounted to the dash in another few years."

"You should sell to your other partners," said Cole, "and apply to the academy at Quantico…"

"Not this again," said Mac, though he smiled as he said it.

"You have a natural gift for investigation," said Cole. "Not many people do."

"I'm twenty-nine next month," said Mac. "Little late to be changing careers."

"Not really," said Cole, "and some people don't come to the Bureau until later in life." He paused, and Mac heard a keyboard tapping in the background. "I have to run. I suspect I don't need to remind you not to discuss this with anyone, especially not reporters."

"Of course not," said Mac. "You know what I think about journalists." He grimaced. "That damned blogger is still going to write a book about the Kelsey assassination."

"The Internet is going to be the death of us all," said Cole. "Good luck with Julie Norton."

"Thanks," said Mac.

Cole said good-bye and hung up.

Mac stared at his phone, thinking. Cole was a veteran FBI agent with the suspicious, methodical mind of an experienced investigator. And his assessment agreed with that of Kristin Salwell. In a moment of depression after the shooting, Doug Norton had likely shot himself. Mac was eighty percent sure that was what had happened.

But he was still only eighty percent certain. It seemed odd that so many people involved had worked for either Morgan Properties or Crest Development. As Cole had said, it was likely because the two companies were major employers in the Brookfield area. And why the hell had Doug written Kristin Salwell's name before he died? Mac had disliked and mistrusted Salwell, but he thought she had been telling the truth about not having slept with Norton.

Perhaps there was something he could clear up right now.

He keyed through his contacts until he found Julie Norton's number and dialed.

A crisp-voice woman answered on the third ring. "Morgan Properties, Julie Norton's office."

That would be Julie's personal assistant, the one who thought Mac was a charlatan preying upon Julie's grief.

"This is Cormac Rogan," he said. "I wondered if Mrs. Norton could spare a few minutes to talk."

There was a long pause, dripping with disapproval.

"Please hold," said the woman at last.

Julie picked up about thirty seconds later.

"Mr. Rogan!" she said. "I wasn't expecting to hear back from you so soon."

"Thank you for speaking with me," said Mac, deciding how to phrase his question. "I've been focusing on tracing Winston Marsh's gun, and I came across a few things I wanted to ask you about."

"Go ahead," said Julie.

"Why did Maggie McIntyre quit working for Morgan Development after the Northwoods shooting?" said Mac.

There was a long pause.

"Oh, boy," said Julie at last. "You don't think...Maggie didn't have..."

"No," said Mac. "But Northwoods High School had three serious problems in a row – the shooting, the teachers who slept with Kristin Salwell, and then your husband's death. I don't think they're connected, but since they happened so close together, there are probably links between them. I'm sure you've done enough due diligence on business deals that felt like walking up to a bush and hitting it with a rake to see what falls out. Investigating anything is sometimes a lot like that."

"I've never heard it put quite that way," said Julie. "Well, Maggie quit because she didn't think Morgan Properties supported her enough in the aftermath of the shooting."

"Go on," said Mac.

"The shooting was awful, and the aftermath was bad," said Julie. "The police and the FBI didn't have any idea who had done it, and people were getting angry. Then the press reported that the FBI thought that two students fit the potential psychological profile of school shooters, and all hell broke loose."

"Parker McIntyre and Ryan Walsh," said Mac.

"It was a mess," said Julie. "They started getting death threats, and I think the father of one of the murdered students attacked Parker and broke his nose. Ryan committed suicide, but Maggie fought back, and hard. Her lawyer proved that Parker and Ryan were playing some sort of online video game when the shooting happened. Maggie wrung a settlement and an apology out of the FBI, and then she started suing every news outlet that had published or mentioned her son's name for libel."

"Why did she quit the company?" said Mac. "I think she would have needed the money."

"She didn't," said Julie. "She's rich, almost as rich as Angie. Maggie was the company's best agent, and she invested well. But Parker's her only kid, and Maggie's not…well, not rational where he's concerned." A wry note entered her voice. "I suspect most men probably think women are irrational about their children, don't they? But Maggie gets intense. That father who punched Parker and threatened him? If Maggie could have gotten away with it, I think she might have broken his kneecaps. As for why she quit, she felt ostracized here in the aftermath of the shooting. I'm afraid she had a point." She sighed. "People were howling for Parker's blood, and we pulled away from her. After the FBI apologized, Maggie marched into a senior staff meeting, announced that we hadn't been there for her in her hour of need, and quit on the spot. Angie tried to talk her out of it, but Maggie's mind was made up."

"I see," said Mac. "Did Doug have any connection with Parker or Ryan?"

"Not really," said Julie. "They were in his classes, but neither one of them was athletic." She hesitated. "I don't think Doug liked either one of them, to be honest. He can't stand computer games, and he doesn't…didn't respect anyone who won't even try to play sports in high school. But he was disgusted by what had happened to them. He had been interviewed by a few reporters after the shooting. But after Ryan killed himself, Doug refused to talk to any more journalists."

"Probably just as well," said Mac. "I've had a few bad experiences with journalists myself."

He doubted that Parker McIntyre or Ryan Walsh had anything to do with Doug's death. For that matter, they didn't have anything to do with Kristin Salwell. Her contempt for them had been obvious. Though no doubt if Parker put his credit card details into the website for Graymont Gentlemen's Club, Salwell would cheerfully take off her clothes for him in front of the camera.

"Maggie worked for Morgan Properties," said Mac. "Do you know where Ryan's parents worked?" He half-expected her to say that Ryan Walsh's parents had worked for Morgan Properties or Crest Development.

"I don't know where his father worked, but I think his parents divorced when he was still a toddler," said Julie. "I do know his mother was an ER nurse at Froedtert Hospital. I think Maggie tried to convince her to join the lawsuits, but she didn't want anything to do with it. Janice Walsh took the FBI's settlement and moved to…mmm, Florida, I think. I suppose she was done with the Milwaukee area after everything that happened here."

"Kind of like Clarissa Chartwell," said Mac. "Can't blame her for that."

"No, I suppose I can't," said Julie. She let out a long sigh. "God, but it's been an awful couple of years."

"Do you have contact information for Ryan's mother and for Maggie McIntyre?" said Mac. "I might want to talk to them."

Julie hesitated. "What for? Janice Walsh has been through enough, and Maggie…is not someone you want to annoy."

"They don't have to talk to me if they don't want to," said Mac. "I'm not going to wait outside anyone's garage. But they might know something important without realizing it."

"All right," said Julie. "I'll send it to your Wester Security email account. But I would prefer that you didn't mention that you got the information from me. The last thing I need is Maggie marching into the building and starting another fight with Angie. She's got enough on her plate as it is, trying to keep Arianna Crest from stealing away the Westview Mall deal."

"Does that happen a lot?" said Mac.

"More than we would like," said Julie. "Crest Development is our main competitor, and with the housing boom, there's lots of work to go around. We win some, and Arianna wins some, but she always seems to win at the worst possible time. I was in the middle of negotiating a big contract when Doug was murdered. God, it's such a small and stupid thing by comparison, but I'm glad we didn't lose that deal. Everything else that year went to hell, so it was nice to have a win."

For a second, just a second, an idea started to form in Mac's mind, two pieces coming together to form a new connection. The sensation was almost like trying to remember something that he had forgotten. Something that Julie had said had triggered a connection in his subconscious, but Mac could not quite grasp it.

"Mr. Rogan?" said Julie.

"Sorry, I was thinking about what you had said," said Mac. "I'm going to keep tracing the gun. If you think of anything else, don't hesitate to call."

"And if you have any other questions, please call," said Julie. "I'm usually in meetings, but I'll get back to you as soon as I can."

They said their goodbyes, and the call ended.

Mac tapped his fingers on the steering wheel for a moment, thinking. Then he got out of the car, opened the trunk, and drew out the file that Julie had given him. A car full of teenagers drove past, making for the Taco Bell's drive-through. Mac wondered why they weren't in school and then realized it was well past three in the afternoon.

He paged through the file and found the address where Winston Marsh had fallen and broken his neck.

Mac wanted to have a closer look.

10

ACCIDENTS HAPPEN

Traffic was heavy as rush hour picked up, but Mac pushed his way through.

Winston Marsh had lived on the eastern edge of the Metcalfe Park neighborhood, in an apartment over a convenience store. Mac drove east on North Avenue, joining the long lines of cars moving back and forth. Commercial buildings lined the street, most of them built of brick and looking worn-down, with a floor or two of apartments rising above stores. Here and there, a newer-looking fast-food restaurant or gas station stood on a corner. Large crowds waited near the bus stops, and he saw three homeless people pushing shopping carts of their personal possessions.

The area where Marsh had lived wasn't exactly dangerous, but Mac would not come here alone after dark unless he had a good reason. He turned off North Avenue and slid his battered Corsica into an angled parking spot. Marsh's apartment had been in a two-story building overlooking the street. The bottom floor held a convenience store with a painted sign over the door that said CARVER'S CIGARETTES & LIQUOR, metal grating over the windows and doors. A glowing neon sign proclaimed that checks were cashed within and that the premises were under 24/7 video surveillance.

After a moment's thought, Mac put his wallet and cell phone in the glove compartment, though he kept some of his cash and a few business cards. He got out of the car and locked it. A white man in a suit drew a few curious stares from pedestrians, followed by indifference. Mac walked past the front of Carver's Cigarettes & Liquor and stepped into the alley.

The files that Mac had read said that Marsh's apartment had an alley entrance, and the medical examiner concluded that he had gotten drunk, fallen down the stairs, and cracked his skull. The alley was narrow, just wide enough to accommodate a city garbage truck, and Mac saw a pair of dumpsters next to a steel door, no doubt where the employees of Carver's Cigarettes & Liquor disposed of trash. The air smelled faintly of garbage, and tiny pieces of broken glass glittered on the concrete.

A steep flight of wooden stairs ran up the side of the building to a metal door on the second floor. A mailbox had been bolted to the brick wall at the foot of the stairs, and the number matched the address for the police report on Marsh's death. Mac stopped at the foot of the stairs and looked them over.

They were in very good shape. They had been built of pressure-treated lumber, and Mac saw no signs of rot or decay. The handrail likewise looked sturdy. The boards of the steps were thick and could support an adult's weight. For that matter, anti-slip treads had been attached to the steps. Had the landlord replaced the stairs after Marsh's death? Mac doubted it. Marsh had died about two years ago, and the stairs looked older than that. Mac supposed it was possible that someone could slip on the stairs and fall to their death, especially if they were drunk at the time, but it would be difficult.

And Marsh had died in July of 2005. It wasn't as if the stairs would have been icy.

"Hey!" came a rough voice. "You looking for something?"

Mac turned and saw a man standing at the entrance of the alley. He was black, and Mac would have put his age at a very weathered fifty. Deep lines marked his face beneath his close-cropped gray hair, and his eyes were bloodshot. The man wore jeans, a T-shirt, and a cardigan sweater beneath a blue apron that said CARVER'S across the chest.

To judge from the way the cardigan sagged on the right, Mac suspected the man had a small revolver in the pocket. He hoped the safety was on.

"Hi," said Mac. "Do you work here?"

"Son, I own the damn building," said the man. "So I've got a reason to ask why you're loitering in my alley."

"You're Mr. Carver?" said Mac.

"Yeah. Jake Carver. Now, I'm going to ask again, what are you doing?"

Mac decided to play it straight. "My name's Cormac Rogan, and I'm a private investigator."

"Private investigator?" said Carver, his eyes narrowing. "What, the insurance company send you sniffing around?"

"No," said Mac. "I'm looking for Winston Marsh's apartment. Did he used to live here?"

"Winston?" said Carver, blinking. "Yeah, he used to live there, but you're out of luck. He died two years ago. Fell down the stairs and cracked his head open, the damn fool."

"I know," said Mac. "Have you ever met anyone named Julie Norton or Douglas Norton?"

Carver leveled a finger at Mac. "I'm not answering any questions until you tell me what you're doing in my alley."

"Last year Douglas Norton killed himself with a handgun," said Mac. "The police said it was suicide. His wife Julie thinks he was murdered and hired me to review the case."

"So what's that got to do with old drunk Winston?" said Carver. "You think he killed this guy? Winston never hurt anybody."

"No," said Mac. "Marsh died in July of 2005, and Doug killed himself in January of 2006. But he used a handgun registered to Winston Marsh to do it."

Carver thought about that for a while, and some of his hostility seemed to fade.

"Huh," he said at last. "Didn't know that old drunk had a gun. Not surprised, though."

"Do you mind if I ask you a few questions?" said Mac. "I'm not looking to make trouble for you or your store."

Carver thought about that some more and then shrugged. "Why the hell not?" He reached into his cardigan and produced a pack of cigarettes and a lighter. "Time for a smoke break anyway. You got until I finish my cigarette."

"If we need to talk longer, I'll buy something from your store," said Mac.

Carver snorted and lit a cigarette. "Well, you got questions, then ask."

"How long did Marsh live in the apartment?" said Mac.

"I'd say it was...mmm, he moved in around November of 2000," said Carver. "I remember it was when the people on TV were losing their shit about the election. Hanging chads and all that nonsense. That was when I had the stairs put in, so I could rent a third apartment upstairs." He nodded at the stairs. "The damn building inspector said the stairs had to meet safety standards, so I paid a contractor too much for them. I passed the inspection...and Winston still fell down the steps and broke his neck. But he was drunk, so the cops said it wasn't my fault."

"Did Winston make a lot of trouble?" said Mac.

"Not while he was alive," said Carver. "The trouble came after he died. See, Winston had only one daughter, and she lives out in California. Hated his guts. Guess old Winston was a crap father. Anyway, after Winston died, I called her, said she could go through his stuff. Daughter said she would, but she never showed up." He gave an irritated shake of his head. "Finally, I boxed up all his stuff and put it in a storage locker, rented out the apartment again. I needed the income, you know?" Mac nodded, encouraging Carver to keep speaking. "Then six months – six months – after Winston died, the daughter shows up. Has a screaming fit in my store that I didn't keep things in the apartment, threatens to sue and call the cops and God knows what else. I told her she could go through the storage locker, and she took off and I never heard from her again." Carver blew out a cloud of smoke. "You own any rental property, son?"

"I'm several thousand dollars in the hole, so no," said Mac.

Carver snorted. "You buy a rental property, you'll get even deeper in the hole, and you'll listen to your tenants bitch about all the things their bratty kids broke as you do it."

"I'll keep that in mind," said Mac. "You don't seem to have liked Winston very much."

"Eh, he was harmless," said Carver. He finished his cigarette, dropped the butt, and ground it out beneath his shoe. Mac thought that meant the conversation was over, but Carver lit a second cigarette. Evidently, smoke breaks involved two or three cigarettes. "He drank too much, that was his problem. It wasn't bad while he was still working. He was a maintenance man for...mmm, I forget..."

"Crest Development?" said Mac.

"Yeah, that was it," said Carver. "But he retired at the start of 2005, and then he didn't have anything to do but sit on his ass and drink." He pointed at the stairs. "He left his apartment twice a week and bought junk food and booze at my store, and then went right back upstairs."

"When you boxed up his stuff," said Mac, "did you see a handgun? Or bullets or anything like that?"

Carver raised his gray eyebrows. "Did I sell it on the sly, you mean?" He seemed halfway between amusement and anger.

Mac decided that trying to placate him would only backfire. "It's got to be an easier way to make money than listening to your tenants bitch about the things their bratty kids broke."

Carver snorted. "That's God's own truth. Right up until you get arrested, anyway. But, no. I don't do anything illegal. I got good relations with the local cops, and I want to keep it that way. Helps keep troublemakers out of my store. Besides, there are too many guns out there as it is."

"I think you've got a revolver in your sweater pocket," said Mac.

Carver actually looked sheepish for a second. "Come on, man. There are too many idiot kids out there who think robbing old Carver's store is the way they're gonna get rich. If the rumor went out that I didn't have some guns, every wannabe thug for miles is going to show up and knock over my cash register. Lose too much to shoplifting every year as it is." He squinted at Mac through the smoke rising from his cigarette. "But you look like a stubborn asshole who doesn't let things go."

"It's gotten me into trouble before."

"I'll bet." Carver tapped some ash from the end of his cigarette. "But I'll tell you what. I didn't see any guns or ammo when I boxed up Winston's stuff. Suppose the paperwork might've been in his file cabinet, but I didn't go through that. And even if I had found a gun and wanted to sell it, I wouldn't have. I was worried that crazy bitch of a daughter was going to sue me or claim I stole her daddy's stuff, so I made a list and took pictures of everything I took out."

"That's very thorough," said Mac.

"I don't like getting sued. You ever been sued?"

"I've been arrested," said Mac, "but I haven't been sued."

"It ain't much fun either way," said Carver.

"I wonder if Winston sold the gun to buy more booze," said Mac.

"I doubt it," said Carver. "Around here, you'd have to be crazy to sell your gun. And Winston wasn't rich, but he wasn't going to be out on the street, either. He always paid his rent out of his Social Security, and I guess he worked long enough at that Crest place that he had a pretty good 401 plan. I think that's why the daughter stopped bothering me. She inherited the rest of the money in the plan and didn't care what happened to the rest of his shit."

Carver inhaled, a distant look coming into his bloodshot eyes. Mac waited, unwilling to interrupt the chain of thought.

"But if you want to know what happened to Carver's gun," said Carver, "I bet his girlfriend stole it."

"Girlfriend?" said Mac.

"Or his hooker," said Carver. "She looked too pretty to have been with somebody like Winston."

Suddenly Mac remembered Kristin Salwell's claim that she had seen a blond woman arguing with Doug Norton.

"You saw him with his girlfriend?" said Mac.

"At the time, I thought she was his daughter," said Carver. "But then I met his actual daughter, and she was so fat she'd have to turn sideways to get into the alley here." He laughed at his own joke. "But the hooker...pretty blond white girl. Great ass on her." Carver snorted. "Way too fine for the likes of Winston, let me tell you."

"How often did you see her?" said Mac.

"Four or five times," said Carver. "She'd come after dark, bring Winston a bottle of liquor. Never bought it from me." He scowled at that. "She'd leave after an hour or two. After Winston died, I didn't see her come around anymore. Probably was a hooker. Winston must have paid through the nose for her because she didn't look like a hooker, not really."

"What did she wear?" said Mac, remembering Salwell's description of a blond woman wearing an expensive coat.

Carver snorted. "What, you into that kind of thing? She didn't leave a business card."

"I think she might have stolen Winston's gun and sold it to the man who killed himself," said Mac. Though he could see several holes in that theory. Douglas Norton and Winston Marsh had no conceivable connection that Mac could see. For that matter, if Marsh had blown some of his retirement savings on a very expensive prostitute, he couldn't see Doug doing the same, or if he had, concealing the expense from his money-savvy lawyer wife.

Carver shrugged. "Jeans, sneakers, a light black jacket. Nothing special."

"You were the one who found Winston's body," said Mac.

"Yeah, that's right," said Carver. "I come at six to open up the store for the day. I saw Winston at the foot of the stairs, and I hurried over, thought he fell and hurt himself. I could tell the poor bastard was dead right away, so I called 911, and that was that."

"Those are really well-built stairs," said Mac. "Good handrail, too."

"Damn right. I paid enough for them."

"Do you think he might have been pushed?" said Mac.

Carver stared at him, smoke rising from his cigarette.

"Suppose it's possible," said Carver. "But when I talked to the cops about it, they said Winston was so drunk he could barely put one foot in front of the other. They said he died at one or two in the morning or so. If he missed a step in the dark, doesn't matter how nice the stairs are."

"Did you see the blond woman the day before he died?" said Mac.

"Don't think so," said Carver. "Couple days before, maybe. But it's not like I have cameras back here, and I do have a business to run. Can't spend all my time watching the alley."

"You spotted me quick enough," said Mac.

Carver grunted. "White guy in a suit shows up and starts poking around, that means trouble."

"That's true," said Mac.

Carver took another puff of the cigarette, glowered at it. "Or maybe I'm full of shit. Handguns are small and easy to steal, that's why there are so many of them. But I'd bet the blond woman took it. Winston didn't ever have any other visitors. Guess he hadn't talked to his daughter for five years before he died. Course, after talking to the daughter, can't blame him for that." He flicked away the cigarette and ground it out. "Smoke break's over. You wanna hang around here more, you're gonna have to buy something."

"No, I think that's all I wanted to ask," said Mac. He produced a business card. "Thank you for your time, Mr. Carver. If you think of anything else, could you give me a call?"

Carver eyed the card like it might explode. "You gonna buy something?"

"Sure," said Mac.

"Okay." Carver took the card and tucked it into the same pocket as his gun. "But I already told you everything. Trying to figure out who stole that gun...you'd have a better chance trying to win the lottery. Speaking of which, we do sell lottery tickets..."

Mac followed Carver into his store. A middle-aged black woman manned the cash register behind a cage of metal and plexiglass, and two black teenagers were opening cartons of potato chips and putting them on the shelves. They all stared at Mac like they expected him to go berserk but then saw him talking amicably with Carver and relaxed. Mac bought a microwave dinner and a go-cup of coffee, paid in cash, and asked the cashier about Winston Marsh's girlfriend. The woman, who was named Tammy, confirmed that she had seen a blond woman visiting Marsh a few times. Tammy hadn't liked the woman, saying that she looked mean.

"She looked like the kind of bitch who'd punch herself in the face," said Tammy, "and then get the cops to arrest you for giving her a black eye."

"Did you ever talk to her?" said Mac.

Tammy gave him a disdainful look. "She didn't come in here and buy anything. Here's your change."

Mac went back to his car and headed out, sipping at the coffee as he did. It was better than he expected. He thought about what Carver had told him as he fought the rush hour traffic. Somehow, that handgun had gone from Winston Marsh to Doug Norton, and there was a gap of almost six months between the deaths of Marsh and Doug. The blond woman seemed the most likely candidate for taking the weapon.

But that hardly narrowed it down. Five million people lived in Wisconsin, half of them women, and a substantial portion of them were blond. For that matter, what had been the woman's relationship with Marsh? In the pictures that Mac had seen, Marsh had looked like what he was – a retired maintenance technician drinking his way to death by liver failure or a related disease. A man like that was not going to have a young, pretty girlfriend, not unless he was rich. Or she was a prostitute, but Mac suspected that the kind of prostitutes Marsh could have afforded would not have caught Carver's attention. Someone like Kristin Salwell would have refused to have anything to do with Marsh without a large amount of money involved.

The next course of action, Mac decided, was to dig more into Marsh. Somewhere he would find a connection that would lead to the blond woman, and then maybe he could figure out what had happened to the handgun. Marsh's daughter, maybe? She had been estranged from her father and hadn't talked to him for years. Probably better to start with people who had known Marsh more recently. His supervisors and coworkers at Crest Development, Mac decided.

He would call them tomorrow.

He pulled into the parking lot of his complex. Most of the spots were full, and he wound up having to park about as far from his building as possible. Mac trudged across the lot with his laptop bag, coffee, and the bag holding his microwave dinner, and climbed up the stairs to his apartment. He changed out of his suit to T-shirt and sweatpants and spent twenty minutes typing up notes from his interviews with Salwell and Carver. Once that was done, he sent them in an email to Dave, who had been a police officer for twenty-five years and therefore was happy when his subcontractors sent him regular written reports.

Mac had skipped lunch, so he heated up the microwave dinner he had bought from Carver. Once it was ready, he returned to the bedroom, sat in front of his computer, and got ready to start a long evening of working on the coding changes that he and Nikolai had discussed.

Solving coding problems was easier than trying to solve the riddle of why Douglas Norton, respected teacher and family man, had decided to shoot himself.

Or how the gun that had killed him had come into his possession.

11

RED FLAGS

On Wednesday, October 24th, Mac got up before dark and dressed for the gym. One week before Halloween, part of his mind noted. Not that he really did anything for Halloween. Kate had liked costumes and Halloween parties, and she had always chosen the sexy version of a costume – Sexy Nurse, Sexy Bunny, Sexy Lumberjack (inexplicably), and others.

He had always appreciated that.

But Mac hadn't seen Kate in years, and his apartment complex wasn't the sort of place that attracted trick-or-treaters. Likely he would spend Halloween night coding for RVW Software.

Mac drove through the early morning gloom to Iron Oswald's gym and went through several sets of weights, working different muscle groups than yesterday. He finished off with a two-mile run, nodded to the sullen Turkish man at the front desk, and headed home to shower. By then, there was just enough light to see that it was going to be an overcast day, the sky filled with heavy gray clouds.

It was about seven by the time he got out of the shower, and Mac sat down in front of his computer and checked his email. Nothing of significance – Nikolai had already reviewed Mac's code changes.

Sometimes Mac thought that Nikolai never slept. Mac would need to implement a few more minor tweaks, but he could do that in a few minutes without difficulty.

Instead, he went to his web browser and found the website for Crest Development. It looked like the typical website for a commercial real estate firm and developer. Mac had probably put together at least forty similar sites over the last few years as freelance jobs. The home page showed a slideshow of various gleaming office buildings, interspersed with stock photos of ethnically diverse actors in formal business attire smiling and laughing or doing Serious Business Things in Crest Development's various buildings. The company owned a lot of properties, and the website touted that both commercial and industrial spaces were available at market-competitive rates.

Mac found the staff page and scrolled through it. The phone numbers and email addresses of various senior staff members and agents were available, but he couldn't find the number or name of the director of maintenance. Mac wanted to talk to the director of maintenance or people who had worked with Winston Marsh, and he doubted the various agents would have lowered themselves to talk much with the guy who fixed the toilets.

According to the website, the main office of Crest Development opened at eight. Mac decided to call the front desk at about half-past eight. Hopefully, he could talk the receptionist into forwarding his call to the director of maintenance or someone else who had worked with Winston Marsh. They might not want to talk while on the clock, but if Mac got some names, he could talk to them later.

He spent the next hour and a half working on the app and uploading the changes to the server. Their web client, Mac thought, was looking pretty good, and the iPhone app was a well-built container for the web client. Mac still wasn't sure if the iPhone would last, but even if people chose not to buy touchscreen smartphones, he hoped the web client would evolve into a nice little revenue stream. He had made progress in paying off the debts he had incurred after his father's murder and the business with Senator Kelsey over the summer, and it would be nice to get out of debt. Or to occasionally eat nicer food than the microwave meal he had bought at Carver's store.

Mac ran through some more code changes, tested them, didn't find any problems, and finalized them. He glanced at the clock in the corner of the screen and saw that it was 8:43.

Time to see if he could find out more about Winston Marsh.

He picked up his cell phone and dialed the main number for Crest Development.

A briskly cheerful female voice answered on the second ring. "Crest Development, how can I direct your call?"

"Good morning," said Mac. "I was hoping to talk to your director of maintenance."

"May I ask what this is regarding?"

"I'm doing some checks on a former employee named Winston Marsh," said Mac. "I was hoping to talk to his former supervisor or some of the people who worked with him."

There was a long pause.

Oddly long, come to think of it. Had his phone dropped the call? Mac found himself wishing he still had a landline, though he hadn't gotten one to save on the cost of the phone bill.

"Hello?" he said.

"I'm still here," said the female voice, a little less cheerful now. "You wanted to ask someone about Winston Marsh?"

"Yes, that's right," said Mac.

"What's your name?" said the receptionist.

"Cormac Rogan."

"Please hold," said the woman, and the call switched over to elevator music.

That was odd. Mac had expected the receptionist to refer him to Crest Development's lawyers or to tell him they didn't hand out employee information over the phone. She hadn't even asked for his credentials.

Maybe she wanted to put him on hold in hopes that he would give up.

Mac shrugged, glanced at the time, and decided to wait ten minutes before giving up.

Arianna Crest was in a good mood when she walked into her office.

Maybe that was understating it. She felt the familiar buzz, the thrill going down her nerves before she took a risk. Halloween was coming, and if her plan worked, Angela Morgan would be too crippled with grief to function. Arianna would swindle the Drummond cousins out of their land, the Westview Mall project would be all hers, and she would make millions of dollars.

All that was good.

But the risk, yes...that was the fun part.

That got her excited.

She had planned it well, and between the guns she had stolen from Nathan Rangel, the cell phone jammer that Rod Cutler had built, and her own planning, the risk was minimal.

It still sent electricity down her nerves.

She walked into her office. It was an overcast fall day, and the light that came through the windows was dim and gray. Arianna sat at her desk with a cup of coffee and started to sort through her email. In addition to her focus on the Westview Mall development, there were a dozen other ongoing problems that required her attention. Nothing so serious as to require the sort of distraction she would use on Angela Morgan, but they still needed some work.

It was hard to concentrate on them. Arianna felt as she did at the moment before she had sent the bullet through her mother's front tire or before she had raised her weapon and started shooting into the crowd of students before the doors of Northwoods High School. No matter how carefully she planned, no matter well she calculated, the risk was always there, and it was an exultant feeling.

Just as well, she thought, that her father's example had instilled a dislike of alcohol and drugs into her. Otherwise, Arianna conceded, she could see herself doing so much cocaine that her heart stopped before she was forty.

Still. Hell of a way to die.

"Ms. Crest?"

Arianna looked up from her computer. Her assistant, a mousy, brown-haired woman named Helen who Arianna had trained to total subservience, stood in the doorway. She would know better than to interrupt for something unimportant.

Her cardigan was hideous. Still, Arianna didn't mind, as she knew the contrast made her look all the more striking when meeting with clients.

"What?" said Arianna.

"Someone named Cormac Rogan is calling about Winston Marsh," said Helen.

Arianna blinked several times.

Cormac Rogan. She had heard that name before. Where, though?

"Did he say why?" said Arianna.

"He said he was doing background checks on Mr. Marsh," said Helen. "You said you wanted to be notified if anyone ever called about Mr. Marsh…"

"Or any of our employees," said Arianna. "Given how litigious our rivals are, we can't be too careful." She tapped her fingers against her desk, her mind racing into overdrive.

It had been over two years since she had pushed a drunken Marsh down those stairs to his death. All the receptionists and customer-facing employees had been trained to forward any requests for information about former hires up the chain to their supervisors, and Arianna had made sure to include Winston Marsh's name on the list. Part of it was a defensive measure to prepare if one of Angela Morgan's lackeys started sniffing around for dirt. Most of it was to defend herself if someone became suspicious.

But why now?

Marsh had been dead for two years, and no one had cared about him at the time. Arianna had visited him a few times, building up his trust while getting him drunk, and then shoved him down the stairs and stolen his handgun. Acquiring another weapon that couldn't be traced back to her was always prudent, and she had used the gun a few months later on Douglas Norton to derail one of Morgan Properties' deals. That hadn't worked out, but it hadn't been traced back to Arianna, either.

So why now?

Why less than a week before Halloween?

Arianna should have been upset. Worry would have been the rational response to the situation. Instead, she felt the thrill of risk strum up her nerves. Perhaps that was why she was so much smarter than most of the other people she encountered – she enjoyed danger rather than cowering from it.

Other people were sheep, really.

But Arianna wasn't deluded enough to believe that she was the only wolf in the world.

"Which line is it?" said Arianna.

"Line seven," said Helene.

"I'll talk to him myself," said Arianna. "Please close the door on the way out."

Helen nodded and obeyed.

Arianna grinned and picked up her phone's handset.

Time to find out if this Cormac Rogan was a sheep or a wolf.

Though Arianna was sure that she had heard his name before.

MAC HAD PLANNED to wait ten minutes for someone to pick up, and he spent the time idly browsing the news on his computer. Most of the political and national news was complete nonsense, as he had learned firsthand that summer after Senator Kelsey's death. It was amazing how many of the details in the reporting about the incident had simply been wrong.

Annoyed, he switched to a tech news site and started reading an article speculating about a potential application store for the iPhone. Thanks to Nikolai's contacts, Mac already knew more about it than the general public, and he definitely knew more than the tech journalist who had written the article.

At four minutes and thirty-seven seconds, the phone clicked, and someone picked up.

"Good morning." It was a woman's voice, confident and a little throaty. "I'm Arianna Crest. I understand you have some questions about one of my former employees?"

Mac blinked. The owner of the company was talking to him? He had been fishing, but he had caught a bigger fish than he had expected.

"Good morning," said Mac, kicking his brain into gear. "Thank you for talking to me, Ms. Crest. My name is Cormac Rogan. I had some questions about a former maintenance technician named Winston Marsh."

"I see," said Crest. "You realize, of course, that I am only legally obligated to confirm the dates of his employment here if you are conducting a background check."

"I am aware," said Mac. "I appreciate your time." Best to be polite.

"However," said Crest, "since Mr. Marsh died in an accident almost two years ago, I'm afraid you have piqued my curiosity. Why are you calling about him? I should also remind you that in this state, it is illegal to record a phone conversation without the consent of both parties, and I do not consent to the recording of this conversation." She said that last part clearly and loudly for the benefit of the nonexistent recording device.

"I had heard you were well-versed in the law," said Mac, trying for a little humor.

To his surprise, Crest laughed. She had a nice laugh, pleasant and warm. "I am famously litigious, you mean? Mr. Rogan, I know my rights, and I defend them vigorously. Now. Why are you calling about Winston Marsh?"

Mac hesitated for a second. Everyone he had spoken with said that Arianna Crest was ruthless and not above playing dirty. The last thing Mac needed was a vengeful, wealthy enemy. For that matter, he didn't want to direct Crest's annoyance at Julie Norton. That might start another round of lawsuits between Morgan Properties and Crest Development, and then both Angela Morgan and Arianna Crest would have grudges against him. Or, worse, express those grudges via a lawsuit.

Perhaps it was best to keep things simple.

"Were you acquainted with someone named Douglas Norton?" said Mac.

"Only in passing."

"In January of last year, Norton killed himself," said Mac. "The weapon he used was registered to Winston Marsh, which was surprising since Marsh died in that accident about six months before that."

"Yes, I remember that part," said Crest. "He still had a life insurance policy through our provider. One of the benefits we offer employees. The medical examiner ruled his death an accident, and so his heir received the payout." The voice hardened just a little. "But what does that have to do with my company?"

"I doubt it has anything to do with you or your company," said Mac. "But at some point between Marsh's death and Norton's suicide, Marsh's handgun found its way to Norton. I'm trying to trace how. I've been speaking to Marsh's acquaintances, trying to see if they can offer some light on who might have stolen the gun from his apartment."

"Quite a chore you've taken on for yourself," said Crest. "The police can't trace stolen handguns half the time. It seems every time some hoodlum robs a liquor store, he uses a stolen pistol. Might I ask why you've decided to push that stone up the hill?"

"The family of Mr. Norton hired me to review the investigation into his death," said Mac.

"I see," said Crest. "Julie Norton, she hired you?"

Mac resisted the urge to wince. "You've met?"

"She's the chief legal counsel for my primary competitor," said Crest. "We've met many times. It was very sad about her husband. She was clearly devoted to him, which I suppose is why she can't accept that he killed himself." It was, Mac thought, a precise summary of the case.

"I'm sorry to have taken up so much of your time, Ms. Crest," said Mac. "If I could speak with your director of maintenance or Marsh's immediate supervisor…"

"Eleven o'clock," said Crest.

"I'm sorry?" said Mac.

"That's your appointment with me," said Crest. "Eleven AM at my office. We'll chat about Winston Marsh."

Mac definitely hadn't expected this. It did not seem like a good idea at all. Given Crest's reputation for litigiousness, he could see her turning an interview into a weapon. She could claim that Julie Norton had hired a private investigator to spy on Crest Development and sue Morgan Properties and maybe Mac himself.

Then again, he supposed, perhaps Crest was fishing as well. Paul and had said that Morgan Properties and Crest Development regularly hired investigators to spy on each other. Maybe Crest was trying to figure out if Mac really was looking into Doug Norton's suicide or if that was only a cover for some sort of corporate espionage.

Mac didn't know anything about the two companies' business enterprises, and more to the point, he wasn't being paid to look into them. If he stuck to the matter of Winston Marsh, maybe that would convince Crest that he wasn't trying to investigate her business. If he persuaded her, that would be enormously helpful – she could tell any of Marsh's former co-workers to talk to him, and a request from the owner of the company could carry a lot of weight.

"Of course," said Mac.

"Splendid," said Crest. "I'll look forward to our talk."

She ended the call.

Mac stared at his computer screen, thinking. Paul Williamson would almost certainly be awake by now. He pulled up Paul's number and hit the call button.

Paul picked up on the second ring. "Don't tell me that you've gotten arrested again."

"Why would you think that?" said Mac. "I've only been arrested once this year. I just need some quick advice."

"Legal advice?" said Paul. "That gets expensive." There was a rushing sound in the background. It sounded like running water. Maybe Paul was washing dishes.

"General advice," said Mac. "I told you about my case from Dave. I called Crest Development this morning, hoping to talk to Winston Marsh's former supervisor."

"Uh huh."

"I am now meeting with Arianna Crest in two hours."

There was a long pause.

"Oh, boy," said Paul.

"Yeah," said Mac.

"Okay," said Paul. "I think she's only talking to you to find out if you're working for Morgan Properties in a business capacity or for Julie Norton personally. If she decides that you're working for Morgan Properties, she'll raise holy hell. Suppose that will be one way to get out of the case."

"I'd prefer not to get sued," said Mac.

"Yeah, that's always a good policy," said Paul. "All I can tell you is to be careful around Arianna. She can be charming, but when it comes to business, she's a goddamn barracuda. Just stick to Winston Marsh, and you'll be fine. Don't talk about any of their projects. And especially don't talk about the Westview Mall development."

"Yeah, I saw some drawings for that at Morgan Properties," said Mac.

"It's a big, big deal," said Paul. "Lots and lots of money on the line. So Arianna's probably paranoid about it. That's why she's talking to you, making sure you're not there to screw up the Westview development. Just talk about Marsh, and I bet she'll get bored and send you to talk to whoever Marsh's supervisor was."

"Okay," said Mac. "Thanks. I..."

The rushing noise stopped, and Mac realized it had been the sound of a shower.

"Are you talking on the phone in the shower?" said Mac.

A woman laughed in the background of the call.

"No," said Paul. "I'm talking on the phone while someone else showers. The barista I told you about yesterday? She needs a ride to work."

He said something, and the woman laughed again.

Mac took a moment to process that.

Maybe he really was in the wrong line of work.

"Okay," said Mac. "Well, good luck with that." Paul snorted. "Thanks for the advice."

"I make my own luck," said Paul. Mac found he was unable to argue that point. "I should wish you good luck, man. Seriously, you're going to need it. Be very careful around Arianna. She's not someone to screw around with."

"Thanks," said Mac. He paused. "Even if I have a chance to get her in the shower?"

"I strongly suspect that she eats her mates after they're done. Don't tell her I said that."

ARIANNA SET the handset back on the phone, her mind going a million miles a minute.

The thrill of risk thrummed along her veins.

Did Julie Norton suspect the truth? Everyone thought Doug's death had been a suicide, except for his wife. Arianna would have said that Julie was irrational, but she knew that Julie was perfectly sane.

In fact, she was entirely correct. Arianna had shot Doug Norton in the head with Winston Marsh's stolen gun, and she had done it so flawlessly that the police were certain it was a suicide.

Not Julie, though. She knew that her husband had been murdered, though she couldn't prove it.

Did she suspect Arianna? It seemed impossible.

And yet...

Cormac Rogan. Where had she heard that damned name before?

She grimaced, unlocked her computer, pulled up a search engine, and typed "Cormac Rogan Milwaukee" into the field.

There were hits in news articles.

Lots and lots of hits.

Rogan had foiled the terrorist bombing at Greenfield Community Church, and he had been present at the assassination of Senator Jack Kelsey. Arianna had been passingly acquainted with Kelsey and hadn't mourned his death. She was rich and influential enough that her business came to the attention of the state's politicians, and so she had given Kelsey just enough campaign contributions to avoid trouble with him.

Arianna recognized another wolf when she met one…and Kelsey had secretly been funding an environmentalist terror group to boost his reelection chances.

Audacious. But stupid.

According to the articles, Rogan had been the one to find Kelsey's plan. Arianna ran her tongue over her teeth as she scanned the text. If Rogan had found Kelsey's plot, that meant he was either lucky or good.

Or both, which would be worse.

Why was he looking into Winston Marsh's death?

Maybe he was telling the truth. Maybe he was just trying to trace the gun.

Or did he suspect what had really happened?

Halloween was coming up. Arianna didn't want any complications.

This was dangerous, having an investigator poke around Marsh's death, especially with the Westview deal hanging in the balance. But Arianna found that she was enjoying the risk.

Still, best to prepare.

She opened a locked drawer in her desk and drew out one of her burner phones. Arianna called up the only contact on the phone and dialed.

It took seventeen rings before Rod Cutler picked up. "What?" His voice was sleepy, irritated.

"Did you spend all your money on prostitutes already?" said Arianna, putting a cold edge into her words.

"Uh…Arianna," stammered Rod. "Sorry, I was sleeping. What…"

"I have a surveillance job for you," said Arianna. "The usual rate. I want you here by 10:30. Park by the front sign and pretend to wash it. Around 11, a man named Cormac Rogan is going to drive to the building." She found a picture of Rogan in one of the articles. He was testifying to Congress about the Kelsey assassination, a hard scowl on his face. "He's white, black hair, blue eyes, a bit wiry…probably a little under six feet tall. Make sure you see him when he arrives."

"Okay," said Rod. "What am I supposed to do?"

"Make sure you recognize his appearance and get his license plate number," said Arianna. "We can use that to get his address." A discreet gift to a low-ranking state employee could unearth all kinds of useful information. "I might need you to follow him."

"Okay," said Rod again. He sounded steadier and more awake now.

"Remember," said Arianna. "I need you here by 10:30. And don't talk to Rogan. I don't want him to remember you."

"All right," said Rod. "I'll be there." He tried for bravado, failed. "Don't forget to have my money."

"Have I ever not paid you?" said Arianna. She found herself looking forward to the day when she could rid herself of Rod Cutler, but it hadn't come quite yet.

"10:30," said Rod.

"Don't be late," said Arianna, and she ended the call.

She put the phone back into the drawer and checked the other item in her desk.

A load Glock 19 pistol.

Arianna unloaded it, checked all the parts, reloaded the weapon, flipped the safety off, and put it back.

She didn't think she would need it. Likely Rogan was just fishing. She would know more once she talked to him.

But if Rogan knew too much, if he threatened her, Arianna would have to take action. Or maybe Rogan had worked out that she had been involved in Winston Marsh's or Douglas Norton's death and wanted a bribe for his silence.

If that happened, Arianna would shoot him in her office, rip up her clothes, beat herself up, and then claim that Rogan had tried to attack her, and she had shot him self-defense. It would be a huge mess, would cost Arianna the Westview Mall deal, and it might likely go to trial. But she was confident she could wriggle out of any charges...a weeping woman claiming that she had been assaulted was a believable figure.

Arianna didn't think it would come to that.

But if it did, she would be ready.

12

CREST DEVELOPMENT

It had been chilly yesterday, and Mac hadn't sweated at all, so he figured his suit was good for another day. He got dressed, collected his laptop bag, his notebook, and his digital recorder, though he suspected that Crest would not allow him to record their conversation. Once he was ready, he left the apartment and headed across Milwaukee for Brookfield and Crest Development's main office.

As it happened, Crest Development was not all that far from Morgan Properties and Morgan Business Park. Arianna Crest's company was headquartered in a four-story office building of polished white stone and glass. According to Mac's research, Crest Development owned the entire building but only occupied the top floor, leasing out the rest of the space to other businesses.

A large, impressive-looking stone sign with black letters stood to the left of the parking lot, listing the businesses within the building. The sign for CREST DEVELOPMENT was the largest by far. A white panel van had been pulled up next to the sign, its side adorned with the logo for a business called "General Contracting." A weedy-looking man in a blue coverall was running a power washer over the stone of the sign, though the sign didn't look like it needed much of a wash. He turned to look at Mac as he drove past. The man in the coverall was wearing aviator sunglasses, with an unfortunate black mustache that looked like something from a 70s action film.

Mac pulled into the parking lot. He thought about taking his laptop bag but decided against it. Doubtless Crest would refuse to let him record the conversation or take notes. Mac felt eyes on him and glanced back towards the sign, but the maintenance man was fiddling with his power washer.

Mac walked into the lobby of the building and took the stairs to the fourth floor. The reception area of Crest Development was behind two glass doors. Beyond was a waiting room, the walls gleaming white. The logo of Crest Development adorned one wall. A counter of polished wood closed off the far side of the room, and a receptionist smiled up at him, a Hispanic woman somewhere in her twenties with a bright smile.

"Good morning," she said. "Welcome to Crest Development. Can I ask the purpose of your visit?"

"Hi," said Mac. "My name's Cormac Rogan. I have an appointment to talk with Arianna Crest at eleven."

The receptionist's eyes widened. Apparently, people did not just show up to talk with the boss. "One moment, please." She lifted her phone and spoke into it and then nodded and set it down on the cradle. "Ms. Crest will be able to see you shortly. Would you care for some coffee while you wait?"

"Please," said Mac. "Straight black, no sugar or milk."

He sat in one of the chairs – expensive dark leather, either real or a very good imitation – and the receptionist emerged with coffee in a ceramic mug with the logo of Crest Development. Mac thanked her, and she beamed again, making him wonder how often anyone was polite to her.

The coffee was very good.

Mac waited. Eleven AM arrived and then crept to five past the hour. He recognized the tactic. Crest was making him wait, highlighting that she was in charge. Mac didn't care. He got paid either way, and it was nice to sit and relax for a bit. If he were to place a bet, he thought that Crest would see him between 11:07 or 11:10. Just enough to flex a bit, but not enough to be truly rude.

At 11:08, the receptionist's phone rang, and she picked up again. "Right away." She set down the phone and stood up. "Mr. Rogan? Ms. Crest will see you now."

"Thank you," said Mac. He rose, set the empty cup on the counter, and followed the receptionist behind her desk and down a carpeted office hallway. They passed offices where men and women in formal business attire worked on computers or talked into phones. Crest must insist on formal wear for her office, and Mac was glad he had gotten a second day out of his suit.

The receptionist led him to the corner office. There was an outer office, and a mousy-looking woman sat typing into a computer. The door to the inner office was open, and an expensive wooden desk dominated the back half of the room, holding a computer and a variety of papers. Four more of those comfortable chairs sat around a low wooden table holding a potted plant. A blond woman in a black jacket and skirt walked around the desk as they entered, keeping her balance flawlessly in gleaming three-inch black heels.

"Your eleven o'clock, Ms. Crest," said the receptionist.

"Thank you," said Arianna Crest, smiling at Mac.

Mac blinked, momentarily taken off-guard. Paul had said that she was attractive. The picture on the website had showed a pretty blond woman somewhere in her thirties smiling at the camera.

But the picture was one thing.

The reality was another.

Something about her was so mesmerizing that a jolt went down his nerves in a way that watching Kristin Salwell had not inspired. Crest was about five foot five, with gleaming blond hair drawn back in a loose bun, her eyes pale and blue. Only the top button of her blouse was undone, but her clothes fit her just tightly enough to convey that she was in very good physical condition.

"Mr. Rogan?" said Crest. Mac shook her offered hand. It was cool and dry and strong. To judge from the veins on the back of her hands, she probably lifted weights. "I'm Arianna Crest. Thank you for coming in on such short notice."

"Thank you for seeing me," said Mac, using the banal pleasantries to get his thoughts into order. He had not expected the sudden attraction to sucker-punch him like this. Mac had not been with a woman in over three years. Contrary to what Paul and Tom thought, he had been with a woman after Kate had left him – a short-lived relationship with a web developer he had met on a contract job. It had been fun, but she hadn't been interested in anything serious, and the relationship had ended when she had moved to Chicago for a new job. Mac hadn't been upset after she had left. In the end, he wasn't ready to move on after his breakup with Kate, and his debts and family problems had held most of his attention.

But now part of Mac wondered if he was ready to move on.

Well. He knew which parts of his body were ready to move on, at any rate.

Mac pushed aside the attraction. He had to keep his wits about him. Attractive or not, Paul had said that Crest was a barracuda, and Mac did not want to acquire another enemy.

"Helen, if you'll get the door?" said Crest. The receptionist retreated, and the mousy-haired woman rose and closed the door. Crest gestured to the chairs. "Would you like a seat?"

"Thank you," said Mac. He waited until Crest had picked a chair and then sat across from her. His eye wanted to linger on the taut skin of her crossed legs, and he made himself look at her face. "I admit that when I called, I didn't expect to talk to the owner of the company."

"Well." Crest smoothed her skirt, the motion drawing his attention to her legs again. "For my part, I have to admit that I did not expect to get a phone call from a private investigator of your notoriety."

"Notoriety?" said Mac.

She smiled. "Modesty is unnecessary. Did you think I wouldn't Google you? Almost everything is on the Internet now. You were the one who stopped that crazy woman from blowing up Greenwater Community Church."

"I was involved in that, yes," said Mac.

Crest laughed. "The FBI agent at your Senate hearing was much more complimentary. I knew Jack Kelsey in passing, and I have to say that while it was shocking that he funded a domestic terror group to get himself reelected, I can't say that I'm all that surprised."

"I wasn't, either," said Mac.

"So." Crest folded her hands in her lap and leaned a little closer, her pale eyes somehow brighter. Mac noted that she didn't wear any rings. "What would you like to talk about, Mr. Rogan?"

"Winston Marsh," said Mac.

"And are you sure that's not a convenient excuse to look for other things?"

"Ms. Crest," said Mac, "I know you're busy, and your time is valuable, so I'll state it simply. I'm trying to trace how Winston Marsh's handgun disappeared from his apartment and ended up next to Douglas Norton when he killed himself six months later. I'm not spying for anyone, and I don't have any interest in digging into any of your business enterprises."

Crest didn't blink. "You were hired by the chief legal counsel of my primary competitor."

"I know," said Mac, "but she's paying me out of her own pocket, not her employer's funds. She wants to know the truth of her husband's death, and that's all."

"So why are you talking to me?" said Crest.

"Because I was trying to talk to Marsh's immediate supervisor, and your receptionist transferred the call to you."

"Touché." A quick smile flickered over Crest's lips. Mac thought she was wearing just a hint of subtle lipstick, not garish enough to be stark against her pale skin. Once again, he made himself stop thinking about her body and focus. "But why talk to Marsh's former employer?"

"Because from what I can determine, Marsh didn't have any friends and was estranged from his only living relative," said Mac.

"He didn't go to church, didn't belong to any clubs, didn't even have a bowling league or a fantasy football team. All he seemed to do is drink and work. So his employer is the logical place to start."

Crest stared at him without blinking for a full five seconds. Mac met her gaze.

"You know, Mr. Rogan," said Crest, "I think I believe you."

"Telling the truth is less work than lying," said Mac, "and I charge by the hour."

A quick smile of genuine amusement went over her face. He thought it made her look radiant. "A good point. All right. Ask me what you want to know about Winston Marsh."

Mac sorted through his thoughts. It was harder than it should have been. He hadn't been this physically attracted to a woman in a long time, and it was distracting.

"How long did Mr. Marsh work for you?" said Mac.

"Seven years," said Crest. "From 1998 to the start of 2005 when he retired."

"What were his job duties?" said Mac, settling into the familiar rhythm of asking questions.

"Maintenance technician," said Crest. "Basically, an odd-jobs handyman. If there was a minor problem at one of my properties, he would fix it. Doors, carpets, mechanical problems, basic plumbing. No electrical. He used to be an electrician, but he let his certification lapse, and we wouldn't let him near the wiring, not with his drinking problem."

"He had problems with alcohol?" said Mac.

Crest's smile turned hard. "The other maintenance technicians used to call him Winnie the Wino. Which, I'm afraid, was entirely accurate. He didn't drink on the job, or else he would have been fired. And if he was on call for an evening or a weekend, he would stay sober. Otherwise, he drank until he passed out."

"Did the drinking ever cause him problems at work?" said Mac.

"If it did, I would have fired him," said Crest. She smirked. "The fact of the matter is that Marsh was a bargain. He was quite good at his job. I understand that he used to be a master electrician, but he was arrested several times for drunk driving after his divorce. I suppose he would have gone to prison, but the laws were less strict back then. Nevertheless, he lost his electrician's license and so had to work for Crest Development for less money than he might have made otherwise." She gave an indifferent shrug. "He was content, so long as he had enough money to drink himself to oblivion. A pathetic way to live, frankly."

"You don't drink or smoke yourself?" said Mac.

Crest's smile widened. "Do my teeth look like I smoke?"

They were very white and even. Which made Mac think about her lips again.

"Not particularly," said Mac.

"Such flattery," said Crest. "I mainly eat lean protein, vegetables, and fruit, and I don't consume alcohol or tobacco." Her eyes grew distant. "A legacy from my parents. Both were alcoholics, and I refuse to follow their example."

"I understand," said Mac, thinking of Monica Rogan, how she had smirked when she had been found guilty of John Rogan's murder.

"But we're not here to talk about me, you wanted to know about Winston," said Crest. "Ask questions, Mr. Rogan."

"You sound like you knew Winston well," said Mac.

"Passingly well," said Crest. "Does that surprise you?"

"A little, yes," said Mac.

"Why?"

"With respect, you're something of a big shot," said Mac. Crest's smile returned at that. "Big shots don't hang around with the maintenance technicians."

"You've met Angela Morgan, I see," said Crest. "I doubt she's done a day of actual work in her life. She sits in her office, takes phone calls, and probably never talks to anyone making less than a hundred K a year. I'm more hands-on, Mr. Rogan. I like to get my hands dirty." Something about the way she said it sent a shiver down his spine. "I make lots of in-person visits to my properties and my construction sites. If I know what everyone is doing, it is harder for anyone to cheat me."

"Very prudent," said Mac. "Did Winston have any friends?"

Crest shrugged. "I don't believe so. He got on well enough with his co-workers and his supervisor, but he wasn't particularly close to anyone. His primary interest was drinking and drinking alone."

"Did you know where he lived?" said Mac.

"An apartment in a crappy neighborhood," said Crest. "I can't recall the address off the top of my head. If you need it, I can have my assistant pull it from the employee records."

"I have the address already, thank you," said Mac. "Were you aware that Winston owned a Smith & Wesson 910 pistol?"

"No," said Crest. "Well, I found out later, once I heard about Douglas Norton's suicide. I wasn't surprised that Winston had a gun. Given the neighborhood he lived in, it would be foolish of him not to own a weapon."

"Do you have any ideas on how that gun might have come into Douglas Norton's possession?" said Mac.

Crest shrugged again. "No. But it was probably stolen, wasn't it? Guns are stolen all the time. I doubt his apartment had any serious locks. His landlord probably sold it. Or someone simply walked in and took it. Then Doug Norton turned out to have a problem with drugs or porn or something, and he bought the gun in a bar somewhere and shot himself."

Mac frowned. "Doug had…problems?"

"Not that I know of," said Crest. "But he must have, right? Else why would he have killed himself? I don't understand suicide, Mr. Rogan. I suppose if I had terminal cancer, I might decide to shoot myself rather than wither away in a hospital bed, but he was healthy."

Her tone reminded Mac of something, but he couldn't quite place it.

"How well were you acquainted with Doug and Julie Norton?" said Mac.

"Passingly," said Crest. Her smirk returned. "More than I would have liked, to be honest. Julie, of course, is the chief counsel for my main competitor. We probably saw each other at zoning meetings and the like more than either would have wanted. I saw Doug a few times at various social events. I have volunteered on and off at Northwoods High School over the last few years, and I saw Doug there at various times."

"You have?" said Mac. Kristin Salwell had seen Doug talking to a short blond woman in an expensive coat. Mac was hardly an expert on women's fashion, but he was certain that Crest had spent a lot of money on the clothes she was currently wearing. And while Crest was average height for a woman, Doug had been six and a half feet tall. He would have towered over Crest, and she would have looked short next to her.

"Yes. That school has had some bad luck." Crest shook her head. "Teachers sleeping with students is bad. Teachers sleeping with the same student, who then blackmailed them, is worse. But the shooting in 2005 was the worst yet. If I was superstitious, I would say that the school is cursed."

"Did you ever visit Winston's apartment?" said Mac.

"I did not," said Crest. "I don't object to socializing with my employees, but Winston wasn't a social sort. All he was interested in was drinking." She shrugged. "A man has the right to drink himself to death in his apartment, I suppose. Frankly, he would have died of liver failure in a few years anyway. I suppose it was a merciful death that he tripped and broken his neck." She snapped her fingers. "Over in a few seconds. Quicker than liver disease."

"Yes," said Mac. "Quicker."

He felt his skin crawl with a sudden visceral memory. His mother had said the same thing many times. Whenever she had seen someone in a wheelchair, or even an obese person driving a cart, she had remarked that such people should be given a merciful death for their own good. Mac had heard the black humor of cops and doctors, but that was a coping mechanism, a defense for when they saw the worst that humanity had to offer.

His mother had really meant it.

Arianna Crest did not look anything like Monica Rogan, but suddenly she reminded Mac of his mother, of how she had smirked when she had been declared guilty of John Rogan's murder and attempting to frame Mac for it.

She seemed to pick up on his disgust.

"I'm sorry, that was heartless," said Crest. "But while Winston was a good worker, I would say he was a thoroughly…depressing man, let us say. Alcohol was his one true love. He was either going to die of liver illness or an accident. It is probably fortunate that he tripped down the stairs rather than driving into a school bus."

"It could have been worse," said Mac. "Did you speak to Winston's daughter at all?"

"Briefly," said Crest. "Winston ought to have counted himself grateful that he was estranged from her. A thoroughly unpleasant woman. She was convinced we had taken out secret life insurance policies on her father and had kept the money from her. Carmen Marsh bothered every single person in my accounting department and my insurance agents. She only stopped when I talked to her myself and convinced her that she wasn't getting a secret payout."

"I see," said Mac. "Will you be willing to share contact information for people who might have worked with Winston? His supervisor, his co-workers. I want to get a general picture of his life and who might have stolen the weapon."

"Of course," said Crest. "I'll have my assistant prepare the list before you go." She paused, tapped her fingers on the arm of her chair. "You realize, of course, that you're probably wasting your time. The most likely explanation is that someone passing by checked the apartment door, found it unlocked, and took the gun as the smallest and most easily salable item."

"Probably," said Mac. "But I have a job to do, and I'm going to do it."

"Indeed." Crest's smile returned, and she rose to her feet. "If you have no more questions for me, Mr. Rogan, I suspect we both have a great deal left to do today."

"We do," said Mac, rising. "Thank you for your time."

"Of course." She stepped closer and rested her hand on his upper arm for a moment. Despite his earlier disgust, the touch made his nerves crackle, and he had a brief and completely inappropriate mental image of closing the distance between them and kissing her. "I have to say you impressed me more than I expected. Tell you what." She gripped his forearm and guided him to her desk. "Here's my card with my personal cell phone number." Crest passed it into his hand, and unless Mac was imagining things, her fingers lingered against his a little longer than was necessary. "If you think of something else you need to ask me, give me a call."

"Thank you," said Mac. "That's very kind."

"No one would ever call me kind, Mr. Rogan," said Crest. "But, well...if you think of something to ask me, give me a call. I'm sure we can think of something to discuss."

Was that a personal invitation? Mac wasn't sure. He wasn't sure if he wanted to know or not. Overall, he didn't think he would like Arianna Crest very much, but his attraction to her might be clouding his thinking.

"Maybe we will," said Mac, and he left Crest's office. Helen printed him off the list of names and contact numbers for people who had worked with Winston Marsh, and he left the building and headed back to his car. The cool fall air felt pleasant after the heat of Crest's office.

No, he reminded himself, Crest's office hadn't been warm. Mac had the one who had been heating up. He shook his head, irritated at himself. At his age, you'd think he couldn't have his brains scrambled by an attractive woman. Then again, he could think of any number of politicians and public figures who had ruined their careers with affairs they should have known would be a bad idea, and some of them had been twice his age.

Mac unlocked the trunk, put the list in his laptop bag, and dropped into the front seat of his car.

"Man," he muttered. He glanced up at the office building to see if Crest was watching him leave but couldn't see past the reflection of the cloudy day on the sheer glass of the windows.

Just as well.

He started the car. Mac would spend the rest of the day working his way through Crest's list and continuing work on the RVW app. Perhaps one of Marsh's former co-workers would have an idea of who might have stolen the gun.

Mac backed out of his parking space, a thought turning over in his head.

Northwoods High School. Somehow this all centered on the school. Douglas Norton had killed himself, or had been killed, in his classroom. Crest had said she volunteered at the school. Norton had written Kristin Salwell's name in his day planner, the last thing he had written before he died. Joshua Chartwell, the first student to die in the mass shooting, had been the son of Morgan Properties' best agent.

Mac had the feeling it was all connected, but how?

It could have been all coincidence. But he had the sense that some single fact, some lone truth, connected them all.

But what?

Hell if he knew.

Mac decided to drive to the high school and look around. He doubted he would discover anything useful, but it would give him a chance to think.

He drove past the sign.

The man with the power washer watched him go and then turned his attention back to his work. Mac wondered how much time it took to wash a damn sign.

Maybe he got paid by the hour.

Arianna sat in her desk chair and turned to face the parking lot, watching Cormac Rogan drive off.

She hadn't decided what to do about him yet.

He had been attracted to her at once, that was obvious. And Arianna did like the look of him. She appreciated wiry, muscular men. Someone like Douglas Norton, so much larger than her, would not have been to her taste.

Seducing Rogan might solve the problem he presented in a most enjoyable fashion.

And yet there had been something off. Something about Arianna had raised his alarms. She had seen it in his face.

Did he suspect the truth?

She remembered Michaela Simpson, the insurance investigator who had looked into her father's death. There had been proof, absolutely no proof whatsoever, that Arianna had killed her father, yet somehow Simpson had known. Some intuitive leap, some faculty that defied logic. Had Arianna left a single shred of evidence that she had killed Andrew Crest, Simpson would have latched onto it like an attack dog.

Would Rogan do the same?

Arianna stared at the parking lot.

The timing was damned inconvenient. Halloween was coming up. Arianna didn't have to go through with it, of course, but she was prepared, and the Halloween bonfire at Northwoods High School offered her the best chance to kill Charlie Morgan and a bunch of other students and make it look like a repeat of the mass shooting from 2005. Arianna could wait, of course, but if she did, she might lose the Westview Mall deal. The negotiations were approaching a critical phase, and Arianna needed Angela Morgan to fall apart from grief, and she needed it right now.

The last thing Arianna needed was a tenacious private investigator poking around her business.

Did he believe that Douglas Norton had been murdered? She didn't think so. Everyone knew that Douglas Norton had killed himself. The problem, of course, was that he hadn't actually killed himself. Arianna had killed him and staged the death to look like a suicide. She had gotten away with it, but what if she had overlooked something? What if there was some link that the police had missed but Rogan dug up?

It seemed unlikely, but it was possible.

She opened her desk, picked up her burner phone, and called Rod Cutler.

"Get his license plate?" said Arianna.

"Yeah," said Rod, and he recited the numbers. Arianna wrote them down. "Got a good look at him, too. You want me to follow him?"

"Yes. Discreetly. I'll pay the usual rate. Don't let him see you," said Arianna. "Keep your phone turned on. I need to do some research. Once I've made up my mind, I'll tell you."

She hung up and reached for her office phone, intending to call her contacts at the state tax office.

The first step was to find out where Rogan lived.

And then she would decide the best way to deal with him. Maybe she would ignore him. Maybe she would seduce him.

Maybe she would kill one of his relatives to distract him.

Or perhaps Cormac Rogan would kill himself just as Douglas Norton had done.

13

NORTHWOODS HIGH SCHOOL

It wasn't all that far from Crest Development to Northwoods High School.

Mac drove across Brookfield and came to an older residential neighborhood with a lot of post-World War II two-story family homes. Some of them had been torn down to make way for larger McMansions or condominium buildings. Good for the economy, he supposed, though he wondered who could afford all these new houses.

Mac certainly couldn't.

He turned a corner, and the Northwoods High School campus came into sight.

The main building was a massive brick rectangle, four stories tall, with narrow windows in gray concrete frames. It looked as if it had been built in the 1930s. The rest of the campus was more modern – an athletic fieldhouse, a football field, and a vast parking lot filled with cars.

Mac drove past the main entrance. A flight of concrete stairs climbed to a wide terrace before the double doors. The stairs and the terrace could easily have held hundreds of people. With the students packed together on the steps, they would make an easy target for even a mediocre marksman. Little wonder the shooter had chosen that time and place.

The opposite side of the street was lined with houses. Agent Cole had said that the school district owned most of the homes on the opposite block in anticipation of future expansion. The house that the shooter had used was in the process of being torn down. A chain-link fence encircled the property, and two dumpsters full of debris sat on the lawn.

Mac circled the block, found a parking space, and slid his Corsica into it. He got out of the car and locked it, buttoning his suit jacket. A single man hanging around a high school during the day was automatically an object of suspicion. Then again, he was wearing a suit, and people were less likely to assume that a man in a suit was up to trouble.

Even if it was a cheap suit that Mac really needed to wash.

He headed towards the high school. Behind the main building of Northwoods High School he could see a large concrete courtyard that looked as if it had started life as a playground but had now been converted into an outdoor commons area, with tables and benches. A few dozen students were there, some standing in groups and talking, others sitting and reading at the tables. Mac supposed it was just cool enough that studying outside would be pleasant rather than uncomfortable. A large electronic billboard was mounted next to the front doors, cycling through announcements for athletic events, a reminder about parking permits, and something called the Halloween Bonfire scheduled for 7 PM on October 31st. Pizza and soda would be provided, no doubt in an effort to keep teenagers off the streets and away from alcohol.

Mac stopped in front of the fence around the half-demolished house. A sign mounted on the fence said that the house was being torn down to be replaced by a memorial garden in honor of those who had been killed on April 14th, 2005. A slightly smaller sign said that the demolition work was being carried out by Crest Development. Arianna Crest hadn't mentioned that. Then again, Crest Development did big construction deals. The Westview Mall thing that both Morgan Properties and Crest Development were fighting over had to be worth tens of millions of dollars. Tearing down one house was a small matter by comparison.

The house's roof was gone, but the rafters were still in place. Cole had said that the shooter had opened fire from a window facing the front doors of the school. That would have been a perfect firing position. The line of sight from the top of the house to the front doors was clear. Five students had been killed and many more wounded, and Mac supposed it was surprising that far more hadn't been killed.

He glanced around, but no one was watching him. Cole had said that the shooter had likely entered the house through the back door and escaped in a waiting vehicle. Mac cut across the lawn and circled to the back of the house. A narrow alley ran behind the row of houses, just wide enough to allow a garbage truck through. The back doors of the houses were secured with heavy padlocks, likely added after the shooter had broken into the empty house. On the far side of the alley stood a thick concrete wall about six feet high. Mac walked to it and peered over. On the other side was a forested patch about sixty feet wide before another residential street.

The sequence of events seemed logical enough. The shooter had opened fire from the house and then retreated through the back door. He might have left his vehicle waiting here, but Mac thought it made more sense that the shooter had left a car parked on the other side of the forested patch. Anyone in reasonable physical condition would have been able to scale the wall without difficulty, and it would have been a quick run to the street. By the time anyone thought to look through the alley, the shooter would have been long gone, and Mac wasn't inclined to believe eyewitness testimony about a white van. People developed tunnel vision in stressful situations, and he had been involved in enough investigations where eyewitnesses gave completely contradictory accounts of the same event.

He turned back towards the half-demolished house. The siding had been ripped off, along with about half of the insulation panels. Had the house still been intact, Mac might have been tempted to walk through it, but he would learn nothing from it.

Yet he could not shake the feeling that the mass shooting was connected to Douglas Norton's death. It had to be, one way or another. The most logical explanation was that the trauma of the shooting had caught up to Doug, and he had killed himself in his classroom using a stolen gun bought from someone. Yet the holes in that theory nagged at Mac. Why would Norton have bought a stolen gun? Given how stridently anti-gun Norton had been, it seemed out of character for him. And why had he put down Kristin Salwell's name before he died?

Maybe there wasn't an answer. Maybe Norton had simply killed himself, and there was no good explanation. The reality was that the truth was sometimes unpalatable, even illogical, and that bad things happened for no good reason.

Mac was staring at the half-wrecked house, so he saw the teenager come around the corner and freeze in surprise.

The kid couldn't have been more than eighteen or nineteen, and the most immediately noticeable thing about him was his size. He was an inch or two shorter than Mac, but he was fat, so fat that he had to be at least twice Mac's weight. He wore an enormous black T-shirt that showed a muscular barbarian warrior battling an orc or a troll or something like that, along with the logo of a popular online game. His hands were in the pockets of his baggy shorts, and he wore flip-flops instead of shoes. He had pale blond hair that had been cut badly, and his blue eyes were wide with surprise in a face that was red with exertion despite the cool day.

"Who the hell are you?" said the kid, his voice strident.

"I'm just taking a look around," said Mac.

"Like hell you are," said the kid. "You're one of those weirdos who wants a piece of the house."

"What?" said Mac.

The kid jerked his head at the house. "Sometimes people try to sneak off with pieces of the house and sell them online. The Northwoods Murder House, they call it. Own a piece of history." He glared at Mac. "Maybe I should call the cops on you."

"You can if you like," said Mac. "But shouldn't you be in class?"

The kid sneered at him. "I graduated in 2006."

"Okay, you can call the cops if you want," said Mac. "But then they're gonna wonder why two men who aren't students and aren't employed by the school are hanging around the murder house at noon on a workday."

The kid opened his mouth, closed it, and thought about it. Not completely stupid, Mac decided.

"That's a really good argument," said the kid.

"You used to be a student at Northwoods?" said Mac.

A cloud went over his expression. "Yeah."

"My name's Cormac Rogan," said Mac. A flicker of recognition went through the kid's eyes. "I'm a private investigator, and I wonder if I could ask you some questions."

"Yeah, I bet you would," said the kid. "Let me guess. One of the parents hired you to find the real killer, and so you've been following me around. My mom's got a really good lawyer, and…"

A suspicion formed in Mac's mind.

"No, I've been hired by Julie Norton," he said.

The kid frowned. "Who?"

"Julie Norton," said Mac. "She was married to Douglas Norton, who used to be a teacher at the school. The police say Doug Norton killed himself, but Julie thinks he was murdered. So she hired me to reexamine the case."

"No shit?" said the kid. Mac nodded. "Well, Mr. Norton killed himself. Everyone knows it. He was really upset after the shooting, and then he just snapped and shot himself." He gave a weary shrug. "Happened to a lot of people."

"Mind if I ask you a few questions about him?" said Mac.

Again, the kid shrugged. "If you like. But you probably don't want to talk to me."

"Why not?" said Mac. "Because you're Parker McIntyre?"

He had guessed right. A thunderous scowl went over the kid's face.

"Oh, so you have heard of me," said Parker. "Was that story about Mr. Norton a lie? Well, you can take your questions about me and shove them…"

"No, it was the truth," said Mac. "And I understand why you're pissed off. I was once arrested for a murder I didn't commit."

Parker blinked. "No shit? I think I heard of you. You're the guy who caught the terrorists who were going to blow up that one church."

"Something like that," said Mac. "But I know what happened to you, and I think you got screwed. You ever heard of a guy named Richard Jewell?"

The wary look on Parker's face didn't go away, but it eased. "Yeah. My therapist told me about him. He was a security guard for the Olympics in the 90s, and he found a pipe bomb before it could go off in the crowd. But the big brains at the FBI thought he fit the profile of the bomber."

"And it leaked to the media, and Jewell went through hell," said Mac. "Same thing happened to you." He shrugged. "Hell, the same thing happened to me, though not quite as bad. I had to testify before the Senate about Jack Kelsey. Reporters followed me around for weeks, and this blogger is writing a book about it. And there are crazy people on the Internet who think that the CIA or the Israelis were behind it all."

"Yeah, I get some of those," said Parker. "I had to delete all my original accounts and sign up under new names." He shifted, wiped his hands on his T-shirt, and then shoved them back into his pockets. "Mrs. Norton really hired you?"

"Yup." Mac reached into his jacket pocket and handed one of his business cards to Parker. "I work through Wester Security. You can call them and check that I'm legit."

"Hang on." Parker reached into his pocket, produced a Blackberry, and dialed the number on the card. Mac recognized the caution of someone who had been put through the wringer by law enforcement.

Parker talked to Dave's receptionist for a moment and then hung up. "Well, she says you work for them, but she can't comment on any individual clients."

"Obviously, you don't have to talk to me," said Mac, "but it would be helpful if you did."

Parker shrugged. "Well, why not? I think Mr. Norton killed himself, but I can see how Mrs. Norton would be in denial about it." He sighed. "Suppose I know something about that."

His best friend Ryan Walsh, Mac recalled, had killed himself after his profile had leaked to the media.

"Did you have any classes with Mr. Norton?" said Mac.

"Yeah," said Parker. "Didn't like him much until after the shooting."

"Can I ask why?" said Mac.

"That sounds harsh," said Parker. "I mean, I could tell Mr. Norton didn't like me. He was a big jock guy, you know?" He gestured at himself. "And I'm obviously not. But he wasn't unfair. Like, sometimes a teacher doesn't like a student, they're jerks about it. But Mr. Norton wasn't unfair. I didn't like him, but I could respect him." He sighed. "And after the shooting, after Ryan…you know," Mac nodded, "Mr. Norton called my mom and said that what had happened to me was unfair and that if she wanted to sue the school, he would testify in my favor."

"Really," said Mac. "Julie said that Doug thought what had happened to you was wrong, but she didn't mention that part."

"Maybe she didn't know about it," said Parker. "So, yeah. I guess Mr. Norton was really upset by the shooting, which is why he killed himself."

"Do you know a woman named Arianna Crest?" said Mac.

Parker's eyes widened. "I don't know her, but I know about her. My mom hates her. See, my mom used to work for Morgan Properties, a big real estate company."

"I've heard of them."

"Crest Development is their big rival," said Parker. "My mom says that Crest is unethical, but I don't really know much about it."

"Did you ever meet a man named Winston Marsh?" said Mac.

"Don't think so," said Parker. "Who was he?"

"He used to be a maintenance technician for Crest Development," said Mac. "Six months before Doug died, Marsh got drunk, fell down the stairs to his apartment, and died of a skull fracture. The gun that Doug used to kill himself belonged to Marsh and was apparently stolen from his apartment after he died."

Parker snorted out a laugh. "Well, that's a lot of bullshit."

"Why's that?" said Mac.

"Mr. Norton hated guns," said Parker. "He wouldn't shut up about it. You know how sometimes teachers go on and on about things?" Mac nodded. "Guns were that thing for Mr. Norton. Sometimes we would try to get him off on a tangent about guns during class to run down the clock. I don't think he would have bought a legal gun, let alone stolen one from anyone."

"Do you think he killed himself?" said Mac.

"Yeah, probably," said Parker. He hesitated. "You...know about my friend Ryan?" Mac nodded. "Back when everyone thought we were the shooters, he couldn't take it. He finally swallowed a bunch of pills." He sighed. "Might've done that myself, but my mom wouldn't let me, and she went after the reporters who said we were suspects. I figure Mr. Norton felt bad about everything that had happened and just shot himself. A bunch of people killed themselves after the shooting."

"But Doug hated guns," said Mac.

Parker shrugged. "I dunno, maybe the gun was like...a statement or something, you know? He hated guns, but the guns won in the end, so he was going to kill himself with one."

Mac hadn't considered that angle. It made a twisted sort of sense.

"Did you know a student named Kristin Salwell?" said Mac.

Parker blinked and then grinned. "Oh, yeah. Well, I didn't know her very well. She thought she was too good for guys like me and Ryan." He laughed. "But not too good for a married teacher, yeah? I saw that site she started. Looked at some of her free videos. I mean, she's sort of hot, but her website seems kind of sad and desperate.

When her looks hit the wall in her thirties, she's going to wind up working as a waitress for the rest of her life." He shrugged. "Most porn on the Internet is free, so I dunno why you'd pay for it. She isn't that good-looking."

"Do you know if Doug had a relationship with Salwell?" said Mac.

"Like, she had sex with Mr. Norton, that kind of relationship?" said Parker. "I don't think so. I know those two teachers went to prison for it. Which didn't surprise me all that much, you know? They were the kind of teachers who would give better grades to girls who were nice to them. Mr. Norton didn't do anything like that."

"Her name was the last thing he wrote in his day planner before he was shot," said Mac.

"Was it? Well, that doesn't make sense," said Parker. She shrugged. "Maybe she called him asking for money or something, and he wanted to record the call. That was how she got caught. I guess she called some of the teachers she was sleeping with and demanded money, and they were smart enough to record it. My mom thinks in a few years everything we do is going to get recorded like in China."

He wasn't wrong. People would be shocked if they knew how easily trackable their Internet activity was. And Mac was sometimes appalled by the things people so casually put on social media. The United States, he sometimes thought, would never have need of a secret police organization. The government could just look at stuff people voluntarily put on social media, and they would know more than the KGB or the Stasi had ever known about their subjects.

Yet something about Parker's words tugged at Mac's thoughts. Some idea, some connection turned over in his subconscious mind, but he could not grasp it.

"You okay, man?" said Parker, and Mac realized that he had been quiet for too long.

"Sorry, just thinking," said Mac.

"Hey, it's my turn to ask a question," said Parker. "Fair is fair." Mac nodded. "Do you think Mr. Norton killed himself or was he murdered?"

"I honestly don't know," said Mac. "When I started this, I was ninety-five percent sure he shot himself. Now I'm down to eighty percent. I still think it was probably a suicide. But you're right, it would have been out of character for him to kill himself with a gun."

"Maybe," said Parker. "My therapist says that suicidal ideation is sometimes impossible to see until it's too late."

Mac wondered how many other psychological terms Parker had picked up. "That's true. Sometimes people never see it coming. The fingerprints on the gun were off. It was like it was wiped clean, and then Doug gripped it once to shoot himself. But if it was stolen, then it might have been wiped down anyway." He shrugged. "I've been trying to track how the gun got from Winston Marsh's apartment to Doug Norton's classroom."

"What're you doing here, then?" said Parker.

Mac shrugged again. "I was on my way through the neighborhood, and I decided to stop by and take a look at the school. I've heard so much about it lately, I wanted to see it for myself, see if any ideas came to me."

"Well," said Parker, "if it turns out Mr. Norton was murdered, I bet the shooter did it. Maybe Mr. Norton figured out who the shooter was, and so he got killed for it."

"Maybe," said Mac, though that seemed unlikely. "My turn to ask you a question."

"Okay."

"Who do you think was the shooter?"

Parker let out a long breath. "Hell if I know, man. And I've thought about it a lot. I don't think it was anyone from the school. The cops talked to literally everyone who had anything to do with the school, and they come up with nothing. Which was why they thought Ryan and I did it, because we were skipping class that day to go on a guild raid..."

"Guild raid?" said Mac.

Parker looked askance at him. Suddenly Mac felt old. "You know, our gaming guild. The guys we play the game with online."

"Right, right," aid Mac.

"I think it was a lone wolf terrorist guy," said Parker. "Maybe it was an al-Qaeda thing, or maybe it was a random crazy person. Like, you remember those snipers in Washington DC a couple of years ago?" Mac nodded. "If they never caught got, it would have been like that." He shrugged. "Or maybe someone was trying to cover something up."

"Cover something up?" said Mac. "What do you mean?"

Parker gave another shrug. "Like…maybe there were two people. One of them shot up the school, and then while all the cops were busy, the second person robbed a bank or something. I don't know."

"Makes sense," said Mac. "If you don't mind the question, what are you doing here? I would think you wouldn't like to come back here."

"I don't," said Parker. "And I don't come when school's letting out or starting, and I stay out of sight. But, well…sometimes I get upset thinking about Ryan and everything that happened, and my therapist says it might be helpful to come back here. I thought that was nuts, but she was right. My mom says they're going to include Ryan's name on the memorial garden, which is good." His expression darkened. "After what they did to him, it's the least they can do."

"Can't argue with that," said Mac. "I don't think I have anything else to ask you. If you think of anything else, give me a call. You have my card."

"Actually," said Parker. "You want to talk to my mom?"

"Your mom?" said Mac. He thought back to what he had heard about Maggie McIntyre. "You think she'd be willing to talk with me?"

Parker shrugged. "Probably. If you were a journalist or digging around the school shootings, I think she'd tell you to go to hell. And then she'd send her lawyers after you. But she knows, like, everybody. Maybe she could help you out with Mr. Norton."

Mac had heard that Maggie McIntyre was not someone to cross. Then again, she would have known everyone at Morgan Properties and likely many of the key figures at Crest Development. Doug Norton's death, whether suicide or murder, was bound up in that world. Perhaps she might know something useful. As he had told

Julie Norton, the process of investigation often resembled walking in circles and beating the bushes with a stick to see what would fall out.

"Sure," said Mac. "If she's willing to talk with me. If not, no hard feelings."

"Great," said Parker. "Would you mind giving me a ride home? I took the bus here."

14

CRASH

Parker didn't want anyone from the school to see him, which Mac thought reasonable. Mac got back in his car and drove around to pick up Parker. He half-expected to see that Parker had left and that the kid had been messing with him for his own amusement, but Parker stood at the end of the alley.

Mac stopped the car and opened the passenger door. Parker levered himself into the passenger seat with a grunt. The Corsica's old shocks made an alarming creak, but Parker didn't seem to notice. He strained a bit but managed to get the seatbelt in place.

"Where are we going?" said Mac.

Parker recited an address in one of the more expensive areas in Brookfield. "You know how to get there?"

"Yeah," said Mac. He pulled away from the curb and entered traffic. A Brookfield police car drove past and turned for the school's street. Mac wondered if someone had spotted two suspicious prowlers by the half-demolished house and called it in. Then again, the police likely did regular drives past the school. "Thanks for the introduction to your mom."

"Just so long as you don't try to sleep with her," said Parker. Mac gave him an incredulous look. "That was a joke, man, that was a joke."

"Right," said Mac. "Do you usually bring home men for your mother?"

"Nah, she has no trouble finding them on her own," said Parker. "She'll go on dates now and again. She thinks I don't know when she has company over for the night, but I do. But I'm home most of the time anyway, so I notice."

"I see," said Mac, who did not want to speculate about the romantic life of Parker's mother. "So what do you do all day?"

"Online classes, mostly," said Parker. "Mom made me sign up since I didn't want to attend college in person. Other than that, I play the game."

"Game?" said Mac.

Parker launched into an explanation of his favorite game, a massively multiplayer online role-playing game where the player could take the role of a knight, an orc, a wizard, and numerous other avatars, and then battle against players of the opposing faction. Mac had never really gotten into MMORPGs due to a combination of lack of funds and lack of time. Parker, however, clearly loved the game, to judge from the way he talked faster and faster while describing it. His conversation was a peculiar mixture of computer geek-speak and psychological jargon that he must have picked up from his therapist.

"I also spend a lot of time making mods for the game," said Parker. "I code them myself." He scratched his head. "Of course, I have to be careful so I don't get banned for cheating. The trick is not to use any mods to generate gold. Besides, it's not like I can compete with the Chinese gold farmers."

"Uh huh," said Mac. He had actually read about that in a cybersecurity site he frequented – apparently, some enterprising Chinese businessmen hired people to play the game eighteen hours a day and then sold their accumulated gold and magical treasures to American players. "What do you use to code those mods?"

Parker started talking about programming languages. Mac asked a few questions along the way, and he was startled that Parker could answer them. The kid had a surprising knowledge of programming and networking for someone his age.

"I'm going to college for computer science, and once I'm finally done with that, I want to get into game design."

"Bad choice," said Mac.

Parker frowned. "Why?"

"Game development is too unstable and doesn't pay enough," said Mac. "The hours are terrible, too. You want something that pays better and has a more stable development cycle. Something like database management with regularly scheduled updates."

"Not to be rude or anything," said Parker, "but you're a private investigator."

Mac sighed. "I was a double major in computer science and criminology. I've done a lot of work as a private investigator, but I've done even more freelance jobs in systems administration and networking."

"That's an odd combination," said Parker.

"Not really," said Mac. "Cybersecurity is a big problem, and it's going to get even bigger. Half the PI jobs I've accepted in the last five years have dealt with computer fraud and computer-related crimes. Hell, you want a stable living, forget about game development and go into cybersecurity. You'll never lack for work."

"So why are you a private investigator instead of a cybersecurity guy?" said Parker.

Because he needed the money. And because Tom was right. Mac was good at digging, and as often as he told himself that he was going to stop, he enjoyed it.

"I do both," said Mac instead. "I work with Wester Security when they need the help, and I do freelance IT jobs. I also started a company with some friends of mine to write iPhone software for law enforcement."

Parker snorted out a laugh. "The iPhone doesn't even have an application store. What, are you going to make web apps?"

"There's going to be one," said Mac. "Not yet, but soon. And in the long-term, we want the software to be cross-platform." He shrugged as they came to a stoplight. "Maybe nothing will come of it. One of my partners thinks the iPhone is the next big thing, but it might be a fad. But we'll see."

"Huh," said Parker. "Something to think about, I guess. Maybe I can convince Mom to let me move somewhere else to go to college. Dr. Random thinks it would be a good idea to have a change of environment at some point, though I don't think my mom would be happy about that."

Mac frowned. "You're seeing a random doctor?"

"What? No, no." Parker laughed again. "That's the name of my therapist. Dr. Mallory Random. Mom made me go see a therapist after the FBI apologized. Guess she was worried I might...you know, like Ryan did." Mac nodded. "I had my doubts about talking to some strange woman about my feelings. Plus, she's got," he cupped his hands in front of his chest, "really nice tits. I mean, not too big, but they're really well-shaped, and it's hard not to stare at them during sessions, and..."

"That's not something you should discuss," said Mac. "Especially when you're looking for jobs."

"I know that, man. I'm not dumb," said Parker. "My point is that I thought it would be weird talking to a therapist about my feelings. Especially when she's hot. Which she is. But Dr. Random was really helpful. Showed me how to deal with a lot of stuff. I still go see her every two weeks. Anyway, both my mom and Dr. Random think that I should be looking at a career. Maybe you're right about the cybersecurity thing. The guild boards go nuts every time someone hacks the game."

They came to a residential neighborhood of expensive-looking houses. Each one had at least four bedrooms and two-car garages, and some of them had swimming pools in the back. Mac's battered old Corsica was the least expensive car he could see parked along the streets or in driveways.

"There's my house," said Parker, pointing at one of the larger houses. Julie Norton had said that Maggie McIntyre had a lot of money, and the house showed it. It had subdued tan and gray siding and a three-car garage off to the side. The lawn was so evenly trimmed and so vividly green it looked like a computer-generated special effect. "You can park in the driveway. Um. I should mention something."

"What?" said Mac as he put the Corsica into the driveway.

"Mom's going to be suspicious," said Parker. "She'll think you're a reporter sniffing around the Northwoods shooting. She'll want to call your company."

"Sure," said Mac, shutting off the engine.

Maybe this hadn't been such a good idea.

Parker got out of the car first, and Mac followed him.

He hadn't gotten three feet from the car when the front door burst open, and a woman stalked out, her expression thunderous.

Mac's first thought was surprise that a woman as small as Maggie McIntyre had a son the size of Parker. If Mac was half of Parker's weight, his mother had to be a third. Maggie was only two or three inches over five feet, and she had Parker's blue eyes and pale blond hair. The hair had been styled into a short pixie-style cut, and while Mac rarely thought that short hair looked good on a woman, Maggie had the cheekbones to pull it off. She looked somewhere in her early forties and wore black yoga pants and a loose blue sweater that hung to mid-thigh.

"Parker," she said, hands on her hips. She held a Blackberry in her right hand. "Where have you been? Did you go to Northwoods again?"

"Yeah," said Parker. "Dr. Random says it's good for me to confront…"

"And who is this?" said Maggie, leveling a finger at Mac. "Are you with the Milwaukee police? Or the FBI? And why are you bothering my son?"

"Neither," said Mac. "My name's Cormac Rogan, and I'm a private investigator."

"Oh, for God's sake," said Maggie. If she had possessed fangs, she would have bared them. "Let me guess. One of the families hired you to prove that Parker was the real shooter all along." Parker winced. "If you try that, I'll have your license and sue you into bankruptcy so fast that..."

"Ms. McIntyre," said Mac. "Julie Norton hired me."

That brought Maggie's tirade up short. "Julie? Why would she hire a private investigator?"

"She wanted me to review the death of her husband," said Mac. "I've been interviewing people who knew him. I was on my way back from another interview and decided to walk by the high school to get a sense of it. I happened to run into Parker there."

"You know everyone at Morgan Properties and the high school, Mom," said Parker. "I figured you would be a good person to talk to Mr. Rogan."

"Did you?" said Maggie. She still seemed annoyed but less suspicious. "I assume you have a card?"

Mac produced another business card and handed it over. "Wester Security."

"Hang on," said Maggie. She took the card, scrutinized it, and punched the number into her Blackberry. Maggie more or less repeated Parker's conversation with Dave's receptionist. She ended the call and stared at Mac, frowning.

"See?" said Parker. "He's legit."

"Maybe," said Maggie. "He could have hired someone to pose as an office manager on the other end of the call."

"No one's that paranoid," said Parker.

"She's right," said Mac. "You've dealt with reporters. You know what they're like."

"I suppose there's one way to find out if you're telling the truth," said Maggie. For a second, she bit her lip, seeming almost nervous. Then she shook her head, scrolled through the contacts on her Blackberry and made another call.

"Hello, Julie?" said Maggie. "It's Maggie McIntyre. I'm really sorry to bother you..."

A short, somewhat awkward conversation followed. Julie confirmed that she had indeed hired Wester Security. A few moments of tentative chitchat about their children followed, the tone that of two estranged friends reconnecting after a gap of several years, and Maggie promised to call again.

She ended the call and turned her attention back to Mac. Maggie had a frank, assessing stare, and Mac met her gaze.

"I was sorry to hear about what happened to Doug," said Maggie at last. "God, I should have gone to the funeral, but I was still upset when it happened. Stupid of me."

"I don't mean to intrude," said Mac.

"Of course you do," said Maggie, though she smiled. "You're a PI. Intruding without breaking the law is your job."

"What I was going to say is that you're not obliged to talk to me," said Mac. "Or if you'd rather talk over the phone or at a different location, I would be happy to do that as well."

Maggie thought it over and then shook her head. "No, we can talk now. Let's go inside."

She turned without another word and strode towards the front door. Mac looked at Parker, who shrugged, and they followed his mother into the house.

Past the front door was a small foyer and then an expansive living room with a high ceiling. The carpet was a cool blue, the walls painted white, and the furniture looked both expensive and tasteful. A middle-aged white woman in jeans and a worn sweatshirt was running a vacuum cleaner over the carpet near the front window.

"Ms. McIntyre," said the woman. "You have a visitor?"

Maggie pointed at her. "Don't pretend like you weren't watching out the window, Melinda." Melinda responded with a sheepish grin. "Parker, why don't you go to your room for a bit? I want to have a word alone with Mr. Rogan."

"Sure, Mom," said Parker, and he turned and lumbered up the stairs to the second floor. He was wheezing a bit by the time he got to the top.

"He'll be playing that game of his in another thirty seconds," said Maggie. She shook her head. "Would you like some coffee?"

"Please," said Mac.

He followed her into the kitchen, which was about the size of his entire apartment, with gleaming steel appliances and polished granite countertops. An island stood next to the fridge, its top likewise granite. A pair of French doors opened onto a patio overlooking a wide lawn encircled by a wooden privacy fence. Maggie took a pair of white mugs from a cabinet, filled them with coffee, and handed him one.

"Have a seat," she said, gesturing for the stools. Mac crossed to the island and waited until she had sat, which earned a brief smile, and then took the stool opposite her.

"If you've been talking to people at Morgan Properties," said Maggie, "then you've probably heard about me."

"Yes," said Mac.

"I can imagine what they said." She took a drink of her coffee. "But they probably told you that I speak my mind, so I'll be upfront with you, Mr. Rogan. I'll talk to you about Doug Norton, but if any of this comes back to hurt my son, I will make you regret it. Professionally, and financially if I can manage it."

"I've got about twelve hundred dollars in my checking account at the moment and a car that's only slightly younger than your son, so that's less of a threat than you think," said Mac, and she snorted. "But I understand. I'm not here to talk about Parker." He decided to offer up a little information. "I was arrested for a murder I didn't commit, so I understand."

"Really." She raised an eyebrow. "Should I be worried? Who didn't you kill?"

"Tom Harkin," said Mac, "who was the campaign manager for Senator Jack Kelsey."

Her eyes narrowed and then went wide with recognition. "That's it." She snapped her fingers. "I thought I recognized your name from somewhere. I guess you really do understand."

"A little bit," said Mac, hoping to give her room to start opening up.

"2005 was an awful year," said Maggie. "Absolutely awful. I thought the worst year of my life was when Parker's father left me after I got pregnant, and my parents disowned me." She shook her head. "When I first heard the news about the Northwoods shooting, I was terrified. I was sure that Parker had been killed. But he was safe… and I felt guilty about how relieved I was. I knew that other women had lost their children. But not me." Her eyes blazed. "But then the FBI started visiting."

"Parker and Ryan Walsh were truant that day," said Mac.

"They were," said Maggie. "In point of fact, they were both here, playing that Internet game. Parker…has challenges relating to people. His therapist…"

"Dr. Random," said Mac.

"A point in your favor, if Parker liked you enough to talk about her," said Maggie. Mac thought it best not to mention Parker's opinion of Dr. Random's breasts. "But Dr. Random thinks Parker is just slightly on the autism spectrum. Not enough to have difficulty functioning or that he would need medication, but he does find social interaction challenging." She sighed. "He's a genius. That's not just maternal pride talking. The kid is an absolute wizard with computers. But he has trouble talking to people. If he gets excited about a topic, he'll talk about it for hours. When he was younger, he would have a different interest every month – spaceships, the planets, a certain kind of animal. He would learn everything he could about it, and that's all he would talk about. Then when he was twelve, he discovered computers, and that's been his obsession ever since."

"He did talk a lot about the game in the ride over," said Mac.

Maggie smiled. "I can imagine."

"I was impressed by how much programming he knew," said Mac. "More than I would expect in someone his age. But he and Ryan were here playing the game on the day of the shooting?"

"They were," said Maggie. "I would have been furious under other circumstances. Parker had trouble with truancy before because he found school so boring. And Ryan was his only friend. I used to take his mother Janice out for coffee once a week. She was an ER nurse, and Ryan was a lot like Parker. We used to bond over the challenges of it, I suppose."

"The FBI decided that Parker and Ryan fit the profile of school shooters," said Mac.

"Absolute bullshit," said Maggie. "Utter and absolute bullshit. Neither the Milwaukee police nor the FBI had any idea who had done it, so they resorted to this psychological profiling crap. Complete pseudoscience, at best. They would have had better luck with tarot cards or that woman who does the late-night psychic hotline commercials. Then some idiot in the FBI office, I still don't know who, leaked it to the press. The reporters managed to put two and two together, and they reported that Parker and Ryan were the chief suspects in the shooting." She drummed her fingers on the edge of the counter, her anger still obvious and hot even after two years. "I remember seeing you on TV testifying to Congress about Senator Kelsey. You know what it's like being on the business end of a media feeding frenzy." Mac nodded. "But, to be blunt about it, your experience was easier. You were a hero. Everyone thought that Parker and Ryan were monsters. The first day it leaked, one of the parents of the murdered students attacked Parker, punched him in the face. I was furious, but I couldn't really blame the poor man. He was out of his mind with grief. But the reporters," her teeth bared in an unconscious snarl, "the reporters were camped up and down the streets. They said the most awful things about Parker and Ryan on TV. Some dumbshit psychiatrist went on the air and said it was proof that video games were the cause of rising crime in the United States and that my son and his best friend were proof of the 'digital radicalization' of the American youth or some crap like that."

"And Ryan killed himself," said Mac.

"He couldn't handle it, the poor kid," said Maggie. "Swallowed a bunch of pills in the bathroom. Janice found him. God, I can't even imagine what that was like. I was terrified the same thing would happen to Parker. So I did what I always do when I'm scared. I went to war."

"You found proof that Parker and Ryan had been playing the game during the shooting," said Mac.

Maggie's smile showed teeth. "And it was so easy, too. My lawyer called the game company, and they were happy to provide the information. If any of the idiots in law enforcement had bothered to check before talking to their snake-oil psychologists, they would have saved themselves a lot of trouble. Once we had that the proof, I started suing every law enforcement agency that had profiled Parker and every media organization that had libeled them."

"How did that turn out?"

Her smile widened. "They mostly chose to settle out of court. Suffice it to say the settlements were large enough that the agreement barred me from discussing the amounts."

"Did it pay for the house?" said Mac.

Maggie laughed. "No, the house was already mine. I did quite well at Morgan Properties." Her mirth faded. "I tried to get Janice to join me in the lawsuits, but Ryan's death broke her. She was done with Milwaukee and everything that happened here, and she moved to Florida to start over. Last time we talked, she was engaged." She paused. "I hope it works out. I did convince Janice to let me give her some of the settlement money from the lawsuits."

"You quit Morgan Properties around that time?" said Mac.

"I did." She sighed again and took a drink of her coffee. "I had become the office pariah. You know how people are. If something's reported on TV news, by gosh it must be true, and people thought my son was a school shooter. After we proved that he couldn't have done it, I'm afraid I made a scene and stormed out. Angela and I are still friendly, but not like we used to be."

"If you don't mind the question, what do you do now?" said Mac. "Are you retired?"

"I could be if I wanted, but I'd get bored," said Maggie. "I got out of real estate entirely, and I do some investing. I'm afraid I've become something of a serial entrepreneur. I own shares of some local companies I'm hoping will be recession-proof."

"Recession-proof?" said Mac.

"I had been considering leaving Morgan Properties even before the shooting," said Maggie. "I think the housing market is heading for an enormous crash in the next few years, and it's probably going to wreck the economy. We'll have either a severe recession or maybe even something like the Great Depression."

"Really," said Mac. "I hadn't heard any of this. I just saw on the news that the stock market hit an all-time high."

"The stock market relates to the health of the economy in the same way that a coat of paint relates to the structural health of a house. In other words, it doesn't. There are big problems coming. The government doesn't want to talk about it," said Maggie. "Do you know what subprime lending is?" Mac shook his head. "Basically, the government made it way too easy to get a home loan, and banks have been making loans to people who can't afford to pay them back. The housing market is a huge bubble right now. To make it worse, there are securities you can buy on this unstable mortgage debt, and a lot of major financial companies have them in their portfolios. The entire economy is essentially gamblers trying to cover their losses before the roulette wheel stops spinning. Just last month, a bank in Britain went bust. It was the first time a UK bank failed in one hundred and fifty years, and I think we're going to see a lot more of that before much longer."

"That sounds troublesome," said Mac.

"It's going to be bad," said Maggie. She shrugged. "Parker and I will be fine. I own the house, I have no debt, and even if I stop working, we have enough money to last for the rest of our lives. Someone like you will probably be fine. You said you don't have much money, and no wedding ring, so I'm guessing you don't have kids?" Mac nodded. "To be blunt about it, you won't lose much because you don't have any assets to lose. But, say, a family of five in a $250,000 house living from month to month with a ton of credit card debt? It's going to be bad, especially in the big cities on the coasts."

"That's the advantage of pessimism," said Mac. "It's good when you're wrong." He paused, wanting to get the discussion away from the economy. "How did Parker handle everything?"

"Badly at first," said Maggie. "I was terrified he was going to hurt himself the way Ryan did. It got better after we proved he couldn't have done it, but he was still depressed. He couldn't go back to Northwoods after all that, so I hired a tutor, and he finished with a GED. It really helped when I convinced him to start seeing Dr. Random. He's taking online classes now for computer science, and I hope it leads to a career." Her eyes narrowed. "You know, considering you came here to talk about Doug Norton, we've been discussing the shooting a lot."

"Yes, for my secret plan to write a book about it," said Mac, and Maggie snorted. "But this has been helpful. Most of the people I've talked to think that Doug was depressed after the shooting and simply had a bad day and killed himself."

"I do think that's what happened," said Maggie.

"How well did you know Doug?" said Mac.

"Reasonably well," said Maggie. "I volunteered for different things at Northwoods since Parker started going there, and I talked to Doug a few times. Sometimes he came to the holiday parties at Morgan Properties. He seemed like a decent guy, if a bit self-righteous. He wouldn't shut up about how much he hated guns, which was why I was surprised when he shot himself." She shrugged. "I couldn't see him killing himself under normal circumstances, but after the shooting? Yeah, I can believe it. That messed a lot of people up. Doug Norton wasn't the only suicide." Maggie paused. "Still, if he was going to kill himself, it seems out of character for him to do it with a gun."

"Have you ever met a man named Winston Marsh?" said Mac.

"No, I don't think so," said Maggie. "Should I have?"

"He used to be a maintenance technician with Crest Development until he retired," said Mac. Maggie's eyebrows rose a little at the mention of Morgan Properties' chief rival. "About six months before Doug killed himself, Marsh got drunk, fell down the stairs to his apartment, and broke his neck."

"What does that have to do with Doug?" said Maggie.

"Doug used a handgun registered to Marsh to kill himself," said Mac. "It was apparently stolen from Marsh's apartment after he died but before his daughter arrived to claim his possessions."

"That is weird," said Maggie. "I suppose Doug bought the gun from whoever stole it. Or he didn't realize it was stolen when he bought it. But that doesn't make sense, either. Doug wasn't the kind of guy to illegally buy a gun. I just can't see him doing something like that." She tapped her fingers on the counter again. "And it's an odd coincidence that Marsh worked for that bitch Arianna Crest."

"It could just be a coincidence," said Mac. "If you include contractors, Morgan Properties and Crest Development have employed thousands of people between them. If you pick any one person at random in the Milwaukee area, odds are they know someone who worked for one of the two companies." Though she was right, it was a strange coincidence. "I take it you do not care for Arianna Crest?"

"Not in the least," said Maggie. "Angela plays for keeps and is a hard negotiator, but she won't do anything illegal, and there are lines she won't cross. Crest is absolutely ruthless and a pathological liar on top of it. I suspect she'll end up in prison for some kind of white-collar fraud. But she's pretty enough and charming enough that she can talk her way out of anything. I've heard Angela and Crest are going head-to-head over the Westview Mall development."

"There's a lot of money on the line," said Mac.

"Oh, yes," said Maggie. "But I hope Angela doesn't win. Whoever gets the development is going to be stuck holding the bag when the economy crashes."

"One last question," said Mac. "Were you familiar with a student named Kristin Salwell?"

Maggie snorted. "The wannabe hooker? I was. My lawyers had gotten Parker cleared when that story broke, so I wasn't talking to anyone at Northwoods, but I still heard about it."

"Kristin Salwell's name was the last thing Doug wrote in his day planner before he died," said Mac.

"Huh," said Maggie. "Suppose he was sleeping with her...no, that doesn't make sense. If she was, it would have come out at the trial. And I can't see Doug cheating on Julie, and definitely not with a student. It would have been out of character."

"So would suicide," said Mac.

"That's true. I think..." She looked towards the ceiling, and a second later, Mac heard Parker lumbering down the stairs. He came into the kitchen, holding a thick gaming laptop with a seventeen-inch screen.

"Hey, you guys still talking?" said Parker.

"We were just about done," said Maggie, and Mac nodded.

"Before you go, Mr. Rogan, I want to show you this," said Parker. He put the laptop on the counter in front of Mac. For a second, Mac thought Parker had somehow uncovered evidence about Doug Norton, but instead, he found himself looking at a gaming interface. "This is the application I wrote for finding the game server with the least load. We were talking about it in the car. If you've got a minute, I think you'll find it interesting."

Mac started to say that he needed to go, but he caught the silent plea in Maggie's eyes and changed his mind.

"Sure," said Mac. "Show me what you did."

Parker spent the next forty-five minutes showing off the various utilities he had made for the game. Mac found that he was impressed. Parker had a solid grasp on the various code libraries and programming techniques, and when Mac pointed out several potential security holes, Parker explained that he had already addressed them.

"Tell you what," said Mac. "I started a company with two friends of mine to write apps for the iPhone."

Maggie frowned. "I thought the iPhone didn't allow user-installed applications." She held up her phone. "Can't see it displacing the Blackberry."

"Maybe," said Mac. "But we also have web-based versions of the software. Anyway, if you're looking for an internship or maybe even a side job, we might have something for you."

Parker frowned. "I still kind of want to go into game development."

"Game development's brutal," said Mac. "Too much unpaid overtime and the business model is too unstable. It's better to sell the tools and services that game developers use. I think instead of spending all your time digging in the hills for gold, it's better to sell the shovels and wheelbarrows."

Parker started to object, but Mac saw that the idea had caught hold in his mind. "I hadn't thought of it that way. I'll think about it, Mr. Rogan."

"He will," said Maggie.

"I said I will, Mom."

"Well, you need to find a job someday. You're not living here for the rest of your life," said Maggie, though she smiled as she said it. "I'll walk you out, Mr. Rogan."

They left the house, and Mac stepped off the front porch. To his surprise, Maggie followed him.

"Thank you for indulging Parker," said Maggie. "I know he can be a bit…overwhelming at the first meeting."

"When I'm not doing PI work, I do various IT consulting jobs," said Mac. "I've met a lot of older versions of Parker. Ms. McIntyre, you were right. He really does have a talent for software. I've known teams that would have had harder times writing some of those utilities. And I'm serious about finding him a part-time job or an internship."

"Thank you," said Maggie. She looked up at him, somber. "I appreciate that. Not everyone is kind to my son. Can I give you two pieces of advice before you go?"

"Of course," said Mac.

"I think Doug probably killed himself," said Maggie. "But Julie's got good instincts. Maybe she's right. If Doug was murdered, I think the mass shooter did it. That's the only motivation I can think of for anyone to kill Doug Norton. So you should watch your back. Someone who got away with that many murders won't like you sniffing around them."

"It's possible," said Mac, though he considered it unlikely. "Who do you think the shooter was? You must have thought about it."

"I have," said Maggie. "I think it was probably a lone wolf terrorist. Some nut with a basement full of machine guns and pipe bombs."

"If it was a terrorist," said Mac, "why wasn't there a manifesto or an attempt to take credit?"

"I don't know," said Maggie. "Maybe the shooter got caught for something unrelated and is in prison for drugs or burglary or something. Maybe the shooter had a close call and decided to lay low for a while. Or he's getting ready to do something else."

Something clicked in Mac's head. "That's why you're angry that Parker keeps going back to Northwoods High School. Not because someone might see him and think he's the shooter. You're worried that he might be there when the shooter comes back."

For a long moment, Maggie said nothing, her brow furrowed.

"People who do illegal things," she said at last, "tend to keep doing them unless they get caught. When I was a teenager, I wasn't like Parker. I was a wild child, smoking and drinking just to spite my parents. My friends dared me to start shoplifting, and I started stealing bigger and bigger items. I finally got caught, arrested, and tried as a juvenile for it."

"You seem to have turned your life around," said Mac.

"I did, and it was hard, but that's not the point," said Maggie. "If I had gotten caught the first time, I would have stopped. But I wasn't, and I kept shoplifting, and I kept going for more expensive items. I escalated. Whoever committed the shooting wasn't caught, and I'm afraid it will happen again and on a bigger scale."

Mac said nothing. Her logic made a disturbing amount of sense.

"Like I said before, that's the advantage of pessimism," he said. "It's good to be wrong."

"That it is," said Maggie. "Good luck, Mr. Rogan." She handed him a business card of her own. "If you think of anything else to ask, give me a call."

Mac nodded, thanked her, and got into his car and left.

The conversations with Arianna Crest, Parker, and Maggie turned over his head as he drove. Arianna was sure that Doug had killed himself, and Parker had been inclined to believe that as well. Maggie was willing to entertain the possibility that Doug hadn't killed himself, but she thought it was probably a suicide. Despite the anomalies, the balance of evidence still seemed to show that Doug Norton had killed himself.

Mac thought of Maggie's speculation that if Doug had been murdered, the killer would notice Mac's investigation and come after him. If Doug had been murdered, his death had been staged as a suicide with exceptional skill. Despite the occasional publicized failure, the police were difficult to fool, and it was exceptionally difficult to make a murder look like a suicide.

Maggie was right. If Doug had been killed, the murderer was not someone to take lightly. Still, Mac had found no links that would lead back to a killer. The only possible clue had been the blond woman that Jake Carver had seen with Winston Marsh before his death.

An odd thought formed in his mind.

Douglas Norton's death had been ruled a suicide. Winston Marsh's death had been an accident.

Unless he had been pushed down those stairs while drunk.

He turned the idea over his head as he drove, examining it for flaws. The stairs up to Marsh's apartment had been well-built, equipped with anti-slip treads and a solid handrail. Marsh would have gone up and down those stairs hundreds of times in the dark while drunk. He would have known them well. Accidents were always possible, of course, but what if it hadn't been an accident?

What if he had been pushed?

It made a disturbing amount of sense. But only if Doug had indeed been murdered. Otherwise, they were two unrelated deaths.

Except Marsh's gun had killed Doug.

Mac frowned as he waited at a stoplight, another disturbing thought occurring to him.

What if Marsh's handgun hadn't been stolen as a crime of opportunity, the weapon finding its way to Doug Norton by chance? What if Marsh had been killed specifically to steal his handgun for Doug's murder? The weapon would have no connection whatsoever to the real killer, especially without fingerprints.

That implied a killer capable of a great deal of careful planning. Especially since six months had passed between Marsh's death and Doug's. Either Doug's killer had been planning his death for that long, or the killer had simply pushed Marsh and taken his handgun on the off chance that the weapon would be useful someday.

That was the sort of thing a sociopath might do. Sociopaths were much less common than TV and movies would have people believe, and those that did exist tended to have low thresholds of self-control and ended up in prison.

But sociopaths with self-control did exist.

Perhaps one had killed both Winston Marsh and Douglas Norton.

Or maybe Mac had just constructed an elaborate fantasy in his head based on Maggie's warning. Still, he had an obvious course forward. Tomorrow he would call all the names Arianna Crest had given him and start digging into Marsh's past. He would also try to contact Marsh's daughter Carmen and see if she could tell him anything. Maybe someone other than Carver and his cashier Tammy had seen the blond woman.

Tonight, though, he would work on RVW Software. Dealing with the puzzles of coding and server configuration would be a welcome change from trying to chase down a murderer who might or might not exist.

He glanced at his car's gas gauge, saw that the needle was dangerously close to the left side of the E. Mac decided to bite the bullet and pulled into a gas station, and winced when he saw that the price of gas was currently $2.79 a gallon. He had heard people say that the war in Iraq hadn't been about Saddam and weapons of mass destruction, that it had been intended to seize a secure supply of oil. Mac hoped that wasn't true, that Tom hadn't gotten wounded for a lie. Certainly, his brother was much more cynical about the government and the senior military leadership than he had been before the war.

And if the US had gone to war for oil, that had backfired, because gas cost three times as much as it had when Mac had been a kid.

He filled up, frowning at the cost, but at least he could charge his mileage for the last few days to Dave. Mac went into the gas station to pay and also bought a sandwich for dinner since he hadn't eaten today and his stomach was growling.

As he walked back to his car, a passing van caught his eye. It was a white panel van with GENERAL CONTRACTING painted on the side. Mac thought it was the same van he had seen that morning at Crest Development. Odd coincidence. He hoped that

Arianna hadn't paid the General Contracting guy too much because he had obviously been dragging his feet on washing the front sign.

The van drove past without slowing, and Mac got into his car and headed for home.

AT ABOUT ELEVEN PM that night, Arianna Crest sat in her car and looked at Cormac Rogan's apartment window through her binoculars.

Her car was unremarkable, a gray 1997 Ford Taurus with numerous dents and rust around the doors, a far cry from her usual Audi. The car was registered to one of Arianna's shell companies, and she used it when she needed to do things quietly and without drawing attention to herself. She had been driving this car when she had first met Rod Cutler, come to think of it, the day she had killed the pimp who had been beating him up for welshing on a debt. That incident had been one of the things that secured Rod's frightened loyalty. His fingerprints, and only his fingerprints, were on that particular murder weapon, and Rod knew that if she ever needed to get rid of him, that weapon would mysteriously find its way to the police.

Or so he thought.

She probably would just kill him herself. He knew way too much about her. For now, though, he remained loyal and useful.

Arianna wasn't worried about anyone seeing her sitting in the car. The street was dark, the nearest light a block away at an intersection. For that matter, Rogan's apartment complex wasn't well lit. The only lights were mounted over the entrances to the buildings, and half of those were broken. The parking lots were pitch-dark, and local police reports noted that drug deals tended to take place here on a regular basis.

The place was a dump. Private investigation didn't pay all that well. But she knew Rogan wasn't rich.

She knew a lot about him now, thanks to the research she had done while Rod had shadowed him during the day.

Arianna watched Rogan's windows through her binoculars. The blinds were pulled, and she caught glimpses of him moving around from time to time. Once she saw him look through the blinds, perhaps responding to a slammed car door in the parking lot.

Then the lights in his apartment went out.

Probably he had gone to sleep.

Arianna put down her binoculars and ran her tongue over her teeth, thinking.

It seemed unlikely he would stumble across the truth – but then again, he found the truth behind the plot to blow up that church over the summer, hadn't he? Rogan was both skilled and lucky, a bad combination for her. His father had apparently been some sort of model police officer who had quit the force to expose a corrupt alderman and had gotten killed for his trouble.

And then John Rogan's son had stopped that church from getting blown up.

He might become a problem.

Especially now, when Halloween was so close. Arianna really needed to kill Angela Morgan's son and make it look like another school shooting. The Halloween bonfire at Northwoods High School was her best chance to do that. Angela would fall apart from grief, Arianna would secure the Westview Mall development, and that would be that.

Unless Rogan found something Arianna had overlooked in the next week.

Maybe she should go into his building, knock on his door until he opened, and then shoot him. That would solve all kinds of problems. She could play the frightened woman, say that she had found something about Winston Marsh that had alarmed her. Arianna would ask for a glass of water, and when he turned to get it, she would shoot him in the head.

The thought of the risk made her shiver.

Or…maybe she would sleep with him first. She had liked the look of him, and he had been attracted to her, she could tell. Arianna thought she would enjoy sleeping with him, and then when he drifted off, it would be so easy to put the gun to his head and squeeze the trigger...

She closed her eyes and shivered in enjoyment at the thought.

No. Too risky. Both approaches were too risky, even for her. Someone might see her entering and leaving the apartment. Arianna might leave DNA evidence behind, especially if she slept with him. And he had just talked to her this morning. That was too much of a link, and the police might follow it back.

And Rogan had been suspicious of her. Some instinct, something in his subconscious, had warned him that she was a wolf while most people were sheep.

Misdirection. That was always better. Julie Norton and Clarissa Chartwell had been in her way, and Arianna hadn't killed either woman. Instead, she had killed Julie's husband and Clarissa's son.

Cormac Rogan had a brother.

Thomas Rogan, decorated Marine sergeant, discharged after taking wounds in Iraq in 2004. Currently worked as an electrician, carpenter, and general contractor, and lived in the same apartment complex as his brother. He was also Cormac's only living immediate family. Arianna had found out all about him during her research.

What would happen if Thomas Rogan was shot?

Arianna grinned in the darkness.

Cormac Rogan would be too busy to poke into Arianna's business any longer.

She started the engine and drove off, planning. Once she was home, she would use her burner phone to contact Rod. He would charge too much, but that was all right.

It was time to arrange a murder.

15

FALSE LEADS

Thursday, October 25th, 2007, was another cold and cloudy day, though it at least had stopped raining.

After his morning workout at Iron Oswald's Gym, Mac spent most of the day in his apartment in front of his computers, working and making phone calls. He made good progress on the web application for RVW Software. The people that Paul and Nikolai had rounded up to serve as beta testers were impressed with the software and were willing to make commitments to spend money on it. RVW Software might actually generate some revenue before the year instead of expenses. Not that there had been very many expenses, save for server hosting and their time.

In between coding the app and checking server configurations, Mac began working his way down the list of contacts that Arianna Crest had given him.

He made much less progress there.

Everyone on the list accepted his call, and all of Winston Marsh's former coworkers had the same things to say. They all remembered Winnie the Wino, but save for the nickname, no one really had anything bad to say about him. Winston had done his work and kept his head down. Not a very sociable guy, but he didn't slack off on the clock. He was almost always hungover on Monday mornings and sometimes during the week, but it didn't affect his work. Everyone knew that Winston had a drinking problem, but no one was close enough to him to do anything about it.

No one could remember seeing Marsh with an attractive blond woman. A few people laughed at the very idea of an attractive woman spending time with him. Marsh's former supervisor, the one who had known him the longest, said that the divorce and the resultant contentious relationship with his daughter had soured Marsh on women in general, and he mostly wanted to be left alone to drink himself to death in peace.

Marsh's daughter Carmen was the last call of the day and by far the least useful. Even over the phone, Carmen's unpleasant, belligerent personality came through. She initially accused Mac of being a reporter until he soothed her by saying that he didn't trust reporters either. Carmen went into a long rant about her father's many failings, how the resultant trust issues caused her string of failed relationships. This expanded into her list of grievances against the women in her office (she worked in claims adjustment), all of whom were "gossipy bitches" and were plotting against her. After about twenty minutes, Mac concluded that it was unlikely that Carmen had anything to do with her father's death and that he wasn't going to get any useful information out of her, so he ended the call as gracefully as he could manage.

Winston Marsh, no doubt, had been a bad father. Then again, after talking to Carmen, Mac could hardly blame the man for ignoring his adult daughter. The idea made him think of his own father. Mac supposed that by some standards, John Rogan would have been considered a bad father, but he rejected the thought. He had taught his sons independence and useful skills, both of which were better than trips to Disney World. John Rogan's biggest flaw, Mac believed, was that he had been devoted to his integrity to the point of inflexibility, which had meant he had no money to his name when he died.

That, and he had trusted the wrong woman once too often.

Mac glanced at the clock. 6:15 PM. He was due to meet Tom for their weekly dinner in forty-five minutes. Well, he had spent enough of the day bashing his head against programming logic and attempting to chase down whoever had stolen Winston Marsh's gun. Mac got dressed in jeans, a sweater, and his heavy black coat, collected his car keys, and headed out.

This week Tom wanted to go to Becker's, where Mac had met Julie Norton for the first time. A couple of months ago, Mac and Tom had both met Dave Wester there for a drink since Dave had wanted to recruit Tom as one of his regular freelancers. Tom had agreed to do one surveillance job, though he hadn't taken another since – evidently Tom had enough carpentry and electrical work to keep him occupied.

Once again, Mac reflected that maybe he was in the wrong line of work. But Tom had liked the burgers at Becker's, so they were having dinner there.

He got to downtown Wauwatosa with ten minutes to spare, though much of that time was eaten up by finding a parking space several blocks from the bar. Unlike the last time Mac had been here, it wasn't pouring rain, but it was colder, with the first bite of winter in the air. He was glad he had thought to wear a sweater and wrapped his coat tighter around himself.

Becker's was about half full, with a crowd of late diners at the tables and early drinkers at the bar. Mac spotted Tom sitting at a table against the wall, glowering at a menu. His brother was wearing a hooded gray sweatshirt, jeans, and work boots. Mac wove his way through the crowd and sat down across from him.

"Trouble?" said Mac.

Tom only grunted and set aside the menu. "The prices went up."

"Prices of everything are going up," said Mac.

"God's own truth," said Tom. A perky waitress in a snug black T-shirt and jeans came over, and Tom flirted with her a bit, which seemed to please her. Mac and Tom got their usual orders – cheeseburgers and fries, and an appetizer of onion rings – and the waitress returned with their beers.

"How's the job?" said Mac, opening his bottle.

Tom shrugged. "I screw boards together and mount wiring. But no one's shooting at me. Can't complain. You figure out if that woman's husband killed herself yet?"

Mac grimaced. "No."

He told Tom about it – the conversations with Julie Norton and Kristin Salwell, Jake Carver and Winston Marsh, Arianna Crest and Parker and Maggie McIntyre. Tom listened in silence, taking a sip of his beer from time to time. He had always been good at listening, but of necessity, his throat injury had made him better at it.

"So," grunted Tom once he finished. "Either Doug Norton found Winston Marsh's gun and killed himself with it, or someone killed Marsh, stole his gun, and then shot Norton with it and made it look like a suicide."

"Yeah," said Mac. "Sounds implausible either way."

Tom shrugged. "Weird stuff happens all the time. Be a stone-cold killer to push Marsh and shoot Norton, though."

"We've met a few of those," said Mac. "What do you think?"

"Norton probably killed himself," said Tom. "Saw a few of those after I got back from Iraq. Always sucks. Always messes up the people left behind. Never really makes sense to them, either." He coughed and took a drink of beer. "But. What you said makes sense. Someone could have killed Marsh, used his gun to kill Doug Norton. Be a great way to do it. Best way to commit murder is with a stolen gun. So long as you don't leave fingerprints."

"Yeah," said Mac. "Of course, that leaves the problem of motive." He shrugged. "Hell if I can find one. I know suicidal ideation isn't always observable, which is why it comes as a shock. But as far as I can tell, no one had any reason to kill Doug. He wasn't cheating on his wife, he didn't have money troubles, he wasn't involved in drugs or money laundering or anything."

"So why'd he write down that girl's name?" said Tom. He coughed again. "What was it..."

"Kristin Salwell," said Mac. "She claims she never slept with him, and I believe her. Besides, she would have had every reason to reveal it when she was arrested."

Tom thought about that.

"Maybe it wasn't about Doug," he said. "Maybe it was about Julie."

"Julie?" said Mac.

Tom shrugged. "Maybe someone killed Doug to get at Julie."

Mac stopped, his beer bottle lifted halfway to his mouth, and then put the bottle back down.

"Huh," said Mac. "I hadn't thought of that." He mulled it over. "Makes sense. I haven't been able to figure out any reason someone would want to kill Doug."

"Would someone want to kill Julie?"

"Not that I can think of," said Mac. "But there would be more reason to kill her. She's the chief counsel at Morgan Properties, handles all these multi-million dollar real estate deals. I mean, yeah, someone might want to kill a teacher over a bad grade or something, but there's a lot more motivation to kill someone over millions of dollars."

"So why not just kill Julie?" said Tom.

"Hell if I know," said Mac. "It was your idea."

Tom snorted a laugh. "I'm not the one getting paid to do this. I'm the devil..." He grunted and coughed.

Mac raised an eyebrow. "You're the devil?"

"Devil's advocate."

The discussion was interrupted by the arrival of the onion rings. Mac and Tom divided the basket into two halves and spent a few moments eating.

"Okay," said Mac. "So why kill Doug to get at Julie? An affair is the obvious choice, but Julie swears that she and Doug never cheated on each other."

"Could be lying," said Tom. "Or deluded."

"True," said Mac. "If someone went after Doug to influence Julie for business reasons, you'd think there would be threats or something first. Julie didn't mention anything like that. I'll have to backtrack through what Morgan Properties was working on."

"Maybe Arianna Crest hired a hitman," said Tom.

Mac snorted. "She's ruthless, but she doesn't seem like the type."

Tom grunted, ate an onion ring, and took a drink of beer.

"What?" said Mac.

"You've got that look," said Tom.

"What look?"

"You like her," said Tom.

"I don't," said Mac. "Really, I don't. Everyone I met describes her as a barracuda or a shark, and that's accurate. And she's cold. When I interviewed her, she said that it was more merciful that Marsh fell down the stairs and broke his neck than dying from his alcoholism."

"Cold," said Tom, "but she's not entirely wrong. Liver failure is a hell of a bad way to go." He looked at his beer, seemed to reconsider, then shrugged and took another drink. "But you do think she's hot."

"She is hot. Physically attractive. Objectively," said Mac. He remembered his former housemate Clare, a graduate student in women's studies, and how angry she had gotten whenever the topic of a woman's looks came up. "Whether I think she is or not."

"Gonna ask her out?"

"Hell no."

"Careful," said Tom. "You're like Dad that way."

"What is that supposed to mean?" said Mac, though he knew. "Dad's problem was that he always tried to do the right thing in the most rigidly inflexible way possible. He had integrity, but he always chose the worst way to act on it. If he wanted to expose corruption in the police department and the aldermen, fine. Collect the evidence and get it to the FBI or the state police. Instead, he quit, made a scene, became a private investigator, and then collected the evidence. All he got for it was bankrupt and murdered."

"That's true," said Tom with equanimity. "But. Dad had two problems." He held up two onion rings to emphasize the point. "The stuff you just said. And women. If Dad was attracted enough to a woman, his brains got scrambled. You know he and Mom still slept together every few months even after the divorce?"

"Yeah," said Mac. It was part of how Monica Rogan had murdered John Rogan and tried, badly, to frame Mac for it.

"Mom's nuts," said Tom. "I figured it out when I was a teenager and cut contact with her. You did too, eventually. Dad always knew, but he kept coming back to her even after they got divorced." He coughed, took another sip of beer. "She must have been good in the sack."

"I do not want to think about that," said Mac.

"But you kind of have the same problem with women," said Tom. "You're attracted enough, your brains turn off. Kate? Kate was bad for you. You should have broken up with her long before she broke up with you. But you've got that same look now."

"All right, fine," said Mac. "I solemnly promise I will not ask out Arianna Crest. Though I'm sure millionaire property developers date broke private investigators and software developers all the time." Tom snorted. "But I think you have a point."

"About you and women? I damned well do."

"About someone coming after Doug to get at Julie," said Mac. "It makes sense. I'll have to call Julie and ask her what she was working on before Doug's death. Suppose I'll have to phrase it just right."

"Why's that?" said Tom.

"Because the most likely possibility still is that Doug killed himself, and Julie just isn't dealing with it well," said Mac. "Sure, maybe someone killed Marsh, took his gun, and then killed Doug for some obscure reason, but maybe not."

"If Julie isn't in her right mind," said Tom, "and she thinks one of her business rivals," he paused to cough, "killed her husband, she might snap."

"Yeah," said Mac.

"Tough problem. Glad it's not mine."

"Very helpful."

The waitress returned with their cheeseburgers, and Mac and Tom discarded conversation for a few moments to focus on dinner.

"You doing anything for Halloween?" said Tom.

"Nah," said Mac. "Probably working on RVW stuff. Or reading

through business deals that Julie worked on if she's willing to share the list. How about you?"

"Probably hit the bar with some friends from the job sites," said Tom. He considered his bacon cheeseburger, reached for a bottle of barbecue sauce next to the napkins and salt, and dumped some onto his bun. "You should come. Better than sitting in your apartment all night. Maybe you'll meet a woman who isn't anything like Kate or Arianna Crest."

"You're one to talk," said Mac.

The door to the street opened, and a group of six people came into the bar. Mac glanced at them automatically. They looked like sober-minded business people – suits, overcoats. Four men and two women...

Mac blinked in surprise.

One of the women was Arianna Crest.

She was wearing a long black overcoat, high-heeled boots visible beneath the hem. Her blond hair had been pulled back in a severe bun. She pulled off her coat, revealing that she was wearing a snug knee-length blue dress with a black jacket.

"What?" said Tom.

Arianna hung up her coat alongside the others at the front of the bar, and then she saw Mac.

"Shit," muttered Mac.

"What?" said Tom again.

Arianna said something to the rest of her group as they headed for the bar, and she walked across the room towards Mac, drawing a few admiring glances as she did.

"Well, well, Mr. Rogan," said Arianna, stopping a few paces from the table. Ingrained manners took over, and Mac rose, as did Tom. "Following me around town as a suspicious person? I do hope you would be more discreet about it."

"No, just having dinner," said Mac. He caught a faint whiff of her perfume. "This is my brother Tom." He braced himself. "Tom, this is Arianna Crest."

But Tom remained grave. "Ma'am." They shook hands.

"I don't suppose you're a private investigator as well," said Arianna.

"No. Contractor," said Tom. "Done some work on some of your properties."

"Have you?" said Arianna. "I suppose I paid for your dinner, then."

"Depends on how much overtime the job had," said Tom, and Arianna laughed.

"What brings you here?" said Mac.

"Was I following you, is that what you mean?" said Arianna, teeth flashing in a smile. "No. I own shares in a commercial complex nearby with my partners there," she gestured at the bar, "and we get together to discuss business every so often."

"I see," said Mac, trying and failing to think of something clever to say. "Thank you again for the list. It's proven useful."

"Has it? Good," said Arianna. "I trust my employees have proven cooperative?"

"They have," said Mac.

"Well, I still think Doug Norton killed himself, the poor man," said Arianna. She smiled and patted his arm. "But it's good of you to try and put Julie Norton's mind at ease. Give me a call if you think of anything else to ask. If you'll excuse me."

"Of course," said Mac.

Arianna flashed another smile at him and crossed the room to rejoin her business partners at the bar. Mac, almost against his will, noticed that the skirt fit her backside very well, an effect further augmented by her heeled boots. He glanced at Tom, saw him noticing that as well, and they sat back down to their dinner.

"Smooth," said Tom.

"Oh, shut up."

Tom grinned. "I'm not the one she gave her number to." He coughed, rubbed his throat, and took another drink of beer. "I know I told you not to sleep with her. But after looking at her, just once might not hurt…"

"You said that would be a bad idea," said Mac.

"Extremely bad," said Tom. "But she did come all the way over here to talk to you. Maybe she wants to go slumming." He grinned. "But once you break it off with her, she might leave a dog's head in your bed or something."

"I don't have a dog."

"She's rich. She'd buy one for the occasion."

Mac shook his head and finished his burger.

"Diet soda, please," said Arianna.

"Still not drinking, Arianna?" said one of the other owners of the commercial complex, a doughy man named Carl Linden. He wanted her to drink so she would be easier to seduce, which was a disgusting thought. Or it would have been, had she not been certain that Carl's heart would give out with any exertion more intense than a brisk walk. During these meetings, she had never seen him eat anything that wasn't deep-fried.

Lucky for Carl that the commercial complex didn't earn enough of a profit to make it worthwhile to kill him.

And at the moment, he was useful in strengthening her alibi. It had been a marvelous stroke of luck that the partners wanted to meet at Becker's, and Arianna had decided to exploit that good fortune.

"I still have to drive home, Carl," said Arianna. She smiled at him. "And I'm a lightweight. One beer, and I'd be dancing on the bar." Or she would lose her temper and stab him in the neck.

Carl brayed out his annoying laugh.

The others chattered about their children and vacation plans. As they did, Arianna slipped a hand into her purse and drew out her burner phone. She tapped in a single word and sent a text message to Rod Cutler's burner.

GO.

With that, she dropped the phone back into the purse and joined the conversation, keeping the satisfaction from her face.

The problem of Cormac Rogan was about to be solved.

In the end, it was too close to Halloween, which was her best chance to kill Charlie Morgan and clear Angela Morgan and her company away as a competitor for the Westview Mall deal. The Halloween bonfire was simply too good of an opportunity to kill Angela's brat and make it look like another random school shooting. Arianna couldn't have someone like Cormac Rogan sniffing around her business. She didn't think there was anything that would lead to her from the deaths of Winston Marsh and Douglas Norton, but there might have been a connection she had overlooked.

Cormac Rogan needed something else to occupy his attention, something completely unconnected to Arianna.

The wounding or potential death of his brother ought to do it.

It turned out that Thomas Rogan had worked on some of Arianna's construction projects, which meant that his information was in her employee records. That included his license plate number since he needed a parking pass at the construction site, and she had located his truck on the way here. Thomas Rogan had parked several blocks away near the mouth of an alley.

The perfect place for an ambush.

The bartender produced her diet soda, and Arianna sipped at it, smiling to herself.

Poor Cormac. She had read up on him. His mother had killed his father, tried to frame Cormac for it, and then ended up in prison. Now his only brother was about to be wounded or killed.

That should give him something to do other than investigate Douglas Norton's death.

16

DRUG-RELATED VIOLENCE

"Before I forget," said Tom.

"Yeah?" said Mac, finishing the last of his fries.

"You've got a box of stuff in my truck," said Tom.

Mac frowned. "What stuff?"

The waitress brought over the checks, and Mac counted some bills out of his wallet and left them on the table, Tom doing likewise. Arianna and her business partners were still at the bar, talking. Mac was annoyed that he was aware of Arianna's presence, that he felt a strong compulsion to look at her.

"Stuff you left at my apartment before you moved out," said Tom.

"I didn't leave anything at your apartment," said Mac. He hadn't had all that much to leave. Most of his possessions had been destroyed in the fire that had burned down his previous building.

"Yes, you did," said Tom. "This box of old cables and these flat gray disk drive things."

"What? Oh, right," said Mac. "The SCSI drives."

Tom frowned. "You left a box of scuzzy hard drives in my living room?"

"No, no, it's an acronym," said Mac. "Small Computer System Interface. It's pronounced 'scuzzy', and...."

"Don't care," said Tom. "Just don't want them in my living room."

"Fine, fine," said Mac. "You sure? Never know when an obsolete external hard drive will come in handy."

Tom gave him a flat look. "I've got enough coasters."

In point of fact, the external SCSI hard drives would make terrible coasters. The chassis were heavy gray metal, and the top was slightly curved, likely a design feature to keep people from setting things atop it, such as drinks.

"All right," said Mac. "Let's go get the box."

Mac couldn't quite stop himself from casting a glance at Arianna as they passed. She was sitting on a barstool, legs crossed, a diet soda in hand as she listened to one of the other women talk. He had the impression that she was bored, but he made himself look away before she noticed.

Annoyed with himself, he followed Tom onto the street. Mac didn't even like Arianna all that much. Her offhanded remark about a merciful death had grated on him, reminding him of his mother. But there was no denying that he did find Arianna attractive, and it was just as well he was unlikely to see her again.

Mac was pleased that he did not look through the bar's windows as they left. Even if he kind of wanted to.

It had been a chilly day, but the night had gotten downright cold. Mac's breath came in visible puffs.

"Where are you parked?" said Mac.

"Three blocks that way, around the corner," said Tom, pointing.

"Why so far?" Mac was going to have a long walk back to his car with the box of drives.

Tom shrugged. "There were more cars when I got here."

That was true. It was past 8 PM by now, and traffic had died off. Most of the businesses along the street had closed, and only a few cars went past. The bars were still open, but it was Thursday night, and the serious crowds wouldn't come until Friday and Saturday.

They turned a corner onto a short side street. It was a block long and terminated at the bluff dropping down to the Menomonee River and the train tracks running alongside it. If Mac looked to the right, he could just see the patio deck at Becker's. Mac spotted Tom's F-150 truck parked next to a pair of buildings with shops on the ground floor and two rows of apartments on the upper levels, a narrow alley between them.

"You could have parked closer," said Mac.

Tom shrugged. "Walking's good for you. Besides. It's hard to park that thing on a tight street."

"You should get a smaller car," said Mac.

"Small cars are great," said Tom, "right up until you need to move some lumber."

Mac didn't have a good answer for that, so he waited as Tom unlocked the truck and opened the passenger side door. A passing car drove past, and Mac glanced around the street, noting details. Part of his mind pointed out that Tom had picked a bad place to park. The only streetlight was on the corner, and it didn't cast much illumination on this dead-end side street. It was an ideal place to mug someone. Then again, downtown Wauwatosa wasn't exactly the most crime-ridden area of the Milwaukee metropolitan area, and someone would have to be drunk or stoned out of their mind to try and mug Tom.

Even as the thought crossed his mind, a flicker of motion caught his eye.

There was someone in the alley.

"Here," said Tom, pulling out a cardboard box full of computer cables and metal drive enclosures. "Surprised it didn't burn with the building."

"It was in the trunk of my car," said Mac, taking the box. There was someone in the alley, he was sure of it.

"What?" said Tom, catching Mac's expression.

A second later, a man in a ski mask ran out of the alley.

He was wearing a dirty coverall that looked like something an HVAC technician would wear, though the name patch had been torn off. Gloves covered his hands, and in addition to the ski mask, he had a scarf tied around the lower half of his face. In his right hand was a small, stubby revolver. Probably a Smith & Wesson .38, but it was too dark to tell for sure. The man came to a stop at the curb, pointed the pistol at Tom, and then looked at Mac. He wasn't sure, but Mac thought the man was surprised.

"Hey," said Tom, his voice calm. "Let's talk about this."

His eyes flicked to Mac, who read the intention in his brother's face.

"Give me the drugs, man!" screamed the gunman, his voice shrill. "Give me the drugs! You gotta give me the drugs! Give me the goddamn drugs, man!"

"We don't have any drugs," said Mac. "We...Jesus Christ!" He made his eyes go wide.

It was a simple trick, but it worked.

The gunman glanced towards the river, and as he did, Mac reached into the box, grabbed one of the metal drive enclosures, and threw it as hard as he could as Tom stepped to the side. Mac's aim was good, and the heavy enclosure hit the gunman in the face. His head snapped back, and Tom moved in a blur that belied his height and size. He seized the gunman's wrist and smashed his hand against the bumper of the truck. The revolver clattered against the street, and Tom pumped his other fist into the gunman's stomach. Mac heard the breath explode from the would-be mugger's lungs, and he dropped the box and ran forward to help his brother.

The mugger reacted with surprising speed, sprinting into the alley as fast as his legs would carry him. Tom took a long step forward, but Mac caught his arm.

"Wait," he said. "The alley leads down to the riverbank and the train tracks. There are no damned lights down there. We'll wander in circles, or he'll get the drop on us."

"Yeah. You're right," said Tom. He looked at the revolver lying on the street. "Hell. What was all that about?"

"A mugging, I guess," said Mac.

They stood in silence for a moment, but the street remained deserted, and no one else appeared. A few cars went past, but nothing else happened.

"We can't leave that gun lying there," said Tom.

"No."

"Do you want to call it in?" said Tom.

Mac's initial impulse was to say no. He had enough negative experiences with law enforcement that his default was to avoid calling the police whenever possible. But as the adrenaline subsided and his brain started working, he realized that was a bad idea. He and Tom had almost gotten mugged for drug money, and neither of them looked like easy targets, especially Tom. If a junkie was desperate enough to attack random people on the street, his next target might not be able to fight back so effectively.

"Yeah," said Mac with a sigh. "Yeah, I suppose we better. That guy's probably going to hurt someone."

He dug out his cell phone and called 911.

SPEAKING with the police proved time-consuming, though less troublesome than Mac had feared.

A uniformed Wauwatosa police officer showed up about five minutes after the call, sealed off the street, and took initial statements from Mac and Tom. Twenty minutes after that, a detective named Scott Armstrong interviewed them separately. Armstrong was black, middle-aged, a bit paunchy, and had a mustache so dense it looked as if it could have been used as a wire brush. Mac had been interviewed by police officers many times, so he knew what to expect.

"You didn't recognize him?" said Armstrong.

"No," said Mac. "Couldn't see anything with the ski mask and the scarf. Didn't recognize his voice, either."

"How did he sound?" said Armstrong. They sat in the front of Armstrong's car, the detective dutifully entering notes into his dashboard laptop. Mac hoped that one day Armstrong would be using RVW Software's products for his reports. "White? Black? Hispanic?"

"Black," said Mac. "Except…"

He thought about it. Armstrong waited.

"It was like he was trying to sound black and not doing a very good job of it," said Mac.

"Like a white guy trying to sound ghetto," said Armstrong.

"Yeah," said Mac. "I don't know what race he was, though. Couldn't see any skin."

Armstrong nodded. "Your brother said the same thing. Is there anyone who might wish you harm, Mr. Rogan?"

Mac blew out a breath. "Well, there are people sympathetic to an eco-terrorist group that burned down my apartment this summer. I was present when a US Senator was assassinated, and a lot of conspiracy people on the Internet think the CIA or the Mossad was involved or something. I've worked as a private investigator for years, and that rubbed some people the wrong way."

Armstrong stared at him for a moment and then grunted. "That's a lot of enemies for a man your age."

Mac shrugged. "How many people have you ticked off while you've been a detective?"

"Fair point," said Armstrong. He sighed and leaned back in his seat. "You and your brother handled yourselves well. We already checked the gun for prints and got nothing."

"He had gloves on," said Mac.

"And he was smart enough to wipe down the gun first," said Armstrong. "Junkies usually don't think that clearly, especially the ones who get desperate enough to start robbing people. But that's probably what happened. We'll run some more patrols through the area and hope we catch the guy before he hurts someone."

With that, the interview was over. Armstrong gave Mac a card with his number, telling him to call if he remembered anything else, and Mac got out of the car. The police were packing up and heading on to the next crisis of the night.

Mac walked to join Tom, who leaned against the side of his truck as he watched the officers leave.

"You okay?" said Mac.

"What? Yeah, I'm fine," said Tom. "Suppose we got lucky. That idiot didn't keep the gun on us. Wonder if Armstrong was right, and it was some junkie who had never robbed anyone before."

"Maybe he was confused," said Mac. "He kept shouting about the drugs. We don't have any."

"Weird coincidence, though, isn't it?" said Tom.

"What?" said Mac.

"You start investigating a suicide and that guy who fell down the stairs," said Tom, "and then someone shows up to rob us."

"Yeah," said Mac. "Weird coincidence." He looked up and down the street. "You're the only one parked here. So either it was a target of opportunity, or someone was specifically looking for us."

"Or you," said Tom.

"Maybe," said Mac. "Or you. Did you piss anyone off lately?"

Tom snorted. "I work with some assholes, but they would punch me in the face, not put on a ski mask and jump me in an alley." He grunted. "You're the one with the long list of enemies."

He was right about that. Yet Mac couldn't shake the impression that the would-be mugger had been looking for Tom specifically and had been surprised to see Mac. He remembered their speculation that someone had killed Winston Marsh, took his gun, and then staged Doug Norton's suicide with it. Assuming that theory wasn't a total delusion, it would take someone with nerves of steel to pull that off. Not the jittery, shouting man who had emerged from the alley.

"I've ticked off a lot of people," said Mac. "But I'm parked four blocks away. I only walked to your truck because you mentioned that box of old drives at the last minute. If this wasn't random, if this wasn't some random crackhead, the guy was here looking for you."

"You've got an idea," said Tom.

Mac took a deep breath. "Remember when you said that someone might have targeted Doug Norton to get at Julie?"

They thought about that in silence for a moment.

"Kind of a big jump," said Tom after a while. "All that based off a suicide and an accidental death." He frowned. "But..."

"But it's a hell of coincidence," said Mac. "And...oh, man."

"What?" said Tom, looking around.

"I just thought of something else," said Mac. "The Northwoods school shooting. The first kid who was shot and killed was Joshua Chartwell. His mother was Clarissa Chartwell, who used to work for Morgan Properties. She quit the company soon after and moved away."

"So you think that the Northwoods shooter might have also killed Doug Norton and Winston Marsh?" said Tom. He paused to cough. He had spoken a lot of words tonight, but more than he had been able to manage a few years ago. "That's definitely a stretch."

"Still," said Mac. "Hell of a coincidence, though."

"Trouble with digging, isn't it?" said Tom. "Might dig up something you don't want to find." He shrugged. "Still. The guy who attacked us? No way he did all that. Too nervous. Too jittery."

"Maybe someone hired him for it," said Mac. "You watch your back, okay?"

"Same," said Tom. "Want a lift back to your car?"

"That's probably a good idea," said Mac, and they turned towards the truck.

"Hell of an interesting dinner, wasn't it?" said Tom.

"That it was," said Mac, and he got into the truck. "But let's skip the attempted robbery next week."

"No argument there."

Tom drove Mac to where the Corsica was parked. For once, the caution was unnecessary. His car was undisturbed, the sidewalk around it deserted. Tom drove off, and Mac dropped the box of drives into his trunk, started the car, and drove for home.

He thought about the would-be mugging. Like Tom said, it had probably been an attempted robbery, a junkie acting irrationally to find enough money for his next fix.

Just as Douglas Norton's death had probably been a suicide.

And Winston Marsh's death had probably been an accident.

And the Northwoods school shooting had probably been another senseless act of meaningless violence.

Whose perpetrator had never been caught, and probably never would be caught.

A lot of coincidences, all of them seemingly unconnected.

But Mac thought about what Tom had said.

What if Douglas Norton had been targeted because he was married to Julie? What if Winston Marsh had been killed because he used to work for Crest Development? What if the mugger had been waiting for Tom because Mac had been investigating Doug's death?

Mac headed for home, intending to do some research before he went to bed.

17

CUTTING LOSSES

Arianna drove across Milwaukee in an absolute fury.

It was past midnight, the streets mostly empty. Despite her rage, Arianna kept her speed a few miles below the limit.

Given the number of guns she was carrying, she didn't want to get pulled over.

She drove the blue 97 Ford Taurus she had used to watch Cormac Rogan's apartment, and she wore a loose boiler suit, boots, and a baseball cap, under which her hair was secured beneath a mesh net. Thin leather gloves covered her hands, and she had more plastic gloves secreted in her pockets.

The night could very well end with her having to kill someone, and she didn't want to leave behind any evidence.

Arianna seethed as he drove, her fingers all but sinking into the steering wheel.

How the hell could Rod Cutler have been so damned stupid?

She knew he was an idiot – a smart man would not have been enslaved to a lust for prostitutes as he had – but nonetheless, he was cunning and capable when carrying out her instructions. He had never screwed up this badly before.

What the hell had he been thinking? Arianna's instructions had been clear. Wait until Thomas Rogan was alone. Shoot him to wound or to kill, either was fine. Make it look like a robbery or a drug deal gone awry. It should have worked. Yet for some reason Cormac had walked with his brother to the truck. Rod should have withdrawn, waited for a better opportunity. Or maybe he had been ambitious and thought he could eliminate both Rogan brothers at once, no doubt angling to get more money out of her in the process.

He had screwed it up.

Badly enough that it might be time to cut her losses with him.

Arianna had two guns with her. Once was a small revolver that fit into the loose pocket of her boiler suit. The second was larger and heavier, a .38 semiautomatic wrapped in plastic. Arianna had used that gun the day she had recruited Rod by killing the pimp who had been beating him to within an inch of his life. She had been wearing gloves at the time and had gotten a dazed Rod's fingerprints on the weapon.

Rod Cutler had been useful, but he knew too much about her, and as enslaved as he was to his vices, he remained cunning. Arianna had instilled considerable fear in him, but if he found a way to save himself by betraying her, he wouldn't hesitate to do it.

Perhaps it was time to rid herself of that liability.

To tie up that loose end.

And maybe she ought to abandon her plan for Halloween. Complications were a bad thing. When she had done her research on Cormac Rogan and his brother, Arianna had realized that he was both lucky and smart. The luck had just been proven by Rod's failed attempt on Thomas Rogan. The intelligence would follow next, and if Cormac started thinking, if he realized that seeing her at Becker's so close to Rod's blunder was not a coincidence...

Arianna knew that Rogan couldn't prove anything. No one had ever linked her to the Northwoods shooting, or Doug Norton's death, or Winston Marsh's, or any of the other various distractions she had arranged for her competitors over the years. Rogan wasn't about to find any proof linking her to any of those deaths because she had been careful not to leave any evidence behind, and certainly not evidence that would hold up in court.

Especially with the caliber of defense lawyers she could afford.

But if Rogan became suspicious of her, a lot of things could go wrong.

Her fingers ached, and she made herself relax her grip on the wheel. Part of her mind focused on staying below the speed limit while the rest of it considered the problem. There were other ways she could kill Charlie Morgan and throw Angela Morgan's attention off work. But repeating the Northwoods massacre was Arianna's best hope of seizing the Westview Mall deal. The resultant media feeding frenzy would focus on the high school, allowing Arianna to negotiate with the owners of the land. The Drummond cousins had struck her as stupid and venal, and while they might have a modicum of sympathy for Angela's bereavement, that wouldn't keep them from selling the land to Arianna for millions of dollars.

And what a risk repeating the shooting would be…

Arianna shoved aside the electric feeling of excitement at the risk. She could decide how to deal with the problem of Cormac Rogan later.

Right now, she needed to decide if the problem of Rod Cutler merited a permanent solution.

She parked a few blocks from Rod's apartment building and shut off the engine. Arianna hadn't decided if she was going to kill him, but if it proved necessary, she didn't want anyone to remember her walking from her car to the building. Still, it was unlikely that anyone would recognize her or even realize that she was a woman. The boiler suit concealed her figure, and her hair was tied up under the baseball cap.

The street was both dark and deserted, and Arianna walked to the front door of Rod's building. The lock had been broken long ago, and Arianna entered the lobby, climbed the stairs to Rod's unit, and knocked on the door. She stepped a little to the side, out of the field of vision of the peephole. Rod might be waiting on the other side with a shotgun, and she didn't want to give him a clear shot.

"Who is it?" came Rod's voice through the thin door.

"I have your payment," said Arianna.

There was a long pause. Arianna heard multiple chains rattle and deadbolts slide back. Finally. Rod opened the door a crack, giving her a wary look.

He had a black eye, she noted.

"Are you here to kill me?" said Rod.

"For God's sake," said Arianna. She didn't need to feign her exasperation with him. "I have your payment. And we're going to talk about what happens next."

"Okay," said Rod, and he opened the door. He was wearing boxer shorts and a ragged black t-shirt, which made him look even spindlier and less appealing. No wonder he had to hire women for companionship. He stepped aside, and Arianna walked into his living room, making sure that she didn't turn her back to him.

Rod's living room was as dismal as he was. A sagging couch faced a large TV with a DVD player and a game console. Posters of naked women had been affixed to the walls. Pizza boxes and fast-food cartons covered the coffee table in front of the couch. The dining room served as a workshop, holding several tool chests and a worktable with equipment. That, at least, was organized and tidy.

The smell was dismal.

If she shot him right now, Arianna wondered how long it would take before someone discovered the body. Probably until someone got around to complaining about the smell or the landlord came to evict him for missing rent. Then again, the place stank now, and no one had complained yet.

Rod closed the door, and Arianna passed him an envelope. "Your money."

He hesitated, and then took the envelope as if afraid of it. Maybe he thought it would explode or she had coated it in poison or something. "You're still going to pay me?"

"Have I ever not paid you?" said Arianna.

"No." Rod set the envelope on the cluttered end table next to his couch. "But, things...well, I..."

"Screwed the pooch?" said Arianna with false cheeriness. "You sure did. Better stick to underage hookers, you're better at it."

"I didn't know!" said Rod, that familiar whine entering his voice. "There was just supposed to be one guy there. You said there would be one guy…"

Arianna looked at him. Rod shut up.

"What happened?" said Arianna.

"Thomas Rogan parked on a side street," said Rod. "It was perfect. He would be alone, and I could ambush him. I was going to shoot him in the gut a few times. You had said that it would be better to hurt him instead of killing him." Arianna nodded. "But Cormac Rogan was there. I didn't know what to do."

"Why didn't you wait?" said Arianna, hiding her irritation. "Follow Thomas and shoot him when he was alone?"

Rod shifted. "Well…I needed the money." Arianna's breath hissed through her teeth. "And they didn't have guns, either one of them. And I figured that you wouldn't mind if Cormac got killed in the process." That was true enough, assuming that the deaths could not be traced back to Arianna. "I pretended to be a junkie. I figured I would shoot both of them and run for it. But Thomas…he was so damned fast. He hit me in the face and the stomach, and I barely got away." A whine entered his voice. "I think he broke my nose."

"You lost the gun?" said Arianna.

"Yeah, but don't worry, I didn't leave any fingerprints on it, I'm not stupid," said Rod. Arianna withheld comment on that topic. "It was an old piece of shit revolver that I bought in a bar. It wasn't accurate past twenty feet anyway."

"If you're wrong," said Arianna, "if you left a fingerprint on that gun…"

"I didn't!" insisted Rod. "And if I did, the cops would have been here by now. My prints have been in the system for years. You know what they're like. If there had been any prints, they would have shown up at my door for a little chat about it."

He was right about that.

"All right," said Arianna. "What's done is done."

"You're not mad?" said Rod, his voice almost plaintive.

In point of fact, she was furious.

She had sent Rod to eliminate a potential problem, and instead, he had created new ones. Her mind clicked into a decision. Arianna was going to kill Rod, right here and now. After he was dead, she would leave behind the gun she had used the day she had met him, and the police could draw their own conclusions. No one had ever come close to figuring out that she had been the one who had killed the pimp who had been beating up Rod, and she would misdirect the investigation onto Rod himself.

Being dead, he would be unable to testify.

Arianna drew breath, intending to ask Rod to get a glass of water. When he turned, she would shoot him in the back of the head.

Then her eyes fell on a brochure lying on the coffee table. It advertised the services of Deluxe Storage in Menomonee Falls.

Which was one of Arianna's companies. Crest Development wasn't the only business she owned, it was just the biggest. Deluxe Storage was a higher-end establishment with climate-controlled storage units. Since Arianna used Crest Development's HVAC technicians to maintain the equipment (all perfectly legal, since one company paid the other and reported the expenditures and incomes on their tax filings), Deluxe Storage turned an unspectacular but nonetheless solid profit every year.

A stray memory clicked.

Before Cormac Rogan had called, Arianna hadn't thought about Doug Norton in years, not since his death had failed to derail the real estate deal that Arianna had wanted to steal. But Doug and Julie Norton had rented a mid-sized unit at Deluxe Storage for years. Arianna had come across that fact while contemplating how best to kill Doug.

Did Julie still have that storage unit?

All at once a marvelous idea blazed to life in her head.

She could solve the problem of Cormac Rogan and throw Morgan Properties into disarray all at the same time.

"Arianna?" said Rod, watching her like she was a bomb about to go off. She had been silent for too long.

"No, I'm not angry," said Arianna. She shrugged and offered him a smile. "Sometimes you just have bad luck. Don't worry. You'll have the chance to earn some more money soon. Keep your phone on."

With that, she turned, left the apartment, and headed back to her car.

It was almost one in the morning by the time she had gotten back to her house, but she was too excited to sleep, the idea like fire in her mind. It felt almost as good as taking a risk, though if she planned it properly, she would be in no danger whatsoever. Arianna went to her basement workshop, booted up her laptop, and logged remotely into Deluxe Storage's management software. The company used a web-based client to manage and assign storage units, and Arianna had her own logon for when she wanted to oversee things.

She scrolled through the listings and smiled.

Yes. There. Doug and Julie Norton had first started renting storage unit 97 in 2002, and Julie paid for it every month. In fact, Doug's name was still on it. Likely Julie had never gotten around to taking his name off the record, or it had simply slipped her mind in all the stress after Doug's death.

Smiling, Arianna rose and crossed to the basement's corner. She found the hidden latch in the floor and opened it, revealing a metal safe door set into the concrete. Arianna entered the combination and opened it. Inside the safe were several stacks of banded hundred-dollar bills, some jewels, and a few certificates.

And several guns wrapped in plastic.

Her father's stories about his time as a prison guard came to her mind. Arianna knew it was a risk keeping any of the weapons she had used for her previous distractions, but she had kept the gun she had used to murder the pimp, intending to lay the blame on Rod himself once it was time to get rid of him.

She had also kept the AR-15 she had used for the Northwoods shooting.

That was much more dangerous. If she was ever caught with the weapon and it was linked to the shooting, that would be the end. There would be no way she could save herself. Keeping the weapon had been a constant risk, but there was a potential payoff.

If Arianna managed it right, she could pin the blame for the shooting on anyone she wanted.

Like Doug Norton.

Imagine what would happen if the weapon from the shooting was found in his storage locker. It would create the perfect news story. People would believe that Doug had been the shooter and that he had killed himself in shame or perhaps fear of discovery. That would set off another media firestorm, and in the middle of it, Arianna would kill a few students at the school's Halloween bonfire.

Including Charlie Morgan.

And as his mother's bereavement paralyzed Morgan Properties, Arianna would snatch up the Drummond cousins' land and make millions.

Now. How to arrange this all?

Smiling, she leaned back in her chair to think.

18

PATTERN RECOGNITION

Friday, October 26th, proved to be another cold and gray day. Mac got up at his usual time, worked out at Iron Oswald's, and came home and showered. A quick check of his email to make sure that Paul and Nikolai didn't have anything urgent for him to do with RVW Software, and he turned his attention to the idea that had occurred to him last night.

It was time to do some research.

Parker had first suggested it, and then Tom had said something similar. If Doug Norton hadn't committed suicide, what if he had been murdered not for his own sake, but to distract Julie? And what if the attack last night hadn't been a random junkie looking for a quick buck, but someone deliberately targeting Tom?

As far as Mac knew, Tom didn't have any enemies who would don a ski mask and lie in wait with a revolver. Nor did Tom have any enemies who would hire someone to attack him. But if the attack hadn't been random, then the masked man had been waiting for Tom. Mac and Tom had parked blocks apart. Which meant the attacker hadn't expected to see Mac.

It had only been sheer dumb luck that Mac had walked with Tom to the truck.

Well, that, and the box of external hard drives Mac had forgotten in Tom's apartment.

He turned in his computer chair and looked at the box, which he had set down against the wall before going to sleep. Maybe that could be an advertisement for that brand of external drive enclosure. Use it to store important data and also bash assailants over the head in a pinch.

Given the trend of technology towards smaller and lighter, Mac somehow doubted it would catch on.

He unlocked his computer and started doing research.

John Rogan had been fond of saying that ninety percent of all investigative work was research, and Mac had found that to be accurate. On TV and the movies, detectives had brilliant flashes of intuitive insight, usually while talking to a friend about something unrelated. Real life, as always, was nothing like what you saw on TV. In an investigation of any kind, the truth was not found in brilliant bursts of insight but usually through the slow, plodding work of sorting through files and records.

Mac broke out a fresh legal pad and started writing things down as he conducted searches on his computer.

He started with the Northwoods High School shooting. According to the investigators' official timeline, the first victim of the shooting had been Joshua Chartwell, who had been standing on the front steps of the school. His mother had been Clarissa Chartwell, the best agent for Morgan Properties, and she had resigned in grief and moved away. Had she been working on something big for her employer before the murder?

March sorted through online property records and press releases. It was amazing how much stuff was available online now, more than most people knew or would have been comfortable knowing. He sorted through the records and found that Clarissa had been involved in several large deals that had fallen apart in the aftermath of the shooting. Some of those deals had gone to out-of-state companies.

One, the biggest of them, had gone to Crest Development.

Disturbed, Mac searched for press releases and land title transfers around January 2006, not long after Doug's death. He found a press release from March 2006 for a condo development, and in the press release, Angela Morgan praised the work of her team, including Julie Norton, who had "persevered under difficult circumstances."

Okay, that put a dent in his theory. Julie had been working on that condo development at the start of 2006, and then Doug had been killed. It would have been reasonable to expect Julie to withdraw from the process, but she had kept going. She had struck Mac as a tough-minded woman. More to the point, with her husband's death, she was the sole support for her children, and perhaps she felt compelled to continue working even if she would have rather not.

On the other hand, if Doug had been murdered and hadn't committed suicide, maybe his killer had expected Julie to collapse.

Who would have benefited from Julie withdrawing from the negotiations?

Mac went back to the press release and scrolled through it. The document noted that the project had taken bids from several "high-profile" local developers and listed off numerous companies.

Including Crest Development.

Mac went to Crest Development's page, pulling up Arianna's bio and picture. Her cold clear eyes stared at him from the screen, her smile a white slash across her face. She looked nothing like his mother, but something about her reminded him of Monica Rogan, who had murdered his father and tried ineptly to cast the blame upon Mac.

Monica, in the end, hadn't been nearly as smart as she believed herself.

What if Arianna was smarter?

Mac already knew she was intelligent and ruthless. What if she had been engineering deaths, timing them to give her an advantage in her business deals? The thought seemed preposterous. Everyone who knew Arianna said that she was a barracuda, but there was a long distance between a real estate shark and a school shooter. It seemed like a wild conspiracy theory.

Yet it was a hell of a coincidence that someone had been waiting to attack Tom just after Mac had started investigating Doug Norton's death. And that Arianna had been at Becker's at the same time. And that Joshua Chartwell had been shot while his mother had been working on a big deal for Morgan Properties. Or that Doug Norton had killed himself. Or that Winston Marsh had tripped and fallen down the stairs and cracked his skull.

A big old cluster of coincidences.

Maybe Mac was imagining things, or maybe he was finding patterns.

More research would help clarify things.

Mac spent the rest of the morning researching, and by noon he had a headache and a growing sense of unease.

A lot of misfortunes seemed to befall the relatives of potential business rivals to Crest Development.

Mac read about unsolved shootings, car accidents, and in one instance, a home that exploded due to a faulty gas line. It took some work to dig out the pattern, but it was definitely there. The families of people who competed with Crest Development tended to run into more than their fair share of bad luck.

Mac stared at the screen. He knew he wasn't stupid, but he couldn't possibly be this smart. How was it possible that no one had seen this pattern before?

Was it because the unsolved shootings and other tragedies were always one step removed from the rivals of Crest Development? If Julie Norton had been shot, that would be one thing. But her husband had killed himself. Clarissa Chartwell hadn't been murdered, her son had. Mac saw a similar pattern in his findings – spouses and parents and children who suffered misfortunes, distracting their relatives from work.

Work that always competed with Crest Development.

Mac leaned back in his chair, got up, and paced in a circuit through his apartment, trying to think.

He didn't know what to do next.

Was Arianna Crest some sort of calculating mass killer? It seemed preposterous. For that matter, Mac had absolutely no proof, only a long chain of disturbing coincidences. If his suspicion was right, he needed proof before he could act upon it.

An even more unsettling thought occurred to him.

Had his interview with Arianna prompted the failed ambush at Tom's truck?

That would fit the pattern of the other misfortunes he had uncovered. Mac hadn't been targeted. Tom had. It had only been sheer luck that Mac had been at Tom's truck during the attack. And what would have happened if Tom had been shot, maybe killed? It definitely would have taken Mac's time and attention away from the investigation into Doug Norton's death. Depending on how things played out, maybe Mac would have dropped the case entirely.

Which perhaps was what Arianna had wanted.

Mac stopped at the dining room window and looked into the parking lot, seeing the usual collection of older cars owned by the apartment complex's residents.

Did he expect to see someone lurking by the door, waiting to shoot him?

"Jesus," muttered Mac. He was getting paranoid.

Then again, if he was right, if Arianna Crest had somehow been orchestrating murders and accidents, Mac had every reason to be paranoid.

What to do next? Telling Julie Norton was out of the question. Mac had no idea how she would react. If Julie confronted Arianna or went to the police, that would end with Arianna unleashing her lawyers upon everyone in sight. Mac had barely recovered from his legal expenses over the summer, and he couldn't afford to hire Paul to defend him again.

There was no hard evidence. Only a disturbing number of coincidences and a chain of logic, and while the theory made sense, it could easily be a product of Mac's imagination. Had Arianna Crest killed Winston Marsh, stolen his gun, killed Douglas Norton, and somehow made it look like a suicide? Had she committed the Northwoods High School shooting and managed to escape?

Kristin Salwell. That had been the last thing Doug had written.

Maybe Arianna had disguised herself as Salwell and walked into the high school to shoot Doug? No, that was ridiculous. Salwell had been in prison at the time, which would have made her identity a poor disguise. For that matter, Arianna was shorter and thinner than Salwell. In spy movies, Tom Cruise could don a rubber mask to impersonate someone, but the real world did not work that way.

Mac needed proof. And if he was right, and if Arianna was a skilled killer, trying to find proof might be lethally dangerous.

In the bedroom, his cell phone rang.

Mac jumped, felt like an idiot, and hurried back to his bedroom. He had left his cell phone next to his computer keyboard. The number on the screen looked familiar, likely one that he had written down during his investigations over the last few days.

He flipped the phone open and lifted it to his ear.

"Hello?"

"Mr. Rogan?" It was a man's voice, a bit wheezy and out of breath.

"Yeah, that's me," said Mac.

"This is Parker McIntyre. You know, Maggie McIntyre's son? We talked the other day about the high school and a bunch of other stuff."

"That's right," said Mac. "How'd the guild raid go?"

"What? Oh, good, good," said Parker. He sounded distracted. "I kind of have to ask you something, Mr. Rogan."

"What's that?" said Mac.

"Am I suffering from paranoid delusions?"

Mac paused, trying to recall the name of Parker's therapist. "I suppose that would be a question for Dr. Random, not for me."

There was a second of silence, and then Parker's bray of a laugh filled Mac's ear. "Yeah, that's true. But after we had our talk, I couldn't stop thinking about some of the things we mentioned."

"Which things?"

"I made a joke about how maybe the shooting was to cover something else up," said Parker.

Mac felt a chill. "I remember."

"I started thinking about it," said Parker. "During the shooting, the first one to be shot was Josh Chartwell, right? He was a good guy. I mean, he was a football player and popular and all that, but he wasn't an asshole about it, you know? Can't think of why anyone would want to kill him."

"It might have been a random shooting," said Mac. "Your mom told me she thought it was domestic terrorism."

"But what if it wasn't?" said Parker. "What if somebody shot Josh to mess his mom up and everything else that happened was…like, what's the word…camouflage?" Mac's own thoughts had been moving in that direction. "Like, Josh's mom quit working for Angela Morgan right after that. What if that was the reason why he was killed?"

"It's possible," said Mac, "but there's no proof."

Parker kept talking. "Mom talks to me about her business a lot, you know? Says it's educational. And she would tell me when things go wrong. A lot of people working for Morgan Properties have had things go wrong. Unsolved murders and car accidents and all that. I started looking at records, and I have a list…"

"Wait, wait, wait," said Mac. "A list?"

"Yeah. You said you were looking at why Mr. Norton killed himself, right?" said Parker. "But Mrs. Norton worked for Angela Morgan. Still does, I think. I looked up some of my mom's real estate records…"

"You did what?" said Mac.

"She keeps telling me to take an interest in something," said Parker. "Anyway, Mrs. Norton was working on a big deal when Mr. Norton got shot. The deal almost fell apart, but Mrs. Norton finished it, and Morgan Properties got the contract. I said I made a list, right? I remembered some of the stuff Mom told me about work, so I went back and looked it up. There's been a lot of bad luck around Milwaukee real estate."

"Yeah," said Mac, and Parker kept talking.

"Like, unsolved shootings, car accidents, fires, that kind of thing," said Parker. "Like someone keeps trying to sabotage deals for Morgan Properties."

"Funny you should mention that," said Mac. "Last night, my

brother and I went to dinner. After we finished, someone was waiting by his truck with a gun."

"Holy crap!" said Parker. "Did he get shot?"

"No, he's fine," said Mac. "But it was a weird coincidence. I start looking into Doug Norton's suicide, and then someone shows up to attack my brother."

There was a pause.

"If my research is right," said Parker, "then that kind of thing has happened a whole lot. I want to show you my list, Mr. Rogan, and see what you think."

Mac hesitated. He didn't want to get Parker involved in this, but it wasn't hard to see why Parker had started researching. The Northwoods shooting had ripped apart his life, and his best friend had committed suicide over it. Parker had never known why it had happened. The prospect of an answer, of ultimate closure, no matter how remote, would have been irresistible.

But if the same person was behind Doug Norton's death and the Northwoods school shooting and all the other crimes that Mac had discovered during the morning's research, then whoever was responsible would definitely not hesitate to kill Parker if he knew too much.

Mac remembered Arianna's cold, unblinking eyes and wondered.

"Okay," said Mac. "You can show me. But don't tell anyone. This kind of thing might be dangerous to know."

"Yeah," said Parker. "You had lunch yet?"

"No."

"Do you want to meet at the McDonald's on Moorland Road in Brookfield?" said Parker. "I'm starving."

"Fine," said Mac. "I'll meet you there in an hour."

He ended the call and stared at his computer screen for a moment. Talking to Parker about this was probably a bad idea. Yet if Mac had reasoned out the strange pattern around Morgan Properties, other people might. Parker certainly could – despite his eccentricity, he most certainly wasn't stupid. And if he pushed too hard or asked questions of the wrong person, Maggie McIntyre might lose her only son after all.

On the other hand, Parker was a legal adult, and Mac couldn't tell him what to do. Maybe Mac could convince him to stop poking around. Though Mac had the suspicion that Parker tended to do what he wanted unless his mother put her foot down. She hadn't been happy that Parker had been near Northwoods High School, but he had gone to look at the half-wrecked house anyway.

Mac sighed, collected his notes and his laptop bag, and set off for Brookfield.

He arrived at the McDonald's on Moorland Road about twenty minutes later. It sat across the street from the Brookfield mall. The McDonald's lot was mostly full, and Mac parked and went inside. A lunchtime crowd filled the restaurant, a combination of workers on their lunch breaks and harried mothers trying to keep their toddlers from flinging their food to the floor.

Parker sat in a two-person booth along the back wall, and he waved when he saw Mac. He had a tray in front of him holding two orders of large fries, a couple of burgers, and a box of chicken nuggets. Mac really hoped Parker wasn't planning to eat the whole thing in one sitting.

"Hey, man," said Parker. "Thanks for coming."

"No problem," said Mac, sitting across from Parker. "I wouldn't give people my card if I didn't want them to call me with new information."

"Well," said Parker. "I thought I was going crazy, you know?" He took a big handful of fries, chewed, and swallowed. "But I couldn't get it out of my head. Like, Josh Chartwell was the kid of someone who worked for Morgan Properties, and he was the first one to get shot. Mr. Norton was married to someone who works for Morgan Properties, and he shot himself. And then you told me that someone tried to shoot your brother? You started looking at all this, and then someone tries to kill your brother? That is a freaky weird coincidence." He reached for a nugget and paused. "Wait, he's okay, right? I sometimes forget to ask stuff like that."

"Oh, yeah, he's fine," said Mac. "Tom was in Iraq until a few years ago, knows how to handle himself. You said you had a list of suspicious incidents?"

Parker nodded, wiped off his hands on a paper napkin, and reached for the laptop bag on the seat next to him. He pulled out a small bundle of printed pages and handed them over to Mac. "Here you go. I thought about writing it down but figured Mom wouldn't mind if I used her laser printer."

"Where is she today?" said Mac, scanning the information. He half-expected Maggie McIntyre to storm through the door in a rage.

"Visiting some of her businesses," said Parker. "I forget which one. I think it does grocery distribution or something. What do you think of this stuff?"

"Give me a minute to read it," said Mac. Parker grunted and started eating more fries.

Whatever else could be said about Parker, Mac thought, he had a knack for research. He hadn't uncovered as many suspicious incidents as Mac had, but he had come close.

"Where did you find this?" said Mac.

"Some of Mom's records," said Parker. "She has access to this land title database that records commercial real estate transactions. And most of the rest of it is floating around the Internet." He shrugged. "People would probably be horrified if they knew how much you could find on the Internet."

"They would be if they weren't posting pictures of themselves and their kids and their breakfasts and every other damned thing they do," said Mac. He handed the papers back to Parker. "All right. You found all this stuff. What do you think of it?"

"Well," said Parker. "It's really suspicious, isn't it? It looks like a pattern. I'm not sure if I'm making it all up in my head..."

"No," said Mac. "No, you're not. It is a pattern. We both noticed it separately. Each incident doesn't stand out on its own. Most of them are accidents – like that county supervisor's wife who was killed in a car accident when her brakes failed – but they all add up."

"Why didn't the police see it?" said Parker. "No, I know why the police didn't see it. The cops couldn't see a bonfire right in front of them. They thought Ryan and I did the shooting. But why didn't someone notice this? Like the insurance companies or something?"

"It's too random," said Mac. "If someone gets murdered over a business deal, their rivals are an obvious suspect. But if that same person's spouse is killed? That's a different kind of investigation. And if we're right, if there is a pattern, it works too well for anyone to realize what's going on."

"What does that mean?" said Parker.

"If my brother had gotten shot," said Mac, "then we wouldn't be talking right now." It also would have been a cruel repetition. Tom had gotten blasted full of shrapnel in Iraq, only to come home and get shot. "I'd probably be at the hospital or getting interviewed by the police. I wouldn't be thinking or talking about this pattern."

"What does it mean, though?" said Parker. "Is someone at Crest Development going around and killing people?"

Mac thought of Arianna's cold eyes, of how something in them had reminded him of his mother. "I don't know."

"We should tell someone," said Parker. "Maybe I should ask my mom..."

"No, don't," said Mac at once.

"Why not?"

"For one thing, we have absolutely no proof," said Mac. "No hard evidence. Just logic and speculation, and those don't stand up in court."

"So why shouldn't we tell my mom?" said Parker.

"If you tell your mom that you suspect Arianna Crest of orchestrating all of this," said Mac, "what will she do? Confront Crest? Hire investigators to dig around Crest's business? None of that will end well. Crest is famous for suing everyone in sight." And if their suspicions were correct, if Arianna really was responsible for Doug's death and God knows what else, then she might well react with violence.

That masked man had been waiting by Tom's truck after Mac had spoken with her.

"I guess that makes sense," said Parker.

"It's the same reason I haven't told any of this to Julie Norton yet," said Mac. "If I tell her that it's somehow possible that Arianna Crest murdered her husband and made it look like a suicide, she'll do one of two things. She'll either laugh in my face and demand her money back, or she'll lose it and confront Arianna. The first outcome would be better, actually." Though he did need the money, which was how he had gotten into this mess. "Less chance of anyone getting killed."

"What are we going to do about it?" said Parker.

Mac's initial response was to say that there was no "we." Parker wasn't a private investigator, and he had no business getting wrapped up in this. But Mac knew anything he said would fail to make an impression. The Northwoods shooting had left too many scars on Parker. Mac had seen this need for answers, for closure, before. Parker would not stop until he had his answers.

Mac understood it himself. He had told himself several times that he was going to stop investigating, that he was only doing this because he needed the money.

But there were other ways to make money.

"Parker, listen to me," said Mac. "If you're going to do this, you need to be careful. Maybe we're seeing things that aren't there. But let's say we're right, and someone has been killing people and arranging accidents. If this person…"

"Arianna Crest," said Parker. He paused. "Or her boyfriend or something."

"If this person realizes that you're looking into his or her activities, they might come after you," said Mac.

Parker shrugged. "I'm not afraid. I want to know the truth."

"You might not be afraid for yourself, but what about your mom?" said Mac. That made Parker pause. "Someone tried to shoot my brother, but didn't come after me. Joshua Chartwell got shot, but not his mom. Doug Norton committed suicide or was killed, not Julie Norton. If there is a pattern, then the killer is going after the relatives of people who get in the way. Are you willing to take this risk?"

Parker thought about it and then let out a breath. "I gotta do this. But you're right, Mr. Rogan. We have to be careful. Can't tell anyone about it. So what are we going to do?"

"Find proof," said Mac. "And it has to be the kind of proof that will stand up in court. Maybe we're right, and Arianna Crest has killed a lot of people. She's gotten away with it so far, which means she's smart and cautious and plans ahead. We need to find proof that can survive her lawyers."

"Where will we find it?" said Parker.

"I don't know," said Mac. "But she's not infallible. No one is. Somewhere she made a mistake. I..."

His cell phone buzzed once in his pocket, followed by a chime.

"Hang on, I think I got a voicemail," said Mac.

"No, that's a text message, I think," said Parker.

"A text?" said Mac, annoyed. He had never really gotten into SMS text messaging. For one, it was too expensive, and the carriers liked to tack all kinds of extra charges onto text messages. For another, Mac had better things to do with his time than squint at his phone's keypad trying to figure out which number corresponded to which letter. If he had a Blackberry with a full keyboard, maybe it would have been a useful tool, but he couldn't afford a Blackberry. "I better not get charged for this." He flipped open the phone and scowled at the LCD display. "I..."

It was a text message from a number he didn't know.

"What?" said Parker, frowning. "What is it?"

The message was long enough that it had been broken into three parts, and Mac keyed through them. The message said:

"I know who killed the students at Northwoods High but I've been too afraid to tell anyone. I know it was Douglas Norton and then he killed himself in guilt. There is proof. Go to storage locker 97 at Deluxe Storage in M. Falls. He hid the weapon there."

Mac stared at the screen.

"What the hell?" he said at last.

"What is it?" said Parker again.

Mac shrugged and turned his phone towards Parker, whose face screwed up in confusion.

"That doesn't make any sense," said Parker.

"No," said Mac.

"Who uses good punctuation and spelling in text messages?" said Parker.

"Not a teenager," said Mac. Which meant that whoever had sent the message probably hadn't been a student. Then again, there was no reason a teenager couldn't use proper punctuation in a text message.

"Who sent that to you?" said Parker.

"I don't know," said Mac. "It could be anyone. I've been talking to a lot of people over the last week, and I gave out my card and phone number. But you're right, that doesn't make any sense at all. The Northwoods shooter was across the street. Doug Norton was inside the building with students. Multiple witnesses can place him. There's no way that he was the shooter."

"Yeah," said Parker. "So why did someone send you that message? Some sort of weird prank?"

"I don't know," said Mac.

But he could think of some explanations. Maybe someone did know a fact about the shooting and had contacted him anonymously. He would have to check, but he was reasonably sure the number the text message had come from would turn out to be a cell phone purchased anonymously at a drugstore or a gas station. Cell phones had gotten cheap, to the point where they had become almost disposable, and they were too easy to track. Mac had read about how smarter criminals and terrorists had begun using burner phones, disposing of cheap cell phones after two or three calls. Likely whoever had sent that message had done the same.

Maybe someone really did know useful information and had been too afraid to come forward.

Or maybe someone was trying to lure him into an ambush.

It was too much of a coincidence. Someone tried to attack Tom last night, and now this? If Mac had not already seen the pattern, he might have assumed the attack and the text message were unrelated.

"What are you going to do about it?" said Parker.

"I'm not sure," said Mac.

"Come on, you should really look into it," said Parker. "I mean, yeah, maybe someone's trying to lure you into an ambush, but that would kind of be a stupid way to do it."

"Why's that?" said Mac.

"A storage place like that is going to have a bunch of security cameras recording everything," said Parker. "Pretty dumb way to have an ambush. Hey, let's shoot a guy in front of twenty cameras. Great plan."

"That's a fair point," said Mac. There hadn't been any security cameras near Tom's truck last night. "All right. I'll take a look at it."

Parker nodded. "I should come with you."

"No."

Parker frowned. "Why not?"

Because you're just a kid, Mac wanted to say.

"One, you're not getting paid for this," said Mac. "Two, you don't have any experience with this kind of work. Three, if we get shot at, I don't want to have to explain this to your mother."

Parker snorted. "You're scared of my mom?"

"She's rich and knows a lot of lawyers."

"I have better reasons that I should come with you," said Parker. "One, a second pair of eyes would be good. Two eyewitnesses are better than one." That was true. "And if I don't come with you, I'll just call a taxi and go there anyway."

Mac blew out a sigh and glared out the window at the parking lot. He probably shouldn't have shown that text message to Parker. "Fine. But do what I tell you, understand?"

Parker bobbed his head. "I will, Mr. Rogan."

"Sure you will," said Mac. "Let's go."

Parker swept the rest of his food into a brown paper bag and followed Mac to the parking lot.

19

MISDIRECTION

"Where is this place, anyway?" said Parker, munching on his remaining fries as Mac pulled into traffic.

"Menomonee Falls," said Mac. "You can see it on the right side of I-41 when you head north." An image of a wide concrete yard with dozens of rows of storage lockers came to his mind. If he remembered right, it had been built five or six years ago, and he had driven past it numerous times during his jobs in the Milwaukee area.

Mac had never visited because he didn't own enough to need a storage locker, and anyway, he had lost most of his possessions when his previous apartment had burned down.

"Mom doesn't have a storage locker," said Parker. "She says that if you have enough stuff that you need one, then you've got too much stuff."

"There's some truth in that," said Mac.

This time of day, the fastest way to get from Brookfield to Menomonee Falls was to take I-94 east to the zoo interchange and then onto I-41. In another few hours, the traffic would be heavy, but for now, it was manageable.

"So, uh," said Parker, rummaging around his paper bag for more fries. "I have some questions."

"Thought you might," said Mac.

"I looked you up on the Internet," said Parker.

Mac sighed. "Of course you did."

"Hey, come on, don't be like that," said Parker. "A private investigator shows up and starts asking questions about the worst couple of weeks of your life, you get curious."

"That was by accident," said Mac. "I didn't know you were going to be at Northwoods High School when I walked by."

"But to be fair, that makes a guy curious, you know?" said Parker. "I did a bunch of research on you before I started looking up the pattern. You've kind of been involved with some big stuff, man. That church that almost blew up?"

"I remember, I was there," said Mac.

"And that Senator who got killed," said Parker. "Jack Kelsey? I remember seeing him on TV. I read this one blog…"

Mac sighed again. "Don't tell me that you read the blog that argues the entire thing was a plot by the CIA to trigger a war with Iran."

"What?" said Parker, taken aback. "How would it cause war with Iran?"

"Because a new Senator was appointed who might be more favorable to a war with…never mind," said Mac. "The theory doesn't make much sense. The simple truth is that Kelsey was a crook, he tried to manipulate an environmental terrorist group to get reelected, and it came back and bit him in the ass."

"I didn't read that blogger," said Parker. "But the one who's writing a book about the Kelsey case…um, Vanessa Portman, that's it…"

"Dear God," muttered Mac.

"Her site mentions that it will be available at all major bookstores in November," said Parker. "She also says that you refused to talk to her."

"Still do," said Mac. "I get an email from her every two weeks like clockwork. She must have put a reminder into her calendar."

"Why don't you talk to Portman?" said Parker. "Might be good for business, yeah? Maybe if you're right about the iPhone being a big deal then it will be good publicity for the company."

Paul was the one who thought the iPhone was going to be a big deal, as did Nikolai. Mac was mostly along for the ride.

"You never want to talk to a reporter for any reason," said Mac. "They've already decided the story they're going to write, and they want to twist your words to fit the role they have in mind for you to play. Talking to a reporter is like making rope and giving it to the hangman." He looked sidelong at Parker. "For God's sake, you should know this. For a couple of weeks, you had people thinking that you were a mass shooter. Your mom told me that you were hassled by reporters."

"Well, yeah, that sucked," said Parker. "But someone from the FBI leaked that I was the shooter, and if you can't believe the honest and hard-working FBI, then who can you believe?" The sarcasm by the end of the sentence was so thick that Mac would have needed a concrete saw to cut it. "But you could have gotten on TV."

"I was on TV, remember, testifying to Congress," said Mac. "That also sucked."

"I want to be on TV. Someday, when somebody figures out who the Northwoods shooter really was," said Parker, "I'm going to be on TV. And then I'll tell everyone who thought I was guilty that they're dumbasses and should be ashamed of how stupid they are."

"Won't make you feel better," said Mac.

"I know, I know," said Parker. "That's what Dr. Random says."

"The therapist with the nice tits," said Mac.

Parker snorted. "You said I shouldn't say that."

"You shouldn't," said Mac. "But she's not my therapist. And she's right." He concentrated on the freeway, waiting for an opportunity to pass a slow-moving truck. "Some things you have to let go, no matter how bitter they are."

Parker didn't say anything. Mac knew the blog that Parker had read and the book that was coming out about Kelsey's death. Vanessa Portman was even less scrupulous than usual for a journalist. She had written a long email suggesting that the reason Mac didn't want to talk to her was because of his experiences with his father's murder and his mother's incarceration. An edited version of that email had turned up on her website, speculating over the reasons Cormac Rogan refused to ever talk to the press.

He waited for Parker to mention it. Mac could all but see the connection in his brain, but Parker only grunted and ate a chicken nugget.

Huh. Maybe Parker had learned better social skills than his mother had thought.

"Guess that makes sense," said Parker at last. "There are still some people I wanna give a middle finger, you know? Wave it right in their faces."

"There are always going to be people like that," said Mac.

A short time later, Mac exited I-41, and Deluxe Storage came into sight.

The facility sat off the freeway in an area that had been a cornfield until a few years ago. The only other business nearby was a small strip mall that was mostly unoccupied, save for a car insurance office and a Subway. Deluxe Storage still looked new, the concrete slab of the parking lot free of cracks, the rows of storage lockers painted white with red metal doors and gleaming red steel roofs. A sign near the gate proclaimed that Deluxe Storage was a premier self-serve storage facility, with 24/7 security cameras and all-hours available access. Climate-controlled storage units were available for a modest fee.

Despite the claim to security, the gate was open, though the parking lot was deserted. Mac pulled the car to the spot nearest the office and shut off the engine. The front office was a small cinder block building. The blinds were drawn, and a sign on the front door said that office hours were between eight and noon on Mondays through Thursdays, with other options available on appointment. A phone & fax number were below the office hours.

Mac and Parker sat in silence, staring at the sign.

"Should we make an appointment?" said Parker.

"No," said Mac. "We're just going to have a look around. Come on."

He got out of the car. Parker heaved out with a grunt, the car rocking a little with the motion. The wind picked up, a few dead leaves skittering across the concrete. The overcast sky had gotten darker during the drive here, and Mac really hoped it wasn't about to rain.

"Don't you need a coat?" said Mac.

Parker blinked, then shrugged and slapped his belly. "Let's just say I don't get cold very easily. I look forward to winter all summer. I can finally stop sweating all the time."

"Right," said Mac. "Let's find unit 97."

ARIANNA LAY on her stomach atop a closed dumpster behind the strip mall, watching Cormac Rogan's car through the scope of her rifle.

From here, she had a perfect view of Deluxe Storage, and specifically, unit 97. Arianna owned the strip mall in addition to Deluxe Storage, and the mall so far had been a disappointment. Arianna was barely breaking even on it. Still, she expected more development here in the next few years.

And right now, it had paid off handsomely.

It made a perfect location to deal with Cormac Rogan.

She watched as Rogan emerged from the beat-up old Chevy Corsica, stark in his black coat and jeans. He really did make for a striking figure. It was almost a pity her plans hadn't required seducing him. But he was too clever and too persistent, and she needed to get him out of the way before the Halloween bonfire.

Arianna had expected the text message she had sent from the burner phone would lure him here.

She had not expected him to come with someone else.

For a moment, she did not recognize the heavyset man who emerged from the passenger side of Rogan's car. He was young and obese, with a bad haircut, a sweatshirt that Arianna could have used as a sleeping bag, loose shorts, and sandals. It wasn't Rogan's brother Tom, and it wasn't anyone else she knew…

No. Wait. Parker McIntyre, one of the two students the media had blamed for the Northwoods massacre. The FBI and the reporters had decided that Parker McIntyre and Ryan Walsh were the perpetrators, and Walsh had killed himself from the attention. Maggie McIntyre had put up a ferocious fight for her son and wound up winning several settlements from news organizations and a public apology from the FBI, which was like squeezing blood from a stone.

So what the hell was Parker doing with Rogan?

The crosshairs settled on Parker's head, and Arianna felt an impulse to pull the trigger. She could just imagine Maggie's grief and rage, and the thought delighted her, to say nothing of the glorious thrill of the risk…

No. Stop.

Think.

If Arianna killed Parker, she would have to kill Rogan. That would create all kinds of problems. The police would go over Rogan's recent activities with a fine-tooth comb. They would realize that Cormac's death and the failed mugging of Tom Rogan were connected, and they might stumble on connections Arianna wanted kept secret. And even if they did not, Maggie had the resources to hire a dozen private investigators for years.

That could be disastrous. At the very least, Arianna would have to abandon her plans for Charlie Morgan and Halloween.

No, misdirection was better. Killing would create too much attention. Best to keep to the original plan.

Arianna swung her scope around to point at storage unit 97 and waited.

MAC AND PARKER walked into the storage yard.

It was deserted, but it had been well-kept. There was no graffiti or litter. The rows of storage units were separated by lanes large enough to admit a truck, and mesh roofs had been stretched between them, strong enough to keep out rain and snow but not enough to block sunlight. At the end of the rows, numbers had been painted. It looked like units one through fifty had no climate control, but units fifty-one through one hundred did.

They came to the row holding unit 97. Number 97 was about halfway down the row, and at the far end, Mac saw the strip mall half-concealed behind bushes and high grasses.

"There it is," said Parker.

Mac took a step forward and paused.

"It's open," said Mac.

Each of the units had rolling metal doors, much like garage doors, and the door to unit 97 was half-open, pale electric light spilling into the aisle. Mac eased forward, peering inside the unit. Plastic totes had been stacked against one wall, and he saw several large pieces of furniture draped in sheets – a bed, an armoire, and a desk, and...

He was about twenty feet away when a man stepped from the storage unit. He wore a dirty HVAC uniform, a ski mask pulled over his head, a scarf wrapped around the lower half of his face.

There was a bloodstain around the collar of his uniform from where Tom had punched him last night, and instead of a crappy revolver he had a semiautomatic, a .38 Smith & Wesson, and the weapon was swinging in their direction.

"Shit!" said Mac, and he shoved Parker to the side.

"What?" said Parker, and the masked man fired.

Mac had acted in time. The two shots that would have hit Parker instead struck the concrete and bounced off, the ricochets whining in his ears. The gunman adjusted his aim, but by then, Mac was already moving. He closed and threw a punch that clipped the gunman's jaw. Mac needed to close and grapple, to get the pistol out of the masked man's hand, and he needed to keep the weapon from pointing at him or Parker...

His surprise was absolute when the gunman whirled and sprinted towards the strip mall.

"What?" said Parker again.

For a moment, Mac wanted to pursue, but reason reasserted itself. Running after an armed man in tall grass was a great way to get shot. Mac watched as the masked man scrambled over the fence and vanished into the bushes behind the strip mall.

"Did he just shoot at us?" said Parker.

"Yeah," said Mac, his brain getting back into gear. "Get out your cell phone and call 911 right now. Right now! That guy might hurt somebody." Parker nodded and fished his phone out of his pocket.

Mac took a long step forward and stared into the storage locker.

One object caught his eye.

There, lying on the plastic-draped bed, was an AR-15 with a scope.

The text message had claimed that the weapon used in the North-woods shooting would be in the Nortons' storage locker.

Mac sucked a breath through his teeth and wondered what the hell had just happened.

ARIANNA WATCHED as Rod Cutler scrambled across the grassy field and into the strip mall's parking lot.

For such a weasel, Arianna reflected, Rod could really move when necessary. Then again, his sense of self-preservation was well-honed and was only overruled by his lust for prostitutes.

And his greed.

Because otherwise, he never would have agreed to take this job for Arianna.

He didn't realize it yet, but his usefulness had just expired.

Rod scrambled into the parking lot and stopped where Arianna lay on her stomach atop the closed dumpster, watching Rogan and Parker through the scope. She rolled off the dumpster and landed, her legs flexing a little to absorb the impact.

"It's done?" said Arianna. Like Rod, she wore an HVAC coverall, her blond hair concealed beneath a black cap. From a distance, they would look like two utility workers. Not that anyone had seen them. The strip mall's parking lot had two driveways, and they had used the one on the far side of the lot, out of sight of the insurance office and the Subway.

"It is," said Rod, breathing hard. "They saw me, I shot at them, and then ran like hell."

"Move," said Arianna.

Rod's General Contracting van had been parked behind the dumpster, and they got in and drove away. Arianna settled back with a sigh, enjoying the remaining thrill. She hadn't personally taken much of a risk, but the chance of disaster had still been there.

But if this played out the way Arianna thought, Cormac Rogan would soon stop sniffing around her affairs.

"I'm getting paid, right?" said Rod.

Arianna nodded. "Don't worry. You'll get paid."

And sooner than he thought.

THE REST of the day turned into an epic shitstorm, and Mac didn't get home until almost midnight.

The Menomonee Falls police arrived first and questioned both Mac and Parker. Their account was met with skepticism until the police summoned the manager of Deluxe Storage, a harried-looking middle-aged woman who nonetheless opened the office and let the police view the security recordings.

Then things started to get interesting.

For one thing, most of the day's footage was missing. The camera system kept two weeks of footage at a time, recorded to an array of camcorder tapes. The recording for the morning was scrambled, almost like someone had held a magnet to the tape. The footage only regained clarity at noon, which meant Mac got to watch himself and Parker walk into the storage yard and get attacked by the masked man.

That got the cops moving. An actual detective arrived, followed soon after by Detective Armstrong from Wauwatosa and two more detectives from Milwaukee. Mac repeated his story to all of them, and the AR-15 was taken from the Nortons' storage locker for immediate rushed ballistics testing.

At some point during all this, Parker sent a text message to his mother, and at around 2 PM, Maggie McIntyre arrived in a towering fury, accompanied by her lawyer, who seemed to salivate at the prospect of a legal battle. Maggie's fury was mollified somewhat when the various detectives informed her that her son was under no suspicion of having committed any crimes, and indeed, had been the victim of an attempted assault.

After that, her anger turned towards her son, and to a lesser extent, towards Mac.

During this confrontation, Julie Norton showed up. The manager had tipped her off that the police were searching her storage locker, and she arrived with her own lawyer, demanding to know what was happening. Halfway through that conversation, she began glaring at Mac and then left, her lawyer in tow.

Mac thought about calling Paul but decided it wasn't necessary. He had been on the business end of police interrogations before, and he could tell they didn't consider him a suspect. Instead, they were baffled, and Mac and Parker were interviewed together and then separately. Mac didn't tell them about Arianna Crest, and neither did Parker. There was absolutely no proof that Arianna was involved in this, and Mac worried what might happen if they mentioned her.

He suspected he might get sued by both Maggie and Julie Norton by the time this was done.

Mac listened to the cops' discussions. The masked gunman had fled towards the strip mall to the north, and unfortunately, the mall was mostly unoccupied, with the only tenants an insurance agent and a fast-food restaurant. The employees at both businesses had seen nothing, and while the restaurant had cameras, they only covered the interior. No one had seen anyone coming or going.

Finally, the police released Mac and Parker to go home at about 9:45 PM, with an admonition that officers might be in touch for additional interviews.

Mac walked to the parking lot with Parker and Maggie. His

Corsica looked particularly run-down sitting next to Maggie's gleaming white SUV.

Best to take the bull by the horns.

"Ms. McIntyre, I would like to apologize for..."

"Go wait in the car, Parker," said Maggie, her voice quiet.

Parker opened his mouth, closed it, and nodded. "Okay. Thanks for listening to me, Mr. Rogan."

He headed towards the SUV.

"I would..." said Mac.

"Okay, okay, I get it," said Maggie. She sighed and pinched the bridge of her nose. "You're sorry. That's nice. You're sorry, and Parker still could have gotten killed. I might be driving to the morgue instead of this crappy storage rental place."

"I know," said Mac. "If I had known what would happen, I wouldn't have brought him with me."

Maggie took a long breath, let it out. "He's not a child, Mr. Rogan. He's nineteen. He's going to make decisions I don't like, probably more than one of them."

"Yeah," said Mac.

"So what the hell do you think happened?" said Maggie.

"I don't know," said Mac. "I've spent the last few days asking all kinds of questions. My best guess is that someone was pissed off about it. That guy in the mask and the HVAC uniform? He tried to rob my brother last night."

"Okay," said Maggie. "Then this guy sent you that text message, told you to look in the storage locker, and he was waiting here to ambush you?"

"I think so," said Mac.

Maggie paused. "Parker said you thought someone connected to Crest Development might be behind it."

"Maybe," said Mac. "I just don't know, Ms. McIntyre."

But his suspicions were hardening into certainties. There had been too many coincidences. He was pretty sure that Arianna Crest, or someone connected to her, had sent the masked gunman after Tom and to Deluxe Storage. Which meant that if the AR-15 in the storage locker was indeed the weapon used at the Northwoods shooting...

That would mean that Arianna was a cold-blooded killer, or maybe a high-functioning sociopath if such a thing existed. She would have shot all those students to simply kill Joshua Chartwell and sabotage Clarissa Chartwell's deal. The pattern fit – the gunman had come after Tom, not Mac himself, and in the other unfortunate "coincidences" that Mac had found, the family members of Arianna's business rivals had been attacked or suffered accidents, not the rivals themselves.

That meant that Douglas Norton's death had indeed been a murder.

Arianna had pushed a drunken Winston Marsh to his death down the stairs, stolen his pistol, and used it to kill Doug Norton, making it look like a suicide. That would explain the unusual lack of prints on the gun. Arianna must have wiped down the weapon and made sure to get Doug's prints on it.

Arianna was a cold-blooded killer who had gotten away with it again and again, and Mac had not one shred of proof, not one. Maybe he could convince Agent Cole of the FBI to look at her, but what would they find? If they went over Arianna's business with a microscope, no doubt they would find some tax irregularities, but likely nothing that would connect her to any murders.

"I just don't know," said Mac again. He took a deep breath of his own. "But I think you should tell Parker to stay away from this."

"I'll try," said Maggie. "But Parker wants to know who the shooter was. I can't blame him. That mess almost destroyed his life." She paused. "He said you saved his life. That you pulled him out of the way when the gunman started shooting."

"I don't know about that," said Mac. "The guy in the mask had bad aim."

Very bad aim, now that Mac thought about it.

Almost as if he had been deliberately trying to miss.

But why?

"Thank you," said Maggie. "For looking after him. He might have run off half-cocked by himself and gotten killed."

"I don't think you'll have to worry about that again," said Mac. "Mrs. Norton looked furious. I think I'm getting fired in the next few days. And possibly sued."

"Good luck, Mr. Rogan," said Maggie. "I think you're probably going to need it."

With that, she joined Parker in the SUV and drove off.

A steady autumn drizzle began to fall, cold and sharp.

Mac got into his car and checked his phone. Tom had called him around seven – no doubt he had heard from his friends in the police that Mac was being questioned. Tom ought to still be awake since it was a Friday, so he hit the dial button.

Tom picked up on the second ring. "You getting arrested?"

"No," said Mac, and he told Tom the story – the pattern he had noticed, the text message, the gunman.

Tom coughed when he finished. "So you think Arianna Crest is killing people who get in her way?"

"Yeah, I do," said Mac. "Or I'm full of crap because I don't have a single piece of evidence. Just a long, long string of very unlikely coincidences."

"Don't know," said Tom. "But if the same guy who tried to mug me shot at you this afternoon, that's a pretty big damn coincidence."

"Yeah," said Mac. "Keep an eye over your shoulder, will you?"

"You, too," said Tom.

He ended the call, and Mac headed to an all-night restaurant not far from his apartment. He hadn't eaten anything all day, and he was ravenous and ordered a burger and fries.

As he ate, he wondered what the hell he was going to do next.

20

TIDYING UP

But as it happened, the question was answered for him. At eight the next morning, Mac got a call from Dave Wester, asking him to come to the offices of Wester Security at 10 AM. It was Saturday, October 27th, and Mac knew that Dave didn't like to work on Saturdays unless he had no choice.

He drove to the offices of Wester Security, which were in an office building on Highway 100 a couple of blocks north of Wisconsin Avenue. A car dealership and a restaurant were across the street, and Mac thought the restaurant had changed something like six times in the years he had been working for Dave. Wester Security occupied a suite on the fourth floor of an unremarkable office building across the hall from an osteopath and a place that administered certification tests.

Mac let himself into the outer office, an unremarkable space with a receptionist's desk and some worn chairs, and then into Dave's office. It looked like the workspace of a former detective – simple furniture, numerous stacks of paper and files, all of it meticulously arranged and organized. Dave's laptop computer, which he hated using, rested on the corner of the desk. Dave Wester himself sat behind the desk, wearing a suit jacket and a shirt with the top button undone.

Julie Norton sat in one of the visitor chairs, her lips pressed into a thin line, her knuckles turning white where they gripped her purse. She looked absolutely furious, and Dave had on a calm, reassuring expression, the one he had used when trying to talk suspects into surrendering.

"Mac, thanks for joining us," said Dave. "Have a seat. Mrs. Norton had some concerns she wanted to discuss."

Mac sat, and Julie erupted.

"Did you plant that rifle in my locker?" snapped Julie.

"No," said Mac. "I didn't..."

"I have been in that locker three times in the last year," said Julie. "I have never, ever kept a firearm in there. Not once. All our guns are in a locked safe at home."

"I'm as confused as you are," said Mac. "I..."

"I suppose you've heard already," said Julie. "The lab rushed the ballistics test. The gun from the locker was the one used in the Northwoods High School shooting."

Dead silence answered her.

They all knew the significance of that. The police and the FBI hadn't come anywhere near finding the Northwoods shooter, which was why the media frenzy had whipped up around Parker McIntyre and Ryan Walsh. This was the first piece of actual physical evidence that anyone had ever found.

"Jesus," said Mac.

"The media hasn't found out about it yet," said Julie, "but you can imagine what will happen when they do." She glared at Mac, her eyes like hard blue stones. "You know what they'll say. Maybe that's the reason Doug killed himself. Maybe he was the school shooter all along. Maybe he hid it from his wife and kids, who had no idea what was going on. The rifle was concealed in the storage locker for years, that's what they'll say. God." She rubbed her face. "So, what? Did you plant the rifle? Maybe you wanted to get on TV, testify to Congress again?"

"You've met Congressmen," said Mac quietly. "Do you really think I would want to talk to them voluntarily?" Julie huffed out a sound that was halfway between a snarl and a bitter laugh. "I don't know what happened. I think the guy who shot at me planted the rifle in the locker…"

"Unless he was working for you," snapped Julie. "Unless you're all working together."

"That's ridiculous," said Mac.

"Mrs. Norton," said Dave in his reasonable-cop voice before either of them could speak again. "We know this is a stressful time for you and that you have every right to be upset. But if we planted the rifle, that meant we were involved in the shooting. Do you really think that is reasonable?"

Julie hesitated and then shook her head. "No. But something's going on. Some conspiracy. How else did that rifle magically appear in my storage locker? Maybe that's why Doug was killed. Maybe he found out about the plot, and they killed him to silence him."

Mac started to say again that he thought the masked gunman had planted the weapon, but he stopped himself. There was a furious glitter in Julie's eyes that unsettled him. He remembered his initial worry that Julie Norton was in denial, that Doug Norton had killed himself and that she simply could not accept it. Maybe that denial was festering into something worse.

"This is going to be a challenging time," said Dave, "but the police are looking for the masked gunman who attacked Mac. Once they find him…"

"They won't," said Julie. "They never found the Northwoods shooter, and they never found who killed my husband, either." She glared at Mac again. "Nor will you."

"Mrs. Norton…" started Dave again.

"No, we're done," said Julie, getting to her feet. "Hiring you was a mistake. I'm not naïve enough to think that I can get my retainer money back, but I don't want to hear from you again. But if you two suddenly find mysterious new 'evidence' popping up at my house or my office, you'll be hearing from my lawyers."

With that, she collected her purse and stalked out.

Mac and Dave sat in silence for a while.

"I'm not getting paid, am I?" said Mac.

Dave sighed. "Better than getting sued, isn't it? But you'll get paid for the hours you put in. You keep good records, Mac, and you did good work. But I have no idea what's going on here or how that Northwoods rifle turned up in the storage locker."

"What do you think happened?" said Mac. Perhaps Dave would have a reasonable theory that fit all the facts.

Dave shrugged. "Hell if I know. Best guess? Some sort of crooked land deal somewhere. You know, a city council was getting kickbacks. You stumbled across that with your investigation, and so they sent the guy in the mask to make trouble for you."

That made sense, except for one detail.

"What about the rifle?" said Mac.

"I don't know, Mac," said Dave. "Maybe someone involved a real estate deal knew who the shooter was, killed him, and kept the rifle..." He gave a shake of his head. "Sounds stupid even as I say it. There's an explanation, but we don't know what it is."

"I'm sorry about all the trouble," said Mac.

"Nah. I'm sorry for dumping this on you," said Dave. "I really thought this would be an easy one. You ask questions for a few months and eventually Julie Norton decides it was a suicide after all. But I guess we're done with it now." He got up. "I'll cut you a check on Monday."

"Thanks," said Mac, rising as well.

Dave grinned. "Next time I have a nice easy surveillance job, I'll send that to you by way of apology."

They shook hands and left, Dave closing and locking the door behind him. A few minutes later, they came to the parking lot behind the building, which was in desperate need of a new layer of asphalt, and Dave got into his truck and drove off. Mac walked to his car, dropped into the driver's seat, and stared out the windshield at the dumpster, thinking.

Like Dave had said, they didn't know what had happened. There was no one theory that fit all the facts.

Except for one that Dave had dismissed due to lack of proof.

Arianna Crest had committed the Northwoods school shooting, and she had killed Doug Norton, in both cases trying to distract people involved in real estate deals. After Mac had interviewed Arianna, she had sent the masked gunman after him, and she had left the rifle in the storage locker to muddy the waters.

And Mac had absolutely no evidence of her involvement whatsoever.

He drummed his fingers on the worn steering wheel, thinking.

This wasn't his responsibility. He wasn't getting paid to investigate this any longer, and he was in dire need of money. His focus ought to be on RVW Software and some more contract IT work, on getting out of debt completely. Douglas Norton's death was no longer his concern.

And yet...

He was too much like his father. Mac couldn't stop digging.

And something that Maggie McIntyre had said tugged at his mind.

She had feared that the Northwoods shooting had been a terrorist attack, that the terrorist might escalate since he hadn't gotten caught.

If Arianna really had done it...what if she did it again?

What if she escalated?

Could Mac live with himself then?

He didn't have any proof.

Maybe it was time to go find some.

Mac started his car and headed for his apartment.

On the night of Saturday, October 27th, Arianna was in a good mood.

The plan had worked better than she had expected.

Cormac Rogan would not be a problem any longer. Leaving the

AR-15 she had used for the Northwoods shooting had been a risk, but much of one. Arianna was certain that she had not left any fingerprints on the weapon. A pity there had been no way to get Douglas Norton's prints on the rifle, but that would have been impossible. She would have liked to have gotten Rod's fingerprints on it, but Rod was too smart to let himself get taken like that.

Besides, Arianna had another use in mind for Rod Cutler. She suspected he didn't know that she was behind the Northwoods shooting and Doug Norton's death, but she didn't know for sure. And Rod, despite his disgusting habits, wasn't stupid. The news that the Northwoods shooter's weapon had been found had touched off a frenzy in the news, with both the FBI and the local police announcing that they were reopening their investigations into the shooting.

Arianna had been delighted to see speculation that the weapon had been found in a storage locker belonging a Northwoods teacher who had killed himself. The conclusion was clear enough – Doug Norton had been the shooter and then had killed himself out of guilt and remorse. Never mind that was physically impossible since too many witnesses could place Doug inside the building at the time of the shooting.

The media had never been known for accuracy.

She prepared for her visit to Rod, loading bundles of cash into a small duffel bag. Beneath the cash, she placed the handgun she had used to kill the pimp and the two prostitutes, the weapon with Rod's fingerprints on it, carefully wrapped in plastic. Once that was done, Arianna emptied a twenty-ounce lime soda bottle and methodically stuffed it full of rags. When the bottle was prepared, she took a stolen .44 semiautomatic and loaded it, taking care not to leave any prints on the weapon. She slid the barrel into the bottle and duct-taped it to the plastic. The net effect was to create a weapon that would have terrible accuracy but would make nothing more than a loud thump when fired.

Arianna tucked the weapon into the duffel bag, out of sight next to the cash, and dressed in boots and an HVAC boiler suit. Her hair went into a net, and she tucked it beneath a black baseball cap. A pair of leather gloves went over her hands. She double-checked all her preparations one last time and then headed for the vehicle in her driveway. It was one of the Crest Development construction vans, specifically one that had been working on the demolition of the house across the street from Northwoods High School. Arianna had taken on the demolition of the house as a charity project for two reasons. One, she derived dark amusement from the parents of her victims thanking her for building the memorial garden.

Two, it accustomed the students and staff to the sight of a Crest Development vehicle near the high school.

Which would come in handy in a few days.

It was almost midnight, and she drove through Milwaukee to Rod's seedy apartment building. Arianna parked several blocks away along a stretch of the street with no working streetlights. She supposed it was possible that she would be mugged, but with the boiler suit, it wasn't immediately obvious that she was a woman, and any muggers who accosted her would be in for a nasty surprise.

Arianna walked to Rod's building and climbed the stairs to his apartment. Her heart started to thump against her ribs as she approached Rod's door. She was about to take a risk, and the thrill of it coursed down her veins, better than drugs, better than alcohol, better than a man, better than anything.

She knocked and waited.

A few moments later, she heard a rattling thump. "Who is it?"

She lifted the duffel bag before the peephole.

The locks rattled and the deadbolts slid back, and Rod Cutler stood in the door, clad in dark sweatpants and a ratty T-shirt.

"Come in," he said, shooting a quick look up and down the hallway. Arianna followed him into his filthy living room.

She made sure to close the door behind her. Interruptions would be unwelcome.

"The money," said Arianna. "All one hundred thousand dollars, just like I promised." Rod dropped onto his couch and looked up at her. "I imagine that will buy a lot of prostitutes."

Rod snorted. "You don't approve. That's always been your problem. You work too hard. You never relax."

She kept the revulsion from her face. "What, are you going to tell me that I need a man to help me relax?"

Rod shifted. "Couldn't hurt."

"Go ahead and count the money." Arianna stepped to the opposite side of the coffee table from him, dropping the duffel bag onto it. She unzipped the top and opened the flaps, revealing the stacks of hundred-dollar bills in their thick rubber bands. "A hundred thousand dollars."

Rod leaned forward, his eyes shining with greed.

In one smooth motion, Arianna reached into the duffel bag, lifted the gun, pressed the end of the soda bottle against Rod's forehead, and pulled the trigger.

The sight of the green plastic of the soda bottle confused Rod for a half-second, and that was a half-second too long. The crack of the weapon, muffled by the rags, became a loud thump, like somebody had just dropped a phonebook onto the floor. Rod's head snapped back in a spray of blood, and he slumped against the couch cushions, eyes wide with shock, a bloody hole in the center of his brow.

Arianna watched him for a second. His body jerked and twitched a few times, but then he went limp. The stench came to her nostrils as his bowels relaxed in death, and her mouth twisted with disgust.

He had been an odious little man in life, and now he was one in death.

Just as well she would never come back here again.

Arianna got to work, stripping off the duct tape and removing the rag-filled bottle with the bullet hole from the end of the weapon and dropping it into her bag. A quick wipe-down with solvent to remove the remnants of the tape, and she pressed the weapon into Rod's right and left hands several times, making sure to get his fingerprints all over both the grip and the barrel.

Then she left the gun on the floor between the coffee table and the couch, where it likely would have fallen after Rod had shot himself in the forehead. Or so the police would believe, once she did a little more work. Arianna took the pistol from the bottom of the bag, unwrapped the plastic from it, and left it on the worktable in the dining room. She took a few moments after that to search the apartment and located all three burner phones Rod had used to communicate with her. Those she took with her. Rod's stash of cash and drugs she left behind. Drugs disgusted her, and she had no need for the cash.

And after Halloween and the Drummond land deal, Arianna would have far more money than whatever Rod had managed to prevent himself from spending on prostitutes.

His personal cell phone, the one he used for his General Contracting business, rested on the end table next to the phone. Arianna cleared her throat a few times, picked up the phone, and dialed 911.

"911, what is your emergency?" said the dispatcher.

"I killed them," said Arianna, forcing her voice into a raspy, growling whisper. "I killed the prostitutes and their pimp, and Douglas Norton and I killed all those kids at Northwoods High School. I'm so, so sorry. Doug and I killed them all."

"Sir," said the dispatcher, "please..."

Arianna growled out Rod's address. "I'm here. I'm guilty. Come and find me."

She ended the call, wiped the phone to remove any spittle she might have left, and dropped it on the couch.

Arianna paused just long enough to smirk at Rod's corpse and then picked up her duffel bag with its cash and left, leaving no trace of herself behind in Rod's apartment. She walked briskly through the halls, out the front door, and left. No one saw her or stopped her as she returned to the van, and she drove away.

About two blocks later, she heard the sirens.

If the waters had been muddied before, they would be opaque now.

Arianna smiled in the darkness as she drove for her house.

Four more days until Northwoods High School's Halloween bonfire.

21

RECORDINGS

Mac spent the weekend at his computer, busy with both his work for RVW Software and with research.

The app was proceeding well, and Mac grew more and more confident. Under other circumstances, he might have put all his time into working on the app, hoping to turn a profit in the next year. Instead, he split his time between working on the app and researching the background and past of Arianna Crest.

He could not leave it alone. He could not stop digging.

Maggie McIntyre's comment kept playing in his head.

What if whoever had committed the Northwoods shooting escalated?

Mac knew this would look bad if anyone found out. For that matter, if Arianna knew that he was looking into her past, there were numerous ways she could cast suspicion upon him. She could claim that he was trying to sabotage her or secretly working for Morgan Properties. Or, more simply, she could claim that he was obsessed with her and trying to gain her attention. Given that Arianna was an attractive woman and Mac was a single man living alone in a crappy apartment, most people would believe her argument.

But he dug into Arianna's background, using both the Internet and various other sources, and a pattern emerged.

Arianna Crest had been born in 1972 in a small town in northern Wisconsin, a place with no more than five thousand people. Her father had been Andrew Crest, a corrections officer at a state prison, and her mother Jacqueline Crest, who had held a variety of jobs. Already the suspicious patterns began – Jacqueline had died in a car accident, and Andrew, an alcoholic, had died in his sleep after choking on his own vomit.

Accidental deaths, both of them.

But more accidents connected to Arianna Crest.

After that, Arianna had gone to UW-Madison. Mac found another pattern of suspicious accidents. The partner of one of her professors had been attacked while bicycling. The husband of another professor had been arrested for drug possession and had strenuously claimed innocence and that someone had planted the drugs on him.

Two more coincidences.

Mac followed Arianna's path as she went into real estate and started Crest Development, rising to become one of the richest women in the state of Wisconsin. Throughout the course of her career, tragedies seemed to befall her rivals, unexplained deaths and accidents in the family.

A lot of coincidences.

Mac stayed up past midnight on Saturday researching. He woke up late and felt vaguely guilty that he hadn't gone to church. His mother, surprisingly enough, had been a regular churchgoer, though Mac suspected that had less to do with any sort of belief in God and more her pride in her Irish heritage, which included Catholicism. Though she had also combined it with an increasing belief in pre-Christian Irish paganism, and sometimes she claimed that she was the reincarnation of an ancient Irish priestess or possibly a princess.

Intellectual consistency had not been among Monica Rogan's virtues.

Tom had started going to church again after he had gotten out of the hospital, and every so often, he invited Mac to come with him. Mac had declined so far, unable to reconcile belief in a righteous God with the manifest injustice and cruelty of the world. Which he supposed did not make him atheist or agnostic, just annoyed with God.

Petulant. It made him petulant, and he smiled at the thought, half-annoyed, half-amused with himself.

Mac spent the rest of Sunday morning working on the app, and at noon his cell phone rang. He didn't recognize the number, and he picked it up. "Hello?"

"Mr. Rogan?" The woman's voice was familiar.

"Speaking," said Mac.

"It's Maggie McIntyre."

"Oh. Hello, Ms. McIntyre," said Mac, surprised and a little worried. He half-expected her to say that Parker had run off in pursuit of Arianna Crest. "What can I do for you?"

"Have you seen the news today?" said Maggie.

"No," said Mac. "I've been working all morning."

"Does the name Rod Cutler mean anything to you?" said Maggie.

"I don't believe so," said Mac. "Why?"

"He killed himself last night, sometime around midnight," said Maggie. "Before he shot himself, he made a call to 911." She took a deep breath. "He claimed to have worked with Douglas Norton to carry out the Northwoods shooting."

It took a moment for Mac to make sense of the words.

"What?" he said at last.

"It's all over the local news," said Maggie, voice grim. "Between that and the rifle at the storage locker, the story's blowing up. Parker already talked to the police about it this morning."

"Parker?" said Mac. "Why would the police want to talk to Parker?"

"Because this Cutler guy was apparently some sort of contractor," said Maggie. "He had a lot of coveralls in his apartment, and one of them had blood on the collar like the one you saw at Deluxe Storage. Parker looked at a picture, and he thinks it's the same piece of clothing. Rod Cutler might be the guy who attacked your brother and who you saw at the storage facility. I just wanted to give you a warning that the police will be talking to you soon."

No sooner had she spoken than someone knocked at Mac's door.

"I think you're right," said Mac. "Thanks for the warning."

He went to the door to find Detective Armstrong from the Wauwatosa police. He had brought pictures, and Mac looked at them. Rod Cutler had been a weedy, balding man with a shifty look to him. He looked vaguely familiar, though Mac couldn't place him.

The picture of the worn, bloodstained coverall, Mac recognized at once.

"That's it," he said. "That's what the guy by my brother's truck was wearing, and it was the same outfit we saw at the storage facility."

Armstrong nodded. They stood in Mac's kitchen since it was the only place with a free flat surface. The detective had taken a long look at Mac's relative lack of furniture but kept his thoughts on the topic to himself.

"It seems like Cutler was the one who attacked you," said Armstrong. He scratched his jaw. "Working theory is that he realized you were investigating Doug Norton's death and then panicked and started following you."

"That doesn't make any sense," said Mac. "Doug couldn't have possibly been involved with the Northwoods shooting. Too many witnesses were with him when the shooting happened. They can't all be lying."

Armstrong shrugged. "Agreed. But we don't know what's going on. There's some thought that the voice on the 911 call wasn't really Cutler. It looks like a suicide, but there are some odd signs. Cutler previously went to prison for solicitation, and the Milwaukee cops found a lot of drugs and cash in his apartment. He might have been dealing or pimping on the side. Maybe he pissed someone off enough to get himself killed."

"Maybe," said Mac. But if an angry drug dealer or pimp had decided to shoot Cutler, then why mention the Northwoods shooting? Why even call 911 at all?

It didn't make sense.

Armstrong asked Mac a few more questions, but they were all routine. Mac had still been awake and working when Cutler had been killed, and the timestamps on the code files for the app would prove it if necessary. But Mac didn't think it would be a problem. The police clearly did not consider him an actual suspect in Cutler's death. He thought the police would decide that Cutler was murdered in a drugs or prostitution deal and the 911 call made to spread doubt, or that Cutler did in fact kill himself and called 911 as a last macabre joke.

The detective left, leaving Mac with another of his cards, and he went to his computer at once.

A brief search revealed a lot of news articles about both the find of the AR-15 in the storage locker and the death of Rod Cutler. The articles noted that Cutler had claimed responsibility for the Northwoods shooting with Doug Norton but said that police suspected Cutler had planted the weapon and mentioned Norton out of some sort of vendetta. That was good. Mac felt bad that Julie Norton thought he had tried to frame her husband for the shooting, though he did not see what he could have done differently.

Mac read what information the articles held about Cutler. He had been a contractor with a prosperous business until his penchant for prostitutes had come to light. After a prison term, he had resumed a contracting business, though with a much smaller clientele. His business had been called General Contracting, and...

General Contracting?

Mac blinked, and then the memory came.

That was where he had seen Rod Cutler before. He had been power washing the sign on the day that Mac had interviewed Arianna. Mac had seen the van again later at the gas station.

Cutler had been following him.

The chains of logic played through his mind. Cutler had been there to watch and follow Mac. But Mac had never met the man, and Cutler had no reason to follow him.

Arianna had sent him.

Mac leaned back in his chair and let out a long breath, disturbed. This was more than a coincidence.

This was proof.

Arianna had decided that Mac was a threat. She had sent Cutler to follow him. And then she had likely paid him to attack Tom, hoping to distract Mac from the investigation.

And the reason that Cutler had left the weapon from the Northwoods shooting at the storage locker was because Arianna had given him the rifle.

"Jesus," whispered Mac.

The enormity of what he had discovered chilled him. He had met some depraved people in his life, people he would have called evil without an instant of hesitation. But this level of coldness disturbed even him. Mac had absolutely no doubt that Arianna Crest had murdered Douglas Norton after first killing Winston Marsh to use his weapon. She had been the one to shoot those five students at Northwoods High School, all to cripple a business rival with grief.

And Mac knew that Rod Cutler hadn't committed suicide. Arianna had used him to attack Mac and leave the AR-15 at the storage locker, casting suspicion away from her.

And once Cutler had reached the end of his usefulness, Arianna had killed him and made it look like a suicide.

Just as she had once done with Douglas Norton.

Mac was absolutely certain of all that.

And he had no way whatsoever to prove it.

No doubt there were financial records proving that Rod Cutler had worked for Arianna. But so what? Mac was sure Arianna's payments to Cutler had gone under the table, perhaps the source of the cash in Cutler's apartment. But all of Crest Development's payments to General Contracting would be aboveboard and filed with the IRS. If pressed, Arianna would claim that she had hired Cutler because he was cheap and that she had employed countless contractors during her years in business, some of whom had criminal records. Unless she screwed up and left a fingerprint at Cutler's apartment, Mac couldn't see that Cutler's death would affect her in any way, and he doubted that Arianna had been that careless.

Which meant that a mass murderer was free to walk about and plan her next atrocity.

It wasn't his business, but Mac could not stand by in good conscience and do nothing. Somehow he and Parker were the only ones to stumble on to Arianna's pattern, and Mac had learned more than Parker. For that matter, Mac had far more experience than Parker.

Yet what could Mac do? Go to the police? The FBI? They required proof before they acted, and Arianna had been clever enough not to leave any behind. Yet she had to have made a mistake somewhere.

But where?

Mac spent the next several days alternating between working on the app and researching Arianna, trying to find a place where she might have left evidence behind. He made little progress. Most of the investigations into the tragedies that Arianna had left in her wake had been closed as accidents or gone cold with a conclusion of "persons unknown." For that matter, RVW Software was taking up more and more of his time. On Tuesday, October 30th, Mac drove to one of the sheriff's departments that Paul had recruited to test the app and spent most of the day in in the conference room of a county law enforcement running a training session for the deputies, showing them how to use the web interface on their vehicle laptops. The deputies were impressed, and Mac realized that the company might start seeing its first revenue very soon.

He didn't have time to keep pursuing an investigation into Arianna Crest. Not when he might finally have a chance at getting out of debt and finding a stable income for the first time in years. For that matter, Dave's check for the hours that Mac had put in had cleared, which would keep his head above water for a few months, but he needed some more freelancing jobs soon to pay the bills.

But what if Arianna perpetrated an atrocity like the Northwoods shooting, something Mac could have prevented?

Then, on the late morning of October 31st, an idea occurred to Mac.

He copied Arianna Crest's official picture off the Crest Development website and spent a few minutes on the Internet locating high-resolution headshots of similar-looking women – white, blond, blue-eyed, and sharp-featured. Mac loaded them onto a flash drive and drove to a copy shop, where he paid too much to print the JPEGs as photographs. Once he finished printing, he tucked the pictures into a folder and drove to Carver's Cigarettes and Liquor.

By then, it was about two in the afternoon. Mac parked a short distance away and walked into the store. As before, Mac was the only white person in sight. Tammy the cashier occupied her post in the fortified booth of bulletproof glass and metal and gave Mac a suspicious look.

"Can I help you?" she said.

"Hi," said Mac. "My name's Cormac Rogan. I was in here last week talking to…"

"Oh, right, I remember you," said Tammy. "You were asking about old drunk Winston."

"Yeah," said Mac. "Is Mr. Carver in? I want to ask him a question."

Tammy jerked her head to the side. "Ask him yourself."

Mac turned his head and saw Jake Carver approaching. The old man wore the same sweater and apron as before, the sweater's pocket sagging from the gun he kept concealed there. This time, though, Carver's expression was much less suspicious, though still warry.

"Well, well," said Carver. "Cormac Rogan again. Still trying find out why that one guy shot himself?"

"I am," said Mac. "I was wondering if I could ask you another question."

"You gonna buy something?"

"Yup."

Carver shrugged. "Then sure. What do you want to know?"

"It's just one question," said Mac. "You told me about the woman who was visiting Marsh before he died."

"I remember her," said Tammy. "Fancy bitch. Never even bought anything."

"Yeah, what about her?" said Carver.

Mac lifted the folder. "I've got some pictures. I'd like you to look at them and see if you can spot the woman who visited Marsh."

"A lineup," said Carver. He snorted. "Been robbed enough. I know the drill."

"I want to see," said Tammy.

"Yes," said Mac. "But I'd like you and Mr. Carver to look at them separately. I don't want you to influence one another."

Tammy didn't look happy but offered a sullen nod. Evidently she had been through this drill before as well.

Mac and Carver stepped to an empty shelf, and Mac spread out the pictures. He had ten in total, and he put Arianna's seventh in the line. Carver looked over the pictures and then nodded to himself.

"Blond white ladies," he muttered. "All look the same to me. But I think it was this one."

He tapped Arianna's picture, and Mac felt a mixture of a chill and satisfaction. Logic and guesswork had led him here, and it sometimes felt like he had been fooling himself, like he had been building an elaborate castle out of nonsense.

But here was more proof that he was right.

"You're sure?" said Mac.

"Pretty sure," said Carver. "Course, she never smiled when she was here. Looked like she had taken a big old bite out of a lemon." He tapped Arianna's picture again. "But she kind of looks like a shark, don't she? Like she's about to take a bite out of somebody."

He was more correct than he knew.

Mac picked up the pictures, shuffled them, and walked to the cashier's booth. Tammy perked up as he approached, and Mac laid the pictures over the counter, covering the advertisements for lottery tickets and cigarettes.

Tammy didn't hesitate and tapped Arianna's picture a few times. "That one right there."

"You're sure?" said Mac.

"Course I'm sure," said Tammy. "Skinny bitch thinks she's too good for Carver's store, never bought anything here. Don't know why she was hanging around with poor old Winston. He just wanted to sit around and drink, you know? What's she doing with him? Nothing good, I'll tell you that right now."

Mac nodded. One witness might have been mistaken identity. But two? Two was more substantial.

"You okay?" said Carver. "You look like you just saw a ghost." He grunted. "What did this girl do anyway, kill someone?" He laughed at his own joke.

Mac didn't laugh.

Carver sobered. "She did kill someone?"

"Probably," said Mac. "Probably more than one person. Can't prove any of it, though."

"For real?" said Tammy.

"Yeah," said Mac. "Listen, you've still got my card?" Carver nodded. "I don't think she'll ever come here again. There's no reason for her to come back. But if you see her, don't let on that you know anything, and give me a call."

Carver and Tammy looked at each other.

"Shouldn't we call the police if we see her?" said Carver.

"And tell them what?" said Mac. "There's absolutely no proof. And bad accidents happen to people who get on her bad side."

He saw Carver get it. "Like falling drunk down the stairs in the middle of the night?"

"Exactly," said Mac.

"Well, shit," said Carver. "Poor damn Winston."

"You've probably got nothing to worry about," said Mac. "But if you see her, please give me a call."

"All right," said Carver. "We'll do that." He leveled a finger at Mac. "But you watch your back. People who ask the wrong questions tend to turn up dead in alleys, you understand?"

Once again, he was more correct than he knew.

Mac bought a cup of coffee and a frozen dinner, as he had promised, and drove back to his apartment. He had found proof that

Arianna was behind Douglas Norton's death, but he could do little with it. Even if Carver and Tammy were willing to testify that they had seen Arianna Crest coming out of Winston's apartment, so what? There was no other physical evidence that Arianna had killed Marsh and absolutely no proof that she had stolen Marsh's gun. Arianna could simply say that she had been visiting a former employee out of concern for his alcoholism.

Mac needed a lot more than that.

But where could he find it?

Arianna would have made a mistake somewhere. As he drove home, Mac thought about where to find it.

The deaths of her parents, he decided. According to the records he had seen, Jacqueline Crest had died in a car accident, and Andrew Crest had gotten drunk and choked on his own vomit. Those were the only deaths he had seen that were closely linked to Arianna, rather than deaths among the families of her business rivals. Probably her mother and father had carried life insurance policies, and the payouts would have been investigated. Maybe one of the investigators had noticed something suspicious.

It was a thin thread, but it was better than nothing.

Mac realized that it might take months, even years, to find the proof that would reveal Arianna's misdeeds. Perhaps it would be better to watch her, to wait until she made a mistake. But he could hardly devote his life to monitoring Arianna Crest's activities.

A darker thought occurred to him.

The Westview Mall development. Julie Norton had mentioned it to him, at least when she had still been speaking to him, and said that Crest Development was their main rival for the project. Millions of dollars were at stake.

What would Arianna do to secure that kind of money?

Anything, Mac realized. Absolutely anything. He was now certain that she had killed Winston Marsh simply to steal a pistol that could not be traced back to her. If she had indeed carried out the Northwoods shooting, she had killed five teenagers to kill Joshua Chartwell and removed his mother Clarissa as a potential obstacle.

For the kind of money that the Westview Mall development would bring?

God help anyone Arianna decided was an obstacle.

Mac pulled into his apartment's parking lot at about 4 PM and let out a long, irritated breath.

The damnable thing of it all was that he could do nothing. The only actual proof he had was two eyewitness statements that Arianna could easily refute. If Mac went to nearly anyone with his suspicions, they would assume that he had lost his mind or had a vendetta against Arianna. Dave had been sympathetic to Mac's position, but he had been a detective for a long time and assumed that the simplest explanation was most likely the correct one. The simplest explanation was that a mentally disturbed Rod Cutler had been the Northwoods shooter and had mentioned Doug Norton's name in his call to 911 as one final spiteful twist of the knife.

It was the simplest explanation.

It just wasn't the truth.

Mac returned to his apartment and settled in front of his computer, intending to work on the documentation for the app. Mac had spent a lot of time writing up both investigative reports and documentation for technology interfaces, and he had gotten pretty good at it. At least Paul and Nikolai both thought that Mac was a good technical writer, and the better the documentation for the app, the fewer support problems they would have down the road.

Mac decided to work until 5:30 PM, and then he would give Tom a call. Tom had invited Mac to go out drinking with his friends on Halloween night, and maybe that was the thing to do. Something other than working on the app and brooding over the case. Maybe an idea would occur to him.

Or maybe he would forget all about Arianna and Doug Norton for a while. Maybe Mac would meet a woman who was nothing like Arianna Crest or Monica Rogan or Kristin Salwell. Tom kept telling him to get a girlfriend, and...

Mac blinked.

Kristin Salwell.

Something scratched at the edge of his mind, but he couldn't place it.

Mac shrugged and got back to work.

At 5:17, his phone rang.

Mac looked at the number on the LCD screen and grimaced.

Parker McIntyre.

He debated letting it go to voicemail, then sighed and opened the phone.

"Mr. Rogan?" said Parker. "How are you? It's Parker."

"Good," said Mac. "What can I do for you, Parker?"

Parker hesitated. "You heard about what happened with the guy who shot at us, right? Rod Cutler?"

"Yeah," said Mac. "It's all over the news, and I talked to the police about it."

"You're not in trouble, are you?" said Parker. "The cops don't think you did it?"

"No," said Mac. "I think they're just trying to figure out what the hell happened. I was working on the RVW app when Cutler was killed, and the timestamps on the files prove it. Besides, from what the police told me, it seems like Cutler killed himself." Just as Doug Norton had killed himself. "His fingerprints were the only ones on the weapon, and the 911 call came from his cell phone." Mac paused. "The cops don't think you did it, do they?"

Parker brayed out a laugh. "Nah. They were very polite around me. I think Mom's lawyer scared them. Besides, I was online playing the game all night. There are timestamps on that, too. Mom's lawyer thinks that this Cutler guy was nuts. Like, he was really into hookers and drugs. He thinks Cutler decided to try to pin the Northwoods shooting on Mr. Norton but snapped and killed himself when we interrupted him."

"I see," said Mac.

There was a long pause.

"You don't think that, do you?" said Parker.

Mac sighed. "You know what I think."

"I wanted to talk to you about that," said Parker. "I think..."

"No," said Mac. "No. We can't do this. The last time we talked about this, you almost got shot. I had to explain to your mom how you had nearly gotten killed."

"I just had an idea I wanted to talk about," said Parker.

"No."

"Come on," said Parker. "I bet you're not going to give up, either. You think Arianna Crest did it. The pattern's right there. All those accidents and murders among relatives of people who got in her way. She did it, didn't she? Both Mr. Norton and the Northwoods shooting, and now that Cutler guy."

"I don't have any proof," said Mac.

"That's a yes," said Parker.

"Look, Parker," said Mac. "This is dangerous. Let's say we're right." He wanted to dissuade Parker, but he didn't know how. It was hard to dissuade someone when they knew the truth. "Let's say it was Arianna Crest. What are we going to do about it? There's no proof. If we go to the cops or the FBI, they'll laugh us out of the room. And then she'll probably come after my brother and your mom if she realizes we suspect her. I am looking into her, yes. But carefully."

"I have an idea about that," said Parker. "We…"

"Parker," said Mac. "You…"

"I gotta do this," said Parker. "My best friend killed himself, five other kids got killed, a whole bunch of people got hurt, and my life was almost wrecked because of the shooting. I gotta find out what really happened, you know?"

"Yeah," said Mac.

"I just want to talk to you about an idea," said Parker. "If you want to meet at McDonald's again, we can talk about it."

"Your mom's going to be pissed," said Mac.

"Mom keeps telling me to get out of the house more," said Parker.

"This isn't what she had in mind," said Mac.

"Besides," said Parker. "Mom's out at Halloween parties with her business partners all night."

"And you didn't go with her?" said Mac.

Parker snorted. "Who goes to Halloween parties with their mom?

And her costume is way too tight." The idea flashed through Mac's mind that Maggie McIntyre in a tight costume would not be an unpleasant sight, but he kept that observation to himself. "It would be embarrassing."

"Fine," said Mac. "But we're just going to talk about the idea. That's all."

"Good!" said Parker. "I'll see you there at...6:30? Will that work? I'll take the bus."

"I'll give you a ride home," said Mac, suppressing a sigh. "Why that McDonald's?"

"I really want some fries."

"Right," said Mac.

He finished up his technical writing for the day, checked over some code changes that Nikolai had made, and then went to his car and drove to the McDonald's in Brookfield. It was a cold night, clear for once, the stars and moon bright overhead. Even at 6:30 PM, there was still a good crowd in the lobby and in the dining area of the McDonald's. Mac saw quite a few parents escorting children in Halloween costumes, evidently getting ice cream after trick-or-treating. Some of the employees had even donned costumes.

Mac spotted Parker in a booth, a tray loaded with fries and chicken nuggets before him. He was wearing a black hooded sweatshirt depicting an armored knight and a green-skinned orc locked in battle, the logo of his favorite online game above them. Despite the chill of the October night, Parker was still wearing baggy shorts and sandals.

"Another couple of weeks, and you're going to need a coat," said Mac, sitting across from him.

"I suppose," said Parker. "But I like winter. It's not so hot."

Mac thought Parker might not be so hot if he didn't eat two large orders of fries quite so often, but that was yet another thought better to keep to himself.

"Anyway," said Mac. "What did you want to talk about?"

"I had an idea," said Parker, leaning closer. "You know how Mr.

Norton wrote Kristin Salwell's name. It was the last thing he wrote before he died."

"Yeah?"

"What if Kristin and Arianna Crest were working together?" said Parker.

"I don't see how," said Mac. "Salwell was in prison at the time of Doug Norton's death. There's no possible way Salwell could be involved, and when I talked to her, she claimed that she didn't have anything to do with it and that she had never slept with Norton."

"She could be lying," said Parker.

"I can see her lying about absolutely anything," said Mac. "But not when her own neck is on the block. She seduced those teachers, but that doesn't matter. She was underage, so it was statutory rape. The only reason she went to prison was that she was dumb enough to extort the teachers and got recorded doing it. If she had slept with Norton, it would have come out. She would have used it as a bargaining chip to try and get leniency." He shrugged. "Might've worked, too. But she made the mistake of letting herself get recorded."

"Arianna could have used her for something," said Parker.

"To do what?" said Mac with a shrug. "If Arianna is as ruthless as we think she is, she would definitely use and abandon Salwell, but I can't think of any reason she would. Salwell wasn't useful to her. It's too bad Northwoods High doesn't have any security cameras."

Parker made a disgusted sound. "You know it's been two and a half years since the shooting, and they still haven't put in any cameras?" He soothed his disgust by eating a chicken nugget. "Mr. Norton used to talk about that."

"Did he?" said Mac.

A shrill cry caught his ear, and he looked towards the door. But it was only a little girl dressed as a ladybug standing with her mother in front of the cash register. Evidently, she wanted her ice cream right now. The cashier, a teenaged Hispanic girl dressed like some sort of superhero, leaned over the register and smiled, probably complimenting the toddler's costume.

"Yeah, he said the way that society was going, we'd all be recording each other all the time in a few years," said Parker. "All the cell phones with cameras, yeah?" He ate some more fries and swallowed. "He said it was creepy, but it might turn out to be necessary to keep everyone honest."

Mac started to say something, and then something else caught his eye.

There was a black dome of a security camera over the teenage girl's register. Nothing remarkable about that. Every fast-food restaurant and gas station in the country had security cameras, both to identify criminals and employees who stole from the registers.

Northwoods High School didn't have any cameras.

The idea that had been scratching around the inside of Mac's head came into focus.

"Oh my God," he muttered.

"What?" said Parker, craning his neck. "That toddler's loud, but not that loud, and..."

"I think I know why Norton wrote Kristin Salwell's name before he died," said Mac.

That caught Parker off-guard enough that he stopped reaching for his fries. "What? Why?"

"Think about it," said Mac. "Norton died in January 2006. Kristin Salwell was arrested for blackmail in July 2005. That's almost six months. That would have been more than enough time to install one."

"Install what?" said Parker.

"A camera," said Mac.

Parker blinked. "What are you saying?"

"What if Doug Norton installed a secret camera inside his classroom before he died?" said Mac.

"Why would he do that?" said Parker. "He could get into a lot of trouble for that. I think it's illegal."

"It probably is," said Mac. "But think about it. A female student accuses a male teacher of misconduct. Most people will believe the student, and even if she's lying, the teacher will probably lose his reputation anyway. What's the only possible way he can clear his name?"

Parker's brow started to furrow with thought. "If there was a video recording of it."

"Right," said Mac. "Salwell gets arrested in July 2005. Norton's a smart guy, and he knows that teenagers mimic each other. Maybe he's worried that a student might falsely accuse him of misconduct. He knows that it would be better to lose his job for a secret recording than it would to go to prison for a fake accusation of misconduct. So he installs a secret camera somewhere in his classroom. Just in case a mass hysteria sweeps the school. And then when Arianna Crest shows up with a gun..."

"He writes down Kristin Salwell's name?" said Parker. "That part doesn't make any sense."

"Because I bet Arianna was watching him," said Mac. "Holding a gun on him and telling him to sit a certain way. He couldn't write down 'hey, I have a secret camera in the ceiling' or something like that. It's hard to think under stress, and he wrote down Kristin Salwell's name, thinking that people would figure out that it meant a camera or a recording. But no one was able to make the connection."

"Wouldn't the cops have found a hidden camera in the classroom?" said Parker.

"Not if it was hidden well enough," said Mac. "And they didn't have any reason to look for a camera. Norton's death was ruled a suicide."

"But he didn't leave a suicide note because he was murdered," said Parker. "And he wrote Kristin Salwell as his final words..."

"Because he was being recorded," said Mac.

They sat in silence for a moment. Parker looked shaken. He had stopped eating, at any rate.

"Do you think the camera is still there?" said Parker.

"It might be," said Mac. "Did his classroom have a drop ceiling?"

Parker frowned. "What's a drop ceiling?"

"White tiles mounted in a metal framework below the actual ceiling," said Mac. "Institutional buildings usually have them to hide ducts and wiring stuff."

"Oh, yeah, those panels?" said Parker. "Every room in Northwoods High has ceilings like that."

"If he hid the camera up there, no one would find it unless the room needed maintenance," said Mac. "Someone would have to stand on a ladder, push up a panel, and look around the plenum space with a flashlight."

"It could still be there," said Parker.

They stared at one another.

"What are we going to do about it?" Parker said at last.

"I don't know," said Mac. "I suppose we should contact the detectives who investigated Norton's death. Convince them that they should look in the ceiling." That would be an uphill battle, though. "I know someone at the FBI who owes me, maybe I could have him make some phone calls..."

"We could look ourselves," said Parker.

Mac shook his head. "That's a bad idea. If we ask them, they'll freak out, and I'm not breaking into a school."

"But it's Halloween," said Parker.

"What does that have to do with anything?" said Mac.

"It's bonfire night," said Parker, and Mac remembered the announcement he had seen outside the Northwoods building. "Every year at Halloween, the school has an open house and a bonfire in the courtyard. I guess the school board thinks it will stop the students from doing drugs and smashing mailboxes, something like that." He shrugged. "It's kind of lame, but it was fun, back when I was able to go."

It didn't seem like a great idea. There would probably be at least one police car there, and Mac didn't have any official reason to be wandering around a high school. For that matter, if someone recognized Parker, there might be hell to pay.

And yet...

The need to know burned within him like a hunger.

"This is a terrible idea," said Mac.

"We're doing it, though, right?" said Parker.

"Damn it," said Mac. "Get your stuff. We're going."

THE THRILL of the coming risk pulsed through Arianna.

Everything had gone as she wished, and it was time to remove Angela Morgan as an obstacle once and for all.

Rod Cutler's death had caused the desired results. Julie Norton released a statement to the press asserting that her husband had been a devoted teacher and had nothing to do with the Northwoods shooting. Given that Doug Norton had been physically seen with multiple students during the time of the shooting, several of whom went on the news to praise Norton's actions, Arianna doubted that anyone seriously thought that Doug had been involved.

But that didn't matter. Julie had fired Cormac Rogan, and Rogan had no money. Without payment, he would have no reason to examine Arianna's affairs, and his penury meant he would have to turn his attention other paying work. She would be free to act as she wished.

The police had spoken to Arianna about Rod Cutler's death, and she had told them the truth. She had known about Rod's criminal history but had employed him anyway because he had done good work and was cheap. Arianna regretted his death but wasn't surprised that he had gotten killed. She would be happy to cooperate with the investigators in any way and had cheerfully handed over all the records relating to his contract work with Crest Development.

The detectives had gone away satisfied. No suspicion had attached to Arianna whatsoever.

She smiled as she worked, loading up the Crest Development van with what she needed tonight.

Arianna only wished she could see Morgan's cold, arrogant mask shatter when she learned the news of her only son's death.

Well. Arianna would just have to imagine it. The money from the Westview deal would be reward enough.

Obtaining a maintenance coverall of the sort used by the janitors at Northwoods High School had been easy enough, and Arianna had tucked her hair beneath a net and a ball cap once again. From a distance, she would look like a custodian working at night. She threw a heavy black tool bag into the back of the van. Instead of tools, it held the modified AR-15 she had stolen from Nathan Rangel, along with spare ammunition and a few other things that might prove of use.

Next to the bag, she put an object that looked like a heavy black metal briefcase. Inside was a powerful radio connected to a car battery. It was the cell phone jammer Rod had built for her. The device would block any cell phone transmissions within five hundred yards. The battery would last only fifteen minutes or so, but that was all right.

Arianna would not need that much time.

Smiling to herself, she started the van and headed for Northwoods High School.

22

TRICK OR TREAT

Mac drove past Northwoods High School, Parker sitting in the passenger seat.

"See?" said Parker. "I told you that a lot of people come to these things."

He wasn't wrong.

Every light shone in the windows of the building, illuminating the sidewalk around the school. Mac glimpsed people heading through the school's front doors, which stood open. A police car sat in front of the front steps, two uniformed officers visible inside the car. Probably the police were there as a favor to the school board, helping people to feel safe at the site of the shooting.

"Is there another way in?" said Mac. He didn't want to walk past the police car at the front doors. They might recognize him, or worse, Parker.

"Yeah," said Parker. "The back doors are open, too. If we cut through the loading dock on the side of the building, we can get in that way. Probably fewer people there right now."

Mac nodded and drove past the loading dock, which was presently empty. He went for another block and then turned and parked on a residential side street. There were quite a few cars on either side of the street already, so he hadn't been the only one with that idea.

"Do we have to walk that far?" said Parker.

"Yes," said Mac. "I don't think there's room at the main lot, and I don't want to get parked in if you get recognized."

Mac opened the trunk and collected his laptop bag while Parker waited. They walked around the corner and headed towards the high school building. At Mac's insistence, Parker kept his hood up. Mac glanced across the street towards the half-demolished house. The chain-link fence encircled the property, the sign proclaiming the future site of the memorial garden, the work done by Crest Development. If Mac was right, Arianna had shot those students from the top floor of that house, and now she was paying for it to be demolished and turned into a memorial garden.

A humanitarian gesture for the mourning Northwoods community.

God, that was cold.

They walked past the empty loading dock, and Mac looked at the crowds in the yard behind the school. There had to be at least a thousand people there, gathered around three enormous bonfires that crackled with cheery light. The crowd was mostly teenagers wearing a variety of costumes, though there were quite a few adults in the mix, likely parents and teachers. Long tables held coolers of punch, pizza boxes, bowls of chips, and platters of cookies.

Mac and Parker circled around the back of the building and came to a patio area with rows of concrete tables and benches. Probably an overflow area for the cafeteria. Parker led him to a pair of double metal doors, and they stepped into a large cafeteria, with dozens of round tables surrounded by blue plastic chairs. The air smelled a bit of grease and old food. The big room was mostly deserted, save for a few pairs of teenaged couples engaged in deep conversation. They turned brief glances towards Mac and Parker and then went back to their discussion.

"Which way?" said Mac.

"Mr. Norton's room was on the first floor," said Parker. "Right around the corner."

A large hallway opened off the cafeteria. It looked like a typical 30s-era high school corridor, Mac thought. An old linoleum floor that had been recently waxed. Cinder block walls painted a cheerful shade of blue, no doubt the shade recommended by educational psychiatrists. Metal lockers stood in rows along the walls.

"Here," said Parker, nodding to a door with a window set into it. The sign next to the door read ROOM 189 – MS. JAMALA HENDRICKS, MATHEMATICS. The lights were on underneath the door. Mac checked the handle – a stroke of luck.

It was unlocked.

He opened the door and stepped into the room where Douglas Norton had died.

It looked utterly unremarkable. Rows of desks sat facing a wall covered in whiteboards. Posters on the other walls showed teenagers looking unreasonably excited about mathematics. The teacher's desk was in the left-hand corner, supporting a monitor and a desktop computer. An LCD projector hung from the ceiling by a black metal arm, pointed towards a smartboard.

"Parker," said Mac. "When you were here, did this room have that projector?"

"Yeah," said Parker. "It was put in just a couple of months before the shooting."

Mac nodded. "Where was Doug Norton's desk?"

"Ah..." Parker hesitated and pointed at a spot on the wall about halfway towards the door. "Right there."

The wall, Mac noted, had been painted sometime in the last few years, probably to remove the bloodstains. There was no trace that a man had died there.

"Hold this, please," said Mac, and he passed his laptop bag to Parker. He opened the bag, took out a small flashlight, and then climbed onto one of the desks. It gave an alarming creak but held his weight.

"What are you doing?" said Parker.

"If I'm right, the camera will be up here," said Mac. He pushed aside one of the tiles in the drop ceiling, the whitish-gray material rough beneath his palms, and looked into the darkness above. The real ceiling was about six feet above, and he saw a heating duct bolted to the steel and concrete of the next level. "But if it's not battery powered, it needs electricity, and I bet there's only one outlet up here."

He clicked on his flashlight and swept the beam back and forth. A lot of dust had accumulated atop the acoustic tiles. Mac saw the steel gleam of an electrical conduit running along the ceiling and followed it with the flashlight. An electrical socket with four plugs was mounted to the ceiling above the projector, and its black cord went through the metal arm to the outlet.

But a second cord was plugged in next to the projector.

A surge of excitement went through Mac.

He followed the line of the cord and found the device tucked into the metal frame of the drop ceiling.

It was a small, compact surveillance camera, a model designed to be installed in hidden places. When Doug Norton had mounted it, he had also drilled a small hole in the nearby tile. The camera had been pointed right at his desk.

Right where he had died.

Mac unplugged the camera and put the ceiling tile back into place.

"Did you find anything?" said Parker with sudden eagerness.

"Yeah," said Mac. "Surveillance camera." He turned the black rectangle over. "Looks like it uses a standard SD memory card. My laptop has a card reader."

"Let's take a look," said Parker.

"Not here," said Mac. "Let's get out of here before Ms. Hendricks comes back or someone sees us."

They slipped into the hallway, but it remained deserted. No, not quite deserted. Mac caught a glimpse of a short man in a janitor's coverall, hair hidden beneath a baseball cap, a heavy tool bag in hand. But the man vanished up the central stairwell, and Mac let out a sigh of relief. They hadn't been seen.

"Cafeteria," said Mac. "We'll use one of the tables."

They returned to the cafeteria and picked a table far from anyone else. Mac sat down, Parker next to him, and unpacked his laptop. He powered it on, and as it booted, Mac examined the camera. The memory card within was thirty-two gigabytes. Expensive – memory card prices had gone down in the last few years, but not that much. Doug had likely wanted to store a great deal of video footage.

"That's Ubuntu Linux," said Parker, pointing at the laptop screen.

"Yeah," said Mac, and he unlocked his computer.

"Hard to play games on Ubuntu," said Parker.

"We're not playing games now," said Mac, and he slid the card into the reader. After a moment, a window appeared on the screen, listing the card's files. As Mac had expected, the card was entirely full. He suspected the camera had been configured to activate whenever it detected motion, and he scrolled through hundreds of video files. Doug had died on January 24th, 2006, sometime before five in the afternoon.

There. A video file about five minutes along, from a little after 4:30 in the afternoon. Mac copied it to his desktop.

"Why are you copying it?" said Parker, his voice little more than a whisper.

"Don't want to take the chance of accidentally screwing up the original," said Mac, his throat dry as dust.

The file seemed to take forever to copy, though it was no more than a few seconds. At last, it finished, and Mac opened the file in the video player.

The image came up, sharp and clear. The recording was in black and white with no sound, but picture was superb. Doug Norton had done an excellent job of mounting the camera, and Mac saw his desk and a space about ten feet around it. In fact, Mac saw Doug Norton himself sitting at the desk, grading papers with a frown on his face.

"God, that's so weird," said Parker. "He's just..."

"Quiet," said Mac.

Arianna Crest stepped into the frame of the recording.

Mac recognized her at once. She was wearing a heavy winter coat, jeans, and boots, but he knew those sharp features. Her hair was hidden beneath a watch cap, and one hand was in the pocket of her coat. Doug gave her a cautious smile and started to speak, and Arianna nodded and answered him.

Her gloved hand came out of her pocket, holding Winston Marsh's Smith & Wesson 910.

Doug froze, his expression sliding from shock and anger to fear and then to a blank mask. A strange look went over Arianna's face, one of almost mad exultation. Both she and Doug said something, and then Doug scribbled something on his day planner – no doubt the name of Kristin Salwell. Arianna glanced at his day planner, frowned, and then lunged forward.

She was quick, and she did it exactly right. Arianna jammed the end of the gun against Doug's head in the exact spot and angle he would have put the gun if he shot himself in the temple, and squeezed the trigger.

Parker flinched as Doug jerked back in his chair.

They watched in grim silence as Arianna arranged the scene. She used her gloved hands to move Doug's body and the gun into the positions they would have been had he shot himself. Little wonder Doug's death had been ruled a suicide.

Arianna finished her work in a few minutes and left. Doug's body remained motionless in the chair. The recording skipped fifteen minutes ahead, likely because the motion detector had switched off. Another teacher came into the frame, gazed at Doug's body in horror for a few seconds, and then ran out of the recording to call 911. If Mac remembered right, that was Raul Torres, the teacher who had the bad luck to find Doug's body and had been the first to call the police.

Mac tapped the touchpad and closed the video file.

"Holy shit," whispered Parker.

"Yeah," said Mac.

There seemed to be nothing else to say.

He removed the video card and tucked it into the camera, and then put both his camera and the laptop into his bag.

"She's screwed, isn't she?" said Parker. "If we go to the police. There's no way she can wriggle out of that. It's all there in black and white. She killed Mr. Norton." Parker shook his head in dismay. "Mom always said that Arianna Crest was ruthless, but...holy shit, Mr. Rogan. We gotta go to the police right now."

"We do," said Mac, fishing in his coat pocket for his cell phone. "But we need to talk to someone competent. Crest's dangerous, and God only knows what she'll do when the police come for her."

"They'll just arrest her, won't they?" said Parker.

"Do you think that she hasn't thought of that?" said Mac. "Someone like her...she won't go to prison. She'll go out with guns blazing and try to take as many people with her as possible." Mac could just imagine Arianna wiring up her house or her office with bombs and setting them off when the cops arrived.

He pulled out his cell phone. Matthew Cole of the FBI, he decided. The FBI agent had proven himself competent and level-headed, and Mac would present both the video and his theory about Crest to him. From there, the FBI could spearhead an effort to take Crest alive without anyone getting killed in the process.

Mac found Cole's number and hit the call button.

NO SIGNAL blinked several times across the screen.

"What the hell?" said Mac.

"What's wrong?" said Parker.

He tried making the call again. Once again, the NO SIGNAL message went over his screen.

"Parker, look at your phone," said Mac. "Are you getting any signal?"

Parker frowned and pulled his phone out of the pocket of his shorts. It was an expensive Blackberry, probably one of his mom's old ones. "I...huh. No. No bars at all."

A dark idea scratched at the edges of Mac's mind.

"Come with me," said Mac, and he shoved to his feet, grabbed his laptop bag, and hurried across the cafeteria, Parker lumbering after.

He headed for one of the teenage couples – a skinny boy with black hair and a somewhat plumper girl with bright red hair. Both looked at Mac with the typical teenaged mixture of disdain and wariness towards unknown adults.

"What do you want, man?" said the boy. "We were sitting here first."

"Do either of you have cell phones?" said Mac.

The boy sneered. "What's it to you?"

"Check to see if you have signal. Check right now," said Mac.

The boy started to say something else, but the girl was quicker on the uptake.

"Brian," said the girl. "Just check your phone quick."

Brian shrugged and pulled out a cheap flip phone, as did the girl. Both frowned at their screens.

"Huh," said Brian. "No signal."

"Me, neither," said the girl.

"Damn cheap phone," said Brian. "I wanted a Blackberry, but..."

Mac didn't wait for the rest of the conversation but ran across the room to the cafeteria doors. There was a phone mounted on the wall next to the doorframe, and he yanked the handset from the cradle and lifted it to his ear.

Nothing. It was dead.

"What's wrong?" said Parker, wheezing a bit as he caught up to Mac.

"Phone's dead," said Mac, shoving it back onto the cradle. "Someone cut the phone line, and someone's jamming cell phones. Something bad is about to happen."

ARIANNA PARKED the Crest Development van about a block from the school. Her company's vans had been parked along the street for the last week or so, and it would draw no notice. She collected the tool bag and the cell phone jammer and strode briskly down the sidewalk, keeping a wary eye on the sidewalk around her. But it was unnecessary – everyone was heading for the front doors of the school, no doubt intending to eat and drink and enjoy the bonfires.

She veered left and headed for the school's truck dock and side entrance. Next to the side entrance was a locked metal cabinet with a conduit sinking into the ground. The main building of Northwoods High School had been built in the thirties, back when telephones had been only an afterthought, and the school's phone connection went through that metal conduit.

Arianna set down her tool bag, produced a pair of heavy bolt cutters, and sliced through the conduit. It took all of ten seconds, though she had to strain to do it. She stooped to check that the wires within the conduit had been severed, then put the bolt cutters into her bag and continued into the building proper.

She found herself in a long, wide corridor that led towards the cafeteria, lockers lining the walls. To her left was a steel door that read STAFF ACCESS ONLY. It opened onto a utility stairway that went directly to the roof. Arianna reached into her pocket, produced a set of keys she had quietly copied from the school's masters, and disarmed the door's alarm. That would be her escape route once the shooting was done. It would be easy to go down the utility stairs, walk calmly to the van, and get the hell out of here. By the time the police and the paramedics arrived, she would be long gone.

One last check for anything amiss – Arianna had seen only one police car outside, as expected, and she wasn't worried about them. They would not be expecting trouble. She walked down the hallway, past the cafeteria, and was pleased to see that the building was mostly empty. The school was holding an open house to accompany the bonfire, but all the food and drink was outside. She saw a few students in the cafeteria, but that was it.

They would be the lucky ones.

Arianna came to the main stairwell and started up it, and froze for a second when a flicker of motion caught her eye. She saw a man in a dark coat and a fat kid in a hooded sweatshirt duck into a classroom. Nothing to worry about – probably a student showing his father a school project.

She hurried up the main stairs to the fourth floor of the school. At the top landing was a narrow metal staircase that climbed to the roof and a closed metal hatch. Arianna ascended the metal steps, pleased that she wasn't breathing hard after carrying the tool bag and the cell phone jammer to the fourth floor. She unlocked the hatch and climbed onto the roof, dragging the tool bag and the jammer after her. For a second, she considered locking the hatch behind her and then decided against it, realizing she might need an alternative method of escape if something unexpected happened.

The rooftop of Northwoods High School was a broad space covered in tar paper, gritty and rough beneath her boots. Some square sections of the roof had been covered with small stones, no doubt to reduce heating and cooling costs. Far to her left was the door that led to the utility stairwell, mounted in a structure that looked like a brick outhouse. A row of heavy air handlers for the school's air conditioners stood on the roof, along with a pair of electrical transformers and some metal chimneys connected to the chemistry lab's fume hoods. A waist-high brick wall encircled the edge of the rooftop, providing some protection from falling over.

Arianna walked to the edge of the roof, dropped to a crouch, and peered over the top of the low wall.

She smiled at the sight that greeted her eyes.

Nearly a thousand people had gathered in the space behind the school. The three bonfires provided a lot of light, more than enough for accurate shooting. Granted, Arianna didn't need to kill all that many people. She only needed to shoot Charlie Morgan and then a few others to make it look like another school shooting.

She opened her bag and readied the AR-15 with swift, practiced motions. Arianna had taken the expended shells with her the last time, but she wouldn't bother now. Her fingerprints would not be on them. If any prints were on bullets, they would belong to Rangel, or maybe whoever had sold him the ammunition.

Once the gun was ready, Arianna opened the case holding Rod's cell phone jammer. She flipped the switch, and an LED on the device turned red, showing that it was operating. Arianna had tested it several times before, no doubt causing her neighbors to wonder why their cell phone service and their Wi-Fi suddenly stopped working, and she knew the jammer worked. The battery would only last for ten or fifteen minutes, but that was more than long enough for what she needed.

Arianna went to one knee behind the low wall, set the rifle on it, and began scanning the crowd.

The final step was to find Charlie Morgan. He would be here, she knew – he was a wide receiver on the football team, and the entire team would attend the bonfire. She spotted a cluster of teenagers wearing varsity jackets – no, the basketball team.

There. The football team was near the central bonfire, perfectly outlined against the flames. A mixture of players and cheerleaders, Arianna thought.

Her eyes flicked over the teenage boys in their letter jackets, moving from face to face.

As soon as she found Angela Morgan's son, the killing could begin.

The anticipation coursed down her veins like lightning.

23

HISTORY REPEATS

"Something bad is about to happen?" said Parker. "What do you mean?"

"The phone line's been cut," said Mac. "Someone's jamming cell phones. I think Arianna's going to do something."

"But that doesn't make any sense," said Parker. "How does she even know that we're here?"

Parker was right. It didn't make sense. Mac was convinced that Arianna had killed Rod Cutler to keep Mac from looking any further into her affairs. From Arianna's perspective, the plan had worked – Julie Norton had fired Mac and Wester Security, and Mac had no more reason to look into Doug Norton's death. Arianna couldn't have known that Mac had guessed how many people she had killed.

Then the pieces clicked together in his mind.

The Westview mall development project.

Julie had told Mac that both Morgan Properties and Crest Development were competing for the deal.

And Mac was willing to bet that one of the key people in Morgan Properties had a child who attended Northwoods High School.

A child who was almost certainly in the courtyard near the bonfires.

"Shit," said Mac.

"What?" said Parker.

"Arianna's here, right now, but she's not here for us," said Mac. "She and Angela Morgan have been fighting over some big land deal or another. Arianna's pattern is to kill the relatives of people who are in her way. I bet that someone high-up at Morgan Properties has a child here right…"

"Charlie Morgan," said Parker, his face going white. "Oh my God. Charlie Morgan, Angela Morgan's son. He's a senior here. Oh my God, Mr. Rogan. It's all happening again. It's all going to happen all over again, and…"

"No," said Mac, grabbing Parker's shoulder before the kid could fall apart. They needed to do something right now.

But what?

The police officers outside? But what could they do? Would they even believe Mac and Parker? And if they started an evacuation, how would Arianna react? During the last shooting, Arianna had fired into the crowds of students near the front door. If the police started an evacuation, crowds of students would bunch up near the entrances and exits. That would make a perfect target for Arianna.

The last time she had fired from the house across the street. But tonight, it would be almost impossible for her to shoot with any accuracy from one of those houses. The bulk of the students were in the courtyard behind the school's main building. If Arianna was indeed here to kill Charlie Morgan and make it look like yet another school shooting, she needed to find and identify him. She couldn't do that from across the street. One of the classrooms on the upper floors? No, that would be difficult. Most of the windows in the building looked as if they didn't open. Arianna would have to smash one of them to shoot through it, and that would make too much noise, which meant…

"The roof," said Mac. "She's on the goddamn roof. Come on!"

He left the cafeteria and ran down the hallway, slinging his laptop bag diagonally across his shoulders. Mac found the main stairwell and took the steps two at a time, grateful for all the hours he had put in at Iron Oswald's gym. Parker managed to keep pace, though he wheezed like a bellows, and his face turned an alarming shade of red. Mac wanted to tell him to stay behind and get the cops in the front of the building.

But he knew Parker wouldn't listen. Parker had lived through a nightmare, and the whole nightmare was about to repeat itself in a new form. There was nothing that Mac could have done to stop him.

They reached the top floor, and Mac saw a steep metal staircase that ascended to a hatch in the ceiling. It was open a few inches.

Someone was up there.

"Keep quiet," said Mac.

Parker nodded, wheezing, and wiped sweat from his forehead. Mac climbed up the steep metal staircase, Parker behind him, and eased open the hatch.

He had spent a surprising amount of time on the rooftops of industrial buildings – sometimes wireless networking equipment ended up on the roof, and Mac had once spent a week on a fiddly contract job adjusting line-of-sight radio transmitters. The roof of Northwoods High School was flat and covered in thick tar paper, with a row of air handlers and electrical cabinets running down the center. Over to the left was a brick cube with a steel door in it – that probably led to a utility stairwell. Square patches had been covered with small stones, likely installed as part of some sort of eco-friendly insulation scheme.

On the far side of the roof, Mac glimpsed a dark figure outlined against the fiery glow of the bonfires. For a second, confusion gripped him – it was a janitor in a loose coverall and a black baseball cap, a tool bag on the roof next to him, along with an open black briefcase that held something that looked like a coil of copper wire and a car battery.

It was the janitor he had seen earlier, the one going up the stairs.

Then the dark figure's head turned a little, and Mac saw the sharp features of Arianna Crest shaded beneath the brim of the ball cap.

She was holding a long black rifle – maybe an M-16, maybe an AR-15, he couldn't tell in the dim glow – pointed at the crowd below.

~

Arianna spotted Charlie Morgan.

The boy stood with the rest of the football team, wearing a varsity jacket. He had inherited his mother's pale blond hair and slight build, which was no doubt why he was a wide receiver. In fact, during her research, Arianna had learned that he was an excellent wide receiver and maintained a high GPA. The boy was his mother's pride and joy.

His death would rip the heart out of Angela Morgan, and Arianna would push aside the devastated owner of Morgan Properties and seize the Westview deal for herself.

Angela Morgan herself was actually at the bonfire, standing with a group of parents. For a second, Arianna entertained the idea of shooting her rival but dismissed the thought. Too likely to lead directly back to her. Killing Charlie, though? Who would suspect Arianna? Come to think of it, Arianna would make sure to release a public statement offering her condolences for Angela in this difficult time. Maybe she would even attend the boy's funeral.

The thought pleased her to no end.

Arianna settled into place, bracing her rifle against the low wall. She peered through the scope and aimed the weapon at Charlie's head. A shot through his skull, she decided, and then she would empty the rest of the weapon into the crowd. With the students packed into the courtyard, Arianna could scarcely miss, and more would be injured during the panicked stampede from the school grounds.

By then, she would be back in the van and long gone.

She slowed her breathing, focusing on Charlie, her finger sliding inside the trigger guard...

Something clanged behind her.

~

Mac eased forward a step.

Arianna Crest hadn't noticed him. Mac really, really wished he had brought a gun. But concealed carry wasn't legal in Wisconsin, and if Detective Armstrong or one of the other police officers he had spoken with over the last week had caught Mac carrying a gun, he might have gotten into serious trouble.

Weapon or no weapon, he had to act right now. Arianna was going to start shooting at any second. Yet she hadn't heard Mac or Parker. If Mac could just get a little closer, he could rush Arianna and pin her against the wall before she fired into the crowd or turned to shoot at him.

He glided forward another step, and then a loud clang went over the rooftop.

Mac shot a quick look over his shoulder. Parker was a half-step behind him, his eyes wide. The damned hatch had fallen shut behind them.

Arianna whirled, leaping to her feet, the black rifle swinging around towards them.

"Down!" shouted Mac, and he shoved Parker to the side.

He was just barely fast enough. The muzzle flashed in the gloom of the rooftop, and the bullet that would have gone through Parker's head instead tore through his left shoulder. Parker let out a bellow of pain, stumbled, and fell behind one of the air handlers. Arianna squeezed off another shot, but it ricocheted off the handler's metal housing.

Mac had taken three running steps towards Arianna, but she turned, the front of her weapon tracking towards him. He threw himself to the side, landing in a patch of stones behind another air handler, and he heard the clang as the bullets impacted into the machine.

ARIANNA'S MIND RACED, her finger ready against the trigger.

Her first react was stark bafflement.

How the hell had Cormac Rogan and Parker McIntyre followed her here?

Pure molten rage followed her a moment later. She would make them regret this.

A mixture of exultation at the enormous risk and cold calculation followed the emotions.

She had to kill them both right now. No other options. They had seen too much, figured out too much. Neither one of them could leave the rooftop alive. Perhaps it was time to abandon her Halloween plan and settle for killing Rogan and McIntyre.

Arianna was sure that she had hit McIntyre but didn't know if the wound was fatal. She knew that she hadn't hit Rogan, that he had taken cover behind that air handler. Had anyone heard the shots? No, probably not. The music was too loud. A few people closer to the building might have heard the gunfire, but Arianna doubted they would have recognized what was happening.

She had to act right now.

Arianna glided forward, weapon ready, intending to finish Rogan.

MAC CROUCHED behind the air handler, looking for something he could use as a weapon.

He could just hear Parker groaning over the music coming from the courtyard. Mac didn't think Parker's wound had been fatal, but he needed medical attention as soon as possible, and if the bullet had hit an artery or a vein, Parker was in trouble.

Arianna would make sure he didn't live long enough for it to be a problem.

He needed something to distract Arianna. Something that would hold her attention long enough for him to get the rifle away from her.

The stones. They were each about the size of an egg or so. Mac grabbed two of them, hefted their weight, and threw one of them over the top of the machinery. It arced through the air and clattered against the rooftop.

A second later, Mac heard two quick shots.

He leaped to his feet and sprang around the air handler. Arianna was facing to the left, rifle pointed towards where the first stone had landed. He flung the second stone as hard as he could, and the rock hit her in the jaw. Her head snapped back with a cry of pain, and she stumbled.

Mac sprinted towards her.

A second later, he realized that was final mistake of his life.

Arianna recovered her balance, her beautiful face twisted with rage, eyes wide and gleaming. Already the rifle was swinging back towards him, and Mac knew he would be a half-second too slow, that she was going to shoot him in the chest at point-blank range...

A howling scream filled his ears.

Arianna hesitated, caught between two targets, and Mac looked to the side to see Parker running towards them, roaring at the top of his lungs. The genial, awkward teenager had vanished, his face a mask of volcanic rage, and Parker thundered towards Arianna, arms extended.

She started to step back, turning the gun towards them, but the instant of hesitation cost her. Parker slammed into Arianna, still screaming, and the gun was forced between them, the barrel pointing towards the sky. Arianna snarled and headbutted Parker, and Mac heard his nose snap. Arianna was in excellent shape, and getting up the stairs had winded Parker, but he was still over twice her weight and had a lot of momentum.

They slammed into the low wall at the edge of the roof before Mac could reach them, fighting for the rifle, and Parker's momentum forced them over the edge.

Mac seized Parker's shoulders as the younger man started to fall after Arianna. Every muscle in his body screamed with the strain, and for a horrible second, Mac thought he would lose his grip. But he planted his feet and strained as he did when performing deadlifts at Iron Oswald's Gym, and Parker's balance shifted towards the roof.

They fell backward and landed hard on the tar paper.

Arianna tumbled over the wall and hurtled towards the courtyard, her mind exploding with anger.

She was going to kill Rogan for this, and then McIntyre. And then she would kill Charlie Morgan and his wretched mother, and then…

But none of that would happen.

In the final instant of her life, Arianna Crest finally had something in common with her mother.

Like Jacqueline Crest, she landed on her head.

24

DIGGING

There had been a furor after the shooting at Deluxe Storage. But it was nothing, absolutely nothing, compared to the shitstorm that followed the death of Arianna Crest.

No one had heard the shooting on the rooftop, but a woman plummeting to her death in the courtyard had been impossible to miss. The two cops in the car outside had been summoned and taken charge of the scene. By then, Mac had switched off Arianna's cell phone jammer and called 911, summoning an ambulance for Parker.

Armies of police descended upon the high school, and Mac spent most of the night answering the same questions over and over again. He told them the entire story – the investigation, the video, realizing that Arianna had committed the first shooting and had been about to commit a second. The detectives had been skeptical. Mac could hardly blame them. In their position, he wouldn't have believed it, either.

But there was the video of Doug Norton's murder.

There was Arianna's corpse, found with the stolen AR-15 beneath it.

There was Parker's account, which corroborated Mac's, which he gave to detectives from his hospital bed, surrounded by his mother and her lawyer. The wound in his left shoulder, thankfully, was serious but not life-threatening. The bullet had gone in and out cleanly without shattering any bones or hitting any major blood vessels. Parker would need surgery and physical therapy, and given his age, the doctors expected no long-term loss of function.

The police descended on both Arianna's house and Crest Development.

In Arianna's basement, they found an entire arsenal of weaponry, enough to arm a small platoon. Most of it had been stolen, and they found considerable evidence linking her to other crimes. The detectives proved more than happy to follow the pattern in Arianna's activities that Mac had discovered, and suddenly a lot of cold cases and closed investigations were reopened.

The news story exploded a few days later.

SCHOOL SHOOTING FOILED, proclaimed news organizations from coast to coast. The story was too rich to resist. A young man, previously accused of having carried out a school shooting, had returned to thwart one at the last possible minute? For that matter, the perpetrator had apparently been a millionaire sociopath who also happened to have been a beautiful woman? The media fixated on the story for weeks. Vanessa Portman began blogging about it multiple times a day and sent Mac a dozen requests for a new interview, all of which he deleted.

He spent much of November dodging reporters or referring them to Paul.

In the end, the district attorney declined to bring any charges against Mac or Parker. Both men, the district attorney said in a news conference, had acted heroically, preventing a repeat of the Northwoods High School tragedy.

A legion of lawyers descended upon Crest Development, and Mac expected the company to get ripped apart by lawyers representing the families of Arianna's victims. Morgan Properties might buy up some valuable real estate on the cheap.

The worst of the media attention came at the Wisconsin State Capitol the week before Thanksgiving. At the suggestion of Angela

Morgan, one of the state senators introduced a motion for an official Legislative Commendation for Mac and Parker, citing their actions in stopping another massacre at Arianna's hands. The legislature approved the commendation unanimously, which meant that Mac and Parker had to go to the Capitol to receive it. Mac was slightly annoyed that he had to spend his birthday in Madison, but he supposed it was important to Parker, so he didn't complain. The governor, a bald man with a toothy smile, presented the certificate, and the entire legislature rose in applause.

Maggie McIntyre beamed with pride from the spectators' gallery.

Afterward, there was a press conference. Mac refused to take any questions, instead reading a short statement that Paul had written for him expressing gratitude that Arianna's plan had been stopped with no loss of life. Parker was more than happy to take questions, his arm still in a sling and a white plastic brace on his nose.

"Mr. McIntyre!" said a TV reporter. "What do you have to say to people who thought you were guilty of the first shooting in 2005?"

Parker took a deep breath, his eyes glittering. Mac braced himself for the torrent of ranting. Then Parker stopped to collect himself, and Mac all but heard the creaking of his self-control.

"Like...Mr. Rogan said," said Parker, "I am just glad there was no additional loss of life."

THE NEXT DAY, Mac had two meetings.

The first was at the Starbucks where he regularly met with Nikolai and Paul about RVW Software. One day they might need an actual office location, but the company wasn't there yet. Mac arrived a few minutes early, his car crunching through the thin crust of snow. He parked near the door and got out of the car, laptop bag in hand.

Parker awaited him outside, wearing his usual hooded sweatshirt. In deference to the growing cold, he had actually donned jeans and shoes.

"Man, that was something yesterday, wasn't it?" said Parker.

"Yeah," said Mac. "I was surprised you didn't yell at the reporters. I know you wanted to."

"Well." Parker grunted and scratched his chin. "Mom talked to me about it. And Dr. Random thought it would be a stride in the right direction if I didn't rant about it. She said it would demonstrate personal growth and acceptance of things outside my control. I guess she was right."

"How's the arm?" said Mac. Parker had been wearing his sling yesterday, but not today.

"Stiff," said Parker. "The physical therapist has me doing all these exercises. It's a real pain in the ass, and it hurts, but it won't last forever. I can still type, though, which is the important part."

"You might miss some gaming sessions otherwise," said Mac.

The sarcasm failed to register. "Yeah, that would be the worst."

"Speaking of typing," said Mac, and they went into the Starbucks.

Paul and Nikolai were at their usual table. Nikolai was busily typing into his laptop. Paul was reading emails on his iPhone and eating a scone, but he looked up and smiled as Mac and Parker approached.

"Saw you two on the news yesterday," said Paul. "Very nice."

"No, it wasn't," said Mac.

"I don't know," said Nikolai. "If you're going to be on the TV, better for something good than bad."

"Agreed," said Paul. "I know you won't like to talk about it, Mac, but it will be good for the company to have our software designed in part by one of the men who foiled the attempted second Northwoods school shooting."

"Ugh," said Mac.

Paul grinned. "At the very least, you should get a date or two out of it, finally."

"Really," said Parker, sitting at the table. Mac sighed and took the last chair. "Girls like that kind of thing?"

"They do if you play your cards right," said Paul.

"We are not here to discuss women or cards," said Nikolai, "but the code changes for the app now that we have paying customers in three different sheriffs' departments."

"You picked a good time to come on as an intern," said Paul. "We have lots of work to do."

"Do women like conversations about application coding?" said Parker.

They all looked at him.

"Well..." started Paul.

Parker brayed out a laugh. "I'm kidding, I'm kidding." He lifted his own laptop, wincing a little. "I looked at the code changes, Mr. Volodin, and I had some thoughts..."

The new intern would fit in at RVW Software just fine.

MAC'S second appointment was at noon, in Dave's office at Wester Security.

He did not expect the crowd that awaited him in Dave's office.

"Hi, everyone," said Mac at last for lack of anything better to say.

"Mac, come in," said Dave. "Better grab one of the chairs out there and bring it in."

Mac put the chair against the right wall of the office, which meant he was facing Dave, Maggie McIntyre, Julie Norton, and Angela Morgan all at the same time. All three women wore formal business clothes – black jackets and suits and slacks. Mac suddenly felt like he was facing a panel of lawyers, even though he knew that Julie was the only one among them who was an attorney.

"I have to admit," said Mac, "that I wasn't expecting to see you all here."

Angela offered a thin, wry smile. "A lot of unexpected things have happened in the last month, Mr. Rogan. I think you wanted to go first, Julie?"

"I do." Julie Norton took a deep breath. "I would like to apologize for the things I said during our last meeting, Mr. Rogan. They were neither kind nor fair."

"That's not necessary," said Mac. "Because you were right. Doug didn't kill himself. He was murdered. I admit I didn't believe you at first. I only started to have doubts after I talked to Arianna."

"That horrible woman," said Maggie. "None of us liked her."

"Let's not mince words," said Angela. "I hated her…but I never dreamed she would do all the things she did. Did you hear that the police believed she killed her father for the insurance money?"

"It wouldn't surprise me," said Mac.

"It was only obvious in hindsight," said Maggie. "But not to you, Mr. Rogan."

"And you were right to disbelieve me," said Julie. "I had no proof at all. But I could never believe that Doug killed himself. Not ever."

"That didn't matter. You were right," said Mac. "He didn't kill himself. You were right, and the rest of us were wrong."

Julie sniffled, took a deep breath, and wiped at one eye. Angela patted her on the shoulder.

"Anyway," she said once she had composed herself. "I have since settled my bill with Dave, who has been very understanding." She lifted her purse and reached into it. "Additionally, Maggie and Angela and I have been talking, and we would like to offer you this with our thanks."

She passed Mac an envelope, and he opened it.

He blinked several times in surprise.

It was a check for seventy-five thousand dollars.

"A token of appreciation," said Julie, "for what you have done for the three of us."

Mac's first impulse was to refuse. But he didn't act on it. The bald fact was he really needed the money. He could finally pay off the last of his debts. He could get a new car when his Corsica finally died. He could buy some upgraded computer equipment for his work with RVW Software.

Hell, he could finally buy an actual bed, though his couch was comfortable enough.

"That's very gracious of you," he said at last. "Thank you."

Angela's wry smile returned. "You didn't refuse. I thought you seemed like an intelligent young man."

"I am sorry again that Parker was hurt," said Mac to Maggie. "That wasn't my intent at all."

"I know," said Maggie. "And…it is an awful thing to say, but this was good for Parker."

"Closure," murmured Julie. "It brought him closure. It did for me."

"Yes," said Maggie. "He would have had that cloud hanging over him for the rest of his life, people thinking that he might have done the shooting. That's all gone now." She shivered. "And you and Parker stopped something worse from happening."

"You and Mr. McIntyre saved my son's life, Mr. Rogan," said Angela. "My only son, the only child I will ever have. That horrible woman tried to kill him, and you stopped her. I won't forget that. I own and manage many properties, and you should be getting calls from their security departments. Perhaps it's time that we switched to RVW Software for our tracking needs."

"Thank you, Ms. Morgan," said Mac.

They talked for a little while longer, and then the women left, leaving Mac alone with Dave.

"Think you made some friends there, Mac," said Dave, leaning back in his chair and tucking his hands behind his head.

"Guess I did." Mac looked at the envelope. "After everything that Arianna did…it seems wrong to take the money…"

"But you really do need it," said Dave. "Mac, let me give you some advice. Take the money. In both life and investigative work, there are good days, and there are crap days…and the day you stopped Arianna was one of the good ones."

MAC SPENT Thanksgiving at Tom's apartment, drinking beer and watching the football game between the Packers and the Lions. Neither one of them was inclined to make a big deal out of Thanksgiving. Mac bought a take-and-bake pizza the night before, and Tom brought the beer.

This year, Mac found himself more reflective than usual.

"I suppose I've got a lot to be thankful for this year," said Mac.

They sat on the couch, beers in hand, the pizza on a tray table between them.

"You do," said Tom. He coughed and took a drink of beer. "And I've got something to be thankful about as well."

"Yeah?"

"When you threw that box of drives at Rod Cutler, I finally got all of your crap out of my apartment," said Tom.

Mac laughed, and they drank their beers and ate Thanksgiving dinner.

THE END

Thank you for reading COVERING FIRE!

Cormac Rogan will return in his next adventure, CORRUPTING FIRE.

If you liked the book, please consider leaving a review at your ebook site of choice. To receive immediate notification of new releases, sign up for my newsletter, or watch for news on my Facebook page.

ABOUT THE AUTHOR

USA Today bestselling author Jonathan Moeller has written over 120 novels, including the bestselling FROSTBORN, SEVENFOLD SWORD, DRAGONTIARNA and THE GHOSTS fantasy series, and the SILENT ORDER science fiction series. His books have sold over a million and a half copies worldwide.

Visit his website at:
http://www.jonathanmoeller.com

You can sign up for his email newsletter here, or watch for news on his Facebook page.

Made in the USA
Columbia, SC
16 September 2021